Pride Not Prejudice

VOLUME I

JENNIFER ASHLEY   CAMILLE DUPLESSIS

KRISTAN HIGGINS   AMALIE HOWARD   KATHY LYONS

SARA NEY   HILDIE MCQUEEN   ERICA RIDLEY

The Price of Lemon Cake

A BELOW STAIRS MYSTERY

JENNIFER ASHLEY

Chapter One

"That's a fine one," Bobby Perry said as she lounged in the studio at the top of Miss Judith Townsend's London townhouse. She regarded the painting taking shape under Judith's capable hands with admiration.

Judith added highlights—or whatever it was she was doing—to the golden hair of the lady in the portrait. Said lady was draped across a chaise, lavender skirts billowing, the painted bodice shimmering as the real one would when a beam of sunlight danced upon it.

"I'm pleased with it," Judith said in her modest way.

Bobby kicked her legs over her chair's cushioned arm and suppressed her longing for a cheroot. No smoking, not in the studio. Judith's rule. *Too many paint fumes, darling,* Judith had explained the first time Bobby had been ushered into this sanctum. *You'll blow us all up.*

The deprivation was worth it. Bobby would give up tobacco altogether to bask with the dark-haired Judith in her aerie, watching those skilled fingers work.

"Surprised you persuaded good old Cyn to sit still that long." Bobby sipped the fine brandy Judith always stocked. There were compensations for not being able to smoke.

"A large slice of Mrs. Holloway's lemon cake and a bottle of Beau-

3

jolais." Judith's lips quirked into her gentle smile. "It helps that I can make a sketch very quickly."

The subject and their mutual friend, Lady Cynthia Squires, was a restless soul, more at home, like Bobby, in trousers and suit coat than skirts.

"For her family, is it? This portrait?" Bobby waved her glass at the painting.

"Indeed. Something nice to hang in the hall, said her aunt." Judith's brush halted in midair as she tilted her head to decide her next stroke.

"Her aunt means something that won't embarrass them." Cynthia's aunt was horrified that her niece put on men's clothing and went about with Bobby, though she'd already realized she couldn't stop Cynthia doing exactly as she pleased.

"I believe that is the intent." Judith's eyes narrowed as she made a precise dab.

Bobby lifted the brandy to her lips once more, then froze in dismay. "Hang about. You won't let my family bribe you into painting *me* like that, will you? In a frock and all?"

Judith's silvery laughter rang out. "Never, darling. You are much different from Cynthia."

"I don't wish to placate my family, you mean?"

Judith glanced at Bobby, her dark eyes coiling need through Bobby's limbs. Bobby blessed her luck every day that Judith Townsend even considered looking at her at all.

"Cyn is in love with her mathematician," Judith said. "The fact that he might gaze upon this painting of her allowed me to coax her into sitting. Not that either of us admitted such a thing."

"I wish them happy," Bobby said with sincerity. "The pair of them would be good for each other. I hope they produce twenty-seven bouncing babies for Uncle Bobby to spoil rotten. Then I'll hand them back when they need changing and bathing and whatnot."

Another glance from Judith, this one assessing. "You are fond of children, aren't you?"

Bobby shrugged, trying to hide her embarrassment. She often

referred to her brother's children as squalling brats, but in truth they were charming little lads. "They're all right."

"Hmm." Judith returned to the painting, leaving Bobby nonplussed. Judith's *hmms* always held a world of meaning.

"Ever think about having babies yourself?" Bobby asked in curiosity.

Judith hesitated. "I doubt I'll have time for that sort of thing," was her light response. "Too much I want to paint first."

A nice, vague answer. Of course, Judith bearing children required a man to touch her. Said man would likely end up in three pieces at her feet if he tried.

Judith could use an actual sword. Learned it in a foreign land for some reason or other, she'd told Bobby, rather evasively. Judith's life had been far more exciting than Bobby's thus far.

Any further speculation on children or life and its profundity was interrupted by a blast on the speaking tube Judith had installed. No old-fashioned, clanging bells for Miss Townsend's grand Mayfair home.

Judith set her brush on the lip of the easel, lifted the ear horn from its wooden box, and spoke into it. "Yes, Hubbard?"

The muffled tones of Hubbard, Judith's creaky butler, came though the tube, his words too garbled for Bobby to discern from across the room.

"Is she?" Judith asked in delight. "Do please send her up. Or, if she doesn't wish to climb so many stairs, we can come down."

There was a pause, followed by Hubbard's indistinct response.

"Excellent," Judith replied. "We shall await her." She laid the horn back into its box and turned to Bobby, her eyes alight. "It is Mrs. Holloway, come to visit us."

Judith adored Mrs. Holloway, who was the cook for Cynthia's family. Maybe *adored* was the wrong verb—Judith admired and respected her, which was saying a lot. Judith didn't have much use for many people.

Bobby swung her legs down, brightening as well. "What a treat. Do you suppose she's brought any cake?"

"She doesn't exist to bake for us," Judith admonished, then her eyes glowed. "Though what fun if she did."

"Now, there's a thought." Bobby sprang to her feet. "You could hire her away from Cyn's awful relations and set her up here as your cook."

"An intriguing possibility." Judith lifted the brush and touched another stroke to the canvas then wiped the bristles and dropped the brush into a jar filled with oil of turpentine. "But I am afraid I'd be a sore disappointment to her. I eat only simple fare. Mrs. Holloway is far too talented to waste on me."

"I could eat your share." Bobby patted her already ample stomach. "I don't mind."

Judith chuckled, but they could say no more because Hubbard opened the door and stated in his lugubrious tones: "Mrs. Holloway."

He might have been announcing the queen. Instead of the mourning-clad monarch who occupied Britain's throne, a much younger lady entered, one with dark hair, blue eyes, and flushed cheeks. She wore a frock of rich brown that was several years out of date, matched by a modest brown straw hat that sported a few black-dyed feathers.

Her best frock, Bobby knew. Today must be Mrs. Holloway's day out, which meant she was on her way to see her daughter. Nothing would keep her from that, Cynthia had told them, which indicated that what she'd come to say was important.

Hubbard withdrew like a ghost, leaving Mrs. Holloway standing awkwardly in the doorway.

Judith, who'd risen at her entrance, quickly drew a chair forward. "Do sit down, Mrs. Holloway. How lovely to see you."

Mrs. Holloway accepted the chair but perched on it uncomfortably. She was very conscious of her place in life—a highly talented cook in a wealthy household in Mayfair, which put her a cut above most people in service.

However, she held with the nonsense that Judith and Bobby were her "betters." Bobby was in truth Lady Roberta Perry, daughter of an earl. Judith came from a prominent and blue-blooded old family—

one half of them practically ran the Foreign Office, the other half, the Home Office. Bobby and Judith might have been born into these privileged households, but Bobby did not see how it made them better than anyone else planted on this earth.

Mrs. Holloway was perhaps a year or two younger than Bobby, but she gazed at them both with the deference of a schoolgirl in the presence of two headmistresses. She planted a dark leather handbag on her lap, enclosing it in her black-gloved hands. The bag was far too small to hold a cake—*bad luck, that,* Bobby mused. Though perhaps she'd left one downstairs.

"I hesitated to approach you," Mrs. Holloway began in her smooth tones. "But I'm at a bit of a loss."

"Not at all." Judith sank down on her painting stool and leaned to Mrs. Holloway encouragingly. "We are always happy to help, for dear Cynthia's sake if nothing else."

Bobby hid a snort. Judith might claim they'd assisted Mrs. Holloway in the past in gratitude for her looking after Cyn so well, but Bobby knew better. Judith liked playing detective for the fun of it. She'd had some exploits on the Continent a few years ago that Bobby was just learning about, such as hunting assassins and other exciting adventures. Judith was always up for intrigue.

"Why don't you tell us the problem, Mrs. H?" Bobby paced to the skylight on the sloping ceiling and rubbed a clear spot on the steamy pane. Judith's house lay on Upper Brook Street, and the studio gave a view over the roofs of Park Lane to Hyde Park in the distance.

Mrs. Holloway seemed both reluctant to begin and impatient to have this errand behind her, but she softened under Judith's kind interest.

"I am looking into a matter for the Countess of Coulson," Mrs. Holloway said. "She approached Lady Cynthia for help—she is worried about her son."

"As she's right to be," Bobby said, turning from the window.

Lady Coulson was the wife of the Earl of Coulson and much despised by Bobby's mother. *A vapid, vacant woman,* Lady Lockwood

—Bobby's mother—always snapped. *Lovely to look at but hasn't got the brains of a mouse.*

Bobby's sister-in-law, Eliza, had snidely confided to Bobby that Bobby's mum had once held a grand passion for Lord Coulson. Handsome and athletic, he'd apparently broken many a lady's heart in his day. When Coulson had married the very blonde, very comely chit who'd become Lady Coulson, Bobby's mum had never forgiven her. Still hadn't, though thirty and more years had passed.

Lady Coulson's second son, Terrance, was a wild and untamable rogue of twenty who routinely ran through his allowance and begged for more. His indulgent mother often convinced his father to give it to him.

"I take it you're speaking of the Honorable Terrance Makepeace, black sheep of the family," Bobby said.

"No, the older son, the Honorable William." Mrs. Holloway adjusted her bag minutely on her lap. "Lady Coulson is worried that Terrance has pulled William into trouble, but she is not certain. She fears the wrath of their father, if this is the case."

Bobby stuck her thumbs into her waistcoat pockets. "Coulson might come down hard on her beloved Terrance if he's led William, the heir and apple of his father's eye, astray," she concluded.

"You know the family?" Mrs. Holloway asked her.

"I know *of* them," Bobby said. "Both sons a bit of a loss, in my opinion. Even my insipid brother doesn't like them. Any reason you're keen to aid these rather wet Coulsons?"

"Is that any of our business, Bobby?" Judith asked quickly, probably afraid Mrs. H. would grow incensed at Bobby's impertinence and depart.

Bobby shrugged. "Merely curious."

"Lady Cynthia indicated to me that Mr. William has attended a few of Mr. Thanos's lectures at the Polytechnic," Mrs. Holloway explained in her patient way. "Mr. Thanos believes that Mr. William has great cleverness and much potential, but he is being dragged into the muck by his brother."

"Ah," Bobby said. She leaned back against the windowsill,

ignoring the cold of the glass. "Thanos hopes you can save young William—and his brother in the process—in case William proves to be a scientific prodigy. Thanos is too good to his fellow men, if you ask me."

Elgin Thanos, the man Cynthia was mad sweet on, though she'd never say so even if her toenails were pulled out, had an immensely clever brain. He was a bloody genius, able to carry long and complex mathematical equations in his head. He knew a damned sight more about everything than anyone Bobby had ever met. He was also a gentle soul and headlong in love with Cynthia—likewise, torture would never make him admit it.

"In other words, you're not doing this so much for the lofty Lady Coulson, but as a favor for Cyn," Bobby said. "And by extension, Mr. Thanos. Or the other way about."

"Indeed," Mrs. Holloway said primly.

"I commend you," Judith said. "But how can *we* help?"

Mrs. Holloway lost her assurance and looked embarrassed. "Well, it's a bit of a cheek, actually. Daniel—Mr. McAdam—has gone to Ireland, so I cannot ask him."

The blush when she slipped and called McAdam by his first name tickled Bobby. Mrs. Holloway was as gone on him as Cyn was on Thanos. So much romance in the air.

"Ask him what, Mrs. H.?" Bobby prompted when Mrs. Holloway seemed reluctant to continue.

"Mr. Terrance has been taking Mr. William to a gambling club," Mrs. Holloway said. "A rather rough one, on the Strand. Called the Adam since it's near a street by that name. Gentlemen only, of course." Mrs. Holloway's mouth tightened, she clearly having second thoughts about her errand.

Bobby saw Judith realize Mrs. Holloway's intent at the same time she did.

"The penny drops," Bobby declared, her anticipation heightening. "You want me to infiltrate said gentleman's club and see what Terrance and William get up to. And then what? Simply report? Or drag them out by their heels?"

Judith's lovely eyes filled with alarm as she pictured Bobby doing the latter. "Mrs. Holloway, I am not certain that we are the best to ask —" she began.

Bobby cut her off. "Nonsense. Of course, I'll do it. Happy to. Only one thing to ask in return, Mrs. H. If I carry out this mission, will you bring us one of your stupendous lemon cakes?"

Chapter Two

Bobby guessed there'd be a row as soon as Mrs. Holloway thanked them and departed, and she wasn't wrong. When Judith returned to the studio from seeing Mrs. Holloway downstairs, her face held a dark scowl.

"Mrs. Holloway is already remorseful about coming here," Judith began before Bobby could say a word. "She asked me to tell you never mind. She will wait for Mr. McAdam to return and have him assist her."

"Rot that." Bobby flung herself once more onto her favorite chair, a wooden structure with soft cushions designed by William Morris. She retrieved a cheroot from the depths of her pocket, remembered she shouldn't light up, and stuffed it back inside. "Mrs. H. needs a spy, and I'm happy to be one. She did agree to the lemon cake." Bobby rubbed her hands. "I can taste it now."

"Bobby."

Judith's admonishing tone made Bobby's ire rise. "Lord, Judes, you sound like my mother. Only you have to say *Roberta*, with your nose turned up so high it's a wonder you can breathe."

"Please be serious." Judith sank to her stool but kept her steady gaze on Bobby. "This idea is highly risky. What if you're caught and arrested? Even if your father could get you off any charge, you'd be humiliated in every newspaper in Britain and beyond. Your father might lock you in his cellar for embarrassing him."

"What should I do instead?" Bobby clenched her tailored cashmere lapels with stiff fingers. "Stuff myself into corset and frock and behave like the insipid society daughter I'm supposed to be? Or wear drab gowns and throw myself into charity work, like the spinster rather long in the tooth that I am? I'm thirty and unmarried—I might as well be dead."

"Do not twist my words, please." Judith folded her arms over her curved waist, her sign that she was uneasy. "I am worried about you. I know you easily blend in with gentlemen in their gaming houses all the time, but this family knows you. Won't Terrance and William be surprised to find Lady Roberta in their midst in a gentleman's suit?"

"Not at all. Their mother and mine made their society debut in the same year. That is the extent of the acquaintance, in the same manner as all titled idiots who went to the same schools know each other. I barely saw Terrance and William growing up, but I heard all about them, mostly from my spiteful mother. They'll have no idea who I am, no fear." And a taste of adventure wouldn't go amiss, Bobby thought, but did not say. Why should Judith have had all the fun?

"But this is a club you've never gone to." Judith rocked a little on her stool, her anger softening to pure anxiousness. "If all titled idiots know each other, as you put it, couldn't someone else recognize you? Friends of your brother's, perhaps? Or one of your childhood acquaintances?"

"My childhood friends either know all about me and wouldn't betray me, or they wouldn't recognize me if I danced naked in front of them," Bobby said with assurance. "You'd be astounded how much people see only what they wish to see. And anyway, I look so much like a bloke, no one has ever tumbled to me no matter where I go. That is why Mrs. Holloway didn't ask Cynthia to run this errand. Cyn can dress in a man's clothes all she likes, but she's very obviously a woman. If she'd cut off her hair, she might fare better, but she refuses."

Bobby rubbed her very short hair, cropped by a barber in the way she liked. So much more comfortable than having all that hair wrapped around her head in styles so complicated it took two lady's maids to dress it. Best thing she ever did was to have the whole mess chopped off.

Judith, whose luxurious hair was a dream to stroke, deepened her frown.

"It is still a risk. What if it's a club where you must have someone vouch for you simply to get inside the door?"

Bobby shrugged. "Then I, like any other disappointed chap, will walk away, hail a cab, and come home. If I don't drown my sorrows at a pub that will let me in its taproom."

"That is another point—what if you get drunk and babble things you should not?"

"Now you are inventing things," Bobby scoffed. "Point the first, I never drink to excess—well, not when I'm trying to be careful. Point the second, what the devil could I babble? I don't have any deep dark secrets. I mostly read books, enjoy my cheroots, watch you paint, and get on with my life. The most I'd admit in a drunken fit is that I didn't really like the latest book by Wilkie Collins." *And that I'm potty about you, dear Judith,* she added to herself.

"It is still too dangerous." Judith crossed her legs, her skirt swinging freely.

Look at her, all tightly wrapped around herself, Bobby mused. She longed to untwist those shapely limbs and have them twine around her instead. End this silly argument with something much more pleasurable.

"I'll be doing nothing more than what I would on a leisurely night out with Cyn," Bobby said. "If you're so worried, come with me."

Bobby only half joked. Judith never had any inclination to dress as a man. She wore frocks designed to her specifications that allowed her less restriction than most ladies' attire and saw no reason to don anything else.

Judith sent Bobby a look that boded no good. "I just might."

She turned her back, took up her brush, and returned to the painting, a signal that the conversation was over.

~

IN SPITE OF JUDITH'S DECLARATION, SHE WAS NOWHERE IN sight by the time Bobby was ready to depart that evening.

"She's gone out, your ladyship," Hubbard told Bobby when she inquired.

Hubbard insisted on using the honorific with Bobby and had gone stiff with horror when Bobby suggested he not bother. She didn't press him, however, because Hubbard was a good soul, who put up with Judith's way of life without a word of admonishment or even of judgment.

"Do you know *where* she's gone out?" Bobby asked somewhat impatiently.

"I could not say, your ladyship."

Which meant he might or might not know. Bobby sighed, wrapped a scarf around her neck, and settled her hat. "Never mind. I'll try not to be too late."

Hubbard liked to bolt all the doors at midnight on the evenings Judith didn't have guests. If Bobby didn't make it by then, she'd be sleeping in the garden or trudging home to her old flat on Duchess Street.

She ought to give up that flat, but she didn't want to presume that her newfound understanding with Judith would last forever. Or that they even had an understanding. Bobby was reluctant to broach the subject.

She said her farewells to Hubbard then stepped into Upper Brook Street, turning toward Grosvenor Square in search of a hansom cab. She soon found one and directed the driver to take her to the Strand.

The Adam Club, which Mrs. Holloway had given them the address of, lay not far beyond Charing Cross railway station. The club was situated in an unprepossessing building of dark brown brick with one small sign on the doorpost to tell passersby what lay within.

Bobby alighted from the cab, noting that the club's windows were either shuttered or too grimy to allow her a look inside. The whole place was unnervingly dark.

The hansom rattled away into traffic that was still heavy, even at this hour, the Strand always full of life. Despite the bustle behind her, Bobby suddenly felt very much alone.

She approached the front door as though she had no qualms and rapped upon it.

The portal was opened by the sort of man Bobby expected to see —well-dressed but large and beefy. Portraying respectability but with the obvious strength to throw out any riotous patron.

"Evening," Bobby greeted him cheerfully. "Anyone welcome here? Or do I need to answer the secret questions?"

In some gaming establishments, if one had to ask such things, then one didn't belong there. Bobby had learned to act the rather dim-witted upper-class twit trying to slum, a ruse that worked like a charm. She might not always be admitted to a place, but she wouldn't be bodily tossed to the pavement either.

It also helped that she had a naturally low-timbered voice and didn't have to take on a false baritone. She bounced on her toes and beamed at the bloke while he scowled down at her.

Bobby knew what he saw—a shortish, plump young man who'd grow stout as he aged, with a square face, brown eyes, and clothes tailor-made for him. Probably had money to burn and not enough sense to hang on to it.

The man abruptly stepped aside and gestured for Bobby to enter. Bobby relinquished her coat and hat to a thinner chap who came forward at the snap of the larger man's fingers. The footman, or whoever he was, tucked the coat into the cloakroom and set the hat carefully on a shelf. She wasn't given a ticket—presumably they'd remember whose clobber went with whom.

Bobby gave both men a salute and dove into the bowels of the club.

The door to the gaming room was obvious, as noise boomed from behind it. Bobby pried open the portal and walked into a wall of smoke. Cheroots, cigarillos, and Turkish cigarettes were in every hand or hung from every mouth. The only things absent were pipes, as those would be leisurely enjoyed in a quieter room, not furiously sucked on over games.

Bobby didn't mind the miasma, as she'd have her own cheroot out soon, but Judith wouldn't let Bobby near her reeking like a smokehouse.

The tables were packed with men from the upper and middle classes who thought they had money to spare for this insalubrious hell. No women present, which was interesting. Often seductively dressed ladies called butterflies circulated in clubs like this one to distract a man from playing his best.

Possibly no need for that here. These gents were frenziedly throwing money to the tables as though they never needed to eat again.

Bobby found an empty chair and squeezed onto it. If the table's entering stake proved too high, she'd shrug and wriggle back out, but if not, she'd place a bet and blend in.

The game was *vingt-un*. Bobby studied her cards, laid down a few crowns—which seemed to be an acceptable wager—and waited for the dealer to toss her another card. A ridiculous game, she thought darkly as her hand's total passed the required amount, more luck than skill. Bobby's coins disappeared, and she dug into her pocket for more.

As she played, she glanced about for her quarry but did not see them. Annoying waste of time if they didn't turn up. She'd learned, though, from Cynthia's stories of Mrs. Holloway's undertakings, that investigating was often more about patience than exciting break-throughs.

The night rolled on, Bobby's coin purse grew lighter, and she never saw Lady Coulson's brats. She recognized gents from other clubs and a few friends of her brother, as Judith had feared. However, those lads had never paid much attention to Wilfred Perry's awkward little sister, and they didn't have any idea who she was now.

Bobby was simply a ne'er-do-well the chaps at the clubs had come to accept. There were enough nouveau-riche young men roaming London these days that who was who had become rather blurred. As long as Bobby didn't try to marry anyone's sister, all would be well.

She lingered for hours, playing cards—losing and winning—enjoying a cheroot and some fairly decent brandy, listening to tittle-tattle, and contributing opinions when asked. Gentlemen often derided ladies for nattering on about other people, but in Bobby's opinion, gentlemen could out-gossip ladies any day.

She saw no sign of Terrance or William Makepeace. There were plenty of young men here wagering out of their depth and losing too much, but none were the two sons of Lord and Lady Coulson.

Discouraged, Bobby at last retrieved her coat and hat and stepped into the night, heading for a hansom cab stand.

She reflected as she walked that a great advantage of assuming man's dress was that no one thought a thing about her being on the street alone, even stumbling along to find a hansom.

If she were in skirts, striding by herself in the Strand at half past eleven, she'd be roundly condemned, by those who didn't try to assail her, that is. Even if she'd been out here through no doing of her own —perhaps she'd been abducted and dropped in this street—she'd be ruined and shunned, as though said abduction would be all her fault.

In her greatcoat and hat, a scarf around her neck against the new falling rain, no one looked at Bobby twice.

A hansom waited at the closest stand, the cabbie on top half asleep. He came awake as soon as Bobby stepped into the cab and called her direction, and they clopped off.

Bobby made it to the house in Upper Brook Street as the nearby church clocks began to strike twelve.

"Let me in, Hubbard. I'm just in time." Bobby gave the butler a grin as he opened the door he'd been about to bolt.

"Did you have a pleasant evening, your ladyship?"

"Tolerable." Bobby handed over hat, coat, scarf, and gloves as Hubbard reached for them. "But happy to be home."

"Very good, your ladyship. Miss Townsend has already retired."

It was early, by Bobby's standards, but Judith was unpredictable.

Some nights she'd stay up until dawn, painting like mad. On other nights, she'd toddle off to bed at eight.

"Then I shall retire myself," Bobby said. "Good night, Hubbard."

"Good night, your ladyship."

Having carefully hung up Bobby's things, Hubbard returned to bolting the doors, and Bobby headed up the stairs.

A light shone under Judith's bedchamber door on the second floor. Bobby took the chance and pushed it open. She had her own bedchamber in this vast house, though most nights she and Judith shared.

Judith was indeed awake, propped up against pillows, reading a book. Nothing unusual in this, but Bobby noted that Judith was slightly out of breath and the book was upside down.

"All's well?" Bobby asked her.

"Oh, there you are, darling." Judith set the book aside and yawned with pretended fatigue. "I wasn't certain whether you'd return tonight."

"Better company here," Bobby said with honesty. "No luck at the hell. Plenty of gentlemen losing their shirts, but the oiks in question never turned up."

Judith sent her a gentle smile. "Ah, well. Never mind. Are you coming to bed?"

Bobby's heartbeat quickened. Judith in her fine lawn nightgown and nothing under it was a beautiful thing to behold.

Bobby regretfully jerked her thumb at the door. "I should kip down the hall. I reek like a chimney sweep."

Judith's warm smile heated the room. "Leave your clothes over there, and all will be well."

Bobby's heart banged even harder. "What an excellent idea."

She disrobed with all speed and soon was burrowing into the comfortable nest Judith had made. Judith turned down the lamp, softening the room with delicious darkness. All as it should be.

~

BOBBY RETURNED TO THE ADAM FOR THREE MORE NIGHTS, determined to not let Mrs. Holloway down. She gambled sparingly, making herself walk away from a losing game, and each night she came home perhaps five guineas poorer than when she'd left.

Judith was always in bed when Bobby returned, ostensibly reading the same book. She never seemed to make any headway with it, marking the same spot every night before she closed it to welcome Bobby home.

Bobby didn't question her. If Judith wanted to pretend she was nonchalantly absorbed in reading whenever Bobby wasn't there, she could do so.

On the fourth night at the Adam, Bobby's vigil was rewarded. Lady Coulson's offspring, William and Terrance Makepeace, swaggered into the Adam Club and eventually joined the card game at Bobby's table.

Chapter Three

The Honorable Terrance, in fact, did all the swaggering. His older brother simply looked worried and out of place.

Another man had come in with the brothers and now hovered at Terrance's shoulder as the lads seated themselves at Bobby's table. This gentleman—Bobby gave him the label with reservations—was about double the age of the brothers, wore a well-made suit complete with gold fob-watch, and observed the two with an eagle-like stare.

Bobby had no idea who he was. She recognized nearly half the gents in this place, most of them sons of peers and wealthy nabobs. Many had either gone to school with her brother or now rubbed elbows with him at the grand palaces of White's and Brooks's.

The other half were the up-and-comers who'd made their fortunes in trade and wanted to hobnob with the peers. They might not be admitted to the closed clubs of St. James's, but they could meet and consort with sons of dukes and earls at the Adam Club without restriction.

This man appeared out of place even here. He had a soft face and a full but well-trimmed beard, and his shoulders spoke of much exercise. His eyes, on the other hand, were like steel ball bearings, devoid of any sort of warmth.

He watched Terrance with an intense gaze, though he did nothing to interfere with Terrance's choices of cards or wagers. If the man was helping Terrance cheat—perhaps signaling what others held in their hands—he was damned subtle. Bobby caught no twitch of fingers or brows that might be guiding Terrance, and in fact, Terrance lost a good deal more than he won.

Now that Bobby had located the lads, she wasn't certain what to do. Note all she observed, she supposed, to relate to Mrs. Holloway.

Her focus on the pair was so avid she lost a hand she could have won if she'd been paying attention. As Bobby slid her markers over, she realized she was twenty guineas down. That was her signal to leave the table or the club altogether. Instead, Bobby took a hefty pull on her cheroot and accepted another round of cards.

Not long into that hand, she found the hard-eyed chap's gaze upon her. Maybe she'd been too obviously staring at Terrance and William. Or perhaps he thought he'd found another mark to fleece.

Bobby drained her glass of whisky in a practiced way and let out an expletive when her hand was beaten. The man's contemplation of her sharpened.

Dash it, Bobby was nowhere near as good at this investigation business as McAdam. He'd know how to find out information without giving himself away.

Bobby held on to her courage and continued playing.

Neither Terrance nor William ever glanced her way, or at anyone else at the table, for that matter. Terrance was fixed on the game, his eyes glittering. William kept his attention on Terrance, except for fearful glances at the hard-eyed man.

William's spying on him too, Bobby realized. *Trying to decide how to save his brother from his influence.*

The game was not going well for either brother. Terrance was playing very deep, and Bobby doubted William could stop Terrance racing to his ruin.

The hard-eyed man gave Bobby another assessing glance, then he removed a folded paper from his coat pocket and handed it to the nearest gentleman at the table.

This gent flicked through the cards inside the paper, grinned, and passed them to the next man in line. Bobby's curiosity grew as the pack moved from hand to hand around the table.

She opened the paper when it reached her, revealing flat pictures in gray monochrome colors. *Ah*. Naughty photographs. Gentlemen often shared such things at the clubs—some of them had whole books of ladies in various stages of undress.

Bobby never minded gazing upon a lovely woman and studied the photographs with interest. Judith was Bobby's only love, of course, but no harm in having a look.

The hard-eyed man had riveted his stare to Bobby while she leafed through the pictures. She felt his gaze skewering her, trying to penetrate her disguise.

Bobby's heart beat faster. She'd told Judith she didn't much worry that she'd be revealed as having the body of a woman, but now she wondered if the blasted man would expose her.

What would these chaps do to her if he did? Bobby had learned some boxing in her day, but nothing that would help her fight her way free of a gang of men and run for home.

She kept her head bent over the pictures, as though examining them thoroughly. One lady was quite pretty, with either blonde or red hair—hard to tell on a photograph that hadn't been tinted. Shapely lass, wearing only knickers, her long legs crossed. She stared with good humor at the photographer, as though having her picture taken without her clothes on was good fun. Bobby smiled back at her.

She felt the man's attention on her lessen, and when she dared look up again, she saw that he'd redirected his scrutiny to William.

Bobby exhaled in relief, then that breath caught. Beneath the picture of the blonde lady, Bobby found a photograph of a comely woman with long, sleek hair and features she knew very well.

She stared, frozen, at the image, her mission forgotten. The woman's dark hair twined about her bare torso, framing the bosom Bobby had grown quite fond of. Like the lady in the previous photo, she wore only the bottom half of combinations, her lower legs and elegant feet exposed. The woman peeped at the camera through a lock of her hair, far more seductively than had the blonde.

When the devil had Judith Townsend decided to pose for bawdy photographs?

She looked younger in the picture, so likely years before she'd met Bobby, but still, Bobby thought Judith would have mentioned it by now. She'd always known Judith had lived a colorful life on the Continent, but she hadn't realized how colorful.

Bobby brought the picture closer to her face. Yes, it was Judith's right shoulder peeking at her, and her slim cheek, those eyes that made Bobby melt into a puddle. On her other shoulder ...

She peered harder, wishing the lighting in the room was better. Instead of gaslight, the club had candles and kerosene lamps, probably to keep the high-wagering gentlemen from better seeing their cards.

Bobby realized abruptly that the woman in the picture wasn't Judith at all. But a dashed good resemblance. So good, that there was only one thing for it.

She shuffled to the next photograph, barely noting that this young woman was completely nude, her back to the photographer, peering saucily behind her.

Bobby went through the rest of the dozen before she managed to drop the pictures all over the floor.

"Damn," she said loudly, then dove for them.

A waiter hurried to help, and together they picked up the photographs. Bobby palmed the one of Judith's double and slid it into her pocket.

She grinned as she restored the photographs to the paper and slid it to the next man in line. "Bit of flesh always makes me tremble," she said heartily, and the gents on either side of her laughed.

The hard-eyed man would know the photo was missing. But with luck, he might think that it was still stuck under the table or that the waiter had absconded with it.

To her relief, the man seemed to have lost all interest in the photographs. The packet made it to the last player, who laid the pictures aside after he'd had his ogle, but the hard-eyed bloke made no move to retrieve them. Terrance glanced at them longingly, and Bobby saw his hand edge toward them.

Had the hard-eyed man been testing Bobby? Suspecting she was not what she seemed? Unnerving.

She must have passed his little stratagem, because he ignored her for the rest of the game.

Bobby decided this would be her last hand. She threw down her cards and her coins in disgust when she lost and slid from her seat. She moved slowly toward the card room's exit, glancing at other games as though tempted to join them, then shook her head and meandered into the corridor.

As much as she itched to hurry, she knew that running out of the club like the hounds of hell chased her would only draw more notice. She made herself pause in the hallway for several more puffs on her cheroot before depositing the end into a bowl set out for that purpose. Only then did she stride to the foyer, calling for her hat and coat.

It was colder outside tonight. The finer weather of early autumn had deserted London, and chill rain pattered to the cobbles. Bobby adjusted her scarf and resigned herself to trudging down the Strand in search of a cab.

A carriage rumbled to a halt in front of her before she reached Bedford Street. Bobby recognized the coach and the figure of Dunstan, Judith's coachman, at the reins.

Torn between annoyance and relief, Bobby yanked open the carriage's door and hauled herself inside.

"Following me about, are you?" she demanded as she landed on the seat next to Judith.

The carriage jerked as Dunstan started forward. Even this late, the Strand was full of vehicles conveying patrons to and from theatres, or revelers to soirees and such. The social Season was long over but that didn't stop anyone still in Town from gadding about to every event they could find.

"I am, yes." Judith sat calmly, her shoulder against Bobby's warm and solid. "Concerned for you. And from your present agitation, I had a right to be."

Bobby pulled off her hat and tossed it to the opposite seat. Ruffling her short hair, she peered at Judith in sudden realization.

"You've been doing this every night, haven't you? No wonder I find your chest heaving like you've been running and you reading books upside down. You've hurried home and leapt into bed, pretending you've been there all along. Hubbard is your partner in crime, damn the man."

"I'm sorry, darling." Judith sounded contrite but not entirely humble. "I have no wish for you to be harmed because you're excited about helping Mrs. Holloway sleuth."

"I don't know how exciting it is." Bobby jammed her arms over her chest, the photograph singeing her pocket. "Interesting, I should say. Lady Coulson's sons came in tonight, by the bye. With their evil mentor."

"I saw them," Judith, who'd just accused Bobby of being too excited about the enterprise, came alight with curiosity. "But I couldn't wait for you to come home before I knew what happened. Do tell."

"Not much *to* tell," Bobby said, hoping she didn't dim the enthusiasm in Judith's eyes. "Terrance seems to be heavily under the man's influence, and William is pretending to be. Probably trying to keep the younger lad out of trouble. Don't recognize the bloke playing nanny to them. He looked at me sharpish, probably wondering why I watched them, but thankfully he lost his fascination."

"Oh, dear. Is that why you're upset?"

Bobby reached into her coat pocket and withdrew the photograph. "Chap didn't unnerve me as much as this did. I thought it was you, but then realized it wasn't. You don't have that."

She pointed to a flower just visible on the woman's shoulder. A tattoo, it was called. Sailors collected them up and down their arms, as did men who wanted to prove they were adventurers. Unconventional ladies occasionally had them done as well.

Judith went very still for several moments. Then she reached out with trembling fingers in dark leather gloves and took the photograph. "Where did you get this?"

"From the chappie with Terrance and William," Bobby said. "He was handing around a stack of lewd photographs, probably to distract the other gents from their cards. There was a lot of losing, that round."

"More to the point, where did *he* get it?" Judith's voice was as steely as the man's eyes had been. "I thought these were all destroyed."

Her cheeks burned red in the coach's dim lamplight, and she pressed her lips tightly together.

Bobby regarded her in bewilderment touched with alarm. "If that ain't you, Judes, then who the devil is it?"

"My sister," Judith said. Sudden tears wet her eyes and spilled to her cheeks.

Chapter Four

B obby jerked herself out of her stunned motionlessness and gathered Judith into her arms. Judith rarely cried—almost never. Now she rested her face against Bobby's shoulder, shaking with sobs.

It was difficult not to be flummoxed. Bobby had learned much about Judith's family—their wealth, high standing, and connections to almost every peer in the land on both her mother's and father's side. Bobby's father was an earl, but Judith's parents could buy and sell him several times over, as well as cast him to the four winds ... socially, anyway.

Judith had an older brother, who, like Bobby's, was busy filling his nursery with heirs and spares. All males, of course. Both families had ceased bothering about their eccentric and unmarried daughters, thanks to all the bonny boys springing up.

Nowhere in the narrative had Judith indicated she had a sister, especially one who resembled her so closely.

"What is it, love?" Bobby asked gently. "Did she die?"

Almost every family had lost at least one child, which was a reason the survivors were encouraged to produce as many as they could.

Judith disentangled herself from Bobby's embrace, sat upright, and took a handkerchief from her pocket. Dabbing her eyes, she drew a long breath.

"Forgive me. It gave me a turn, seeing her picture. I thought all those photographs had been destroyed."

Judith still held hard to it, fingers squeezing the card as though she'd never let go.

"It's none of my business," Bobby began. "If you don't want to tell me the tale, that's all right." She was dashed curious, but she knew from experience how painful another's prying could be.

"No, I want you to know." Judith's shoulder bumped Bobby's as the carriage jerked over a hole in the road. "You'd have liked Lucetta. She was a free spirit, determined to choose her own path. Still is, I hope. She is very much alive ... I think."

"You *think*?" Bobby's eyes widened. "Good Lord, that sounds dire. What happened?"

"Nothing so awful as you are imagining. Lucetta lives somewhere on the Continent. At least, that was the last I heard from her, ten years ago. She blamed me and cut the tie, but I still worry about her."

"I've changed my mind," Bobby said abruptly. "You must tell me all." She softened. "If I can help ..."

Judith shook her head. "It's not an uncommon story." She gave her cheeks a final dab and returned the handkerchief to her pocket, but her eyes remained too bright.

"Lucetta was beautiful and bold." Judith smiled shakily. "Like me, she declared early that she'd never marry a tedious boor and be under his thumb the rest of her life. My parents were incensed with her. They'd already resigned themselves to me being an artist and removing myself from the rules of society. They decided to give up on me, and so expected Lucetta to be the good and obedient daughter. She was to marry a respectable gentleman of the correct lineage and become a model wife and mother. They misjudged her terribly."

"Bit hard on the poor gel," Bobby said with feeling. "I'm no stranger to being pressed to follow that path. Luckily, dear Eliza and Wilfred are so fruitful. Wilfred's children are far more valued than mine would be, in any case." A daughter, in Bobby's family's view, was an appendage, useful only for making a connection with another prominent family.

"As you can imagine, Lucetta rebelled," Judith went on. "She was always more audacious than me. Unfortunately, her adventuresome spirit landed her in the clutches of a bad man. I liked Mr. Arnott—Stephan—at first, and I encouraged my parents to leave her be."

"But?" Bobby reached for Judith's free hand and squeezed it. "There is a *but* lurking in that sentence."

"Arnott was an artist, a photographer. Lucetta met him at one of the parties I took her to. His work was very good, and he was personable enough. I saw no harm in him. He supplemented his income, as many photographers do, by selling racy pictures to publishers, collectors, and anyone else who would hand him the money. I didn't blame him for that—it is difficult to make one's way in the art world, unless one has a wealthy patron."

"Lucetta posed for him?" Bobby asked. "Of her own free will?"

"She was proud to do it. Lucetta said she was helping him. Artists must do what they can to eat, she told me. She was certain that the commission to make him rich would come along any day, and they'd be married."

"But it did not," Bobby supplied.

"No, which turned Stephan bitter and angry. He pressed Lucetta to do more and more pictures, and then he wanted to hire her out to undress in salon gatherings—you know the sort of thing."

Such parties had been all the rage at one time. Unclothed or barely draped young women turned up in the drawing rooms of the rich to pose as Greek statues. Rather silly, in Bobby's opinion, but people thought it showed they were both very modern and had good taste.

"She objected?" Bobby asked.

"Not at first. But Lucetta didn't like having to stand perfectly still, in a draft, while gentlemen walked around her and ogled her. It was one thing to pose for a photograph alone in a studio with Stephan, another to share her body with strangers. She declared she wasn't a prostitute and refused to do any more. But Stephan had already promised her to several more soirees and ribald parties, and he stood to lose a bit of cash." Judith's mouth tightened into a grim line. "He took it out on her."

"The bounder," Bobby growled in rage. "Did you put your boot up his backside?"

"In a manner of speaking." Judith's tone told Bobby she'd not gone easy on Mr. Arnott. "I got Lucetta away from him, and I spoke to friends who made London too hot to hold the man. He fled his creditors to the wilds of Canada, I believe."

"Where there are many bears," Bobby finished with satisfaction.

"I imagine he tried his luck on the gold fields. He was that sort." Judith waved him away. "We've never heard from Stephan Arnott again, which is the best conclusion. I gathered up all the photographs and destroyed them. Lucetta helped me—she enjoyed it. But our family shut her out." Judith gazed down at the photograph in regret. "They disinherited her, cut her completely. Told me I wasn't allowed to have anything to do with her. Lucetta had ruined herself, and now she must live with the consequences."

"Very compassionate of them. I take it you ignored this command?"

"Of course, I did. I loved Lucetta. I decided I'd travel for a time on the Continent and took Lucetta with me, out of their reach. She deserved a life, happiness. But while she appreciated my assistance in getting her away, she also blamed me for the family shunning her. If I'd not rebelled first—if I'd taken up the mantle of the good daughter and made an advantageous marriage—Lucetta could have had her own life—*my* life—without censure. In her eyes, I stole that from her. Plus, she'd met Stephan through me and my art circles. Her resentment ran deep. I know she simply needed someone on whom to take out her disappointment, but it hurt."

"Poor Judes." Bobby rested her head on Judith's shoulder. "None of it was your fault."

"I knew that, logically, but my heart said otherwise." Judith slid her hand over Bobby's, her leather gloves soft. "It *was* my fault for striding out without a care for what anyone thought of me. I left Lucetta behind to struggle and then founder."

"*Really* not your fault," Bobby repeated. "Lucetta could have cut off the blackguard at any time instead of trusting him, could have asked for your help in leaving home before that."

"I know you are right." Judith's voice was strained. "Yet, I can't help what I feel. One night, Lucetta and I had a terrible row. We were in Paris, living in a hotel. She wanted nothing more to do with me, and I told her she'd be a fool to refuse my help. We said many more things, all of which I regret now. She stormed off." Judith let out a shaking breath. "I've not seen her since."

Bobby saw her pain, which awakened a hurting in her own heart. Judith had kept this locked inside her, trying to put it behind her and move on. But she'd never truly been able to, and no wonder.

"I imagine you didn't leave it at that," Bobby said quietly. "You must have tried to find her."

"Of course, I did. I remained in Paris for a long time, searching, but Lucetta was gone. None of her acquaintance had seen her—or so they said. I began checking the city morgue, just in case. Thankfully, she never turned up there." Judith's grip tightened on Bobby's hand, the clasp conveying the fear she'd gone through. "Eventually I accepted that if Lucetta wanted to contact me, she would. About that time, I met Miss Morisot, the artist, and started to paint with her. I was grateful to her for her instruction and decided to stay on in Paris for several years. I never ceased looking for Lucetta, but I also never found her."

"You met McAdam there too." That story Bobby had heard, how Judith had posed as McAdam's wife and flushed out assassins bent on killing men who knew how to make weapons. Exciting times.

Judith's smile returned. "Assisting Mr. McAdam helped take my mind off my worries. I realized when hunting those men that there were far more things at stake in the world than my family troubles."

Bobby disagreed that Judith's worries were of less consequence than the fate of nations, but she kept that thought to herself.

"Is this one of the scoundrel's photographs?" Bobby asked, touching the picture still in Judith's hand. "Or a more recent one?"

"No, this is Stephan's work." Judith's brow puckered. "I swore we destroyed them all. I must discover how this man at the Adam Club got hold of it."

Judith's trembling had subsided, her voice returning to its usual determination. When Judith set her mind on something, woe betide any person, even an assassin, who got in her way.

Bobby's worry eased—Judith upset was not something she liked to see. She preferred that her strong-willed, quietly stubborn lady be free of difficulties.

"Well," Bobby said, trying to sound optimistic. "We'll find out exactly who this chap I saw at the club is, and ask him."

~

JUDITH'S SOLUTION FOR RUNNING THE HARD-EYED MAN TO ground was to interview Lady Coulson's sons.

She arranged to meet them, by methods unknown to Bobby, in Regent's Park the following afternoon. Likely Judith had used the network of servants she seemed to command, starting with Hubbard and her extremely loyal and discreet lady's maid, Evans.

However the word got passed, at three o'clock, Judith and Bobby descended from the coach and moved sedately to the entrance of the Royal Botanical Gardens in the southern portion of Regent's Park.

At least, Judith strolled sedately—Bobby was bouncing with impatience. She was ready to shake Terrance until he told her all he knew, but she reined herself in and let Judith take the lead.

Terrance and William had actually obeyed Judith's summons. The brothers waited near the gate at the Inner Circle—the lane that bounded the botanical gardens.

William stood ramrod stiff in a fine suit, autumn coat, and tall hat. Terrance, on the other hand, was red-eyed and pasty skinned, with rumpled coat and cravat twisted as though he'd slept in it. From the looks of things, he probably had. William was dressed for an afternoon's ramble in a park, while Terrance still wore last night's evening dress.

Judith halted when she reached them, nodding with extreme politeness. William tipped his hat and gave her a courteous bow.

Terrance belatedly seized his headgear and lifted it the barest inch from his head, but he kept his back rigid. Bobby concluded that if he tried any sort of bow, he'd fall over.

"Bit heavy on the tipple last night, eh?" Bobby asked, letting her voice boom. "Feeling delicate, are we?"

Terrance winced and screwed his eyes shut for a painful moment.

William sent Bobby a startled look. "Hang on, you were at the Adam last night, weren't you? Do I know you?"

Bobby straightened the lapels of her coat, its cut as smart as William's, before she stuck out a gloved hand.

"Mr. Robert Perry, at your service."

William clasped Bobby's hand, flinched slightly at her firm grip, and quickly let it drop. Terrance didn't bother offering to shake hands, but then, it probably hurt him to lift his arm. He'd already been well into his cups when he'd arrived last night, and he must have imbibed quite a bit more after Bobby's departure.

"Mr. Perry mentioned that you had a gentleman with you last evening," Judith said in her even tones. "I would like his name and address, please."

Terrance gaped. With his open mouth and red-rimmed, watery eyes, he resembled nothing more than a startled fish. "Why the devil should I tell you that?"

"Terrance." William's admonishment held shock. "Is that any way to speak to a lady? Apologize at once."

Terrance curled his lip. William might be shadowing his brother, trying to keep him out of trouble, but Terrance was by no means docile.

"It's none of her bloody business who he is," Terrance snapped. "Why do you want to know, eh? It's a fair question."

William became more and more distressed at Terrance's language. Judith, who could swear like a sailor when she had a mind to, withstood the onslaught without wavering.

"I have reason to believe he has something that belongs to me,"

Judith said smoothly. "Or knowledge of it. I will not tell him from whom I obtained his direction, if you do not wish me to."

When Judith began speaking like an instructor at a finishing school, most gentlemen became embarrassed and fell all over themselves trying to be on their best behavior. William certainly flushed and cleared his throat, but Terrance, who must have one hell of a hangover, only glared at her in defiance.

"Blackmailing you, is he?" Terrance chuckled, a sound like a boot on eggshells. "Maybe over some indiscretions with your gentleman friend?" He swept Bobby a knowing sneer that held some admiration. Bobby rolled her eyes.

"Certainly not." Judith's voice became ice cold. William's flush deepened, and even Terrance's sarcasm fled him. "This is of great importance. I am doing you the courtesy of asking you first, before I take up the issue with Lord Coulson."

"You never would." Terrance's aghast answer floated out, his face losing what little color it had.

Bobby, standing a pace or two behind Judith, mouthed, *Oh, yes, she would.*

"It is no matter," William said quickly. He seemed as adamant as his brother to keep his father far from their exploits. "His name is Joseph Moody, and he has a shop where he sells all sorts of things. Moody's Emporium, he calls it. On the Commercial Road, in Shadwell."

Terrance glared at William but realized it was too late to stop him. "A place no lady ought to go," Terrance said with derision. "Have a care for your reputation, love."

Bobby took a step forward. "Have a care for your tongue, lad, or you'll get a punch in the nose."

Terrance looked Bobby up and down. Bobby had no great height, but she was sturdy, and had rather enjoyed her boxing lessons.

"I'm only giving her a friendly warning." Terrance faded next to William, becoming sullen. "Shadwell is a dangerous place."

Judith jotted the name and direction into a small notebook she'd removed from her pocket. "Thank you," she said to William. "Why are you with such a gentleman, in any case? From what Mr. Perry says, he is not the most honorable of men."

"None of your affair," Terrance said, trying to imitate Judith's cool tones, and failing miserably.

"My brother likes to gamble," William said. "I am trying to dissuade him of the habit."

"I see." Judith skewered Terrance with a shrewd gaze. "You owe Mr. Moody some winnings."

"Quite a bit of them," William answered while Terrance spluttered. "Mr. Moody bought up all Terrance's gambling debts from the clubs and now wants to be paid. He follows us about—Terrance swears he'll win the money he owes, but of course he never does."

"And if he cannot pay?" Judith asked.

"Our father is very wealthy." William reddened again. "Mr. Moody threatens to take the money from *him* if need be. We truly do not want this coming to his attention."

Bobby broke in, "You could always confess all to your dear papa. Let your brother face the music, and be right out of it."

"Obviously, you do not know my father," William said, with the first hint of humor Bobby had seen in him. "We both will bear the brunt. Best we solve this on our own."

"Why are you spilling to them?" Terrance demanded. He focused a bleary gaze on Judith. "Who are you? William only dragged me here because he feared what you'd tell our pa about what we got up to. Friend of our mum's, are you?"

"A friend of Mr. Thanos," Judith said calmly. "He says you have much potential," she added to William.

William started and then looked pleased behind his worry. "Yes, he's a clever gentleman," he said with admiration, while Terrance wrinkled his nose. "I hope to return to his lectures as soon as I can. If there is anything else we can do to assist you, you have but to say the word."

"That will not be necessary." Judith snapped the notebook closed and returned it to her pocket. "Again, thank you."

"My brother is an ass, but he is right about one thing," William said quickly. "You should not go to Shadwell, not on your own. Perhaps I could ..."

He left the offer to escort her there hanging. Terrance let out a taunting snort, then put a hand to his head as though even that effort had pained it.

"Thank you for your concern, Mr. Makepeace," Judith replied. "I never said I would go there myself. Good day, gentlemen."

William tipped his hat, opened his mouth, probably to ask if he could guide her somewhere—anywhere—but then snapped it shut and gave her another polite bow. "Good day," he managed.

Terrance swayed and grabbed William's arm to steady himself. "Tart," he snarled.

Bobby raised one balled fist. Terrance's alarm grew as Bobby came at him, and he hurriedly ducked behind his brother.

William held up wavering hands to halt Bobby's onslaught. "I apologize, Mr. Perry. My brother is an idiot and had a late night. He has no idea what he is saying."

Bobby stopped close enough that the brothers understood the threat was real, though she had no real intention of battling these pups. Scaring them would suffice.

Judith paid the encounter no attention at all. She was already walking along the road toward her waiting carriage, her elegance like a song.

Bobby held out her hand, her gaze on Terrance. "Hand them over, please."

Terrance peered at her from behind William's shoulder. "I don't know what you mean."

"I saw you pinch those photographs from the table last night," Bobby said with conviction. "Thought you'd ogle them at your leisure at home, did you? Let's have them."

Bobby had seen Terrance slide the pictures surreptitiously into his pocket as she'd left the table last night, and she'd taken a chance he still had them on him. It was obvious he hadn't been home for a good grooming and change of clothes since the club—the stench of him was indication enough.

William, growing more the stern older brother by the moment, turned severely to him. "Give them to him, Terrance."

With a growl deep in his throat, Terrance yanked the folded paper out of his coat pocket and thrust it at Bobby. She glanced inside to see that, indeed, all the photographs were there before she tucked them neatly into her own pocket.

Bobby tipped her hat to both of them. "Behave yourselves, gentlemen. Oh, just a friendly hint—I'd stay far from Mr. Moody were I you. I have the feeling things are going to become very bad for him. Up to you, of course."

She slapped her hat back to her head and swung away, hurrying to catch up with Judith.

Judith, ahead of her, moved briskly, her skirt swaying with her smart, upright walk. Bobby's heart flooded with joy to watch her. She loved this gifted, clever, and generous woman who could put anyone in their place. Bobby now and always blessed the day that Cynthia had introduced her to the wonderful Judith.

Chapter Five

J udith, true to her word, never set foot in the Commercial Road. She sent a flurry of telegrams instead, one to a known associate of Daniel McAdam.

That associate was Mr. Fielding, who on the surface was a respectable vicar, but who'd at one time lived on the other side of the law. Mr. Fielding—or *his* associates—would know how to find Mr. Joseph Moony of Shadwell, and indeed, he did just that.

Two days after their meeting with Terrance and William, Bobby accompanied Judith to a vicarage in the heart of the East End. Mrs. Holloway, informed by Judith that they'd cornered the man causing Lady Coulson so much heartbreak, had insisted on joining them.

Mrs. Holloway carried a box that Bobby suspected held one of her feather-light cakes. Not for them, Bobby surmised, as the box on her lap remained firmly closed and tied with a string during the coach ride across London.

Mrs. H. had changed a bit since Bobby had first met her a few years ago. Instead of trying to hide her shock at Bobby's comfort in men's dress, she now accepted Bobby as she was. Mrs. Holloway was good at that, Bobby reflected. She saw the truth of a person and didn't require that person to change to suit her expectations.

Mrs. Holloway was much more disapproving of Mr. Fielding,

however, who was a wolf in sheep's clothing. He was a slim man, handsome, some ladies would think, with a trim beard and lively blue eyes.

Mr. Fielding met them in the parlor of his vicarage as his long-suffering housekeeper hauled in a loaded tea tray. Bobby sprang up to take the tray, setting it on the tea table in front of Mrs. Holloway. The housekeeper had also brought in the cake, which Mrs. Holloway had handed her upon their arrival, now sliced on a plate.

Mr. Moody was present, sullenly planted on a straight-backed chair. He did not rise when the ladies entered. Mr. Fielding leaned one shoulder against the wall next to Moody, seemingly nonchalant, but Bobby felt Mr. Fielding's tension crackle.

"Is this to be an interrogation by skirts?" Moody shifted his gaze over Mrs. Holloway and Judith, who'd seated herself next to Mrs. H., and let it come to rest on Bobby. "That one *should* be in skirts. Thinks no one knows."

Bobby hid her start. She'd sensed Moody's keen observation at the club but believed he'd dismissed her. Now his assessing gaze held avarice, as though he wondered how much he could blackmail Bobby for.

"Keep a civil tongue." Mr. Fielding's voice was deceptively mild.

Moody flinched, which made Bobby wonder what Fielding had done to get the man here and make him behave relatively tamely.

Mrs. Holloway, unasked, poured out tea, carefully adding milk and sugar to each cup. Judith handed the cups and pieces of the cake around, as though she served tea at the vicarage every day of her life.

Mr. Fielding took Moody's portion from Judith's hands and shoved it at the man, which kept Judith from having to go near him. Bobby nodded her thanks at Mr. Fielding, who gave her a hint of a nod in return.

"Now then, Mr. Moody," Mrs. Holloway began. She was a cook, a woman in service, and yet she effortlessly commanded the room. "I am thankful to Mr. Fielding for inviting you here, so that I may speak with you. I would like you to cease your acquaintanceship with the Honorable Mr. Terrance and the Honorable Mr. William Makepeace.

Forgive Mr. Terrance's debts to you, break the association, and trouble them no more."

Moody's bearded face went slack with surprise, then his lips began to twitch. "Oh, yes? I should do that for you? Why?"

"Because it is the right thing," the unflappable Katherine Holloway returned. "The two young gentlemen do not need you dragging them to their ruin."

Moody's lip twitching became a full-blown smile. "To their ruin? I have that much power, do I? If I drop the lads, what do I get in return? They owe me nearly a thousand pounds. Eh, love? What'll you give me?"

His leer had Bobby almost on her feet. She hadn't actually punched Terrance's nose, but she saw no reason to hold back on this man.

Mr. Fielding swallowed a sip of tea. "A *civil* tongue, I said." The flint in his voice made Moody abruptly lose his smile.

"You will have nothing in return," Mrs. Holloway informed Moody. "But turn your attention to other tasks, please."

"Bloody hell." Moody glared up at Mr. Fielding. "You ain't police. I'll do what I choose, and it's no business of this woman with a teapot."

Mr. Fielding emitted a sound like a growl, and Moody snapped his mouth closed.

Bobby, realizing Mr. Fielding had things in hand, slouched back in her chair and had a nibble of the cake. Not Mrs. Holloway's coveted lemon cake but a lovely buttery one. Bobby took the time to enjoy it.

"You *will* leave them be," Judith stated. "But I have another matter to take up with you. Where did you obtain the photographs?"

Moody blinked at her, clearly baffled by the question. "Photographs?"

Bobby touched the packet of them safely in her pocket. They'd proved to be very interesting and not in the way most people would think.

"The photographs of young ladies you handed around at the

club," Judith said. Her back was straight, her dignity splendid. "Where did you get them?"

"Bought them, didn't I?" Moody leaned forward to stare at Judith more intently. "Hang about. One of them was you, wasn't it?" His leer returned.

"Hardly." Judith's crisp tone sent Moody into confusion again. Bobby took another large bite of cake, letting herself be entertained.

"Bought them from whom?" Mrs. Holloway asked.

"A shop, in Paris," Moody said in irritation. "What of it?"

"Which shop?" Judith persisted.

"I don't know, do I? On one of them boulevards somewhere."

"I'll wager you've never been to Paris," Bobby said from the depths of her chair. "You had them from a secondhand shop or some such here in London, who told you they came from a studio in Paris. Didn't you?"

"What does it matter?" Moody asked testily.

"It matters very much, indeed." Judith's tone remained neutral, but Bobby sensed her disappointment. "Never mind. I suggest that you release Mr. Makepeace from your clutches, shut down your store —I imagine the origins of some of your goods would not stand up to scrutiny?—and try your luck on shores far from here."

Moody sprang up. "Shut your gob, missus. You don't know nothing. I'm finished here."

He swung to the doorway and found Mr. Fielding somehow in front of him. Moody was a few inches taller than Fielding, but Fielding was a solid pillar, and it was Moody who shrank back.

"I said, you ain't police," Moody snarled. "Who are you? Your gents only told me you knew something to my advantage. What is it?"

"That it would be to your advantage to not linger in London," Mr. Fielding said without changing expression. "I suggest you cut your losses, leave from here, and start anew."

"Start anew? Why the devil should I?"

Judith answered him after she took a calm sip of tea. "Because your shop has already been seized. I know many people who run things, Mr. Moody. As you say, none of us in this room are police, but

I have connections to those who instruct the police in their duties. Quite a number of constables are now going over what sort of items you have on your premises. Others will be in wait to escort you to a magistrate, unless you take our advice and flee."

Moody stared at her in stunned disbelief, then switched to Mrs. Holloway and Bobby, as though hoping they'd contradict Judith. "You're lying. You're nothing but a pack of females."

"Packs of females can have extraordinary influence, Mr. Moody," Judith said. "Are we not made to adorn and inspire?" The words held scorn. "I have inspired the Commissioner of Scotland Yard to take a great interest in you and your doings."

Sweat beaded on Moody's forehead. "Damnation. I'll have you for this, the lot of you. I wouldn't sleep soundly, were I you." His hard eyes became even more stony, the look he shot Mrs. Holloway and Judith bordering on brutal.

Bobby set aside her cake with regret, in case she had to help Fielding throw the man to the pavement. But again, Mr. Fielding placed himself solidly in front of Moody.

"I wouldn't suggest it." Mr. Fielding didn't raise his voice, but Moody studied him uncertainly. "Other gents like the ones who escorted you here are ready to guide you to the river and push you onto a boat. I have men on that boat to make certain you reach another destination. Or a magistrate can send you to Newgate. It is your choice."

Moody glowered. "I don't take orders from trumped-up vicars."

"I'm a bishop now, did you know?" Mr. Fielding informed him. "But it isn't my ecclesiastical associates who are assisting me. It is ..." He leaned forward and whispered something into Moody's ear.

Bobby didn't catch what Mr. Fielding said, but it had a profound effect on Moody. He drew a sharp breath, and his face went nearly green.

"You—" Moody regarded Mr. Fielding with stark fear, and then he charged for the door.

This time Mr. Fielding let him go, giving him a wave on the way.

Mrs. Holloway came to her feet. "He ought to be arrested," she said, her disapproval sharp.

Mr. Fielding's lighthearted expression faded as he turned to her. "This is best, Mrs. Holloway. That fellow is a slippery one. If Moody goes to a magistrate, he'll lie like an innocent babe, and the evidence against him will somehow evaporate. He's done it before, which is why he's walking about free to pull young aristos into his power. Much better that he's running for his life to some far corner of the earth."

"If you say so, Mr. Fielding." It was apparent Mrs. Holloway did not agree with him, but she ceased arguing. "I thank you for your assistance. We will take up no more of your time."

"Nonsense." Mr. Fielding's good spirits returned. "Stay and enjoy tea. It isn't every day I have the company of such great ladies."

"Yes, indeed, let us remain," Judith said. "Why let the likes of Mr. Moody ruin our day? This cake is excellent, Mrs. Holloway."

Bobby plopped down and forked up another hunk of cake. Judith was right—it was jolly good stuff.

Judith was not as serene as she appeared, Bobby saw from the stiffness of her fingers as she ate a dainty bite of cake. Judith had hoped Moody would have more information about her sister, and her frustration at his lack was evident.

Bobby kept herself from blurting out her own news, which she'd saved to surprise Judith if Mr. Moody had no further information. She liked Fielding, but the man didn't need to know all about Judith's personal life. What Bobby had to say would keep.

She contented herself with observing the curve of Judith's beguiling cheek and enjoying the devil out of Mrs. Holloway's butter cake.

~

AFTER THE TEA WAS DRUNK AND THE CAKE DEVOURED, MR. Fielding saw them to the gate of the churchyard, where he, ever the gentleman, handed Mrs. Holloway and then Judith into her coach.

Bobby pulled herself into it after them. She was full and growing sleepy—perhaps she and Judith could nap when they returned home.

Judith thanked Mr. Fielding graciously and he stepped back, waving them off, grinning like the rogue he was.

"Thank you both very much for your help," Mrs. Holloway said as they rolled toward Whitechapel Road. "I will tell Lady Cynthia to inform Lady Coulson that her sons are safe from Mr. Moody's clutches. Perhaps they will have learned their lesson."

From her expression, Mrs. H. didn't believe they would, and Bobby agreed with her. At least Terrance wouldn't learn, but maybe William could keep him tamed.

Mrs. Holloway turned to Judith with keen perception. "You hoped to learn something about the photographs you mentioned. I know it is hardly my business, but if I can help?"

Judith, who wasn't foolish enough to dismiss Mrs. Holloway's powers of reasoning, drew a breath to speak, but Bobby cut her off.

"Before you go into the entire, sad tale, I've been doing some sleuthing myself." Bobby pulled out the folded paper that contained the photographs. "Sending telegrams like mad, hither and yon."

Judith's chest rose sharply, and Mrs. Holloway leaned forward, avidly curious. "What are those?" Mrs. H. asked.

"The photographs Terrance stole from Moody," Bobby said.

"One was of my sister," Judith began, morose. "She—"

"Hold on," Bobby interrupted. "I've had a good squint at these photographs, at the backs of them, I mean. Peered hard at them through a glass. The light in here is a bit dim, but perhaps we can see."

She withdrew from her pocket a small mother-of-pearl handled magnifying glass, a surprisingly thoughtful gift from her sister-in-law. She opened the paper, the photos facedown, and trained the glass on the back of the top photograph.

"There's a mark, just there." Bobby pointed her gloved finger at it.

Judith took the glass and the photograph and raised both to her eyes. When Mrs. Holloway, across from her, caught sight of what was on the *front* of the picture, her brows went up, but she said nothing.

"LM," Judith announced after a time. "That's all I can make out."

"I thought it was likely the name of the studio," Bobby said. "One of the pictures also helpfully has the word *Paris* stamped on it. It's quite smudged—these pictures have been passed about a great deal—but I could just discern it."

"I saw nothing on my sister's photograph," Judith said, lowering the glass.

"Because it was not from the same studio," Bobby said. "The one of Lucetta was taken by her blackguard sweetheart in London, about ten years ago, you said. These others are more recent. You can tell from the clarity of the photographs—techniques have improved in the last decade. Also, the backdrops have more modern furnishings in them, and fashions in combinations and corsets have also changed."

Mrs. Holloway nodded, as though approving of Bobby's deductions.

"Ergo," Bobby continued. "These were from a different studio. As I say, I cabled like mad to some chums in Paris, and they hunted down the business for me. The photographer in that Parisian studio informed my chums that she had sold the pictures to a gentleman from London last year—an aristo, not our Mr. Moody. The aristo must have tired of them, or didn't want his wife to see them, so dropped them at a shop that sells such things. Probably got his valet to do it for him." Bobby shrugged.

"*She* had sold the pictures." Judith fixed on the pronoun, ignoring the rest of Bobby's speculations. "The photographer is a woman?"

"Yes, indeed." Bobby couldn't suppress a grin. "She owns the premises and takes portraits—likely dabbles in these off-color ones for the extra income. Calls it *LM Studio de Photographie*. Uses initials to hide her sex because so many want a business to be run by a man."

Judith turned her intense stare on Bobby. Bobby couldn't look away, though she felt Mrs. Holloway's interest from across the carriage.

"What does LM stand for?" Judith asked. "Did you learn this?"

"Lucetta Mercier." Bobby tightened, waiting for Judith's reaction. Would she be excited or unhappy that Bobby had decided to pry? "That's her married name."

Judith stilled, lips parting. "Lucetta—" Her throat worked. "You found her."

Bobby kept her voice gentle. "I appear to have."

Judith continued to stare, round-eyed, then suddenly she launched herself at Bobby, wrapping her in a tight, desperate embrace. Judith's mouth landed on Bobby's cheeks, lips, and neck, her passion unleashed by her shock and joy.

Bobby would love to explore how they could celebrate in this carriage, but poor Mrs. Holloway sat across from them. She'd edged her feet back as Judith's sweeping boots nearly kicked hers.

"A trip to Paris might be wise." Mrs. Holloway's calm tones slid through Judith's exuberant kisses. "If this lady is your sister, she will want to see you."

Judith unwound herself from Bobby and plopped to the seat, fishing out a handkerchief to wipe the tears from her face. A clean, neatly folded handkerchief, of course.

"She might not welcome me," Judith said.

"Do not be so certain," Mrs. Holloway replied. "Am I correct that it has been many years since you've seen her? And that you lost touch?" Trust Mrs. Holloway to understand the full story from the bits and pieces she'd just heard.

"Yes." Judith swiped at her cheeks again. "It was not an amicable parting. I have often wondered ..."

"Go." Mrs. Holloway sent Judith a sage smile. "You must try to make amends. It is clear that you love her still. Now, we have reached Cheapside. If you will have your coachman stop here, I will continue on foot."

She was off to visit her daughter, Bobby understood—the charming little girl who had the same dark hair and pretty eyes as her mother. Mrs. H. couldn't admit to the daughter, lest she be dismissed from her post, but Bobby and Judith could keep a secret.

"Of course." Judith knocked on the roof and ordered Dunstan to halt. She opened the door for Mrs. Holloway herself, and Bobby leapt out to guide Mrs. H. safely to the ground.

"Do greet your girl for us," Bobby told her. "Here." She fished

49

into her pocket and pulled out a farthing. Any larger sum, and Mrs. H. would be too proud to accept it. "Let her spend that on sweets, or a dolly, or some such."

Mrs. Holloway flushed but took the coin. "Thank you kindly, Lady Roberta." She shook out her skirts on the dusty road. "And thank you both for your assistance. The promised lemon cake will be forthcoming."

"Excellent." Bobby grinned at her. "I await it with lively anticipation."

Mrs. Holloway ducked her head, always humble, then turned from the carriage. Her steps grew eager as she headed for the lane that must hold the house where her daughter lived, looked after by Mrs. H.'s oldest friend.

"I much admire her," Judith said once Bobby was back inside, and Dunstan started the coach again. "A very clear-headed woman. We all should be as steady."

"I agree." Bobby pulled Judith close once more, hoping for a return to the enthusiastic kissing. "Shall we do as she says and go to Paris?"

"I'd like to." Judith snuggled into Bobby's shoulder. "But what if Lucetta doesn't want to see me?"

"I wager things have changed," Bobby said. "Could be she doesn't believe you want to see *her*. But good for her for becoming a photographer herself. All artists in your family, eh?"

"I'd love to have a look at what sorts of things she's done." Judith's tone turned more hopeful. "Yes, let us plan a journey. Scandalize our families by traveling alone together."

"Hardly alone, with Evans dogging your steps," Bobby said with a laugh. Judith would never leave her lady's maid behind. "We can pretend to be man and wife. Mr. and Mrs. Perry. Such fun." Bobby tried to push aside a qualm. "If you'll have me?"

The smile Judith turned on Bobby transformed the gray London street into the brightest paradise.

"Of course, my darling Bobby. Do you even have to ask?"

Bobby's pulse sped. "I do have to ask. You know how fond I am of you, Judes." She drew a breath and then decided to shuck her reticence. "No, not fond. I mean—I love you. There, I said it."

Bobby sat back, her heart banging. She'd never confessed her true feelings to Judith, fearing the response. Would Judith give her a kind smile and then explain that she didn't share the sentiment? Judith had always seemed just out of reach, like a fine-plumed bird who flew off as one stretched out a hand toward it.

Judith turned in the seat with a rustle of fabric, the scent of tea and buttery cake clinging to her.

"Dearest Bobby." Her voice was soft, taking on the note of desire it did in the dark of night. "The anchor in my swirling world. I love *you*, my silly darling."

Happiness welled in Bobby's chest, displacing the sharp ache that had nestled there. Tears stung her eyes, but she swallowed them down. It would never do to become a blubbering fool. She had better things to do at the moment.

Bobby hid her shakiness by tossing her already crushed hat to the seat Mrs. H. had vacated. "Well. That's all right, then."

Judith's answering smile nearly undid her. Bobby had often wondered what she and Judith could do in a carriage, bumping alone together through the middle of London.

Her blood warmed as Judith brushed a hand over Bobby's cheek ... then Judith carefully pulled down all the shades and proceeded to show Bobby exactly what was possible.

THANK YOU FOR READING! THE CHARACTERS OF BOBBY and Miss Townsend are from the Below Stairs Mysteries, a Victorian-set mystery series featuring Kat Holloway, a cook in a Mayfair home. More information can be found on the website: https://www. jenniferashley.com

About the Author

Jennifer Ashley is a *NY Times*, *USA Today*, and *Wall Street Journal* bestselling author of more than 100 novels and novellas in romance, mystery, fantasy, and historical fiction. As Jennifer, she writes historical, paranormal, and contemporary romance, historical mysteries, and historical fiction; as Ashley Gardner, she writes historical mysteries; and as Allyson James, she writes urban fantasy as well as some sci-fi romance. She lives in the Southwest and enjoys traveling, cooking, walking, knitting, and building dollhouse miniatures.

For information on her novels as Jennifer Ashley and Allyson James visit www.jenniferashley.com. Also see http://www.gardnermysteries.com (Ashley Gardner) for her other works.

The Kraken and The Canary

A PREQUEL FOR LIKE SILK BREATHING

CAMILLE DUPLESSIS

For N. (Above all.)

Author's Note

This will appeal to anybody who liked Mr. Paul Apollyon and possibly wanted me to be nicer to him. It may also appease anyone who wondered why *Like Silk Breathing* opened with him, but not Tom or Theo. If you're a member of one of these categories, you'll notice Paul's public house is called The Queen Anne, not The Shuck. It isn't an oversight: we're just getting a story before her name does change. (The detail-oriented among you may recall that Alastair initiated the change after a drunk patron was convinced he saw Old Shuck in one of the upper-floor windows. That happens after all of this.)

If you're new here: welcome!

I'm so pleased to have written this, because it was in my head all along. I really hope you enjoy it.

Chapter One

"Can I hide in your cellar?"

The question came from a delicious nightmare of a man swathed in faded black clothes and topped in a low-slung hat that would have been in fashion last century.

Paul, standing across The Queen Anne's taproom and behind the bar, eyed him for either a full minute or possibly just a moment. His mind would be screaming for caution if he could manage to figure out where he'd so quickly lost it, or if he could account for why he'd misplaced it upon seeing a man whose appearance breathed trouble. In his own taproom, no less.

Things happened in it. Little brawls and melodramatic scenes. But not anything like this.

"What?"

"If it's your cellar," the man continued. He studied Paul, perhaps deciding he didn't look seasoned enough to own a public house. "Or your employer's." That was fair. Paul had only managed the place all on his own for two months and he supposed it might show. He was confident and competent, but still adjusting to his mother's recent death. "I'll take an attic or a cupboard. Anywhere. I'm not picky, but I am being chased."

"Hide?" Though he was usually a man of minimal speech, Paul

generally employed more than one word at a time. "Chased? And it's not my employer's... it's mine."

"Well, can I?"

"I suppose."

"Thanks, mate, thank you." Relief wove through his voice, blatant as the pine scent that wafted from his person.

"Don't thank me. I'm only giving you a place to hide, not solving your problems. It's not every day a man comes demanding to be let into my cellar."

"Does that make me special?"

Inconveniently, Paul was coming around the bar as the nightmare asked his coquettish question. He rammed his thigh into the varnished corner, which he hadn't done since he was a boy. Back then, he was more prone to clumsiness — but visions of the future would've distracted or exhausted anyone.

They usually came in dreams and could occasionally appear while he was awake. He'd never seen anything too grisly, but he also knew his sense of the macabre was skewed because of what he did see. The first premonition he recalled was about the family dog dying, only he'd been too frightened to mention he'd seen it before it happened. It became less simple to deny he could see the future as he got older, but it also wasn't easy to own up to certain things.

How could he tell his brother he'd seen exactly *how* his broken arm would snap as he fell from a tree — even if he knew that might help prevent it in the first place?

More usefully, he'd been able to advise on things like a chandler who was later charged with theft, and a horse who died of what seemed to be a bad heart. In the thief's case, they found another chandler before anything was stolen from The Queen Anne, and poor Bishy the horse was retired before he collapsed with anyone riding him.

Bishy was the primary reason his parents had suggested he not talk about his ability. They were kind, but he could tell they were unsettled for one reason or another. Either they believed him or they thought he was mad — and he knew they believed him because they'd already enacted some of his advice. He'd been thirteen when they finally told him never to mention any of his premonitions away from family. It made sense to him. Just as he hadn't been able to talk to Edward about how he'd *known* his arm would break, it had been nearly as difficult to tell Father the horse might accidentally kill him.

So, even when it portended good things, he tried not to talk about what he could do. He wasn't sure what to make of a stranger who impacted him like a premonition.

"Ah... yes. You are special. I mean to say... no. You're not, but you do seem..." Paul frowned and fingered the keys at his hip. "This way. The attic is too full and... you wouldn't fit in any of our cupboards, either. You're too big."

"I'm Alastair."

When he didn't add a surname to the forename and came to his side, Paul said, "Just Alastair?" He kept a step between them and did not breathe too deeply of Alastair's pine-needle scent. It wasn't from the world, anyway. Along with the premonitions, other things came to him. Smells and colors, personal attributes that weren't legible in the same manner as wrinkles or freckles.

"Eh, better if I am. For now."

They passed into the adjoining corridor. Paul nodded to the trap-door when they reached the end. "Nothing special down there. Kegs and the like." He cleared his throat. "We're not in the habit of hiding people, or acting as a..." he stopped and considered the nicest way of saying they didn't serve as a hiding spot for either smugglers or their contraband, both of which were still common in the area, though the widespread practice had waned somewhat. He was making assumptions, but he didn't think he was wrong about them.

Then he shrugged and met Alastair's dark eyes. Perhaps there wasn't anything to say to a charming stranger asking to hide in your cellar but yes. There was an air of intrigue to it that Paul enjoyed, and there was all manner of smuggling underfoot. Interested parties would arrange drop points just offshore or inside various businesses who looked the other way, and the water — the sea, or the Broads — served as opportune roads free of taxes.

But Alastair looked more dashing than his presumable peers. It could have been the tattoos that barely crept out from under his collar, most of which likely went unnoticed, or the impish smile. In his day, Father had served known free traders and fences without hesitation, but possessed no special arrangements with them. Paul recalled meeting a few in passing — they were disappointing to his young mind, which had built them up to be roguish protagonists.

He'd read too many novels.

"I see," said Alastair. "Who're you, then?"

"Hm?" Paul couldn't look away from him. The corridor was darker than the taproom and wrapped Alastair in shadows, but he seemed more comfortable away from windows and the street.

He said, gentle as a kitten's whisker flicking against an outstretched hand, "What's your name?"

"I'm Mr. Apollyon."

"Thank you, then, Mr. Apollyon."

"I'll... if you tell me what to look out for, I'll come and let you out after it's over."

"You'll know when it's fine."

"I will?"

"Yes."

Unsure if he would know, and wondering if this was an elaborate ruse to steal something — not that there was much to steal — Paul hefted the trap door open and motioned him down the rungs of a sturdy ladder. "Go on." When Alastair brushed past, the slight contact beckoned to him. He said primly, "I assume you aren't a murderer, or you'd have murdered me already."

"At two in the afternoon in a public house on a well-traversed road? Please, I'm not a fool. I would wait until cover of darkness, my man."

Taken aback by the teasing and enamored with the thought of him returning after dark, Paul shook his head and couldn't resist smiling himself. "If you wanted to go to all the trouble, I can already tell you there would be little to gain from murdering me. I just inherited this place, but I still have to work. Can't even find my mother's silver." He knew he shouldn't be saying so much.

"Don't be so sure," said Alastair, his head tilted up to listen, "there could still be something to gain." Then, he winked.

Paul could think of no reply but letting the trapdoor fall closed, and it didn't close quickly enough to muffle smug chuckling.

Returning to the taproom, which now felt curiously devoid of life, he waited. As he dusted the top shelf behind the bar, he thought, *I'd consider holding lifted goods if it meant seeing* him *more than once.* It wasn't rape or murder; it wouldn't hurt anything except for laws. He already hurt those in his personal life, anyway.

As fast as the thought came, he tried to dismiss it. He really should carry on as normal whenever Alastair saw himself outside.

Something in him understood, though, that anything resembling normalcy had shifted.

HALF AN HOUR PASSED BEFORE PAUL KNEW WHAT Alastair meant about knowing when it was fine. "Good afternoon, Mr. Apollyon."

His back was to the door but he recognized the voice. It was Mr. Sykes, a fisherman who recently fancied himself more of a rogue and whose daughter was about to marry a hostler in Norwich. The Sykes family had known the Apollyons for a generation, though not especially amicably.

Mr. Sykes once suggested Paul propose marriage to Muriel within Mrs. Apollyon's hearing. Muriel was fifteen at the time, Paul sixteen. Mother feigned a sudden headache upon hearing the remark and excused herself. It was widely understood that Mr. Sykes abused Mrs. Sykes, and later turned his ire upon their daughter after his wife died and his reliance on drink became more entrenched. Everyone seemed to like Muriel; few liked her father.

"Mr. Sykes."

"I hate to trouble you," said Sykes. That was a lie, for Sykes rarely seemed concerned with politeness unless it could get him something.

"No trouble. The afternoon is quiet, as you see."

"Then maybe you'll be able to help."

"Happy to do what I can," said Paul. That was a lie of his own.

Sykes sat at the bar. Paul was about to ask what he wanted to drink when foreign sensations entered his mind, sharp as winter cold through an open door. *Oh, fuck. Not now.* There was naught to do but pretend they weren't there.

So he stood in the taproom he'd known all his life while — somewhere else — he ran fingertips through dark, gray-streaked hair mussed against a white pillowcase. Well, it was infinitely preferable to the discussion he was about to have with Sykes. He forced himself to ask, "Can I... get you something?"

"Beer, if you please."

"Of course." Relieved to turn his back as the experience demanded his attention, Paul closed his eyes and drank it in for just a moment. They were not always pleasant, these glimpses into futures, but this was. And mostly, he experienced them as an observer of a play.

But this particular one found him well within his body. Alastair — no one else of his acquaintance had tattoos, and besides, the longer Paul was pulled, the more he saw his face properly — moaning beneath him on his bed, his skin burnished by afternoon sunlight.

Paul might think it was a daydream, except he'd cultivated the discipline not to daydream much about this topic. With internal difficulty and external grace, he procured the beer for Sykes and set it before him. "How can I help?"

He prayed that whatever the answer was, it wouldn't involve him stepping out from the bar, for his trousers had gone tight.

"I'm asking around to locate a certain rogue who's stolen something from my dear Muriel."

Composed, grateful for all the times he'd had to practice concentrating on a conversation while something else provoked sensations in his body, Paul said, "Oh? I'm sorry to hear it."

Sykes took a long drink, then nodded. "He's rather tall. Dark-haired. If you're eagle-eyed, you might notice he's tattooed on the neck. And on the hands, but he's likely wearing some sort of gloves to cover them. Well-spoken for a thug, yet treacherous, you see."

Paul had studiously not looked too much at Alastair's hands, else he'd be tempted to wonder what those hands could do. He might have been wearing gloves. "I see."

"Goes by Alastair, but I'm not convinced that's his real name."

"If he's a thief, I'd guess it might not be."

"Exactly."

"Might I ask what he stole from Muriel?"

Sykes shook his head and took another drink. "It's a family matter."

Knowing better than to take Sykes at his word, awash with curiosity, Paul inclined his head. "Of course. I'll not pry." He smiled his false smile for the patrons he disliked; it always worked a charm. "I'll offer my congratulations on her engagement, though."

That roused a dry chuckle from Sykes. "She's not looking forward to marriage, but she'll do as she's told if she doesn't want to end up a spinster facing a poorhouse."

The callousness made Paul's skin prickle. He didn't feel guilty he hadn't proposed to Muriel, which seemed to be Sykes' expectation even if it wasn't shared by Paul's parents; he'd always supposed his discomfort with marriage would have a poor effect on a wife. But he couldn't wish her father's attitude on anybody.

At least he was no longer dwelling on fornicating.

He found he didn't know what to say, so he kept to more inane politeness that meant little, but would appease Sykes. "I enjoy Norwich, myself. My brother went into business there with his wife not so long ago. Perhaps things will turn out well for Muriel, and the change of scenery will do her good." He remembered her as a boisterous, curious girl with a mass of dark hair and a loud laugh. She'd terrified him, but a dormouse could have scared him at the time.

"Perhaps." Sykes pushed back his seat and stood. "Seeing as you've not seen him..." He moved to leave payment on the bar, but Paul motioned for him to stop.

"For your trouble," he said. He knew the small gesture would make Sykes feel more esteemed than he truly was, which seemed wise. "You haven't even finished it, after all. Consider it a drink from a friend."

"Thank you. The bastard can't have gone far."

When Sykes had showed himself out, Paul rushed to the window and lingered out of sight as he watched the street. He waited for Sykes to disappear into another doorway, then crept to the trapdoor, wrenching it open. Alastair was leaning against the old ladder, gazing at him from under the brim of his hat.

"Well." Paul pursed his lips.

Alastair said, with a nod to the space just under the bar, "Could hear everything from that end. I suppose you want to know the truth of it?"

"I'll admit, I'm interested." Paul actually wanted to know how Alastair felt arching beneath him. And to feel how soft his hair really was. Since a vision of his had never been false, he didn't know whether to be encouraged or nervous.

But he could start with learning why he'd asked for safe harbor from Sykes.

PAUL LOCKED THE FRONT DOOR SO THEY COULD EXCUSE themselves. Jack and Ned, who took rooms next to and opposite his own, would still be able to leave if they chose. Years ago, Father had installed a particular lock so he could secure the premises while allowing residents or guests freedom of movement.

Anyway, Paul didn't think either of them was in, which was all the better if Alastair wanted to reveal dubiously legal things in confidence. Ned was prone to eavesdropping. Jack had been in residence for three months, but still wanted to make incessant conversation. Sometimes he tried to talk through the shared wall between their two bedrooms, which was jarring when one wasn't expecting it.

As Paul unlocked his own door, he was pleased neither man was on the stairs or in the corridor. His windows were ajar to admit the breeze and they allowed for a good view of the beach and sea beyond. Alastair went immediately to the largest one in the back parlor, turning his back, giving Paul a good look at his long hair glimmering with a few threads of silver. After a moment of study, Paul decided there could be a decade between them, or possibly a little more than that.

"I love the sea, but I rarely get to look at it properly. Not from inside a cozy room, anyway."

"Really?" said Paul. "I look at it all the time, but I've never been on a proper boat in my life. Would do, but... haven't had the chance."

"Were you born here?"

"Yes. I assume I sound like it," Paul said. He smirked as Alastair turned to face him. Newcomers weren't generally enthusiastic about the idiosyncrasies. Alastair grinned, showing well-kept teeth that hinted at means, and Paul's expression faltered. By way of distraction, he mused on those teeth: one didn't need to have respectability to have money.

He also wouldn't be unhappy if those teeth ever bit him.

"You do. I haven't spent much time here, but I hear it. That's not a bad thing. Not to me." His eyes were exceedingly kind. "My views might not be what you're used to."

Paul sat on a low sofa under the large window and walked closer to Alastair than was strictly necessary to get there. "Always seems a bit banal to bring up accents, doesn't it? What'm I hearing? Edinburgh?"

"Close enough."

"Haven't been. But more often than you'd think, we get someone from the Athens of the North."

"Jesus, are people still calling it that?" Alastair removed his hat and put it on a little end table. When he ran his fingers through his hair, Paul almost had to sit on his own hands because the desire to follow his was so invasive.

"I don't know. Not that I've heard. I was just making a quip."

Alastair chuckled. "I saw rougher things compared to all those learned men, I guess." Pacing a little, seeming more curious than restless, he picked up a red book with gilt on the cover only to put it down. Then he went to the fireplace and looked in the tarnished mirror above the mantel. "These are your rooms, but the rest are to let, aren't they?"

Watching him, rather enthralled, Paul said, "Yes. It's been a public house since its earliest days, this place, with the handful of rooms above being let from time to time. There are two men taking rooms on either side of me." Fondly, he added, "Bless her, The Queen Anne is starting to show her age and she can't compete with the hotels. I don't try."

Though babbled a little, he succeeded in not telling his guest these rooms had been his family's. That he and his brother had shared the smaller bedroom, now a study where he could keep track of the accounts, and his mother and father had used the larger bedroom where he now slept. That this large middle room with exposed beams and an uneven floor had served as their parlor, though they'd had the run of the place.

And how, despite valuing solitude and privacy and possessing a handful of good friends, he felt quite alone.

He said none of that.

"But it's clean and quiet," said Alastair. "I think it's charming."

"Our cook is also wonderful," said Paul, followed by yet another smile. This stranger had him smiling excessively. "She was a maid at the Langham and one of the chefs tried to carry on with her, so she had to go. Found it was best to leave London entirely. At least she picked up some knowledge for her trouble. She says the patrons treated her like shit."

"I'd believe her."

"Oh, I do. We get all sorts who feel they're better than those who are poorer than them. I've not had much of that because I won't tolerate it. I've turned down custom before. But... can't say I haven't seen it."

With a slyness in his expression that Paul definitely enjoyed, Alastair circled back to the sofa and sat next to him. Not close enough to touch, but closer than most strangers would. So, Mr. Apollyon, if you're so stern regarding what you tolerate from others, I suppose I don't get to know your name. Would be uncouth for me to ask, wouldn't it?"

"Paul," he blurted. He had not wanted to blurt, or at least he wanted to sound more dignified while he blurted.

"Well, Paul... thank you again for allowing me to use your cellar."

One time hearing Alastair say his name and he was lost. He knew it. He didn't have to like it, but he knew it. "You're lucky I despise Sykes."

"Do you? That *is* lucky."

"He's awful. Reputedly violent... and pretends to be many things. Most recently, I heard he thinks he's a smuggler now. He's just one of those types who likes to seem dangerous." Paul snorted and shook his head. "There are plenty of smugglers around who are, I assume, good at what they do. And I suspect many are more principled than a man who hurts his daughter."

"You'd win that wager," said Alastair. "And he is. Awful. Never been violent in front of me, but I think it's there, simmering under the surface."

This was probably as good as he'd get that Alastair was adjacent to crime, and he didn't care. Pausing to think before he spoke, Paul said, "Why was he chasing you?" He rose from the sofa with the aim of sitting right back down after he'd secured them a drink. "And do you like cognac? I haven't any whisky up here, if that's what you prefer, but if you take cognac... I've a good one." He shouldn't assume that someone from Scotland always wanted whisky, but it was out before he could stop himself saying it.

"What kind of question is that?"

Paul went to a sideboard opposite the fireplace and poured them each a large measure, mindful not to trip over the uneven floorboards and look a fool. He handed a squat, crystal glass to Alastair, lulled by the heat between their fingers that did not even touch.

Then he sat, careful to sit even nearer than he'd previously been seated. If Alastair noticed, he didn't comment, and instead he raised the glass in a silent toast before sipping. Feeling there was little to say, and it was somehow more momentous to say nothing, Paul did the same.

After his sip, Alastair said, "Thanks. Shit, that's lovely. He chased me because his daughter hired me to do something for her, and he saw me in her room. I was able to get out through a window, but he did tear after me. And for a fucking drunk, he's quick."

Puzzled, Paul tried to understand. He couldn't even summon a laugh at Mr. Sykes being characterized as a *fucking drunk*. He was, but in an obdurate, unobtrusive manner that didn't make him a loud public nuisance. Just a simmering private one.

"Muriel... paid you..." He knew where *his* mind wandered when he looked at Alastair, and he wasn't naive enough to think women couldn't pay men for fucking. He was sure they might engage in the practice if they had money and time of their own. "Is she all right, now?"

"What do you mean?"

"Well, if she hired you to do something in her room..."

"Ah, I see. No, it wasn't for that... she was out when this happened. He wasn't able to confront her or anything. But I should have met her somewhere else."

"So she's not... paying you... for..." Paul waggled his head a bit, not reluctant to say anything vulgar, but unprepared for the envy he felt.

Apparently delighted by his attempt at being tactful, Alastair laughed. "No, not at all, though I'm flattered you think she would. She's had me deliver certain correspondence."

"Oh?"

"Yes, letters. Little parcels, sometimes."

"How did you even become acquainted?"

"Her father is the most obnoxious fence I've ever met... he's not a smuggler, but he arranges certain things for... them." *Them* sounded more like *us*. "Including me. And I... happened to come by his cottage one evening." Alastair exhibited no shame, but Paul gleaned that he phrased things genteelly. "And Muriel took me aside on my way out. She was on her way in from work and overheard some of our conversation. She thought I'd be well-suited to helping her transport these letters, and I am. But I won't take her money."

"You won't?"

"How well do you know her?" Alastair seemed to be silently evaluating his face for signs of distress; Paul hoped he did not look very flummoxed.

"Not very." Paul sipped and considered how long he had known Muriel, but how little he knew of her as a person. Part of that had been her father's doing, because he did not encourage her to be social unless there were connections or advantages to be gained. "We've known each other since childhood, but I can't say I was an outgoing boy. So... not well."

"You don't seem especially shy now."

"I..." Paul cleared his throat. It was possible that Alastair was flirting. A glint to his eye gave it away more than his tone. Generally, Paul made no such assumptions, yet he would have thought so regardless of the premonition. The signs were subtle, written in tiny clues. "I suppose I'm not, now."

"Well," said Alastair. He leaned closer, smiling just a little. "I'm not fond of gossip, but I think I can be frank with you."

To have something to do that wasn't initiating a kiss, Paul drank more of his cognac.

"She has a lover," said Alastair. "And I deliver their correspondence."

"Does she?"

"Mmhm, a Miss Abigail in Overstrand."

It did not strike Paul as much as it would others because he wasn't strictly normal himself. When Alastair slid him an even wider smile, he nodded and grinned. "And she's supposed to marry some man in Norwich."

"Yes, well, not if she has anything to say about it. She's determined to run away."

"No vicar would marry two women."

"Of course not. But you don't need the church to be married."

"I've often wanted..." Paul corrected himself. "Wondered if such a thing could be possible."

With some pity, Alastair inclined his head and murmured, "Of course it is. She's been saving money for months and she says she's put enough away to help them set up house, so they're trying to make good their escape. It was harder, she said, before she met me. I've just been dealing with her father for the last few weeks, and it's only been a fortnight since I've been delivering things to Abigail."

It explained why Paul had never noticed him before. One didn't have to come inside for him to notice them. From the taproom windows in particular, he saw many people on their daily business and could glean their habits. Chances were, if Alastair had been around longer than those few weeks, Paul would have seen him. "I assume she'd be ready to change her name, start again entirely somewhere else."

"Yes."

After a long pause, Paul asked him, "But why are *you* helping? And without payment? You're not her friend."

"I want to think such a thing is possible for anyone with a good heart. Or at least good intentions."

"That's noble."

"It isn't nobility," Alastair said. He drained the rest of his cognac.

"What is it, then?"

Setting his glass down on the narrow table before the sofa, Alastair replied, "I should have liked the chance, myself. I don't have it, but that doesn't mean others can't take theirs."

With a frown, Paul looked over at him. "You can't come tearing in here demanding to be let into my cellar, then say something like that, without me wanting to know more about you."

∾

"THIS IS TERRIBLE BUSINESS PRACTICE, YOU KNOW," SAID Alastair, both by way of replying and changing the subject. For now, he would ignore Paul's desire to know more about him. That would be like opening Pandora's Box.

"What?"

"You can't run The Queen Anne with its door closed to customers."

Paul seemed, for a moment, perplexed by what he meant; Alastair smiled at him.

Then his eyes widened, and he looked a bit less guarded within his bashfulness. It was endearing, although Alastair tried to be stern with himself. He didn't live in Cromer even if he had been spending time here of late. He might be able to sleep the night once or twice with Paul, but anything more would be tricky. Especially with Sykes swooping about.

He needed to help Muriel as expeditiously as possible, and so he would. But he gave himself a moment of contemplation. Paul was younger than him: his face bore fewer lines and his umber hair didn't have any traces of gray. Age could be hard to guess in one with such a calm bearing and so many responsibilities, but he judged Paul to be somewhere in his early twenties.

And even though he wasn't against casual arrangements, he couldn't muster the same cavalier approach he usually had to other men who'd caught his eye. Instead, he felt protectiveness, something he'd not felt for anyone but dear friends or his wife.

And you never felt for Evie the way you could for a man, anyway. By the time they married, Alastair already knew he couldn't. Evie became a wonderful friend, but she couldn't ease his restlessness.

Fortunately, she never fell in love with him. She was far too sensible. She'd elected to keep the same lover, a wonderfully jovial baker named Arthur, for almost the entirety of their marriage and until her death. It hadn't been so long ago that Alastair left behind Arthur and Evie's recently sixteen-year-old son, whom he'd raised as his own, feeling too young and inexperienced himself as he did so.

Evie and Arthur chose to withhold the truth from James, but Alastair still wasn't convinced it had been for the best. Loving another man's son posed no issue for him. But subterfuge did in this context, even if he could understand why they clung to it. Their truths never came into the open. It helped that he was rather intimidating, Arthur was rather endearing, and James took entirely after his mother.

Nobody of their acquaintance, even if there were suspicions about James' true parentage, dared ask questions. Everyone knew Alastair wasn't exactly the most upstanding man, even if nobody could say exactly what he did — engaged in what the polite called *free trading* — and he tended to charm whoever met him. The intimidation was chiefly visual, found in his stature or tattoos if they were visible, so he leaned on making a certain first impression. Relied on his way with words after that.

No one wished to cause trouble for James or Evie or even Arthur, known to be a friend of the family, because no one wished to cause trouble for Alastair. But the time came when he could no longer stand to be entrenched in a place where he was a widower, where even if nobody spoke about his wife sleeping with another man, they all knew.

Once James was working for Arthur, he felt rather better making plans to go. The lad wasn't a child, and he would have a way to support himself.

Although he felt immense guilt upon leaving, the freedom was equally immense. That bred more guilt, which he tried to assuage by writing and sending James money. There weren't any replies. But the money left his account, so he assumed James was making use of it. He was a pragmatic and staid boy, but they were different as could be: Alastair needed romance and action. He supposed that was how he'd ended up running from Sykes and into this pub.

"I can't?" said Paul. "Why... can't I keep the door shut? Neither of the lads I've hired is down there. They're not due until half-five. That's when things pick up. And Bess won't return until six. She's the cook."

Alastair tried to school the conflict from his face. Had he not tried to be an upright man before simply returning to the demimonde, his life would be considerably simpler. He said, clarifying, "But what if someone wants a drink? Or a room? And you've locked the door?"

"It's... not as busy as it used to be, here," said Paul. He shook his head like he was clearing it. "When my father died, there was little loss of trade. Almost none. Those who stopped coming just thought a woman couldn't manage as well as he did, and I say good riddance to them."

"Your mother." Alastair wondered which of the two he favored.

"Yes. And yet... when *she* died, it did slow more noticeably. Not at first, because I think those who knew us felt sorry for me. Father passed unexpectedly, and Mother didn't hang on much longer. But more recently it's been so..."

Waiting, Alastair just listened.

Paul shrugged his svelte shoulders and tried for a smile. "I'll make it. Things aren't horrible and I think they'll pick up. I just never knew how much my mother and father meant to regulars." Then he added, "And my younger brother is more amicable than me. People came to see him. But he's in Norwich now. He got married before I did." He laughed softly. "Not that I'll ever..." Paul blinked and stopped his thought, but it wasn't a difficult one for Alastair to finish. "That's where his wife's family are."

Distracted from protesting that he thought Paul was amicable, Alastair said, thinking this indicated good things about the younger Apollyon and the way both of them were brought up, "He went there to be with her... and not the other way around? He didn't make her come here to live with him when you've a business. Huh."

"Well, he never wanted this place. He was happy at the thought of letting me take responsibility for it, which was always our parents' plan. He liked Norwich better anyway... and when he met Emma, it turned out that her people kept a pub. He didn't propose to her for that, though. It's a love match."

"Fit right into things, then, from the sound of it." Watching Paul's face as he spoke, Alastair tried not to fixate on the yearning he managed to convey when he said *love match*.

"Edward could fit anywhere," said Paul, without bitterness, but with a little wistfulness. "Happy lad, happy man, excellent with people."

Wishing to reassure Paul that he was just as likable, despite knowing it was a bit ludicrous when he only knew one of them, Alastair listed toward him. "Eh, but that's a bit boring, isn't it? I know I tend to prefer a little more complexity."

He was extremely gratified when Paul's breath caught, just a little. "That's not Edward. He's quite straightforward. Not that *that's* a bad thing at all. I envy him, sometimes, if you want the truth. Just... it's easier when you want what you're supposed to want. A wife, a child." Paul lowered his voice. "I didn't think it would ever bother me, seeing him married. But it's prompted me to wonder if my mother and father *were* secretly disappointed in me and just... never said."

It was cryptic, but it was clear. A cultivated way of owning to certain personal qualities.

Then the question came that Alastair dreaded. Given the subject of their conversation, it was unavoidable.

"Sorry. All of that is nothing to do with you. Do you have a family?"

It was innocently asked, kindly meant, and still, he resisted. "No." How he wanted to tell the truth of things. But he was afraid of being reviled for his slew of either impulsive or unusual choices.

"I expect it's easier in your line of work not to have one," was Paul's diplomatic reply. Nonetheless, he stared at him. Alastair knew he knew something was being withheld. Part of it was his overall air, which was decisive and furtive as a fox. The rest was in Paul's eyes: Alastair wagered they saw more than he ever said.

And Alastair knew he shouldn't be so fascinated. "Think I've taken enough of your time..." He didn't really belong in this setting, a warm parlor in a family business that'd been passed down to someone who suited it.

"No, it's all right," said Paul. "You didn't take me away from anything but tidying, and if I gave myself to that all day, nothing else would ever be finished."

"All the same..."

"Stay."

"Why? You don't know me."

"My business is getting to know people. Sometimes when they don't want me to, but some get so loud over drinks. This..." he motioned with his own glass to the both of them, "is preferable to unwillingly listening to loud, drunk conversations."

"You want to get to know me," said Alastair, ending it on less of a question. He supposed that much was clear, or Paul wouldn't have invited him upstairs. They could have found physical satisfaction anywhere.

"Yes," said Paul. There was a subtle but unmissable note of desire in his voice, yet more genuine curiosity pervaded his expression than anything else. "Stay," he murmured again.

Alastair's reserve eroded. The murmur was more effective than any siren's call. "That still doesn't answer the why."

Paul dropped his gaze, at that. "No reason, really." It felt like a lie even if Alastair couldn't explain the reasons. Boredom might be one, but he sensed there were more.

On a sigh and despite his better judgement, he said, "Fine. If you think Mr. Sykes won't return, perhaps we should go downstairs? I don't feel right taking the landlord out of his milieu." He softly nudged Paul's knee with his own. "If you know the area, perhaps you can help me come up with a way to help Muriel. All I really know are cellars and boats and backroads, and I don't think any of them will be useful at this juncture."

～

THERE WAS LITTLE IN THE WORLD THAT WOULD HAVE enticed Paul to move away from that gentle nudge. He'd never been so overcome by such a small touch. He cleared his throat and said, "We really don't need to go down. He didn't suspect me, so I don't think he'll come back, but we can stay here."

"All right. The problem is meeting her, especially now."

"You might not have noticed, but I've a whole building at my disposal."

"Which is right in the middle of everything."

"Where does Muriel work these days? Has she said?"

"No."

Alastair was lying again, judging from his delivery of the word, but Paul didn't push him. "Well, it must be nearby. Sykes would never let her take work elsewhere until she's gone and married. What if you met with her here? I don't mean the taproom or the common areas... I mean, up here. Sykes isn't welcome in my flat."

When Alastair seemed to give it some thought, Paul persisted. "There's a way to get to the stairs in back that she — or you — could use. All of our deliveries come round back, anyway. Wouldn't be strange." He brushed away the idea of Alastair using those stairs for a nighttime assignation.

His intentions to ignore such a ribald suggestion were dashed when Alastair met his eyes, and Paul knew he had the same idea. It was legible in the slight lift of his dark brows, the sudden heat in his expression. "Not a bad thought," was all he said, though.

"Right," Paul said. "Then... tell her. Somehow. I never see her, so... tell her however you can, set a time, and I'll just try not to be surprised if the two of you are drinking my cognac when I come upstairs."

"Why?"

"Pardon?"

"Why are you doing this?"

He couldn't explain how he was motivated in part by phantom scenes of the two of them in bed. Likewise, he couldn't tell the other truth, which was that, like Alastair, he wanted somebody to have a chance at bliss even if it couldn't be him. He'd long decided he was too strange to be lovable. Sleeping the night with someone or stealing a few hours with him was a different matter.

Love wasn't always, and didn't necessarily need to be, present in those moments. When it was, he bloomed under it, but he didn't expect it. Nonetheless, he did yearn for a friend who could love him completely. Whether it was possible was another question. Well, perhaps he could tell a version of that particular truth. The one having nothing to do with premonitions or the unnatural. "I think Muriel deserves this chance."

Alastair took a moment, then nodded.

"You'll need keys." Paul slipped one from the ring at his belt. "This opens the back door. If you turn to the left, you'll come to the stairs that lead up here." He took another. "And this one opens *my* doors." Holding them both out, he was surprised to see Alastair's disbelief. "What is it?"

"You really don't think I'm going to just rob you..."

"No."

"This could be a sham."

"It could, but it would be very elaborate indeed. How would you know how much I dislike Sykes? How could you know I'm a fanciful romantic? How would you know I'm the only person in charge of this place?" He laughed a bit. "And there's nothing to take, as I said."

Eyes wide, Alastair accepted the keys and put them in a pocket in his coat. Paul glanced at his hands and noted fingerless gloves did conceal the bulk of what seemed to be intricate tattoos. They must have been what Sykes had meant. As Alastair's hands slowed and stilled in his lap, Paul realized some of the designs were on his fingers, above where the gloves ended. "People don't often trust me."

"That's fair, though," said Paul. He leaned close. "You look like a miscreant. A very tidy one, but still... a bit dangerous." He sighed when Alastair looked not at his eyes, but his lips. The shift in attention was tiny, yet blatant.

"Maybe, but that... seems to have been effective in this case."

"Well, something about you read as 'trustworthy' to me, so... yes... it was..." Paul trailed off. Alastair gave the barest of small, closed-mouth smiles. "It was effective. Let's help Muriel, shall we?"

ALASTAIR HADN'T COME TO CROMER TO FIND ANYTHING.

He'd run simply to run and ended up there. He'd drifted with naught but restlessness and a certain skillset that could be put to use for good money. This business with Muriel had been introduced by chance; he'd embraced it by choice. He couldn't have refused her when her desire was to love and be loved.

It was something he wanted dearly for himself and he never spoke of it, fearing speech would give the need more life and then the need would strangle him. As Paul listed nearer, Alastair felt *Don't* war with *Please* as both of them sparred with *This isn't wise* and *If you don't kiss me, I'll go mad.*

Their lips met carefully, then with more verve. He couldn't say who chased or who capitulated. It didn't matter when the kiss felt sublime enough to nearly make him forget what they'd been discussing.

But the very rightness of it made him pull back. "I'll come with Muriel in tow or arrange to meet her here. Don't be alarmed if I'm sitting in front of your hearth, or we two are."

"Ah... I won't," said Paul, after a swallow. He looked as lost as Alastair felt. Not aimless, but consumed. His cheeks were slightly pink, as was his nose. "I gave you the keys, after all."

"I know."

"Sorry, should I not have..."

"I don't know which of us shouldn't have," said Alastair, and he brought his fingertips gently to one of Paul's flushed, freshly-shaved cheeks. "But I'd rather not continue." He didn't expect the words to ache as they did and he frowned. "It's nothing to do with you."

Wanly, Paul gave him a smile and finally drew back from his knee, creating a small amount of space between them, and leaned away from Alastair's fingers. "I know."

"I... didn't mean to open an old wound?" Alastair let his hand fall to the top of his own leg, eyeing Paul curiously as he wondered who else had said anything of the kind to him. It had never served him well to judge people by appearances, for they could hide a multitude of things. He wouldn't be taken aback to learn this quiet Mr. Apollyon took lovers. The thought garnered annoyance, even envy, but it didn't seem implausible. Paul was lovely in a subtle, keen way and he imagined others found it attractive.

"I make it sound like I have a gaggle of men after my charms." Paul sighed. "I don't." He looked wistfully at Alastair. "It's nothing, truly. I just... I'm nobody. Boring. Run a pub. Break up bar fights. Keep books. Why would you, of all people..."

Why would I, what? "Trust me, you're..." Alastair sighed. "You're not the problem." He wanly considered all that he yearned to say, everything about his mad little escapades and the convoluted family that would make Paul cringe.

"I'll still help you and Muriel, so don't worry about that."

A pair of gulls flew past the open windows, bickering as they went, and Alastair gathered his thoughts while he listened to their chatter. He stroked at the few days of grayed stubble on his face. "That's not my concern."

Never mind his past. All of that would be more straightforward than explaining how no other kiss ever felt so intimate. It could sound preposterous or predatory, and the last thing he wanted was for Paul to regard him as manipulative. There weren't many men who'd open their homes and businesses to a stranger looking like him, or to any stranger at all. That said Alastair could take a chance on speaking up, and he might not be rebuked. But he still worried that talk of one wee kiss setting his soul fully alight would sound opportunistic.

No matter that arousal was in Paul's eyes as he asked, "Then, what *is* your concern?"

Alastair said, "It's all ridiculous. You'd never believe me."

"I believe a lot of things." There, again, was a look saying Paul knew more than others, not because he was smug, but because he had access to knowledge nobody else could gain.

It reminded Alastair a little of a wise woman his mother had befriended. All of her neighbors said she could see the future. Even if she couldn't, she still had an eerily accurate way of reading people. Paul shared her air of having one foot here, the other there. Wherever *there* might be.

She'd told Alastair he should keep a canary instead of a cat, assuring him he'd find good luck where there were canaries. They'd been talking about cats because he was trying to convince his mother to permit him one, and she respected her friend's advice. But the wise woman just went on about canaries instead. It meant even less to him now than when he was a boy.

While he didn't know what she'd really meant, or if she'd seen anything at all, he'd remained fond of canaries and yellow. But everyone expected his favorite color to be black and his favorite animal to be something with fangs.

Even though he wanted to, Alastair wouldn't say he believed a lot of things, too.

~

IT WAS HALF-PAST THREE IN THE MORNING WHEN HE USED Paul's keys to let himself into the silent Queen Anne.

The night air was cool against his flushed skin; Alastair had broken one of his few rules and gotten absolutely drunk. When he'd first walked into a life of usually bloodless vice, he'd quickly discovered it was best to be mostly sober. Otherwise, it was too easy for well-crafted plans to collapse under the weight of careless words and actions.

At first, he'd been on his way to the cramped room he was letting from an old widower with many missing teeth and a propensity for very few words. The man's disposition didn't matter, because he was only staying long enough to complete Sykes's transactions and move some innocuous contraband.

Then his feet took him on a different route, his hips wobbling as he went, all of him beckoned by a new ally.

Everything was dark inside as well as outdoors, but he always had been able to see well at night and quietly found his way to the back stairs, only pausing when he'd reached the top and was in the short corridor that led to Paul's flat. Taking a breath, he decided to proceed.

The flat was as still as the rest of the place. A faint sound of waves was still audible and someone's congested snores came through a wall, but they enhanced the peacefulness. As though it was a bed that had been made for him, he fell onto the sofa he and Paul had occupied earlier, feeling it was the right and proper thing to do. Though his mind believed he didn't belong here, his body was now an apostate entirely against that belief.

It had led him back.

As he closed his eyes, the sofa felt like it was dropping out from under him.

He'd be mortified to learn he wouldn't wake until tomorrow afternoon.

~

"IF YOU'D WANTED TO STAY THE NIGHT, YOU COULD HAVE stayed. I wouldn't make you sleep in *my* bed, you know," said Paul from somewhere to his left, a laugh in his measured voice. Alastair kept his eyes shut. "Unless you wanted to."

"What?" He might be dreaming. He might be hallucinating.

"I wouldn't have made you sleep alongside me unless you wanted me. But I'd have let you sleep here if you'd needed to."

"Course I did. Of course I wanted you. God," breathed Alastair, too taxed and sleepy to filter his responses. He couldn't recall anything past leaving The Bell, a coarser pub than The Queen Anne, then stumbling through the streets. He recognized by the voice and smells that he was in Paul's flat, resting on something comfortable but firm and narrow. The sofa. If he concentrated, he caught distant chatter and soft clunks from the ground floor.

"Good. I want you, too. Will you open your eyes?"

"Maybe. Maybe I won't. Don't know if I can look at you. Did we... we didn't do anything, did we?"

"I don't fuck men who are as pissed as I expect you were. Don't think anybody can consent in that state."

Alastair was considerably less worried, then. Chuckling reluctantly, he said, eyes still shut, "On that, we agree... just... humor me. How'd you know I was drunk and not just asleep?"

"Besides the way I found you sprawled in my parlor as I came out of my bedroom, intending to start my day?"

"Yes."

"You smelled like a distillery," said Paul, and if Alastair wasn't overly hopeful, there was a grin in his voice. "It's just not as obvious, now."

"Thank Christ. Love drinking, hate the smell."

"Well, you could thank Christ... or all the open windows. And me. For opening them."

"Thought it was a little cold."

"Better the chill than the smell. And aren't you from the north?"

"Doesn't mean I'm fond of the cold. How'd I get here?" Alastair didn't want to say he'd lost himself because of this very connection between them, the one that had led him to wander here, the one presently rousing smiles and gentle banter despite a thundering headache.

"As to that, I don't entirely know."

Sighing, Alastair opened his eyes and looked at Paul, who sat on the tufted footrest just across from him. He held a cup and wore a smile in his eyes. "I haven't done this in years," Alastair said, transfixed. That coy, almost non-smile, combined with the flat's scents of beeswax, salt, and ink, made the place feel more like home than anywhere else.

"Been drunk? I'm sure you've been drunk before now. How old are you? At least thirty, I'd bet, and likely a few years past that, right? Though, don't get me wrong, you look good."

Alastair rolled his eyes and immediately wished he hadn't. It made him dizzy. "I haven't been *that* drunk in years. I don't even remember coming here."

"Well, you weren't covered in blood or missing any clothes, so I assume you didn't cause much havoc or injure yourself."

"Does anything rattle you?"

"Not the things that are supposed to, apparently. Besides, what's there to be rattled about?"

"I just appeared in your flat. That's not at all unsettling?"

"Some might say a beautiful man appearing unbidden is a boon."

Finding nothing witty to say to the assertion that he was beautiful, Alastair stared at the light on the ceiling's crossbeams and realized what time it was. "It's well past morning."

"It is," said Paul. He gently brandished the cup. "It's beyond noon. If you can sit up, drinking this might help you feel less like horse shit."

The liquid within the cup smelled a little like horse shit. "What the hell is it?"

With a playful air, Paul said, "A friend taught me to make it. She has to deal with many men who overindulge, and this seems to help them trundle along out of bed and get on with their days."

Alastair mumbled a halfhearted "Shit" as he hauled himself precariously upright. His body felt several feet away from his floating head, but he didn't gag. Looking around at Paul and sifting through his choice of words, he said, "Your friend has many men in her bed? Sounds exhausting."

"She doesn't have them all at once. Collectively, I meant. Think she's done two at a time, though. Here." He leaned forward a little to hand over the cup. "I make it like she does. Had to use it a few times for regulars and it seems to work the same as what she's made."

"Ever had to take it yourself?"

"I'm only human."

Caring less what was in it and more that Paul had bothered to make it for him, Alastair just leveled it back without trying to taste it. He wasn't uninitiated in home cures for a morning after too much drink. None were palatable. "Are you sure about that?"

"Yes. I don't abstain," Paul said after a frown. "I just learned my limits *very* early. You tend to if you grow up in this trade. Or... you don't. But I wouldn't want to be that kind of proprietor. The drunk kind. Especially now that it's only me and Bess, and the two lads... wouldn't want them feeling uncomfortable."

Teasing just as much as he dared, Alastair said, "I meant, given those eyes..." he settled back on the sofa and a blanket fell from his lap as he stilled. Paul must have covered him. And removed his boots. Unless he'd removed his own boots and forgotten. "You might not be human at all. You could be a good spirit. Or a bad one."

It was probably just abstraction bred by his exhaustion, but his mind was drawn to the lore he'd heard as a child while his mother completed her seamstress' work near the fire and told him stories of fairies and elves, kelpies and selkies.

Paul scoffed. "I'd know if I was a spirit."

"Sounds like what a bad one would say to make me less suspicious."

"Well, what would a good one say?"

"Nothing. A good one would just show up with a cure for too much drinking. And before that, they'd remove my boots for me. Give me a blanket." He beamed when Paul blushed. Then he set aside the empty cup. "Thank you. This is mortifying."

Regaining some of his drollness, Paul said, "I'm a bad influence on you."

There were a few things Alastair would say before claiming that, surely. He sighed and ran a hand through his tangled hair before reaching for a leather thong wound around his belt. Taking his time to respond, he said to Paul, "You're telling me a man with a reasonably successful, legal business is a bad influence on me. You've got it wrong, I think."

Paul eyed his hands on his hair as he tried to subdue it, and Alastair wasn't displeased when he scooted the whole footrest closer to the sofa. Gently, he took the bit of leather and deftly bundled Alastair's tresses away from his face. "When we were boys, Edward kept his hair this long for an age and it was as wild as yours. He wanted to be a highwayman or a pirate, you see. Our parents didn't care, they even thought it was funny... but eventually, he cut it off. He had too much trouble taking care of it. I always had to help him tie it back."

"Oh." Alastair almost remarked how Edward might have liked to know there was some speculation, proudly on his late, onerous father's part, that they were related to a somewhat infamous pirate with the same family name. But he was captured by the feeling of Paul so deftly managing his hair and couldn't make conversation.

Done, Paul trailed steady fingers just along the back of Alastair's neck and said, "Haven't seen tattoos this closely before. I'm never this near anyone who has them. Certainly never touched any. I thought they might feel a little different from the skin around them, but they don't."

It took a moment for the words to make sense because those fingertips trailed sunlight. Alastair made himself answer. "No. And they don't *all* mean something, if you wondered."

"Oh, that'd be exhausting, trying to come up with that much significance. Better to get mostly pretty, mad, meaningless things and have done with it."

"Exactly." Though he didn't believe in God, Alastair almost began to pray when Paul's fingers slipped lower, under his collar.

"What's this one? Can only see a bit of it along the back of your neck. Looks like a... tentacle?"

"Mm... that one. Sea monster. Big fucking squid."

Paul chuckled. "Right. *Big fucking squid.* Are you covered in them, then?"

"More or less." Alastair twisted to glance at him. Happily, the room didn't wobble too much. "Most people don't notice. Just easier to hide them. I've got to be in various states of undress for everything to be visible."

With an inviting smile, Paul said, "That's all right with me."

Alastair clambered forward for a kiss, then, fear and sense and headache be damned.

But firm, quiet footsteps fell outside the flat's second entrance, the same one he'd used last night, and he stopped himself at the last moment. Paul mumbled something indeterminate, and as he stood, appeared irked by the interruption. That gave Alastair some hope for the unexpected visitor's identity, and that there'd be kissing later.

He gazed at Paul's back as he walked away and asked, "Do you need me to hide?"

"Doubt it. Nobody uses this door unless I want them to. But if you'd feel better being out of sight, you can. Bedroom is just through there."

That brought salacious thoughts. "Best stay put if that's the option."

"There's the study, too, but you'd take up half of it. Used to be Edward's and my room, if you can believe it. Should duck your head in and wonder how we didn't end up murdering each other."

A crisp knock followed the footsteps. Paul opened the door before another could come, and Alastair swore quietly when he saw the woman at the threshold.

"Muriel?" said Paul.

By listening to the single confused word, Alastair discovered what might rattle the unshakable Mr. Apollyon.

PAUL JUST GAWKED. HE COULD ONLY GAPE AT HER BECAUSE most of his blood wasn't in his brain, and they hadn't spoken for some years.

"The back was open," she said. "I just took some loaves of bread through to your kitchen. That new baker brought them. He's quite good, you know, so you've done well to try him. Then I recalled your mother letting me hide in these stairs, once... and just last night, Mr. Gow told me to come to your flat around now... so I thought I'd show myself in."

Then Muriel looked past him with evident relief. She expected Alastair to be there, that was clear. The rest was rather a whirlwind of details. When she'd stopped talking, Paul half-turned and stared at Alastair.

"That's your surname? Is it really? Like the pirate?"

"Unfortunately."

"Right. No, it makes sense."

Evidently, the subject wasn't to be under discussion for the moment; Alastair pointedly leveled his attention at Muriel. "Miss Sykes?"

"You said to meet you here at one. I confess I didn't expect you to be awake after how pissed you were last night, so I've just come early to get it over with."

Understanding that he was not going to get a proper greeting, Paul said, trying to piece things together, "You saw him last night..."

"Oh, yes," said Muriel. "He was *very* drunk at The Bell. I wouldn't let anyone else serve him, but then he just started to drink from his flask." That explained where she was working: The Bell was an old public house that mostly catered to the likes of her father.

Just as he did not expect a hello, she did not seem to find it necessary to clarify why Paul harbored Alastair. She appeared to just accept the two men in the flat. "Then I made him sit in the corner while I closed up, but after that... I suppose he... came here."

A persistent, gentle hope flared as she spoke. If Alastair had wandered here while drunk, he ideally wished to be present while sober. "Come away in," Paul said, gesturing her into the room. She stepped inside and sat in the wooden rocking chair beside the hearth, bringing with her a scent of tea roses that he was almost certain was true perfume and not one of his spirit's tricks.

"My gran used to say that," said Alastair. "Hell, sometimes *I* say it. You sure all your people are from here?"

Muriel interjected before Paul could reply. "He was talking about you all night, Mr. Apollyon." She smirked. "About your eyes and how they reminded him of the sea at dusk, although now that I'm looking at them... they're a little more greenish than the sea, aren't they... and he went on about your shoulders and your..." her words trailed away as Alastair gave a flustered snort. "Well, he should tell you that other part himself. I don't have any experience with admiring men. I'm sure I'd mangle his admiration."

"Please. Just... Paul." If they were going to discuss personal matters, they could all be using given names. He couldn't look at Alastair, then, because an unreasonable amount of glee bubbled to the surface of his mind and its effervescence remained.

She smiled and inclined her head a little. "Very well. Though, if I have my way, I'll be gone by sundown and won't be speaking to you much." With a note of teasing, she added, "I don't care what you call me." Then, addressing Alastair, she explained, "Abigail made it in last night. That note you took her last Sunday did it. She was upstairs in The Bell the entire time. We're leaving tonight."

On a huff, Alastair said, "I wanted to meet her, though. Why'd you not bring her down?"

"You were in no state to meet anyone. And when I said you shouldn't, you were adamant that I needed to see you here before I left. For what, I don't know. But I've come to regard you as a strange sort of friend, so..." she shrugged and beamed. "You may visit us, you know."

"How would you let me know where you've settled, then?"

"Don't you recall what else we spoke of? If you do what you wish, it'll be easy for me to find you. I can write."

"I don't think he recalls anything," said Paul. He sat on the sofa's arm closest to Alastair and Muriel's eyes travelled between the two of them. Though he didn't know why she'd be so pleased about it, she seemed heartened by their proximity to each other. "He asked me how he got here."

"It's not so far between here and The Bell," she said dismissively. "Mr. Gow, you kept telling me you wanted to stay in Cromer. Many times. And then you'd say you shouldn't, or you couldn't — but you wanted to."

"Alastair," he said, as Paul's hand seemed to travel with its own mind to his shoulder. "Please. 'Mr. Gow' was my father, and he was an awful man. Why did I say I wanted to stay?"

"All right. I know you've already told me to ignore formalities. It's just habit." She grinned. "But you said you wanted to stay on account of Mr. — Paul. That much I gathered while you were slurring. For what it's worth, I believe you do."

They could have heard a mouse scamper across the floor in the silence following her words. Paul hadn't taken his hand back. He moistened his lips with the tip of his tongue before he spoke. "We've just met." He added, "We only met because he asked me to hide him from your father." But he knew what he wanted Alastair to do, even if such a want was possibly shortsighted.

Muriel chuckled and shrugged, a fluid gesture that suited the inky blue of her dress and brought to mind deep water's movements. "Hearts are strange. Time may not matter, much. Abigail and I met at a haberdashery when she asked for the last yard of the same violet ribbon I was after. Frankly, I despised her at first."

Despite having seen himself in bed with Alastair after they'd just met, Paul found it curious he didn't see more to do with Muriel or what was ahead for her. But then, they weren't close and probably weren't in a position to become closer. Perhaps it followed that he couldn't see a thing.

"Alastair has told me just enough." He smiled because he knew who Abigail was. "But she's your..."

"My everything."

Her simple words filled Paul with warmth, and he said, "I assume you won't be remaining nearby." She shook her head. That made sense; her father could try to find her if she decided to live so close to him. "If, though, you need a place to stay for a day or two in Norwich, say... The Swan is Edward's and his wife's. It's just near the market. I'm sure they'd look after you until you decided what you were going to do."

"That's kind. I'd pay them, of course."

"Did I really say I wanted to stay?"

They both looked at Alastair, who'd spoken with mild wonder. Paul tried not to tighten his grip on his shoulder. Muriel glanced at Paul. Then she said, "Yes."

"And... the bit about his eyes. And... the rest of him. I said all that, too."

"Oh, yes," she said. "It disappointed the women sat on either side of you, I can say. But despite that, they did seem interested in Paul's... well, his arse. And his prick." She smirked at Alastair upon revealing this. "Or in your speculations about them, anyway. Sorry, Paul."

He just shrugged and prayed he didn't look too eager.

Quiet while Alastair appeared to think about all this, Paul wondered what it would be like for him to remain. It felt as though they were old friends returning to each other for the first time in years. He found he could imagine months, years alongside him. It didn't matter that he didn't know Alastair's favorite jam or which side of the bed he slept on or whether he preferred green to red. Whatever the answers were to those kinds of questions, they wouldn't feel surprising.

But he didn't know if someone like Alastair would stay in a place like this. Paul enjoyed his life, yet if one was used to variety or even danger, he could guess mundanities might become monotonous. He didn't know how Alastair would react to his stranger qualities, either.

"Then they should prepare for more disappointment," said Alastair.

"What?" said Paul.

"I... look, I do feel like shit, and both of you know I was pissed. But I'm not now... and I still don't want to leave." Paul wanted to kiss him, yet this seemed like an important thing to let him articulate. "Would it be all right? If I stayed. I don't know how it'll be, of course, seeing as I've definitely set Sykes against me and I look like, well, me, which might not be good for your trade, but... it isn't just physical attraction... it's..."

Shaking his head, Paul ducked down a little and kissed him gently, mindful of the state of him after so much drink. But it was Alastair who made the kiss more sinuous, and Muriel who laughed and brought them both back to earth. Alastair laughed a little, himself, and pulled away just a hair from Paul.

"From the look of things, it would be a pleasurable arrangement," Muriel said. "But I should get back to Abigail now that I know you didn't break your neck. The Bell isn't unsafe, but it's rowdy. Don't want to leave her alone too long."

"Do you need anything before you set off?" Alastair asked.

"I don't think so."

Tracing his own lower lip lightly with his pointer finger, Paul said, "Wait." He rose and went into the study to retrieve a number of coins and notes, evidence of last night's trade. Even doing only a cursory tally in his head, he knew he wouldn't miss them much. "Just in case." He held out the money for her to take, and she did after a moment's hesitation.

Alastair's eyes burned on his back as Muriel said, though it was more a breath in the shape of a word, "Why?"

"Something might come up. Or you might want to celebrate. I hope it's the latter. Think of it as a wedding gift."

Muriel stood and kissed Paul on the cheek. "Thank you."

"Of course."

She hesitated, then met Paul's eyes again. "I wonder if you'd do me a favor... Abigail brought her canary with her, only I don't think a bird is the sort of thing we want to carry around the country. I didn't want to hurt her by insisting she leave it, but..."

Although Alastair still said nothing and hadn't moved, Paul felt a keen intentness continue to radiate from his direction as she quieted. After pondering for a moment, he said, "They're popular, but I've never lived with one." Plenty of canaries were bred in Norwich and more locally. "Are they difficult to care for?"

"No. Not really. I just feel she would be cumbersome on a journey, the poor thing." She looked at him so beseechingly that he resigned himself to inheriting a new pet. "Not to mention, I think she'd be frightened by all the change."

"Bring her here... or tell someone to bring her here... and I'll... make sure she doesn't die. Can't be any different from a fern, can it?" The several potted ferns downstairs were the only dependent things besides horses and drunks he'd kept alive. Maybe Edward, too, sometimes.

Muriel laughed. "Only a little."

By the time Muriel left through the same door she'd used to enter, Alastair had almost sorted through the shock that followed her bequeathing Abigail's canary to Paul. It wasn't a bad surprise to learn what the wise woman had meant, or at least to see what she'd alluded to in her hazy manner. Not only did he want to stay, he knew then that he should.

With resolve, he stood. "You didn't have to give her anything. It's not as though you're wealthy. Or you're really friends."

"I know. And you didn't have to help her, either. It's not as though you're in the business of helping."

"Good, as long as you know," said Alastair. The floor creaked under his steps as he came closer, moving deliberately due to his head. But Paul didn't turn to him. "And... canaries *are* popular here."

"Mm, they've quite a history in Norwich." Paul nodded, then slid him a kind glance. "You seemed rather overcome by the, uh, sudden inheritance. Are you... afraid of birds? We don't have to keep it if you are, but I should take it until I can find it a home. Between you and a canary, I'll have you."

"No, I'm fine with them. How'd you know I was? I didn't even say anything."

"Just... felt it. I just knew."

"Hm," said Alastair, and he tentatively reached for one of Paul's hands. "That does follow."

Paul took it. "Does it?"

"Of course it does. You'd just know. You're my shrewd spirit."

"Yours?" Compulsive skepticism seemed to be laced within the word.

But longing shone in Paul's smile, and Alastair said, "If that's acceptable."

Without saying more, Paul inched up for a kiss. This time, Alastair snaked his free hand along his waist. When their lips came together, he held fast.

PAUL WAS BUSY WITH A SMALL BUT DEMANDING EVENING gaggle, so it hadn't taken much to slip away to Sykes' neglected little cottage. It required even less acumen to break into it. Knowing Muriel was gone, Alastair felt no qualms over cornering Sykes.

Before, he'd resisted because she would have been trapped had it gone poorly. But now that she'd made her escape, he wanted to make it clear he wouldn't allow Sykes to antagonize anybody. Soon enough,

Sykes would discover Muriel wasn't coming home and her absence would infuriate him. While Paul wouldn't be implicated because there was no way to connect him with Muriel's vanishing, if Alastair stayed near him, he could potentially draw him into undue conflict.

So he waited in an old, empty chair beside a table that still bore a couple of partially-filled cups. The sky fully darkened through the curtains as he sat. When the front door squeaked open, he turned his head.

To Sykes' credit, he seemed immediately aware that something was different. Without lighting any candles or divesting himself of coat or hat, he said into his own tiny sitting room, "Who's there?"

"A ghost," Alastair said acridly. While the pain in his head had mellowed considerably, he wasn't in any mood to entertain fools or brutes.

"You."

"Me."

"You've seduced my Muriel."

"I thought I'd *taken something*. That's what you shouted out her window after me."

"Doesn't fucking matter. What decent man would be in a girl's room?" As he'd expected, Sykes drew a knife that glinted like teeth in the near dark. "You've ruined her. You'd ruin her reputation if this got out at all. You're lucky she's to be married so soon, or I'd never be rid of her. I should gut you."

Carefully, Alastair rose from his seated position and looked down at Sykes, not intimidated. The man, as he often was, was pickled. He could tell by his gait. Some might manage both their weapon and their drink at once, but he didn't believe Sykes was capable of it. "Careful who you threaten."

"I'm not afraid of a nasty, dark criminal."

Hearing similar words many times hadn't left enough calluses for them not to hurt. But Alastair was still used to the bile, so he pressed on. "Well, because you're not very clever. You've just contradicted yourself, too... aren't you worried about Muriel's reputation? Doesn't that scare you?"

"Get out."

"Only after you listen. Don't worry. I won't take long; I despise it in here."

"It's already been too long," said Sykes, taking a step closer. "And I don't listen to the likes of you."

It had been clear during their meetings that Sykes did not think much of those who actually dirtied their hands with the direct illegalities he avoided. He felt he was above everyone, but clearly didn't mind reaping the money from others' risks. Whoever had first used Sykes as a fence, Alastair thought, didn't think it through. Anyone with foresight would've seen he was too petty, too overindulgent with his intoxicants, and too disdained by locals to be a good intermediary.

"Here it is: if I hear of you harming or harassing anybody," said Alastair clearly, without malice but with careful emphasis, "there'll be hell to pay."

"The fuck are you on about?"

"Just what I say. Stop being yourself. Be decent."

The curtness provoked Sykes in a way Alastair didn't expect, and he wouldn't have called the man pleasant by any definition.

A snarl parted from Sykes's mouth as he brandished the knife.

Alastair quickly shifted slightly to the side, prepared to disarm him in the next moment. Sykes mirrored the movement. But his left boot caught on the edge of a thick rug, and when he tripped, there were no dull thuds of knees or hands on the wood floor. No cursing, no labored breathing.

Instead, the cups juddered as Sykes's forehead caught the table's edge. The impact knocked his head as the rest of him slumped down. He was already limp when he came to rest, and the knife clattered from his open hand while his hat went askew.

After several moments of abject stillness, Alastair knew he wouldn't rise again.

"Fuck's sake," he mumbled, stunned, careful not to alter where the body now rested. He edged away from the blood that began to seep from Sykes's forehead, leaving an even darker stain in the lightless room. Since he had no intention of attracting attention while he left, he imagined most everyone would just accept this as Sykes's logical, fitting end.

He knew a decent man would probably care more, but Alastair hadn't considered himself decent for a long time. Still — given all recent events — even if he couldn't be decent, he might be persuaded to believe in God again.

After a moment of thought, he cautiously took the knife from Sykes' limp grasp. He could either take it with him, or try to put it away in a place that made sense. Rather than take any chances, no matter how slim, he pocketed it with a grimace. It felt odd to have something of Sykes' on him, as though the man's cruelty and peevishness might seep into his own temperament.

THREE HOURS PAST MIDNIGHT AS CANDLES BURNED LOW on the bedside table, Alastair murmured, "Sykes is dead."

"Ah, is he?" Paul tried not to be amused after he realized the words were in earnest. He wanted to understand what the hell had happened, and why, and how Alastair was feeling about it. And decency dictated that amusement wasn't the right response to anybody's death, even if the person wasn't well-liked and the circumstances of its divulgence were a little comical.

But Alastair had only announced the news after they'd shed their clothes, found their way to bed, and made far too much noise within it. Even this late into the night, Paul waited for Jack to pound on their shared wall behind the headboard. While he was fortunate in his lodgers' ambivalence about his private life, he'd understand if they took issue with their sleep being disturbed. He'd had men home before and nobody passed remarks on it, so it was also possible that no one knew.

He'd be incredibly lucky if they were unaware now. With a burning, permission-seeking look that Paul had answered with a nod while they were both entwined, Alastair had covered his mouth with a careful palm to muffle his sounds. But both the look and warm pressure had just induced Paul to moan more readily.

He was still hoarse right this moment.

"Very," said Alastair. "Damn dead."

"Is that where you were earlier tonight? With Sykes?" He'd slipped outside at the same time a little crush of patrons had arrived. Too occupied to think about it, Paul assumed he was going to gather his meager possessions, and he did return with a small leather bag.

"I was," said Alastair. "I didn't do it, if you were wondering."

"No... not particularly." *Only a bit.* But if anything, the idea of Alastair killing a man like Sykes titillated him a little.

"Would it bother you if I had?"

Studying his face and his brown eyes soft as velvet in the weak light, Paul shook his head. "No. It'd be a welcome murder, actually."

Seeming pleased with the response, Alastair kissed his forehead. "I'm not a clandestine assassin or an indiscriminate killer, just so you know."

There had to be many things he was, clandestinely, but *assassin* didn't feel like one. Paul said, "No, you're too sweet."

"Known me for just a moment. How would you know? Fuck you, I'm not sweet." The second kiss to the forehead said otherwise, as did the tone devoid of spite.

"How'd he die?"

"I'd gone to see him. I talked. He balked. He tried to threaten me with a knife and tripped over a rug."

It sounded oddly banal. "One does have to be careful with rug placement."

"He hit his head on a table and didn't get back up."

Blinking, Paul asked, "Where... were you?"

"His cottage."

"Right. Did anyone see you come or go? Hear you? Hear him?" It was the only fear he had around the news; Sykes himself roused neither sympathy nor nervousness. He'd had no living family besides Muriel, and she was well away by now. Given her usual hours at The Bell, Sykes probably hadn't even realized she was gone yet. Paul also didn't imagine his contacts or peers, such as they were, would think to check on him until he didn't show for something.

Once they did, it would be difficult to construe that type of injury — especially suffered by someone under the influence of drink — as foul play without any evidence of more trauma to the body.

"No."

"Good." He trusted Alastair's experience enough to believe him if he said he hadn't been noticed. "Well, I should think it's the way most of us thought he'd die... if not in a puddle of his own vomit. A peer will probably find him, sometime, but he hasn't any family besides Muriel, so we needn't worry about that."

"Remind me never to cross you," said Alastair with a smile. "You're eerily pragmatic."

"I told you. I don't like Sykes. And anybody could die that way... I think about it all the time while I'm downstairs. Watched so many almost-deaths." He chuckled. "And it's not just people who've been drinking... it's everybody. One thoughtless step and... hell, *I've* almost bashed my head on things."

"Hush."

Paul thought of something else, though, and did not hush. "Wait. What did you do with the knife?" He assumed, in any event, that someone like Alastair would know to do something with it. There might not be any signs of a struggle, but if he was discovered still holding his knife, there could be suspicions about what had transpired.

"You're a clever lad to think of that." Alastair almost purred the words, and it went directly to Paul's cock. "Took it with me. Thought about leaving it in an innocent sort of place, a table or something, like he'd just left it there himself. But... better to be safe."

"I'm just happy you're all right. I don't think this will come back to haunt you, if you want the truth." He supposed he'd know if he suddenly dreamt about something coming of it, but until then he'd assume the matter was finished.

When Alastair began to work gently at the largest knot in his right shoulder, Paul suppressed a low noise of pleasure and tried to think beyond this contentment. Tomorrow would dawn. With it would come realities, some less quotidian than others, and he couldn't fathom hiding his premonitions from Alastair even if he was afraid to expose them. Among the list of subjects he wanted to broach, it lingered in his mind because of how they'd passed the night so pleasurably.

It wasn't what he'd seen while trying to serve Sykes a beer — without looking like he was somewhere among the stars as he spilled it onto his lap.

In what he'd experienced, Alastair's hair was less dark, more gray, and his face was a little more worn. It sported more of a beard. The bed had been awash with afternoon light, and he had a tattoo at the base of his throat where there weren't any at present. It was a canary, Paul now knew, thinking back to what he'd seen. He just had better context to recognize the type of bird.

All of these details gave him hope.

"I told you," said Alastair. "Hush."

"I didn't say anything."

"Your brain is saying a lot. I feel it chattering and burning in your skull."

"I hope it isn't. Fevers can be awful."

"Not like that." Alastair chuckled. He rubbed the same knot until it began to give and Paul couldn't stop himself from groaning, then. "You're thinking ahead."

"Aren't you?"

Also of some comfort, Paul was sure Alastair needed to say things, too, and he would accept whatever was freely given without angling for more.

"Oh, a little. But right now... I'm still taken by all your delicious little noises." Alastair punctuated the words with a firm thumb on tense flesh.

"More of that, please."

Grinning, Alastair said, "Gladly." He was quiet for a spell, shifting so both of his hands were on Paul's shoulders. Then he coaxed him to roll more properly onto his side.

"Where do you want me?"

"If you rest with your back facing my chest, like this... I can get both of your shoulders *and* that gorgeous neck that doesn't look like it's moved for years." He kissed the side of Paul's throat, his tongue lingering as though catching the juice of a ripe plum.

"My..." he writhed, pleased when his arse scarcely brushed Alastair's prick. "Um, *what* about my neck?"

"I'm going to melt you. You're too tense." Soft lips spoke against his ear, then kissed his temple. "You have too much going on in here."

"Good luck."

He heard the smile in Alastair's voice. "Give me time. I'll manage."

"Will you?" A trace of vulnerability strayed into his voice, but he tried to give himself over to Alastair's warm hands and reassurances.

"Think so. I have faith in how this feels. I trust the man who let me hide in his cellar... who gave his night's earnings to a woman running away... and takes in her lover's fucking canary. I trust *you*."

"You..." Paul went from feeling arousal to gratitude to mild shame. "Wait." His pulse quickened out of nerves.

Alastair's hands paused. "You all right?"

"Yes, I just have to tell you something." He sat up with great reluctance, gathering the sheets over his lap and angling his back against the cold metal headboard.

To Alastair's credit, he didn't try to stop Paul or coerce him into carrying on. He just looked up at him warmly and rested one of his hands atop Paul's thigh, slipping it under the covers. "What is it?"

Paul drank the sight of him in, his hair spread on the pillow, all the raveled tattoos that were revealed as he undressed, just as he'd said they would be. "Will you do me a favor?" Apprehensive, he used the tip of his pointer finger to trace the edge of a scalloped design atop Alastair's collarbone.

"Just tell me, angel. Whatever you're not saying."

Huffing, Paul supposed his anxiety was clear enough. "Well, you might think I'm mad."

"I'd never call you mad. Dunno if madness actually exists. *Life* is mad, really."

"If you trust me, I want you to know..." he sighed and kept tracing the tattoo, watching Alastair's chest move as he breathed. "I *need* you to know... before you really decide that you do..."

"Whatever you've done, I've either done worse or seen worse. And if you're mad, it's both of us who are."

"It's nothing so interesting," said Paul, and he had to meet Alastair's eyes with a smile. Despite himself, he trusted Alastair fully even though he knew there was much to learn about him. "You sweet man. Besides, I doubt you're as monstrous as all that."

"Go on, then."

"I saw us doing this, but we were older. I mean to say, I saw you under me on my bed; I didn't see myself. But *you* were older, so I must've been." Paul considered it. He'd been so engrossed by how it felt that he hadn't tried to catalogue his future surroundings. But he could hazard a confident guess that they were in this bedroom. "Same bed, though."

And it had all exited in a jumble that wasn't fully cogent. There was no scaffolding to explain how he'd seen it, or even that he could see the future. He winced. Alastair's hand stilled on his thigh; Paul stilled his finger on Alastair's skin. "But, we were fucking and it was glorious. And the entire time I was seeing it in my head, I had to act like you *weren't* here — Sykes was sniffing around."

Then it fell so quiet that Paul could hear the tick of the clock in the next room, intermingling with his and Alastair's breaths and someone else's smothered snores. The window was open just a sliver and allowed the waves to be heard, a low, underlying comfort.

When Alastair did speak, his voice was a soothing rumble. "You've got the sight."

The equanimity wasn't what Paul expected, not in a time of science and progress. He'd braced himself for denials and questions, or some manner of derision. "I... don't call it anything. Like that." It sounded like something out of an Arthurian legend, not anything he'd apply to his own humdrum life.

Then, perhaps upon hearing Paul's stunned tone and realizing how taken aback he was, Alastair began to laugh. "Jesus, you'd seen *that* by the time you came back to fetch me, and you could still walk? Look *me* in the eye? Pull *Sykes* a pint? I'd have to go find a quiet room and a bed. You should consider being a fence... you didn't falter at all."

Relieved at the feeling of having *said it*, or more precisely, Alastair having said it, Paul began to smile. "You're... not angry, or... frightened?"

"No."

"No?"

"One day, sooner rather than later, I'll tell you all about my mother's friend — a wise woman who told me I should keep a canary. I'm fairly certain she had the sight, saw visions; I think she could do what you do."

"She said you should keep a canary?" Paul frowned a bit. Then he took a breath as the awareness hit him. "Oh, fuck. The canary. Muriel's... Abigail's, I mean. Well, mine now. Ours? Ours now."

"Mmhm." Alastair's hand crept up his back and urged him down, short nails slowly raking against Paul's skin. "Ours. And I'm as astonished as you are. But for now, you deserve pleasure."

Coming to rest on his side and gazing at Alastair's profile with unbridled joy, Paul said, "Of course I do. But it'll be morning for me, soon. Do you have any idea what I actually have to do to keep all of this going? How early I get up?"

"You'll have a lot to teach me. But I'll help you rise before the sun, no problems there."

"That is an awful joke, that is." But Paul rewarded him with kisses, first on his cheek. Then he littered another on the edge of his jaw.

～

THE NEXT EVENING, ALASTAIR SAID HE WISHED TO TAKE A walk with Paul and they waited until after closing to go.

They were careful not to look too enamored as they wandered

outside The Queen Anne, then down the promenade, then finally to the water's edge. As it was late, there were not droves of people about, but there were enough to remind them they weren't alone.

Twenty minutes passed in a companionable silence of the sort Alastair had rarely experienced. He found the quiet didn't agitate him at all. He enjoyed watching Paul draped in the light of the stars and moon, and fancied that he was indeed some bewitching entity who was forced to live among men. When they'd wandered far enough from any casual bystanders and Alastair was sure they wouldn't be seen — he always trusted his own assessments of such things — he halted Paul with a soft touch on his wrist, and smiled.

As he pressed a gentle kiss to Paul's mouth, he took Sykes' old knife from his pocket. He wanted to be rid of it; he didn't want it anywhere near this new life.

Dreamily, abstracted by the kiss, Paul asked, "What've you got?" He pulled his face away, barely. He hadn't looked between them yet.

"Just some rubbish."

At that, Paul did look down. "A knife?" He looked back up.

Alastair raised his eyebrows eloquently, meeting Paul's eyes without a hint of guilt or nerves. "Yes."

Paul knew whose it was immediately. "You're not the sort to keep trophies, then," he said.

His seer, his spirit, dripping with silver under the moon, was quick. "Hm..." He took a couple of large steps back so he could throw the knife as hard and far as possible, even with the wind blowing. "Wouldn't say that."

Paul watched as the knife sailed away from them. The metal shined gently against the sky and sea's blacks, blues, and indigos. "You... can't be. Interested in mementos. If you're throwing it out into the tide." The knife disappeared before he finished the sentence.

Alastair turned to him. Smiling, he cupped Paul's breeze-cooled cheek with his palm. He wore no gloves tonight, so Paul's skin was soft under his touch. "I didn't need the knife. I've got my prize right here."

About the Author

Camille is a thalassophile who sadly spent too long residing in Chicago, where there's just a very large lake and no sea. An enquiring and possibly over-educated mind, she's been described as "the politest contrarian." Though everyone believes she's tall, she's not. Likewise, she doesn't dress in all-black.

To Be Fair, They Were Pleather

KRISTAN HIGGINS

Chapter One

"I wish *I* was gay," said Hannah, my best friend since kindergarten, when she let me undress her Barbie doll so I could see what boobs looked like. "It would make life so much simpler. You and I could get married, adopt a border collie and train her to bring us coffee."

"That *is* the dream," I said, sipping my martini, then wincing. They were candy cane martinis, something that shouldn't exist in mixology. "But you're assuming you're my type. Sorry."

"Well, shit," Hannah said. "There goes my chance at lesbian heaven."

I huffed, well used to the running joke. Like so many straight women, Hannah had this fantasy that if she were gay, all her relationship troubles would evaporate. That because women were so intuitive and emotionally intelligent, there was never a cross word or disagreement in Lesbian Land. They were wrong.

Hannah and I were hiding from the rest of the guests at her parents' annual Christmas party. Half of Stoningham, Connecticut, our hometown, was here, and we'd grown tired of that well meaning but repetitive holiday chatter—*Hi, Mrs. Winston, how are you? Great, great. Nope, not married. No, no kids. Not that I know of, anyway, ha ha. I think I'd remember being pregnant... Yep, still at the fire depart-*

ment (me), or *Still teaching fourth grade* (Hannah). We were in that weird *grown but still kids* zone, never to be viewed as a legit adult, since most of these guests had watched us grow up.

My parents were here as well, and I'd seen Mom sniffing the air for a hint of homophobia, a maternal bloodhound ready to pounce, leopard-like, and defend my honor. She lived for that, inviting commentary with three gay pride bumper stickers (rainbow flag, of course; *Proud Parent of a Gay Firefighter*, and *I love my gay daughter*). She often handed out my number to women she assumed were gay. "I have excellent gaydar," she said, which was a bald-faced lie. My dad, on the other hand, was a lot more chill, agreeing with everything Mom said and did, gamely cracking the occasional Dad-joke, the sweetest guy in the world, and the king of nonconfrontation. Theirs was an opposites attract situation.

Hannah nudged me. "Come on. It's twelve degrees out. I'm freezing *and* starving. Let's go in."

"My torso says yes. My legs say stay a little longer until the sweat freezes." I'd worn pleather pants, a tactical mistake.

"Did someone tell you pleather was a breathable fabric? Did they, Samantha Lewis? You're a firefighter. Do those look like you could escape in case of emergency?"

"Why did you convince me to buy them, then?"

"Because your ass looks magnificent." Hannah laughed and patted my butt. "Damn. Seriously. I wish I was gay."

"Yeah, yeah."

"Where's Judith, by the way?" Hannah asked. I'd known it was just a matter of time. "Oh, wait, let me guess. Something...came up." She made finger quotes around the last two words.

"Something came up," I concurred. Something always came up when Judith was supposed to appear with me.

"You deserve better, Sam."

I didn't respond.

"Okay. I'm off to get another disgusting martini and eat some of those chestnuts wrapped in bacon. I'll save you one."

"Save me ten," I said. She opened the sliding glass door, the sounds of the party slipping out, then cutting off as she closed it behind her.

I did deserve better than Judith. Well, Judith was amazing as a person. As a partner...a girlfriend...not so much. We'd been together for six months, and we were exclusive, something we agreed on the first date. We saw each other two or three times a week. At her place, mostly, sometimes mine, and almost never in public. She wasn't closeted about being gay...I think she was just closeted about being with me.

The thing was, her reasons for blowing me off always seemed so reasonable, so logical, so *British*. Something *had* come up. This time, it was work. Judith was a gallery artist who sold giant, colorful post-post-modern paintings and the occasional sculpture. When I reminded her that she made her own hours, she said it was an emergency commission with a fat price tag. How could I argue with that? I could not.

Last weekend, she'd had "a cold." She texted the news, told me to stay away so I shouldn't catch anything, and was sorry to miss "your thing." (Drinks with friends, so I could introduce them to her, and vice versa). I offered to bring soup, was told it wasn't necessary and brought it anyway. I heard her singing in her apartment, but she didn't answer the door. Nor did she sound particularly congested or scratchy. I left the Tupperware on her doorstep. She didn't mention it. I'm not sure she even ate it.

Just before the Stoningham Fire Department's *fabulous* Christmas party earlier in December, she'd had to "ring up" her sister for a chat since "it's been ages. I'll be quite quick. Off you go!" The call began ten minutes before we were supposed to have left and lasted all the way till the end of the party. When I told her how disappointed I was, she said, "But Samantha, it's my *sister*! You know how Cressida can be." I didn't, of course. Judith never talked about her family.

I wasn't stupid. It was clear she wasn't comfortable with our coupledom, not yet. I hoped it would change. It had to, right? I tried to talk to her about it...did she *want* to be a couple? "Of course, you silly duck," she said. "But I need space. As do you, of course."

And so my questions and insecurity (and irritation) would melt at the sight of her Paul Hollywood-blue eyes and the kiss-kiss on each cheek. When we did see each other, it could be magical. "Darling!" she'd exclaim. "You're here! Brilliant." Like most Americans, I got weak in the knees at the sound of a British accent. "Tea?" she'd ask, and even though I viewed tea as dirty, flavorless water, I would accept a cuppa and listen to her talk.

Judith Baines was beautiful and talented. She was a visiting artist, courtesy of Sadie Frost's gallery. Last summer, I'd been invited to the opening, since I went to grammar school with Sadie. On that balmy evening, I wandered around, admiring Sadie's pretty skyscapes, then stopped in front of one of the guest artist's work. To me, it looked like a kindergartener had guzzled a liter of Coke, eaten fistfuls of Coco-Puffs and grabbed some fingerpaints. To the critic from the *New York Times,* it was a searing image of suppressed female rage and feral beauty.

"What do you think?" asked a British voice. I turned, looked into the bluest eyes I'd ever seen, and fell in love. "It's not *terribly* awful, is it?"

"It's so..." I grasped for a word, any word, to impress the magical creature in front of me. "So emotional."

"Thanks." She smiled. Her dark blond hair fell in a perfect satin curtain to her shoulder blades She was slim as a reed, dressed in a silky black dress and Doc Marten boots. "I'm Judith."

And so began my painful, glorious, wretched relationship with a woman who made it clear she had no desire to marry *anyone*, ever. She didn't want children. She didn't want a cat. A woman who said things like, "I adore you provincial Americans" in response to a comment I made about a book, movie or painting. Who chuckled when I told her I loved her, but said nothing back. Whose smile was as beautiful as a Hawaiian sunset, whose small, plump breasts were utter perfection, whose twinkly smile made my heart leap with delight, whose toes were the most adorable things I'd ever seen. The sex was so hot that this firefighter staggered home. Because I was *always* sent home, even though when we were at my place, she always stayed over.

I sighed. Another ten minutes on the Grimaldis' deck, and I'd freeze to death. Time to go inside. I drained the last of my sugary martini, appreciating the buzz if not the flavor, and went inside to the roar of the party. There were my parents at the end of the vast living room. I could hang out with them, since Hannah was my only true friend here. Sure, I'd babysat for a lot of these folks, or their kids had babysat me. I'd just have to wind past sixty or eighty people, all of whom knew me. Some I'd seen at their worst—a broken hip after slipping in the shower, a roll-over because they'd been doing 80 instead of 45, a fire where they sobbed as we tromped through their house.

The sweat on my pleather-clad legs was making the fabric stick like glue, and there was a small *meep* of friction every time I took a step. "Hi, Mrs. Churchill, how are you?" *Meep.*

"Lovely to see you, dear. How's your brother?"

"Oh, he's out in Seattle, being perfect," I said. It was true. Vincent, seven years older than I was, had nabbed the title of best child while still in utero. "We barely made it to the hospital!" Mom liked to crow at every opportunity, in case people wanted to hear stories of her vagina. "He came out like a greased otter. It barely hurt! Now this one," she'd say, pointing to me, since I always seemed to be present for these stories. "She was stuck right at my pubic bone. They had to use a vacuum to pull her out! I had a third degree tear, and it took months to heal. Months."

But my brother was a great guy, and he'd gone to school with one or two of the Churchill boys, so I pulled out my phone and showed Mrs. Churchill a photo of the three of them—Vincent, Ashley and James, my two-year-old nephew.

"They're beautiful. How about you, Samantha? Is there anyone special in your life?"

I tried not to cringe. "When I get married, Mrs. Churchill, you'll definitely be invited." She smiled in pleasure, and I kept going. *Meep. Meep.*

"Samantha!" cried Courtney Finlay. She was the type who liked to pounce on me to prove she wasn't a homophobe (because she was). "How is Stoningham's *bravest* firefighter?"

"You're a firefighter?" asked her husband, whose name I could never remember.

"I am, but of course, we're all equally brave," I said, forcing a smile. They were a bit older than my parents, and I fondly remembered Mom, infuriated after a library board meeting, saying she'd met puddles deeper than Courtney.

"Tell me, Samantha, how is the *L-G-B-T-Q-I-A plus* scene around here?" Courtney asked, proudly pronouncing all of the letters distinctly. She glanced around to ensure everyone heard her being woke.

"Rather than tell you, Courtney, why don't you come out with me? We can see a drag show, go to some gay bars, maybe hit a few pride parades, paint rainbows on our boobs and run naked through the streets. I bet you've never been kissed by a woman, so scrunch up those wrinkled old lips, Courtney, and let me do the honors."

Obviously, I didn't say that. I just smiled and meeped my way past them. Being out in your hometown, where everyone knew everything, could be tiring. I just wanted to be me and have my sexuality not be such a topic of discussion.

"Hey, Sam," said Emma London. She was a little older than I was, but in a town this size, we also knew each other just because. "How's it going?"

"Not bad. Merry holidays." I shifted, and my pants meeped.

Emma looked around for the noise, which I pretended not to notice. "Same to you. Any special plans?"

"Here you go," said Miller, her honey, handing her a glass of wine. "Oh, hey, Sam. How are you?"

"Good, Miller, thanks for asking. How's Tess?" His daughter, a beautiful little girl with crazy blond curls, had come to the firehouse with the rest of the kindergarteners last week.

"She's great. Guess what she wants to be when she grows up?"

"A firefighter?" I guessed. "My work here is done, then." Emma laughed, and Miller put his arm around her and smiled at me. They were good people, those two. A lovely couple. The kind I'd like to be with my person, except my person had something come up. And, said the honest, irritating part of my brain, Judith wasn't really my person.

Suddenly, I wanted to cry. Emma's eyebrows rose, but I said, "Oh, there are my parents" and kept going. *Meep. Meep.* "Is there a cat in here?" asked Mrs. Greene, looking my way, then flinching as our eyes met. She was of those uber-wealthy church ladies who thought I'd be going to hell and shouldn't be allowed in public, and especially not near children. She'd written a letter to the editor after the kindergarten visit saying so.

"Merry Christmas, Mrs. Greene!" I said. "Isn't it lovely to celebrate the birth of the brown-skinned immigrant who hated the rich? It must inspire you to give away hundreds of thousands of dollars. Harder to get a rich man in the kindgom of heaven than getting a camel through the eye of the needle and all that." I crinkled my nose at her in a big fake smile. *Meep, meep, fuck you, Mrs. Greene, meep.*

Finally, with people who loved me. "Hello, parents," I said, relieving my father of his drink and taking a long slurp. The candy cane that served as a garnish almost poked me in the eye. "Having fun?"

"Where's Judith?" Mom demanded. "I thought you said she was coming. I can't believe you've been dating someone for half a year and we haven't met her yet!"

"Inside voice, Mom. Something came up at work."

"She's a *painter*," Mom said. "Can't she put the brush down and come out for an hour so you don't have to make excuses for her?"

It was a terrible thing, being understood by one's parent. "Apparently not," I said.

"You always were a glutton for punishment," my mother said. "Stop feeling guilty for being gay, honey, and choosing these horrible women to date." She glanced around for homophobes to comment so she could fight them.

Another gulp of Dad's martini. "For one, I *don't* feel guilty about being gay, and two, Judith isn't horrible."

"We love you *just the way you are*," Dad said. "We don't *care* who you sleep with."

"Of course we do, Ted!" said my mother with an eye roll. "We want her to sleep with a decent, caring person! Not one who stands her up time and time again and makes her look like an idiot!"

"Filter, Mom. Filter."

"Well, sure," Dad said sheepishly. "We want that, punkin pie. That is, we *don't* want that. We want the first part, not the second."

"Okay, I'm gonna find Hannah," I said. "Enjoy the party."

I ducked out of the Grimaldis' living room, meeping along, and went upstairs. I practically grew up in this house, and I had to go to the bathroom. My legs were so sweaty that I imagined there'd be a splash of sweat hitting the bathroom floor when I peeled them off. Hannah's bedroom, sporting the same décor it had when she'd redecorated it at age twelve, was the last door on the hallway. I went in, paused to appreciate the purple walls, and went into Hannah's loo (a word I'd co-opted from Judith, since it was so adorable), and locked the door. Took a look in the mirror, literally and figuratively.

I should've looked happier. My cheeks were pink thanks, to the martini and a half. My fresh pixie cut looked super-cute thanks to Robert, my hairdresser. The white sleeveless cashmere sweater showed my perfectly sculpted arms, and the cropped top gave a glimpse of my toned stomach. Being female, I had to be twice as fit as the guys on the department and also to make up for Denise, the only other woman firefighter, who complained constantly about working with men, still couldn't figure out how to attach a hose to a hydrant and was afraid of heights (I know).

But tonight, I'd dressed for Judith, wanting to look gorgeous and chic and effortless. I really thought she'd come. This was a huge Christmas party, and at the very least, she'd have been able to schmooze and talk up her art. We could've held hands, maybe kissed under the mistletoe (briefly, because Judith hated public displays of affection).

And here I was alone, as I had been last year, and the year before that, and the year before that.

I sighed, unzipped my pants and sat down on the toilet, the cool air heavenly on my damp legs. I grabbed the hand towel and fanned them. Yeah. I'd stay here a few minutes and dry off, then see if Hannah and I could sneak off to my apartment, which was quiet and small and no candy canes in the martinis. I could swap this outfit for a pair of PJs and take off these cruel and beautiful shoes. Yes, I wore high heels, and I rocked them, thank you very much.

It was when I stood up that I realized I had a problem.

Pleather. Sweat. Super-skinny cut (to make my fabulous ass look even more so). The pants didn't want to come past my knees. "Oh, come on," I muttered, tugging. They didn't budge. I pulled harder. A centimeter, maybe two.

I hopped, pulling harder. Jumped. Wriggled. Pulled them down to my ankles, thinking I could get some momentum going and heaved. Nothing. "For God's sake," I hissed. I mean, how hard could pulling up pants be? I tugged for another minute. I dried my legs with a hand towel, but it was fabric that was a problem. Maybe I could get them off, then just borrow a pair of normal pants from Hannah.

With the pants choke-holding my calves, I gave one last tug. I lost my balance a little, staggered because of my bound legs and crashed against the door.

And then I fell. It was both slow motion and over before I knew it. The edge of the sink hit my eye with a ugly thud, my hands still gripping the truculent waistband of the pleather pants. Ouch. That would leave a mark, I thought as I continued to fall. There. Done. I lay on the cool tiled floor, which felt *incredible* against my mostly bare legs.

Then I felt the sting. Putting my hand to my eyebrow, I winced. Shit. I was bleeding. I sat up slowly—I was an EMT as part of my job, so I knew the drill. Shit. Blood poured down the side of my face, splotching onto my white sweater. That would be hell to get out. And eesh, it was still splotching.

A little dizzy, I grabbed the sink and pulled myself up, pants still clutching my legs in a death grip. Oh, boy. It was a really good cut, about an inch, right in my eyebrow. Blood was in my eye now, and the side of my face was horror-movie nasty—blood now dripping off my chin into the pure white sink. Grabbing a face cloth, I ran it under cold water and pressed it against my eye. Jesus H. Roosevelt Christ! I'd have a huge shiner in a day or two. And I couldn't take tomorrow off, because it was Christmas Eve and I was working for Titus, who had little kids.

This wouldn't have happened if Judith had come with me, I thought. I hoped she'd feel *very* guilty about this and possibly sleep over my house and take care of me. Unlikely, but it would be the least she could do.

Well, I was still gushing blood, and my pants were still stuck below my knees. I needed Hannah. Where was my phone?

Yeah, where *was* my phone? It wasn't in my pocket, because these lovely pants didn't *have* a pocket. Right. I'd tossed it on Hannah's bed before coming in here.

With my legs locked together by the red bondage material. I opened the bathroom door, then walked, penguin-like, to the bed, still holding the sodden face cloth against my eye, and flopped down next to my phone. Texted Hannah with one hand.

Please come to your room asap. Pleather emergency.

If I took the face cloth off my eye, blood might get on Hannah's pristine white duvet, so I lay back on the hardwood floor. Looked at my phone. The text had been read. Thank God.

Just then the door burst open. "Samantha?" It was Hannah's mom, Lisa. "Honey, I don't know where Hannah is, but her phone lit up, she left it on the table with the egg rolls, and I saw the message, and you said it was an emergency, so I...what's...oh, my God. Oh. Oh, God, what happened? Samantha? Are...are you...am I..."

Lisa Grimaldi crumpled. "I'm fine!" I said, sitting up. "I'm fine. My pants got stuck, and I hit my eye—"

Nope. She was out cold. I scooted over to her side, rolled onto my knees, and put my hand on her shoulder. Great. More blood for everyone. Also, I was so glad I'd wore a thong tonight, so my still-sweaty ass could appreciate the nice draft that came in from the hall.

"Lisa? Mrs. Grimaldi! Wake up, Lisa." Splats of my blood fell on her white face. Shit. I'd left the facecloth back at the base of Hannah's bed.

"So, Sam, what's the emerge—" Hannah sauntered in, then jolted to a stop. "Oh, my God! Mom? What happened? Mommy?" She and her mom were really tight "What happened? Why is she bleeding? Daddy, call 911!"

"Oh, please don't," I said.

Hannah looked at me and did a double-take. "Jesus, Sam! Did my mother *hit* you?"

"No! Of course not." Downstairs, I heard someone shouting to someone else to call 911. "I hit my head on the sink. Your mom saw my face and fainted."

Mrs. Grimaldi began to stir. "Why am I lying on the floor?"

"You fainted, Mom." Hannah looked up at me. "Why are your pants—"

"Because they're *pleather*," I hissed. "Tell your dad everything's fine. We don't need an ambulance."

But, of course, it was too late. Party guests were pummeling up the stairs like a herd of buffalo. Dr. Talwar (the wife) came into the room. "Oh, dear, what's happened? Is that her blood? Where is she hurt?"

"She's not," I said, but my words were lost as Hannah's dad bellowed, "Honeybun!" and collapsed to his knees beside her. More people crowded into the room.

"Should we start compressions?" someone asked.

"She does not need compressions," said Dr. Talwar (the husband).

"I'm fine," Mrs. Grimaldi said weakly. "I fainted, that's all." She looked around the room, saw me, and passed right out again.

"Call the police!" someone called. "There's been an assault."

"No!" I yelled. "No one's been assaulted."

I was abruptly aware that my pants were around my knees, my face was bloody, and my girl parts covered by a teeny scrap of deep green silk. Also, there was an unconscious woman next to me.

And yes, here came the sirens. I closed my eyes, scooched backward to the far side of Hannah's bed. "Mom?" I called. "Can you get me a towel and help me get my pants back on?"

· · ·

121

My pants were not back on by the time the Stoningham Fire Department, D Platoon, arrived at the Grimaldis'. To be fair, our response time is one of the best in the state. By then, Mrs. G. was sitting up and nursing a glass of whiskey her husband had pressed into her hand. I was still hiding on the far side of Hannah's bed, sneaking looks at the scene. Mom had found a unicorn-printed fleece throw in Hannah's closet, so at least I was covered. She Mom stood over me, shaking her head and patting mine simultaneously.

"Merry Christmas," came Cupcake's voice, so named because of his perpetually foul mood (we firefighters like irony). "What have we got here?"

"Oh, it's not me," said Mrs. Grimaldi. "I just faint at the sight of blood. Samantha Lewis, though, she's got a *massive* head wound."

"No, I don't," I called. "I'll be fine. Maybe a couple stitches, but my mom can—"

"Samburger," said Jake, the lieutenant. He appeared over me, grinning. "What happened, kid? Drink too much?"

"Not enough, actually," I said. I could hear James, another D platooner, asking Mrs. Grimaldi what day it was.

"You're quite a bleeder," Jake said, kneeling in front of me. "You a Romanoff or something? What happened?"

"Well, my pants got stuck when I was in the bathroom, and I was jumping around, trying to pull them up and I fell and hit my head. Mrs. Grimaldi saw the blood and fainted."

He bit down on a smile. "A wardrobe injury, then?"

Yep." I pulled up the throw at my ankles to show him the tight pants. "You try getting these off."

"Is that an invitation?"

"It is not." I cracked a smile. Jake was a decent guy, happily married with four kids, but he was good at flirting, too.

"Might need the Hurst tool for the pants." He lifted the towel from my eye and grimaced. "Yikes. Good thing you're already ugly."

"Thank you. In my time of pain, truly, thank you for your kindness."

"Yeah, yeah, your poor baby. This'll teach you not to wear tight pants." He stood and gestured to the guys. "We're gonna transport you, Samburger. Already got the stair chair."

I glanced over my shoulder to see the three other guys—Fumble, so named because he once dropped a fully charged hose and had to chase after it as it whipped around—Legend (pulled a kid out of a burning building) and James were all there, grinning like kids seeing Santa. "Absolutely not. No transport. Fumble, put that phone away, you idiot, or I will sue your scrawny ass." I looked back at LT. "I can drive myself. Or my parents can drive me."

"Actually, honey," said my mother, "we've had a little bit too much to drink. Candy cane martinis, Jake. Have you ever had one? Delicious." She'd been his piano teacher.

"Just come with us," Legend said. "It's faster."

I looked at Jake. "I'm wearing a thong," I whispered.

"Me, too," he whispered back. "Don't worry. I'll keep you covered."

With a sigh, I gave in. "Fine. But I'm walking down those stairs."

"Nope. Not with a head injury," he said.

And so, I had a cervical collar put around my neck (so uncomfortable) and was bundled into the stair chair, a device I'd used a hundred times but never had the pleasure of riding on, and was carried out of the room, down the hall, transported down the stairs in front of a hundred people as I clutched Hannah's purple unicorn fleece around my hips.

"I'll try to get there as soon as I can," Hannah said over her shoulder. "I need to make sure Mom's okay. Daddy, too. Did you see his face? I thought he might have a heart attack!"

"Stay here, Han. I'm fine. I'll text you."

The guys got me off the stair chair and onto a stretcher, complete with super plush backboard (I'm kidding, those things are murder).

"So you got tangled up in your pants?" Fumble said as they loaded me into the back of the ambulance.

"That's what she said," James quipped.

"I wouldn't mind being tangled up in your pants," said Fumble.

I glared from beneath the gauze they'd given me to replace the wash cloth. Jake could flirt. Fumble harassed.

"Do not make sexual innuendos to your coworkers, asshole," said the lieutenant.

Fumble looked terrified. "I was just kidding! She knows that. Right, Sam? She's not a snowflake, not like Denise."

"Shut it, Fumble, before I suspend you."

James and Legend loaded me into the back of the ambulance, and Diane, an EMT I knew through similar calls, put a blood pressure cuff on me.

"Text me so I know how you're doing, Burger," Jake said, and I gave him a wave.

The doors slammed shut.

"Tangled in your pants?" said Diane. "That must've taken some work."

"I'm terrible pain right now and don't want to talk," I said with a little smile. My head did hurt, and it would hurt more in the morning.

"Same thing happened to my four-year old. But then again, he's four. BP's 124/55, pulse a little high at 102." She looked under the gauze Jake had used. "Ouch. I'm guessing five stitches. Maybe six. If you're nervous, ask them for some Xanax. Just have someone drive you home."

It was 10:49, and my cut was really throbbing. My whole head ached. My shoulder, too, from where I'd hit the floor. I'd definitely need some ibuprofen later. Too bad I was working tomorrow, but I was covering for Titus, who had little kids.

"What have we here?" asked Bruce, who worked in patient transport. He was waiting in the ambulance bay.

"Just trying to change things up a little this holiday season," I said.

"Looks like you did a good job," he said. "Let me whisk you away, my lady."

To be fair, it was kind of fun to be wheeled from the ambulance, up the elevator and handed off to the ER. I thought about waving, queen-like, and opted not to. I knew too many people, and a few nurses jerked their chins or said hello.

"Someone will be in to see you in a minute," said Bruce. "Feel better."

"Thanks," I said. The door closed, and I was alone.

Alone in the ER on December 23rd, all thanks to an unfortunate wardrobe choice to impress my unimpressible girlfriend. With a fair bit of pettiness, I texted Judith. The least she could do was feel guilty.

Hey. Had a fall at the party and need stitches. In the ER now. Pretty bad cut, lots of blood.

The phone whooshed as I hit send.

It was immediately marked delivered. Then read. Any second now, I'd be getting those three dots and some pithy Britishism about stiff upper lips or the like. Maybe she'd come dashing down to the hospital here, her true feelings of deep love brought to the surface by my injury. It could happen.

I waited. Waited some more. Maybe she'd turned the phone volume down really low, though usually when she worked, she put it on Do Not Disturb.

But stupid technology told me she'd read my message. Five minutes passed. Ten. Sixteen. My throat grew tight with tears. This, I couldn't overlook. This wasn't being British. This was being...heartless.

I laid back on the bed and swallowed hard. Tears leaked out of my eyes. Another look at the phone. Nineteen minutes now. Nothing. She'd read that I was hurt and had opted not to respond.

A nurse came in pushing a computer on a stand, and I quickly wiped my eyes. "Hey, Samantha!" It was Irena, a high school class-mate. "Great to see you, minus the bloody part. You feeling okay?"

"Yeah. Just cracked my eyebrow on a bathroom sink." I adjusted my unicorn blanket. "How are you? How are the twins?"

"Oh, they're demons. I do not recommend having children spawned by Satan." She smiled fondly. "Want to see a picture?"

"Of course!"

She pulled out her phone, clicked, then showed me a picture of two cherubic boys. "At least they got your looks," I said. "No horns yet, though I can't be sure about cloven hooves." I smiled at her. "They're gorgeous."

"Thanks," she said. "So, did you faint before or after your fall?"

"Nope."

"Had you been drinking?"

"Yeah, a little. It was the Grimaldis' Christmas party. A martini and a half, probably."

"How's Hannah?"

"Oh, she's great." On cue, my phone chimed.

You okay? Should I come? I feel so bad about this!!!

"Here's Hannah now," I said, holding up my phone as Irena wrapped the blood pressure cuff around my bicep. I dictated my text. "I'm fine. With Irena Hanson from high school, she says hi. I'll be done soon." I glanced at Irena. "Right?"

"Well, we're kind of busy, so you might have to wait a little. Sorry." She hooked me up to a pulse oximeter, and I craned my head to see, wincing a little. O2 sat 99%, pulse 72, BP 120/62.

"Okay, Sam, someone will be in to stitch you up. It was really nice seeing you, despite the circumstances."

"You too," I said. Then she was gone, the door clicking closed behind her. I checked my phone. Texts from Mom, Dad, my brother in Seattle, who had been alerted by our parents (told you he was nice), Mrs. Grimaldi and Lieutenant Jake and Legend.

And still nothing from Judith.

When we'd first met, everything had been so magical, so electric. In those first two months, I'd felt smarter, prettier, funnier, and Judith had fucking adored me. I realized we didn't know each other well enough for actual true love, but it had sure felt that way. I'd gotten used to being someone she loved...or at least, seemed to love. I honestly thought she was the one. Once, she called me just to hear my voice. She *said* that. "Sorry, but it seems I can't get through the day without hearing your voice." If that didn't make a person weak in the knees, what would?

Growing up in the super-progressive, wealthy little burg of Stoningham, Connecticut, had been lovely. My brother, five years older, was calm and likeable and rarely fought with me, even though we'd shared a bathroom. When it became apparent I liked girls (I was thirteen and abruptly realized that Rachel from *Friends* gave me *feelings*), none of my friends deserted me. If anyone said something derogatory, I was always well defended and, being tall, athletic, and smart-mouthed, could defend myself just fine.

Around the same time, two of my friends came out as well, though Lydia's lesbian phase lasted only until Blake Simpson asked her to the prom. Our graduating class of sixty-two had three gay guys, two of us gay girls, and about eight other kids who identified as Q in LGBTQ. I mean, people could be assholes, but there was more of a price to pay if you were seen as a bigoted asshole.

College...well, I went to Bryn Mawr. Being gay was so unremarkable there, it was weird if you weren't. I had my first girlfriend and studied philosophy and film to guarantee I wouldn't be able to get a job. After graduating (with honors), I moved home, wondering if I'd become a bartender or a barista and save up for grad school. Then, on a whim, I applied to the fire department in my hometown.

It was a good life. It was a *wonderful* life, as they say at this time of year. I had friends, loved my job, had union benefits and some decent coworkers, some asshole coworkers, as was true at any firehouse. There was nothing like jolting out of bed to the sound of the tone, answering Dispatch on the radio and pulling out of the firehouse in a big-ass engine. Being female, I made sure to do everything at least as well as the senior guys and way better than the jamokes hired after me. I rent an apartment in an old house off of Main Street, and Mrs. Peters lets me muck around in the garden every spring. I have a cat. Arthur, named for the once and future king. He has a catnip toy shaped like a sword, even, and he lives up to the nobility of his name.

But I'd never been in love before Judith. I'd been in serious *like* while at Bryn Mawr, and had gone on dates here and there, which always resulted in eventual friend-zoning or being friend-zoned. No hard feelings, a couple new women to meet for drinks or bowling.

But love? No. Never, until Judith. That first night, I'd felt the thunderbolt, and from then on, when she answered her door with a big smile, or laughed at something I said over dinner, I'd feel like a rock star, literally tingling down to my toes. This beautiful, rare creature was with me. Me. She had chosen *me*. This British artist with the huge eyes and paint-stained fingernails, this woman whose work was praised by influential reviewers, who had lived all over the world, was my girlfriend. She kissed me like we were on the deck of the Titanic in its final moments. She was completely confident with sex—no shyness, no pretense, lots of enthusiasm, lots of noise, lots of variety.

We'd been so happy. That was the worst part. We'd so good together, so crazy in love (I thought). For those two months, the whole world was sparkling, and every day was beautiful and fresh, and we couldn't get to each other fast enough. It wasn't just the fabulous sex. It was the conversation, the laughter, the little touches, the making of dinner, the cuddling as we watched TV. It was all I ever wanted, everything I hoped for.

And then, in the third month, Judith began to pull back. She wasn't as available. Needed to focus on her work, though I didn't see her painting more. Now when I was at her house, she made calls and talked to friends or family members while I waited for her, trying not to feel awkward. She wasn't so eager to come to my place, which she'd originally found so cute. Movie nights were now spent not cuddling, her tapping away on her phone, mind elsewhere.

I knew she was losing interest, and I could almost understand it. In my family, my brother was the star. Mom did ninety percent of the talking. Dad and I just...were. My firefighting career was the most interesting thing about me to most outsiders. Maybe I just wasn't that interesting, certainly not for someone like Judith, who had lived in Peru, Australia, Portugal, and San Francisco.

She was an artist. I was a blue-collar worker who, maybe once or twice a year, actually got to save a life. But even with those stories, Judith shut me down. She was squeamish, she said, and hated hearing about a pileup on I-95 or an accidental drowning. Fire was something she feared, she now said, and she'd appreciate it if I could find "something of mutual interest" to talk about. That shut me down instantly. Did we even have mutual interests? But just weeks before, we couldn't stop talking to each other. Now, I had to wrack my brain for conversation that was up to snuff for Judith the worldly artist. The pressure was awful, and all I wanted was to go back to those perfect two months.

I'd sensed our breakup was coming. I just didn't see it coming like this, me with a gash in my head, her just ignoring me at the one time when she really had to show up in some way. *Any* way. She couldn't just...ignore.

But she was doing exactly that.

Someone knocked and opened the door. A tall woman dressed in blue scrubs, brown hair pulled back into a ponytail. "Hey, there," she said. "I'm Delilah Burrows, your PA. Tell me what happened."

I pulled back the unicorn blanket to reveal my bondaged legs. "Wardrobe malfunction. I pulled my pleather pants down, couldn't get them back up, fell and hit my face."

"I see." She pressed her lips together to keep from smiling.

"It's okay. I'm aware of the ridiculousness of my situation."

"Red pleather, huh?" Delilah said, pulling on some gloves. "Kind of awesome."

"You can have them because I'm clearly never wearing them again. They're very dangerous pants."

She laughed. "I bet you looked great, though."

I smiled a little. "I won't lie. I did."

She pulled the blanket back over my legs and tucked it in around my feet. "Let me take a look at your cut," she said, pulling up the stool. "You look familiar. Do we know each other?"

"I'm a firefighter in Stoningham. We transport folks off here all the time."

"Okay, sure." She lifted the gauze. "Wow. Nice cut. Any loss of consciousness?"

"I wish, but no. Someone else fainted, though."

"This sounds like a story I have to hear." Delilah smiled again and pushed the button to lower the bed to flat. "I'm going to stick you with some lidocaine, which will sting a little, then wash out your cut, and then I'll staple it closed, okay?"

"Sure. Will I have a scar? I kind of want a scar."

"I'm sorry to say, you probably won't be able to see it in six months."

"Damn. If I'm injured by pleather pants, I should have a bad-ass scar."

She smiled again, the crow's feet around her eyes crinkling. She was maybe a few years older than I was, and she had three small gold hoop earrings in her left ear, two in her right. She smelled nice, too, even over the sharp antiseptic of the hospital.

"I like your name," I said.

"Thanks. My friends call me Del, so you should, too."

"Thanks. I'm Sam most of the time."

Another smile, this time with eye contact. Lovely eyelashes, and without mascara, too. Delilah opened a drawer, pulled out a vial, unwrapped a needle and loaded it up. "Time to be brave, Firefighter Lewis."

"Yes, ma'am."

It's weird to be so close to someone you don't know. In this case, it wasn't so bad. I closed my eyes, winced a little as the needle went in above my eyebrow, took a deep breath. Another prick. She was right about the stinging. It was enough to make my eyes tear.

"Hang in there," Del said, handing me a tissue. The needle pricked, the liquid stung.

"Thanks." I wiped my eyes and sneaked another look at her. Thirty-five, maybe? Only four years older than I was. "Do you have kids, Del?" I asked.

"I don't. Not yet, anyway. Someday, hopefully, but the situation hasn't been right. How about you?"

"No. Same deal. Maybe someday."

She irrigated my cut with saline solution. "Staples are next," she said, disposing of the needle in the sharps receptacle. "I'm sure you know the drill," she said. "You must see some pretty gory stuff in your line of work."

"Oh, sure," I said. "Last month, we had a motorcycle accident where the guy's leg was ripped off just above the knee."

"I was here that night!" Del said. "That was a big deal."

"Yeah. I had to go into the woods, looking for the leg in case they could reattach it."

Del took out the stapler. "I bet that wasn't on the job description. 'Must hunt down severed limbs at night.'"

I laughed. "Not exactly, no. But I did find it." She clicked the first staple in, and I felt pressure, but no pain.

"I remember seeing that leg lying in the tray. Very hairy."

"That's the one. Do you know if they reattached it?"

"Well, you know the rules about patient confidentiality, but let's just say it was a positive result. Marathon not out of the question." She smiled. "Thanks to you."

"Well. If I didn't find it, someone else would have."

"But you did find it. I bet that guy will think of you every day of his life now." Her kind words caused my eyes to tear. The contrast between Judith's refusal to listen to my job stories and Delilah's immediate, positive response felt like a knife in the ribs.

"You okay?" Delilah asked, frowning at my tears. "I'm sorry if the staples hurt. The lidocaine usually does the job, but—"

"No, no...it's not...I broke up with my girlfriend, that's all. Well. I'm about to."

"Oh." She sat back a minute. "I'm sorry. That must be tough."

I looked away. "No, it's been coming for a couple of months."

"Even when it's for the best, it can be hard." She leaned forward again, bringing in that nice citrusy smell, and clicked the stapler twice more. "I always thought we as humans should come up with a better way of breaking up. Like, we should have a code word or something, so we wouldn't have to talk about all the reasons. Because I think the other person knows, right? It never comes out of nowhere. You could just say 'cinnamon,' and boom. Breakup complete."

"That sounds good to me. And my significant other would probably love it."

She smiled and checked her work, then wiped the area with alcohol and taped some gauze over the staples. "Very bad-ass," she said. "I'm gonna check with the doc and see if we want to get you into

CAT scan, but I don't think you'll need it. Anything else I can do for you right now?"

"Um...could you cut off my pants?"

Her laugh was warm and genuine. "Absolutely." She opened the cupboard and took out a pair of surgical scissors. "Love the blanket, by the way."

"Unicorns are my favorite." I pulled up the fleece so she could get at the pleather. As she snipped, the pants finally lost their python grip on me. I wiggled my feet happily.

"You're free," Del said. "I'll get you some scrubs to ear.. Unless you want to go home without pants." She winked.

"Not this time," I said. "It's a tiny bit cold out there, so scrubs would be great. Thank you."

"Be right back." I watched as she left, her ponytail swinging. Most people were really nice, I'd found. Especially in situations when a person needed help. Being on the lesser end of that equation tonight, I was glad Del was looking after me. Another person might have made me feel stupid. Or ignored me. I checked my phone. Still nothing from Judith. Unbelievable.

A minute later, Del came back, her arms full. "Got a nice warm blanket here, in case the unicorns aren't enough." She moved Hannah's fleece and tucked the warm, white blanket around me, then put the unicorn blanket on top, tucking it firmly against me.

"Oh, that's heaven." I hadn't realized my legs had gotten cold until the warm blanket was against my skin.

"Just one of the many services we offer here. Here are the scrubs for when we send you home. We just had a car accident, so I'm afraid you might have to wait to hear about the CAT scan."

"No worries. This is the most relaxed I've been in weeks."

"Excellent. Back in a bit. Oh, and hey. It's snowing. We might have a white Christmas after all." Another smile, and she was gone.

Sometimes, being taken care of by a kind stranger was better than anything. I wasn't lying about feeling relaxed. Yes, the vodka in the candy cane martini had an effect, but mostly, the feeling of being just hurt enough to get a pass. The past month, I'd worked nine overtime shifts for all the guys who had kids (Denise and I were both childless) and holiday stuff to do. On the personal end, my life had been full of shopping, decorating, baking with Gram at her house, having more than the usual outings with friends and my mom, nights spent decorating my apartment for my cat and me, wrapping gifts and watching *Love, Actually* as often as possible. I loved the holidays, but they were a lot.

My phone rang. Mom. "Hi," I said. "I'm fine. Just a couple of staples."

"Will you have a hideous scar?" she asked.

"I hope so. It'll make up for the humiliation of everyone seeing my ass."

"You have a perfectly nice ass," she said.

"Thanks, Mom." I smiled.

"Do you have a ride home? I assume Judith is with you? Or Hannah? Daddy can come get you. He's sleeping now, but of course he'll be happy to get you if you need him."

I knew he would, dear old Dad, but glancing at the time, I figured it was too late for them. Plus, it was snowing. "All set there, but thanks." I'd take a Lyft or see if anyone was driving at Stoningham Taxi.

Just then, Hannah texted, insisting that I call her for a ride, saying she was so sorry I was hurt (and could I send a picture of the wound. She was creeptastic that way). I'll get a Lyft, I texted.

The hell you will. You fell at my house in the pants I made you buy. I am so your ride.

Okay, bossypants. Speaking of pants, the pleather had to be cut off me. Very dramatic. Cute PA, too.

I take it Judith had something come up?

I sighed. Yep. At least she's consistent.

Okay, babe. Call me when you're ready. Love you.

Best friends were...well...the best.

I also had texts from Legend, LT and the Chief, asking how I was. I answered them all. Closed my eyes and dozed a little, the clatter and voices outside my room comforting in that odd way...

Grownups were in charge, and I didn't have to be one of them right now.

I woke up, my head throbbing again. Not too bad, just pulsing. Glanced at my phone. Another text from Hannah, saying she was going to bed, but she had her phone on. One from her mom, checking to see if I was okay.

Nothing from Judith. Still.

Suddenly, I was furious. With myself. What an idiot I'd been these past few months! What did Maya Angelou say? The first time someone shows you who they are, believe them. Sorry, Ms. Angelou. I'd forgotten that.

Being with Judith was like death by a thousand paper cuts. The little insults, the sense of superiority, her availability only when it was desirable for her. How *dare* I let myself be treated like that? Seriously, why? Because she was pretty and creative and British and hot? Fuck that. I deserved better.

I snatched up my phone again and typed.

In case it's not clear, I can SEE that you read my message, you selfish twat. (Some of her Britishisms had rubbed off on me.) I'm in the HOSPITAL and you can't be bothered to type back? If that's not a definitive way to tell me how little you care, I don't know what is. We're done. Merry Christmas, and fuck you very much.

Then I deleted that and typed, Hey. I think it's better if we don't see each other anymore. Best of luck with everything. Sam.

The three dots began waving immediately. For God's sake.

Sorry, darling, what? I just now saw your text. Just getting into the car now to come see you. My poor little bear!!!

It was 1:45 a.m. She'd read the text at 10:52 p.m. Almost three *hours* ago.

I called her. She didn't pick up. Of course not. Now that she wasn't a hundred percent in control, she was abruptly interested in me. She'd be here, angel of mercy, cooing over me *because* I'd just dumped her, not because I was hurt.

God, I was sick of her games. Games in general. Why couldn't people just be honest? I didn't want to have to outmaneuver Judith to get her to like me. I didn't want a relationship where we had to fight or bicker or ignore or read each other's minds. I wanted someone who'd be happy to see me and wanted nothing more than to just... share my everyday, ordinary, happy, meaningful life.

I texted again. Please don't bother. It's snowing, and you're terrible driver anyway. I'm fine and really don't see the point of you coming.

Whoosh. Delivered. Read.

No answer.

I sighed and closed my eyes, resting my head against the pillow. I guess I dozed off again, because the next thing I knew, Judith was breezing into the room, dressed in a black cape, black leggings, black leather boots and a red wool cap. Glorious, deep red lipstick. I guess makeup and wardrobe were part of her rush to my side. "Sa*man*tha!" she cried. "Oh, darling, look at you, your poor mite."

She swooped in at my face, and I pulled away, pushing her shoulder to avoid a kiss. "Judith, come on. Knock it off."

"Knock what off? I'm concerned! Darling, I didn't get your text until just a little while ago. You know how cell service is out here."

"Cell service is fine, Judith, and guess what? Your phone tells me when you've read a text. You've known I've been here for hours now. Drop the act, okay?"

Her big smile twitched a little. "Don't know what you're talking about, love. I was chatting with my sister."

Oh, really? Because she'd had a five hour convo with her sister last week. She'd told me she'd be working. I held up my phone. "See? This handy little device has a setting, which you've apparently checked. So *delivered* tells me that the message landed on your phone, and *read* tells me that you opened the text and, presumably, looked at it."

"I just told you, I was talking with my sister. It's been ages since we talked.

"You're mixing up your reasons for blowing me off, Judith. The sister chat was for my department party. Tonight was your big dead-line for the commissioned painting."

"Am I only allowed to talk to Cressida once a month?"

"Whatever, Judith. Even if it is true that you didn't see my text, we both know you did, you're only here because I'm dumping you. So just go, okay? No hard feelings."

She sat down and looked at me, her elegant brows drawn together. "I'm sorry, I've no idea why you're so upset."

"Because!" I barked. "Because you make me feel like an abandoned puppy unless we're in bed together, after which you kick me out and ignore me until the next time you want to get laid. You don't want to hear about my work, you won't meet my family, you barely want to be seen in public with me, and I deserve better than that, Judith. I'm tired of being the eighth or ninth thing on your mind. That's not a relationship. That's not friendship, and it sure as hell isn't a romance."

"Well, *we're* quite full of demands, aren't we?" Judith said. "I thought you were a grown woman with interests of her own. Apparently, you're a needy child. Or a *dog*, according to you."

"I'm not making demands, Judith," I said wearily. "I just wanted you to fall in love with me. And stay that way."

"You Americans and your notions of romance really cock up the works. You and I have a perfectly nice relationship, and you're simply overanalyzing it. Grow up, darling. You're almost thirty."

"We don't have a relationship because we don't relate, Judith. We don't talk or laugh or...or cuddle or go for walks or get coffee. We used to, and now we don't. Now, we hook up when you're horny. I want more, and that's it."

"That bump on your head is making you silly. Don't let's be mad at each other. Please. I care about you, you know I do. We have such fun together."

"We have orgasms together."

"Exactly." She lifted her eyebrow and smiled, her small white teeth shocking against the matte-red lipstick. "Come on, then. When can we get you out of here? I'll bring you home, set you up with a hot toddy and make you some toast. Or we can go to your place so your cat can cuddle with us."

She'd make me toast and a hot toddy, eh? Now that I thought of it, she'd cooked dinner for me twice in six months, both times in those first passionate weeks. I cooked dinner for her twice a week—it had been like a bribe, getting her to spend time with me, and each time, we'd end up in bed. Before she sent me home that is. And I didn't just cook for her. I plowed her driveway when it snowed Thanksgiving weekend. Ran errands for her, pathetically thinking it was a sign of intimacy that she wanted me to pick up some tampons or toothpaste. I brought her pastries from Zest, bought her ten tiny round gourds for Halloween, fixed her leaking shower-head.

What had she done for me? Allowed me to be in her hallowed presence when it suited her. And if it didn't suit her, she'd stand me up, cancel, make a tepid excuse without a single pang. I let her, time and time again. My face went hot with shame. If someone treated Hannah that way, I'd kidnap her until she came to her senses. She'd told me, more than once, that I deserved better.

There was no one to blame but myself. That thunderbolt had short-circuited my brain. Maybe the knock on the sink had reversed the damage.

Just then, Delilah came in. "Oh. Hello," she said to Judith. "I'm Delilah Burrows, the PA."

"PA being what exactly?" Judith asked.

"Physician assistant," Del said. "How are you feeling, Sam? Need any ice or Tylenol?"

"I'm fine," I said. "Just a little throb."

"Excellent. I knew you were a bad-ass. But don't be afraid to ask for something if you feel worse. I'm sorry you've had to be here so long."

"Is there a consultant we can see?" Judith asked. "I'm worried about her scarring."

"That would be me, and don't be. In a couple of months, you'll hardly be able to see anything."

"But you're not a doctor, are you?" Judith said. "I'd like her to be seen by a plastic surgeon consultant."

"Judith, enough," I said. "I'm more than capable of speaking for myself. I don't care about a tiny scar. Do I have to wait for a CAT scan, Del?"

"No, but I'd feel more comfortable if you had someone stay with you tonight." She glanced at Judith, then back at me.

"I have someone," I said.

"Me," Judith said.

"Not you, actually. My friend can come over." I could feel Judith bristle.

"Okay, then," Delilah said. "What's your friend's name and phone number?"

"Hannah Grimaldi." I recited the number.

"And she's a responsible adult?"

"More or less." I smiled, and Del smiled back.

"Are you seriously ending it with me?" Judith asked. "Here? In hospital? In front of this stranger?"

"Um...yes," I said, and I swore I saw Del's lips quirk in a smile. "We had some good times, though, and I'm glad to have met you, Judith."

"Well, it appears I've been dismissed," Judith said. "Ciao, Samantha."

"Bye." I watched her go, cape swirling dramatically. The door eased closed.

"I assume that's your freshly dumped ex?" Del asked.

"Correct."

"Ciao, huh?"

"Those artistic types," I said. "You know how they are."

"Well, good for you," Del said. "Now, do you want me to call Hannah for you? I have your discharge papers."

"I'll call her. Thank you so much, Del. You were great."

"Well, you were my favorite patient of the night," she said. "Take care, and hope to see you again. I mean, not as a patient though. Just... bringing in a patient. As a first responder. Or just around town. You know."

She blushed.

She *blushed*.

"Right," she said, recovering her professional vibe. "I'll leave you with these, and when your friend comes in, we'll get you out of here. Very nice to meet you."

"You, too." I took the papers from her and shook her outstretched hand, which was warm and smooth. "Thanks again." I liked her eyes. There was a lot of kindness there, a lot of intelligence.

Then she released my hand and left, and that was that.

I read the papers—the instructions written as simply as possible. *You have sustained a HEAD WOUND REQUIRING CLOSURE WITH STAPLES. For the next twenty-four hours, you should have a RESPONSIBLE ADULT with you. If you experience NAUSEA, VOMITING, DIZZINESS, CHANGES IN VISION, OR CANNOT BE AWAKENED, call 911 and return to the Emergency Department IMMEDIATELY.*

Del's notes came next.

Chief Complaint: laceration of the forehead, left eyebrow.

The patient is a good-natured and otherwise very healthy member of the Stoningham fire department. About 30 minutes prior to arrival, the patient fell and hit her head at a Christmas party after struggling with her pants. To be fair, they were pleather.

I laughed out loud.

The rest of her report was standard...where my cut was, how long, how many staples, no recommendation for a CAT scan based on my mental status (alert and oriented x 3, ladies and gentlemen). She ended with instructions for me to return in ten days to get the staples removed.

I hoped Del would be on ten days from now.

Good-natured and very healthy. Hm. I'd take it. I was, in fact, glad she noticed.

I texted Hannah, who said she'd be right there, and then changed into the scrubs provided by Del. My poor white sweater was splotched with blood, but hopefully the stains would come out.

"How are you feeling?" Hannah said when she got here. "You look very hot with that metal in your eyebrow. Very 90s punk, very Goth."

"Thank you," I said. "Bring me home, Grimaldi."

"Yes, my queen."

As we walked through the ED, I didn't see Delilah. I waved to Irena, getting a wave back, as Hannah told me about the party after my departure, who had made the best comments about my pants, my thong, and how her father almost fainted once her mom was done fainting. "I think he'd had one too many candy cane martinis, really. It's not like him to get so weepy."

"About those martinis," I said.

"Yeah. Never again. I still have candy cane stuck in my teeth."

We went outside, and there was winter in all her nighttime beauty. The snow clung to the branches, bending the hemlocks. We stopped for a minute, taking in the quiet hiss of falling snow, the fat flakes so happy and fast, the pinkish lights from the streetlamps and the mystery of being awake when most people were all snug in their beds, vision of sugarplums, whatever those were.

"Wow," I said. "Hope we don't lose power. I'll have to work OT on Christmas if we do."

"Become a teacher," Hannah said. "I have vacation until January third."

"Your job is way scarier than mine."

She linked her arm through mine, and we started off to her car.

"Hey, um, Sam?" came a voice. We turned, and it was Delilah.

"Hey. Did I forget something?"

"No, no." She stood there a second. "I just wanted to say Merry Christmas. Happy holidays. All that."

"You too, Del."

"Let me know how you're doing, okay? I...I wrote my number on your discharge instructions."

"Oh. Okay," I said. "I definitely will."

"Great. Well. Bye."

"It was great to meet you," I said. "Happy holidays, Del." My smile was huge. Delilah gave a cute wave and disappeared back inside the hospital.

"Somebody likes you," sang Hannah. I didn't deny it. Just smiled. "I like her much more than Judith," she added.

"Whom I dumped an hour ago, by the way," I said.

"A Christmas miracle!" said Hannah. "Tell me everything. No. Wait till we get to your place, and I'll make us scrambled eggs with cheese, and then you can tell me everything."

I stopped. "I love you, Han," I said.

"Love you, too," she said, and in that moment, I had everything I ever wanted...a great friend, a beautiful town, a loyal cat waiting for me, a workforce who'd make merciless fun of me for the rest of my life...

And maybe...probably, even...a really cool woman who liked me.

It was going to be a very happy new year. I already knew it in my heart.

About the Author

Kristan Higgins is the New York Times, USA TODAY, Wall Street Journal and Publishers Weekly bestselling author of more than twenty novels. Her books have been translated into more than 20 languages and have sold millions of copies around the world. Kristan has been praised for her mix of "laugh-out-loud humor and tear-jerking pathos," which the author attributes to a diet high in desserts and sugar-based mood swings.

Kristan's books have received dozens of awards and accolades, including starred reviews from People Magazine, Entertainment Weekly, Good Morning America, Kirkus, the New York Journal of Books, Publishers Weekly, Library Journal, National Public Radio and Booklist. She personally responds to every reader letter she receives, even the mean ones.

Kristan is the mother of two ridiculously good-looking children and the grandmother of the world's cutest baby. She lives in Connecticut and Cape Cod with her heroic firefighter husband, a rescue mutt and indifferent cat. In her spare time, Kristan enjoys gardening, easy yoga classes, mixology and pasta.

To sign up for Kristan's always entertaining newsletter, visit www.kristanhiggins.com.

Lady Waverly's Lover

AMALIE HOWARD

Chapter One

The Marchioness of Waverly was, without a doubt, *the* reigning jewel of London.

Ask anyone. They all said so. Not many of the illustrious *ton* knew that that carefully cultivated persona was a lie. A pretense. A mask she wore to the world while the real version of her was withering inside its flawless, gilded prison. She was reserved, accomplished, impeccable. Never a hair out of place, always unfailingly perfect.

Sumptuous clothing, exquisite manners, and unfailing poise were her hallmarks. Even her smile was curated to precision: not too big, no showing of teeth, *just* touching the eyes.

And the right kind of smile could decimate.

Needless to say, Margot Foxglove's legendary cool hauteur was both envied and hated. Debutantes coveted and dreaded her notice. Ladies resentfully catalogued and copied her every move. Gentlemen begrudged the marquess's deuced luck at winning *such* a prize.

Though now that he was dead, Margot was finally free of him.

Freedom in the *ton*, however, came with caveats. A widow still had to perform for the masses and the ever-judgmental peerage, lest she be relegated to persona non grata. Certainly, she had more leeway than most in her position, but she was still expected to play the part society demanded of her. There were rules that had to be obeyed, and Margot did not care to eschew the lofty throne she had fashioned for herself.

She let out a small scoff. She supposed she was being overly histrionic. And besides, England already had its queen.

"A toast, my darling," Lady Honoria Englewood, the Countess of Rawdon, said as she lifted an obscenely full glass of French brandy. "May that cowardly bastard rot and get what he deserves."

"Hear, hear," Margot said, gulping down her late husband's prized Maison Gautier cognac that was over a century old, and relished the delicious burn down her throat. He'd have no need of it wherever he was, and it gave her perverse pleasure to finish every last precious drop.

She glanced up at her best friend, who let out an unladylike belch, her green eyes bright and blond hair tumbling out of its hold. A drunken flush lit her cheekbones, and Margot knew hers suffered the same, as evidenced by the half-empty bottle between them. Feeling audacious, undoubtedly from the absurd amount of liquor she had consumed, she yanked the last of the pins from her own hair, letting the deep brown waves spill over her shoulders. She kicked off her slippers and unrolled her stockings for good measure.

"Look at you letting loose," Honoria crowed and promptly imitated her before going one step further to loosen the laces of her bodice and corset.

Margot wouldn't go *that* far, and besides, hers were fastened in the back. There was no one here to judge them. The staff had been dismissed, and they were in the privacy of her own home. And Honoria had seen her through the worst of everything, through the bruises and the tears, through the callous words that landed harder than hands ever could. She shook her head to clear it of the memories and wrinkled her nose.

"So how does it feel?" Honoria asked. "To finally breathe?"

Margot considered the question. "Strange but exhilarating."

Twenty-four months was a long time to mourn someone, especially a man who had been half-dead and on his death bed for the last few years of their marriage and still controlled her until the very wheezing end. Margot intended to burn every black bombazine dress she had been forced to wear out of some skewed idea of respect, when the truth was, she would have danced on the bastard of a marquess's grave in every color of the rainbow if it wouldn't have scandalized the *ton*.

Lord Waverly had been a rotten man, a rotten husband, and a rotten lover.

Lord Rotten. That should have been his name.

"Suffer in purgatory, you piece of shit," she swore through gritted teeth.

Honoria cheered. "More bad words, Margot, you can do it!"

"*Fuck* that soulless prick!" Her cheeks burned at the crass oath, but it felt extraordinarily good. One shouldn't speak ill of the dead, but Waverly was truly the exception.

Some arranged marriages turned out well. A couple might get to know one another, and sometimes, a man and wife could find companionship, passion, or even love. Not her, however. Behind closed doors, Margot had found nothing but degradation and pain. Her husband had bedded her without fail every week during the first few months of their marriage until she became pregnant with their son, before warming his bed with a mistress.

Margot treasured sixteen-year-old Percy. He was the light of her life and the only thing she did not regret from her marriage. She'd been betrothed to a man thrice her age at barely a year older than Percy was now, enduring his constant criticism and abuse.

I saved your family from squalor and from sending you to the workhouse.

Know your place, you stupid, useless girl. You're my property.

That pedestal you think you're upon is because I allow it.

He'd tolerated her accomplishments because having such an esteemed paragon for a wife had made him the envy of every peer in London.

"Shall we toast to the future once more, Honoria?" she hiccupped and said to her best friend, who gamely filled their brandy glasses to the brim.

"We shall have a devil of a headache in the morning, but at least it'll be worth it. I always hated your father for practically selling you off to that man. The bride's father should dower the groom, not the reverse."

Margot swallowed. "It saved us from ruin."

"Saved your papa's gambling debts," Honoria muttered.

"And I got Percival out of it so all wasn't lost," she added.

Honoria smiled with genuine fondness. "Where is that dear boy? Eton still?"

"He's off at Cambridge," Margot murmured. "And thriving with his peers."

If it was one thing she was grateful for, it was that Percy had taken after her in spirit. He had the same wide-eyed delight she'd had at that age. Though unlike her, he lived life with avid exuberance, his impulsive nature not buried under a thousand layers of civility. Her son was a thrill-seeker with a brilliant mind who laughed long and often. She supposed it was easier for a man to be himself. As a woman, she'd had to carve space for herself within the rules of society.

Spontaneity became sensibility.

Excitement became thoughtful ennui.

Impetuousness became an abundance of caution.

She squirreled away power where she could, and out of hardship, the unassailable Marchioness of Waverly had been born.

Thankfully, Percival was nothing like Waverly, the cruel streak her husband had harbored hadn't seen fit to replicate itself within their son. And Margot had shielded Percy as best as she could from the evidence of his father's rages. It was a miracle Waverly hadn't targeted his son, but hubris was a devil of a thing. A strapping, smart, and handsome heir to carry on the line was the desire of every peer. Margot huffed a dry laugh. At least she hadn't failed in that duty or her life might have been infinitely worse.

She'd been raked over the coals for not producing a spare.

"I forgot!" Honoria shouted so loudly that Margot nearly spilled the contents of her glass. "I have a gift for you! A bugger-your-slag-of-a-dead-husband gift!"

"Honoria," Margot chided with a horrified laugh. She might wish to be impulsive and free, but years of rigid comportment were hard to ignore. She accepted the small piece of cardstock plucked from Honoria's reticule that only had an address in Covent Garden written upon it. "What is this?"

"A lesson in indecency." The grin that curled her best friend's lips was pure devilry. "A portrait by a celebrated new artist. Trust me, darling, you need this, and her work is to die for. Everything's been paid, you only need to show up for the sitting."

Honoria was famous for her support of the arts, especially in the demimonde. A widow herself, although Margot suspected Honoria's husband had *not* expired from natural causes after a carriage ride gone tragically wrong, her friend did not give a whit about what the *ton* thought of her. She'd opened a private art gallery on New Bond Street, which had cost a fortune to build, and she enjoyed being perversely contrary to the Royal Academy of Arts with her flamboyant choice of artists, women especially.

"How do you do it?" Margot had asked her once, after her husband had passed. "Not care about the gossip?"

Honoria had been quiet, delivering her response with heartfelt ease. "No one has the power to control you, Margot. You are the only one who can *give* them that power."

"But what if they...spurn me?"

Being relegated to nothing, when her husband had taken so much from her, was one of her greatest fears. That, and hurting Percy. Her reputation was tied to him, after all. Honoria's expression had softened with something that looked too much like pity. "If it was a matter of my personal joy, does it honestly matter what anyone else thinks? If being part of some elite group makes you *not* true to yourself, then you have to consider whether that's worth it."

Honoria's words had stuck with her. But when it came to doing anything that toyed with the lines of respectability, Margot had always leaned toward restraint.

She glanced down at the cardstock. This wasn't too daring as far as gifts went, even if it was in the dubious West End of London. She flipped and squinted at the card, a bold name written in cursive on the back in flowery strokes: Ara Vaughn.

The slightest thrill slid through her blood.

What's the worst that could happen?

"I'm due for a new portrait anyway," she said. "Thank you."

Honoria laughed, her cheeks brightening and eyes dancing with mirth. "No, my dearest. You misunderstand. This is a *nude* portrait. All the rage, I assure you."

Margot's mouth slackened as she blinked violently, certain she'd misheard, though from Honoria's leering countenance, she hadn't. The cardstock singed her fingers. Even now, staring anew at the stiff rectangle, a part of her was compelled to throw it into the hearth, but another part of her vibrated with something unfamiliar. "I couldn't," she whispered.

"You can." Honoria winked. "Choose yourself for once, Margot."

And that was why, a fortnight later, Margot found herself at the address on the card in Covent Garden, her heart in her throat and her morals left firmly at home.

The coach had stopped in front of a small, narrow building nearly hidden among a warren of crowded streets, past the market square that was thronged with peddlers with carts, flower girls, cramped stalls, and costermongers. She'd dressed simply and taken the plainest of her carriages, but even her coachman seemed averse to leaving her.

"Are you certain this is where you need to be, milady?" he asked.

"Yes, I am sure, Farrows. Please return for me in two hours." That would be enough to appease Honoria, along with her own fleetingly absurd sense of adventure that seemed to be fading by the second. Descending, she knocked on the bold red door before she lost the dregs of her courage.

"I'm choosing myself," she whispered. *And hopefully, not ruination.*

～

ARA VAUGHN SQUINTED CRITICALLY AT THE SEA landscape painting she'd just finished. It was a commissioned piece, another for the Countess of Rawdon, one of her most ardent supporters. It featured a folly at the edge of a stormy ocean. Banal enough at first glance until one looked closely at the sprites frolicking in the breaking waves...frolicking if not so much as enthusiastically fucking. Lady Rawdon had a shameless sense of humor.

"I want to shock the sticks from their collective arses, my dear," she'd said, vocal in her scathing opinions of the *ton*. "This one is a birthday present for my mother-in-law."

She was devilishly impenitent, too.

Ara suspected that the brazen countess had desired a lot more than just her art, and while the lady was appealing, Ara tried not to mix business with pleasure. Not that being on the arm of someone like Lady Rawdon wouldn't have opened many doors to wealthy patrons in the aristocracy—the countess was well-connected in the art and theater world—but Ara preferred to succeed on her own merit.

As it was, her paintings were already in some demand, and she did have Lady Rawdon to thank for that. A few pieces had been purchased by a young duke with an eye for color who was rumored to be part of the prince's set, as well as by Lord Alfred Douglas, the youngest son of the Marquess of Queensberry.

Word of mouth was definitely not unwelcome.

Besides, it wasn't as though Ara were destitute. Her father had been a prosperous vintner in France and had left her a comfortable fortune when he died. For a woman in her position, she was lucky. That inheritance allowed her to own this entire building a stone's throw from the lovely Floral Hall, which included a few rooms on the upper floors for paying tenants, Ara's cozy private apartments on the second level, and a spacious painting studio on the ground floor.

A sharp rap on the door had her frowning. Should she have been expecting someone? Ara glanced at the clock in the corner of the studio and balked. Goodness, was it four o'clock already? And today was Wednesday, if she recalled. No, no, it was Thursday! When the muse took her under, sometimes it took full days for her to resurface in the real world. She'd begun this painting at the start of the week.

She dimly remembered speaking with Lady Rawdon a few weeks ago about a special favor to paint a portrait for one of her recently widowed friends. And though she'd been happy to agree...an artist was ever on the hunt for different inspiration, the minute she'd been given the name, she'd cringed.

The Ice Queen herself.

Ara exhaled. Everyone with a pulse in London had heard of the aloof, proud diamond of the aristocracy, the Marchioness of Waverly. It wasn't that she wouldn't be a delight to paint—not with such breathtaking bone structure—but the arrogant marchioness was rumored to be the biggest bitch this side of the Atlantic.

One cutting look from her and a girl's whole come-out could be ruined before it began. Grown men shivered in her presence. Admittedly, Ara had only seen her once at the Crystal Palace years ago during an aeronautical exhibition and her fingers had itched back then to sketch the razor-sharp lines of that angular, coldly beautiful, unsmiling face. The sheer *presence* she'd exuded had been entirely too aphrodisiacal.

Bloody hell, was that *her* at the door?

Ara glanced down at her paint-splattered shirt, loose trousers, and bare feet, and lifted a palm to her short mess of curls that had gone uncombed for days. No matter. How bad could it be? People had to expect that artists might be unkempt and greasy, and who cared what Lady Waverly thought anyway. She was likely here to bow out of the arrangement. Ara could hardly fathom that particular marchioness sitting for a portrait in *her* modest studio.

It probably wasn't even her.

But when Ara shook her head and crossed the space to open the door, her mouth instantly dried. An elegantly gloved hand was partially lifted to knock and full lips parted on an intake of breath. The Marchioness of Waverly stood on the threshold in the very resplendent, very haughty flesh, a pair of mesmeric stormy gray-blue eyes widening in cool surprise.

From where Ara stood on the stoop, it put her in direct view of that unforgettable face, and the artist in her could not help but greedily catalog the features she'd only perused from afar: wide brow, winged dark eyebrows over thick-lashed eyes that glinted with wintry blue flame, a bold nose bracketed by sharp cheekbones and softened below by the decadent arch of lips that glistened as if they'd been moistened a heartbeat before. Her chin was proud, with the tiniest dimple at its center, and that exquisitely hewn jawline was a painter's fantasy. Dark hair, swept up in artful curls, surrounded her face and offset her pale, creamy skin.

This close, Lady Waverly was, without any doubt, the epitome of pulchritude.

Ara forced herself to breathe and meet that gray-blue gaze once more.

"Miss Ara Vaughn?" That voice was both husky and imperious, and shot straight between Ara's thighs as if the lips and tongue that housed it would be quick to follow.

She clenched her legs together and cursed inwardly. *Bloody hell, gather thyself!*

"That's me," she replied in a tone that thankfully did not wobble or emerge like she was a starving urchin being offered a crust of bread and willing to drop to her knees to beg. Or to do other things.

Silently fuming, she bit her cheek so hard she winced. "And who might you be?"

As if she didn't know.

As if the world didn't know a goddess stood on its dirty cobblestones.

The marchioness's head tilted slightly, the left side of that tight-lipped mouth quirking slightly as though she absolutely knew that Ara was lying through her teeth. "Margot," she said.

"What?" Dear God, why wouldn't her bloody tongue work properly? She felt fucking brainless, the sound of the given name twisting her insides into knots. Weren't the peerage excessively particular about their forms of address? And why did the small deviation sound so unfairly *provocative*?

"My name is Margot Foxglove...Lady Waverly," the marchioness said.

"I'm Ara," she replied dimly.

"Yes, you've said." A flicker of something brewed in those storm-ridden eyes, the palest blue around the pupil brightening for a moment as the hint of amusement danced through their depths. But Ara must have imagined it because this marchioness was famous for her icy, *unamused* composure. "Countess Rawdon sent me."

Ara cleared her throat. "Yes, please come in and mind the mess. I was finishing up with a piece."

She wasn't exaggerating—the studio looked like a tornado of chaos and color had hit it with old newssheets and random rags spread out over every inch of the floor. Paintings on canvasses lined the walls, some stacked along the floor and others fastened to whatever wall hangings she could find. With some horror, Ara belatedly realized that the chaise longue in the corner and the two mismatched armchairs were covered in clothes she hadn't bothered to have one of the local washerwomen launder. Good God, was that a pair of dirty drawers?

Ara winced. Sometimes when the muse hit and she started to sweat from the effort, her clothes went flying. Cheeks hot, she skirted the periphery of the room and kicked the offending garment under one of the armchairs before hurriedly grabbing the rest strewn about and tossing them into an inconspicuous pile. She kicked those under the chair, too. There. That was marginally better.

But Lady Waverly wasn't interested in the cluttered disarray. She was gliding toward the easel, which had Ara's latest creation upon it. Despite the satin and taffeta layers of her very fashionable royal yellow dress, the woman's sinuous body moved like water over rocks, a study in poetic motion. Her gaze flitted from painting to painting...from portraits to landscapes to animals and still-life subjects.

Biting her lower lip, Ara sucked in a breath and held it. She wasn't a person who was low in confidence when it came to her art. But for reasons unknown, she *wanted* this marchioness to be impressed. Lady Waverly stopped in front of a mangy-looking dog on a small, framed canvas.

It was an odd choice for her to settle upon, but one of Ara's personal favorites, considering its central placement over the small hearth. The dog was a stray. Pink tongue lolling out of his mouth, the look in the mutt's adoring brown eyes held a wealth of emotion, of so much unconditional love. The purity in those eyes juxtaposed with his patchy fur and gaunt body still fascinated Ara. That a simple, starving animal could emanate so much *hope*. Hence the name she'd chosen for the piece.

"That's Lucky," she said. "He's the market dog, but I feed him sometimes."

The marchioness's slender shoulders stiffened as if she'd forgotten Ara was there. "It's a lovely piece. I had a dog once."

Had. From the slightest, barely audible tinge of melancholy, Ara surmised that the dog in question had meant a lot to her, but the marchioness didn't offer anything else. She studied the painting for a handful of seconds more before moving on to the next—a half-eaten apple with mottled reddish skin and the flesh bruised with the imprint of teeth as if it had been discarded mid-bite, lying near an outstretched palm. Two dark seeds rested on the surface beside it. Ara had labeled it *Cyanide.*

"Apple seeds can be toxic when chewed," she explained.

The marchioness didn't speak, though her mouth tightened infinitesimally before she walked to the last on the easel. The Countess of Rawdon's piece. A soft hum of delight flew from her lips, the sound incongruous as if it wasn't one often made. Not by that self-possessed mouth. "Naughty," she remarked.

That word did all sorts of untoward things; Ara felt her nipples tighten beneath her shirt and crossed her arms over her chest in alarm. "Lady Rawdon intends it as a gift for the dowager."

The reply was dry and couched in fondness. "Of course she does."

Such affection suggested that they were close companions and not just acquaintances. That was good to know. While Ara had been reluctant to do the painting for many reasons, she liked and trusted the countess. Ara usually was a decent judge of character, considering her innate artistic ability to see beyond surface levels, but *this* woman had already gotten under her skin in a matter of minutes. That did not bode well...at least for Ara.

It had been months since she had experienced an attraction this intense.

Unrequited attraction, she reminded herself. And the marchioness might not even be of the persuasion to return her sentiments. In the theater and art world, dalliances of all sexes were an open secret, but Lady Waverly wasn't from this world. Mayfair might as well be another planet. Ara wasn't naïve, however. Such relations certainly *did* happen behind closed doors, no matter the station. But the aristocracy had more to lose with the duty of primogeniture and such, and scandal could ruin entire families.

By law, a man of any social class could receive a prison sentence for *gross indecency*. Ara bit back a derisive growl. As though love in any form was something indecent or shameful. Love was like air—free, vast, and open to all. She was in the minority with that opinion, however.

Moving to the right side of the room where she started to reorganize her messy supplies to find an unused canvas, Ara surreptitiously observed the lady in her space. It was the strangest thing. Despite Ara's initial hesitancy, the marchioness's presence in the studio felt like cool wind on a sweltering day.

One would expect that someone so standoffish might be unsettled and feel out of place. She was elegant perfection; Ara's studio was chaos incarnate, much like her own nature. But the marchioness seemed to slot in like a missing cog...like she somehow already belonged there. It was oddly alarming to Ara, a candle being lit in front of an unsuspecting moth.

A positively stupid moth that should keep its distance from beautiful flames.

Ara could feel the singe of futility already. "Shall we begin?"

Chapter Two

M argot turned, her attention drifting from the fascinating compositions toward their creator, and quelled her erratic pulse. What had possessed her to offer up her given name like a complete philistine? No one but Honoria called her Margot. The truth was, she'd been struggling to keep her legendary cool façade in place the moment that red door had opened.

When their eyes had first met, it had been as though every lucid thought in her head had ceased to exist but one—the desire to climb into this woman's bright, radiant aura and to be enveloped in all that blistering, creative energy. Never had Margot felt such a magnetic pull, and at four and thirty, she was a woman of the world who had seen almost everything.

Yet, this ingénue had stolen the very air from her lungs.

Honoria had failed to mention what Miss Ara Vaughn looked like. Not that it would have mattered. It wasn't about her looks. Disheveled, barefoot, covered in paint—were those crumbs in her hair?—and barely garbed to receive company, she *gleamed*. Here was a woman who thrived on living in her own skin, on being just who she was.

And her art...dear God, such *feeling*.

Every sweeping brush stroke on the canvas carried a wealth of sentiment—delirium, wonder, sorrow, joy, eternal hope—as if the artist herself had cleaved a bit of herself onto paper with each piece. The dog had made Margot's heart swell with nostalgia and Honoria's painting with its frisky sprites had made her want to smile. But the discarded apple had hit hardest. It had made her eyes burn as if that ruined fruit with its poisonous seeds had paralleled the darkest, most jaded parts of her soul.

Margot had wanted to possess every single one of the paintings, if only to preserve a living part of the woman who brimmed with such inexhaustible passion. Even now, she trembled with an odd mixture of anticipation and dread. How would a portrait of her even compare?

Reproaching herself, she settled her thoughts with a measured inhale and reached for the cool composure that had never failed her. She removed her gloves carefully and tucked them into her reticule. "How do you want to do this? Shall I strip or is there some etiquette for these things?"

A pair of amber eyes collided with hers, that expressive face not doing a lick of a thing to hide the flare of mischief. "If you require a lesson in etiquette to take off your clothes, you're in the wrong place, Lady Waverly."

Margot felt her cheeks start to warm, and she forced that reaction into ruthless submission. She was the bloody Ice Queen...why was she acting as though melting was in her nature? She froze things. That was what ice did.

Ice could also burn.

She shoved that inane voice away as Ara approached, the scent of sweet vanilla interwoven with turpentine and linseed oil in her wake. It was an odd combination, the latter a by-product of her profession and the oils, but then everything about this woman was a compelling contradiction. Who knew the smell of paint could be so...rousing?

No, no, no. That was the completely wrong word.

Off-putting. That was what she meant.

"One moment," Ara said, dragging the chaise longue into position against one of the wainscoted walls. She stepped back and sucked her lower lip between her teeth, eyes squinting in contemplation. She tossed one cushion against the end and considered it again before adding a second. "That should do, I think. Now, you can get undressed." Margot's ungloved hand fluttered to her throat and Ara's eyes tracked the motion, though there was no playfulness in them now, only that of a master studying her craft. "You can put this on," she said, handing Margot a lace-embroidered *robe de chambre*.

The luxurious fabric pooled in her numb fingers when Margot grasped the dressing gown. Cashmere lined with silk. Definitely not what she was expecting a starving artist to own. The faintest waft of burnt vanilla rose from the dark blue and gold folds. Was this Ara's? Did she expect her to wear this and nothing else? Margot's cheeks flushed at the utter indecency of it.

"What's the matter?" Ara asked, reading her expression. "Changed your mind? This kind of session isn't for everyone. We can do something...more sedate, if you wish. Something more suited to a woman of your temperament."

Sedate? Her *temperament*? Margot's eyes narrowed. It took talent to couch an insult along with a challenge in the same handful of words. The utter audacity of this brat. Margot lifted her chin and peered down her nose with all the frost she could muster. "Of course I haven't changed my mind. Where shall I disrobe?"

Not bothering to hide her smirk, Ara pointed at a screen toward the back of the room. "Let me know if you need help with your laces or, ah, anything else."

A pained sound was obscured by a patently false cough.

That small detail made Margot feel marginally better about her own nerves. Good. She would hate to think she was losing her edge because of some jejune artist with expressive eyes much too large for her face, a tangle of curls better suited to a ragamuffin than a grown woman, and a tongue that clearly wasn't afraid to take the most feared marchioness in London to task.

"How old are you?" she asked from behind the screen as she got to work with the laces on her outer gown. She'd chosen the ensemble specifically for its ease of undress without a lady's maid.

Was that a low laugh? "Three and twenty. Why do you ask?"

Heavens. Her fingers faltered over the fastenings of her blouse. The girl was a full decade younger than her. "Young."

"Youth has no bearing on talent, if that is your concern."

Again, Margot had the feeling that Ara was laughing at her expense. She did not like that one bit, but she graciously gave her the point. "No, you are quite right. Your art speaks for itself." And then because she couldn't help herself and the idea of losing ground to anyone, "But there's no real substitute for experience, is there?"

Dead silence and then, "Trust me, Lady Waverly, I have plenty of experience."

Why did that seem like she was speaking about something else entirely? Flushing and glad she was behind the screen, Margot opened her mouth and closed it. She would not stoop to engage in a battle of innuendo, no matter how inexplicably piqued the challenge made her. She had to understand the playing field first.

Standing with half of her clothes off, she eyed the robe and frowned. "Do you need me to be completely undressed?"

"Whatever makes you feel comfortable, my lady."

Despite her well-honed sangfroid, Margot was decidedly *uncomfortable*, but what was the point of coming here without actually seeing the thing through in its entirety? Honoria would roll her eyes skyward if she went out there in her corset and petticoats like a timid neophyte. A nude portrait implied no clothing, didn't it?

But still, for some reason...Margot balked.

Shedding her clothes felt like forsaking armor. And that she could not do.

To distract herself from the agitation swirling in her veins, she asked, "Where did you study?"

"Paris."

Margot's fingers worked the ties of her petticoats before she stepped out of them. "Where anyone who wants to imitate the greats did, I presume."

"How astute of you, Lady Waverly."

Heavens, that *mouth*. Curled upward in seemingly perpetual amusement, it wasn't afraid to bite back just a little. Parts of her tingled in pleasant surprise at the tart reply. Most women, especially younger ones, were terrified of her, and afraid to speak out of turn for fear of being on the receiving end of her far-reaching influence. A cut direct from the formidable Marchioness of Waverly was a fate worse than death. But while she could eviscerate with a glare, that didn't mean she didn't appreciate the occasional bit of backbone.

Occasionally.

Removing the last of her outer garments as well as her corset and slippers, Margot tugged on the sumptuous robe that felt much too decadent against her bare arms. What would it feel like if she wore nothing at all? As it was, the soft lawn of her chemise and drawers chafed against her over sensitized skin. She clutched the lapels of the robe, which were only secured by a cord with tassels at the end, with numb fingers. The soothing scent of vanilla curled around her and Margot inhaled deeply.

She peeked around the screen to where Ara was perched on a stool, a sketchbook and a pencil in hand. Late afternoon light filtered in from the window, catching her lean silhouette in a buttery shaft of warm sunlight. One bare foot was propped up onto a rung, emphasizing the lines of her lean leg in a pair of snug trousers. Short, messy rust-colored hair curled into a brow that was furrowed with concentration as she sketched the outline of the chaise.

"I'm ready," Margot said.

Ara didn't look up, nor did her fingers halt. "Get situated on the chair in any position that feels good to you, and we'll go from there. Depending on how long this takes, you might be there for a little while so make sure you're comfortable."

"My coachman is due return within the next hour," Margot said.

"Then we'll just have to work quickly."

Ara still hadn't raised her head, and with some irritation at being treated thus, Margot walked toward the chaise and arranged herself in a prim position on the edge. She couldn't recall the last time she'd been so nervous about anything. Discreetly, she sniffed the collar of the robe again, the vanilla scent an unexpected balm to her scattered senses.

After a moment, Ara unfolded sinuously from the stool as half-hooded eyes canvassed Margot's frame. She might as well not have been wearing a single scrap for how exposed she felt under Ara's intense scrutiny. It wasn't salacious in the least. It was simply focused, but that didn't stop Margot's body from heating beneath the robe. She gripped her palms as Ara closed the distance between them.

"May I adjust you?" she asked politely. A pulse streamed at the base of Ara's long neck, and Margot had the oddest urge to press her lips to that fluttering point. The thought of those slender artist's hands anywhere on her body left her extraordinarily breathless. Peculiar indeed, considering how much she disliked being touched.

Mortified at the unwelcome slant of her thoughts, Margot instantly defaulted to her cultivated, icy mien and clenched her jaw. "You may."

ARA FORCED HERSELF NOT TO SWOON WHEN THAT sculpted jawline hardened ever so slightly. How could a bloody jawline be so entrancing? The marchioness both confounded and attracted her. She was as stiff as a corpse, condescending and rude, and yet, somewhere deep down, Ara sensed vulnerability. If she hadn't seen a flare of apprehension appear briefly in those slate-gray eyes, she would not have guessed that the woman was capable of feeling anything at all.

A frisson ran through her as the sudden indescribable desire to make the marchioness come completely undone filled her, and then she reprimanded herself in the same breath. Lady Waverly was *not* someone whose cold, dead heart needed to be resuscitated; she was a very powerful aristocrat sitting for a portrait, and one who could quash Ara like a mouse. That was all.

"Scoot back against the cushions," Ara said. "Relax. You're like a piece of wood."

The tiniest sip of air slid past the marchioness's lips. "This *is* me relaxed."

Ara snorted, and that gray gaze drilled into hers. Bloody hell, they were so glacial that frost practically slicked over Ara's shoulders. She stifled a shiver and focused on the work ahead. Despite her disposition, the marchioness's face was divinely hewn with her features in faultless proportion. And that *body*. Even under the robe belted so tightly at the waist that it might have been cutting off her circulation, she'd be a Renaissance painter's wet dream. Botticelli and Titian would have been beside themselves with giddy excitement.

Ara bit back a chuckle. She was practically in the same boat.

Unquestionably, the end result would be a lovely portrait because the marchioness was a lovely woman, but for some ungodly reason, Ara wanted more. Why settle for prosaic when something unparalleled could be achieved? Ara wanted passion drenching that cool, austere gaze, tension riding the tendons of her throat, and lust bruising that smooth porcelain skin as though she were on the cusp of release.

Perhaps the last might be stretching it a bit, but Ara had to get the lady to unwind.

If not by orgasm, then perhaps by liquor.

She rocked back onto her haunches and stood before walking over to the mantel. "What do you like to drink?"

"I don't usually imbibe," the marchioness replied. "In fact, the last time I did was a fortnight ago with Honoria when we raided the late marquess's supply of brandy. I had regrets."

Ara remembered having read of the Marquess of Waverly's passing two years ago. She remembered having an idle thought that his heir was so young to inherit, barely a man. Then again, with a mother like his, chances were the young marquess had been groomed to walk in his father's shoes since boyhood.

"Regrets you say?" Ara asked with interest. She'd give anything to see this reserved woman reduced to the middling, plebeian state of being cup-shot. Ara simply couldn't imagine her losing one ounce of that fastidious control.

"Yes. We were quite foxed. Honoria is hard to resist at the best of times and, well, I suppose we were celebrating the end of my...

mourning period. I realize that's exceedingly unusual, but well, I'm glad to be done with it." She let out a sharp hiss of displeasure, as if peeved with herself. "I don't know why I'm telling you this."

Ara walked back with a glass of red wine. "I'm easy to talk to."

"Perhaps." The marchioness accepted the outstretched offering. "Or perhaps I'm at odds because I've never been en déshabillé with anyone except my lady's maid and late husband."

Ara stilled. Oh, for the love of mercy, could a woman become *more* attractive with two simple words of French?

"Sip," she ordered in a voice that sounded much too airless for her liking.

In truth, she would have been disappointed if an imperious eyebrow hadn't vaulted at the command, but Ara arched her own brow and waited. It was a silent, categorically fierce eyebrow standoff, and when one delicate hand lifted after a protracted moment to press the edge of the glass to her lips, Ara felt the capitulation deep in her soul.

"Another," she said, and the second order was obeyed with only a hint of temerity. "Good girl."

"I am no girl," Lady Waverly said, studying her over the rim of the glass, though the quick rise and fall of her chest betrayed the sharp bite of the reply.

Did the cold marchioness enjoy being praised? Ara filed that tidbit away for later. For artistic purposes, of course. Every advantage helped to draw out the muse...and she suspected that this one might require an obnoxious measure of coaxing.

"No, you're not," Ara agreed and then smirked. "But we'll see how good you are, all the same."

Bloody hell, stop flirting, you half-wit!

Without waiting for a response, Ara crouched down again and watchful gray eyes with a hint of blue tracked her movement. "Bend your left knee for me." Ara reached out and she couldn't help but notice the slight recoil. That was odd. She frowned, but made sure to keep her movements unhurried. "Tilt your head and arch your back slightly. May I?" When the lady gave a short nod of consent, Ara reached over to adjust the cushion so that it better supported her spine. "There, that's it. Keep the glass where it is and don't be afraid to indulge as needed."

"This is excellent wine," Lady Waverly murmured.

"Thank you. I do have a few discerning preferences upon occasion, a decent French vintage being one of them. My father owned a vineyard in the Loire Valley."

The marchioness swirled the red liquid. "Is this one of his?"

"It is." Ara rolled back onto her heels, observing the arrangement with a critical eye. While not as impassioned as she would like, the pose was good enough for now. She lifted a palm to the lady's expertly coiffed hair. "May I?" she asked again, and this time, Lady Waverly rolled her lower lip between her teeth before nodding.

With no small amount of care, Ara removed the pins holding that silky wealth of hair in place, and watched with pleasure as it tumbled down onto her shoulders and the velvet fabric of the chaise longue. Lady Waverly's fingers imperceptibly tightened on the glass, and Ara's own hands shook when she gently adjusted a few of the curls away from the marchioness's face, once more waiting for tacit permission before doing so.

"Are you well?" she asked, noticing the slight tension at the corners of Lady Waverly's mouth.

Gray-blue eyes flashed. "Yes, of course. Why wouldn't I be?"

"No reason." It was frankly none of her business.

Ara moved back behind the easel, though she did not reach for any paints. Small thumbnail sketches were necessary to narrow down the composition and depth of the piece. A charcoal dash of a line served as the chaise, but her fingers deftly drew the marchioness in several poses, inspired by the graceful curves of her body. Her inner muse took over as she sketched a few ideas, letting her imagination run. Ara moved between the stool and the chaise two more times to arrange the marchioness to her needs until she was satisfied.

"Did you attend a school for art in Paris?"

The soft question was so unexpected that Ara nearly dropped her pencil. "No, but I studied with a private tutor. In Paris first and then Italy."

"You're well-traveled for someone so young."

Ara huffed a laugh. "Again, Lady Waverly, not so young."

"Margot." The whisper was instantly followed by a much sharper, "Since we're clearly past formalities now."

Smiling, Ara shook her head. "We're probably well into the realm of scandal so maybe it's high time we move to a nickname."

There was a shocked beat of silence before the sparest sound that might have been laughter filtered through the studio. "And what would you choose? I've quite a few already. I'm fond of Ice Queen, Frigid Heart, and my personal favorite, Frost Quim."

Ara's pencil nearly snapped in half. "Innovative," she pronounced with a dazed laugh. "Though I'd have to judge for myself."

The air turned solid at that, and Ara belatedly realized the double entendre of her words. She meant she would gauge the level of iciness...not the last. *Definitely* not the last.

"I beg your pardon," she ground out in dismay when the tension seemed to expand. "I meant you being icy. Not *there*. In general. Like an all-purpose frostiness, not just your...er...down there." Horrified that she was making it worse, she licked dry lips. "Oh, ballocks. Ignore me please, I implore you."

"But why should I when you're so very entertaining?" the marchioness countered, a startling wealth of dry amusement in her low-pitched voice that continued to do insufferable things to Ara's willpower. "Besides, I'd hate for you to be disappointed."

I could never.

Ara didn't respond for fear of saying something that she couldn't take back—*give me thirty seconds on my knees to prove you wrong*—and renewed her concentration on the sketches.

When she was finally happy with the different options, she selected the one that had the most pleasing lines and then switched to another page, where she drew it larger and with a little more detail. Her pencil skimmed over the robe tucked neatly over stockinged feet, the closed lapels hiding every inch of skin to the collarbones.

She cleared her throat, glancing up. "So Lady Rawdon paid in full for a nude portrait, but I can do whatever you're comfortable with. Or use my imagination, if you prefer."

"You can do that?" the marchioness asked. Clearly, that earlier surge of humor hadn't vanished when she shocked Ara yet again. "Very well. As long as you promise no icicles on my down-there."

Bloody hell in a handbasket, was that...a *joke*?

Ara's mouth fell open. "I must confess, you surprise me," she said with a wry grin. "I didn't think you had it in you."

"To jest?"

"To slacken that spine of yours. You do have quite a fearsome reputation, you know."

Her head canted. "I'm aware."

They didn't speak for a while after that, and Ara was worried she'd made a horrid faux pas by pointing out her awful reputation. But she forced herself to concentrate instead of making conversation, and the time passed quickly. When the knock on the door came, signaling the arrival of her coachman, the marchioness rose without a word to go behind the screen.

Well, that was over, at least.

Ara loosed a tight breath and rolled her neck, studying the canvas that was prepped with a warm sepia imprimatura hue over the lightly penciled lines of the composition. She would erase the lines later and then add a color wash as well as individual paint color in the first pass. She wasn't truly satisfied with her effort thus far...but perhaps the muse would appear later on.

The Marchioness of Waverly, put back to immaculate rights, emerged. Her stern expression gave nothing away, not one iota of her feelings, but Ara couldn't help noticing even from where she sat that those mercurial thunderstorm eyes leaned toward blue than gray. Her breath hitched as she wondered what that portended. Was she pleased? Displeased? About to unleash hell?

The marchioness's lips parted. "Same time next week."

It wasn't a question, but Ara couldn't do more than nod, her foolish heart taking absurd flight at the thought of seeing her again.

She knew she should have said no, communicated that she was busy, or that she was out of town. One measly sitting with a woman who was no good for her nerves at all, and Ara was already hopelessly infatuated, the artist in her desperate for more. Damn those blue-tinged, winter-fire eyes.

Ara was doomed.

Chapter Three

I t had been nearly six weeks of visiting the small studio in Covent Garden, and each Thursday, an additional article of clothing remained behind the screen. Whether that was a conscious decision on her part, Margot did not know. Today, only two pieces of clothing remained. She both dreaded and anticipated what ridding herself of both would mean. Would that signal the end of their sessions? The finale of this astonishing adventure?

Gnawing her lip in a rare moment of indecision, Margot exhaled a breath and divested herself of the embroidered silk drawers. The cool air kissed her bare skin beneath the hem of her filmy chemise and she shivered before pulling on the robe that smelled more like her now. Vanilla had been replaced with gardenias.

It wasn't so much the actual nudity beneath the garment than the scandalous suggestion of it. Nudity implied intimacy. And certainly, the last handful of weeks had been filled with that.

One portrait had turned into an entire series.

Six stunning works later, Margot was practically addicted.

To the chaise longue. To the robe. To the intense caress of Ara's eyes.

No wonder more and more of her clothing had been left behind. What would that golden gaze feel like on her exposed body?

Oh, she was a fool twenty ways to Sunday, Margot knew. How utterly gauche of her to be smitten with the artist paid to paint her portrait! It was as bad as the women who swooned for the quixotic poets and the romantic novelists. Perhaps slightly more forgivable, considering she was unclothed and that led to a forced, if false, sense of affinity. More fool her.

But that wasn't all of it.

She'd been the Ice Queen for so long that she'd forgotten who she was underneath all that hoarfrost...or what the warmth of summer felt like. Coldness was in her blood, instilled in her very heart. Much of that was pure survival, but for the first time in forever, Margot wanted to remember how to feel, how to be admired for *who* she was rather than what she could offer.

She yearned to bask in the sun that was Ara.

In this studio, in Ara's space, Margot felt seen *and* she felt safe. In Mayfair, the mantle she wore was heavy. It felt ridiculously good to leave it behind, to be her true self inasmuch as that was possible. Without judgment. Without fear.

Ara's opinions, expressed with such optimism and perpetual joy, made her want to smile more than she'd ever had in her life. Her outlook on life was through rose-colored glasses, while Margot's view was exceedingly plain. Ara was pure fire; she was frost. They couldn't have been more contrary in nature, and yet, Margot couldn't stay away.

Ara was too bright, too bold, too *everything*.

And her talent was outstanding, Honoria hadn't exaggerated about that.

"So what do you think of my little Ara?" Honoria had inquired the week right after the first sitting. "Did she thoroughly impress you?"

Her Ara? Margot had faltered on her reply, which of course hadn't gone unnoticed by her very observant best friend. "Yes," Margot said.

"Did you take off *all* your clothes?" Honoria had asked with a sly look.

Her ears had burned hot. "No."

"Did you want to?"

Margot had frowned and refused to answer.

But perhaps it was those very four words that had encouraged her to be more daring the second time. By the fourth and fifth sittings, it had become almost a challenge to herself to be bolder, to seek that comfort in her own skin as Ara did. And on top of that, the easy camaraderie and the underlying hum of *awareness* that made her inexplicably short of breath on occasion were a potent mix.

During their quite candid conversations in the studio, Margot had come to realize that Ara was attracted to women. It was a curious thing, considering that she'd been married off herself at seventeen, without much of a chance to discover her own personal desires. She'd simply assumed she'd be wed to a man, which she had. One thing Margot did know was that no one deserved a fate like hers. No wonder her body had become completely uninterested in sexual congress at the hands of the late marquess. Pleasure was non-existent.

At four and thirty, *this* was the most indulgent thing she'd ever done for herself.

And in all honesty, Margot wanted more. Though what *more* was, she could not articulate. Friendship? Companionship? There was a definite imbalance of power, considering Margot was paying for Ara's portraiture, but she had the distinct impression that Ara also liked her company. It wasn't only one-sided. Still, Margot wanted to tread carefully. Respectfully.

"I'm ready," she said, stepping around the screen and walking across the room.

Each time, her position had been different, and despite her aversion to touch, Margot had enjoyed being situated according to Ara's whims. She'd seen the earlier paintings, of course, and could hardly believe they were of her. For some reason, despite the exquisitely shaded detail, down to the freckles on her shoulders, Ara had chosen to conceal her face in each composition. It was either turned away with a hint of profile or not visible altogether.

Each piece was all about the body of art...in this case, *Margot's* body.

And once each piece was complete, Ara hid them away.

"It's a surprise," she'd told her with that sunny smile. "Trust me. We're telling a story. The final impact will be worth the wait."

Honestly, Margot did not care about the wait one bit because the completion of every piece brought them closer to their inevitable conclusion. Ara could not paint her forever, after all, much as such a fantasy appealed to Margot. Being painted was like having one's superfluous layers stripped away until only one's authentic core remained. There was an inherent honesty in it, at least in Ara's work, that could not be fabricated or replicated.

Her talent was indeed extraordinary.

Ara was already in position in front of her easel, bronze curls tucked behind her ears, as she cleaned out her brushes and pored over the paint selections. She wore a loose blue muslin dress today and her grin was infectious as she glanced up when Margot reached her side. "How are you today, Lady Waverly?"

"Very well, Miss Vaughn. How have you been this week?"

"Better now that it's Thursday and you're here." Ara's smile lit her eyes to gold, and Margot was mesmerized by the unfiltered warmth in them. It was a wonder how open and expressive that gaze could be. She hid nothing of herself, this woman. "How is that handsome son of yours? Making ladies swoon all over London, I see?"

Margot's brows pinched. "So you've read the newssheets then? God, he'll be the death of me one day, I swear."

"He's every poet's dream at the moment," Ara said with a laugh when she paused by the fresh canvas that already had a preliminary thumbnail sketch on one corner. It made Margot flush to think how intimate Ara already was with the lines of her body, at least with a pencil and a paintbrush. "Defending the honor of a lady, who was insulted by a degenerate toad of man, is quite newsworthy and gallant."

"The Marquess of Waverly was brawling! In public. It was a scandal!"

Ara sniffed, though her smile remained. "And I suppose that goes against every decorous bone in your body, does it?"

To say the least! Margot's jaw tightened and she couldn't help but notice the sudden darkening of Ara's amber eyes and the sharp intake of breath. Margot blinked at her. "What is it?"

"You look quite displeased, right now," she said, her cheeks tinting scarlet. "It's distracting. With you in that robe, I mean. Like you'll be rapping my knuckles next for bad behavior." She cleared her throat in embarrassment. "I must admit, this impassioned side of you is quite invigorating. You're normally so composed."

Pleased for no reason, Margot made her way to the armchair, and sat, letting the soft fabric part over her legs, though everything else remained covered. "Percy has always been the only one to get under my skin."

"The only one you *allow* under your skin," Ara said softly.

"Is there a difference?"

Ara's expression begged to differ but she didn't argue. "Let's not lose the light today. The weather has been a bit off. Lean against one arm, both knees bent and hooked over the other. When you're comfortable, loosen the tie and turn toward the back of the chair. Let your right sleeve fall off one shoulder. Pull the ribbon from your chemise so that the neckline loosens as well."

She paused while Margot obeyed her instructions. Extending her legs, Margot wiggled her bare toes, watching as the panel slid over her calf and exposed her from ankle to knee. Though she flushed at the impropriety, her inhibitions had lowered considerably since the first week. The human body was a natural and beautiful thing, and as Ara had said more than once, hers was first-rate. Margot exhaled and untied the cord to let the fabric pool as instructed.

"Yes, that's lovely," Ara said from behind her. "The sheerness of the linen limning your skin adds a level of color complexity in this light that works remarkably well."

Margot felt the press of Ara's gaze like a tangible stroke over her exposed nape and suppressed a tiny shiver. It was uncanny how one could *feel* a stare. Or perhaps that was just Ara. With their proximity over the past weeks, they'd become intuitively aware of one another.

There was a rustle of movement, footsteps, and then Ara was at her back. Margot froze as the quiet "May I?" came, requesting permission, which Ara did without fail. That was another thing about her... she was observant. They had never discussed Margot's aversion to touch, and yet, Ara had always taken such care with her.

Margot inhaled and nodded—Ara's gentle motions never bringing any fear or panic with them. One careful fingertip tugged on the gaping neckline of her chemise, loosening it more and lowering it nearly below her shoulder blade. Margot caught her breath as the fabric dragged over her too-sensitive breasts. She must be nearing her courses—they didn't normally feel so full or tender.

She reached up with both hands to remove the pins from her hair and was stalled by a light palm on her wrist. The touch was visceral, making heat spark like wildfire beneath it, running along her skin and into her tense muscles. Thank God her chemise covered her chest because her nipples instantly peaked. Margot frowned, though did not react any further than that. Her nipples weren't responsive, and other than a source of nourishment for Percy sixteen years ago, she barely noticed their existence.

She noticed them now, however.

"Hair up today," Ara whispered, warm breath gusting against the shell of her ear. "That swanlike neck of yours is the focal point of this piece." A light touch tilted her chin just so, fingers skating fondly over the line of her jaw. "Like this. Shoulders back."

Once she was content with the final position, Ara got to work and they settled into their routine. Periods of silence were interrupted by pleasant conversation as well as the faint swish of bristles on paper and the frequent shifting of Ara's body. Margot tried to remain as still as possible, though Ara didn't seem to care whether she moved or not. During the second hour, Margot usually reclined and watched Ara work, allowing herself to fully be at ease.

Ara's pink tongue peeked out from between her lips as she squinted at her progress. Her blue dress was splattered with paint and a smudge of blue was on her chin. She looked thoughtful and entirely too becoming.

"Why art?" Margot asked as she curled up on the seat. "Why do you like it?"

Bright amber eyes met hers before dipping back down. "I like the medium, and the texture of paint on canvas. I like how each brush stroke can transform something from ordinary to extraordinary." She lifted one shoulder in a shrug, and smiled, the sight of it lifting Margot's spirits like nothing else could. What *was* it about that honest, simple expression? Was it the way it lit her entire face? Or was it the fact that it was directed at *her*? "I like painting what I see, though that doesn't always match the reality."

"And what do you see when you look at me?" Margot asked before she could stop herself. Ara rubbed her nose with the back of her hand. She hesitated as though she wasn't sure how to answer or whether her words might wound. "Go on, I can take it," Margot said, not actually sure if she could.

"A beautiful rose who has wrapped herself in so many thorns, she doesn't even recognize the sight of her own petals." Ara let out a small sigh, her voice lowering. "Or how much she needs to be nurtured. To be loved. To be told that she is enough just the way she is." She met Margot's eyes over the edge of the canvas, her amber gaze so vivid that it shone. "A woman who has been so deeply hurt that to protect her heart, she hid it away, but you have so much more to give, Margot, if you would only give yourself the chance."

Margot shivered at the reverent sound of her name on Ara's lips, more of the ice around said heart melting away. "Oh."

The silence stretched between them, with what felt like so many things being left unsaid, and then Ara put down her brush. She hesitated for a second, but then hiked her chin. "Come somewhere with me," she said. "To a party this Saturday. Let loose just a little outside of this room."

"A party?" Margot frowned, the warmth departing slightly. "Where?"

"At the Floral Hall."

Instant dread flooded her veins, the thought of anyone seeing her like this made her feel much too vulnerable. Much too *exposed*. Some aristocrats from her circles, much like Honoria though hardly as discreet as her, attended these things. What if she were recognized? "I can't—"

"It's a masquerade, if that helps," Ara said softly, as if she could see right through her fears. "You can wear whatever you want."

A knot formed in her throat. "I shall see. I have a...soirée."

SHE DID NOT, IN FACT, HAVE A SOIRÉE.

Heart pounding, Margot stood at the threshold of the extravagantly lit glass-and-iron domed hall that was decorated in a kaleidoscope of vibrant color, and felt panic close around her ribs. Alexandre Dumas coined the word *demimonde* in his play nearly a half-century ago, and it literally meant half-world...a society that existed on the fringes of the real world where hedonists thrived in their search for pleasure. Drugs, gambling, and wanton vices were rife.

The incongruity was almost too much because the Marchioness of Waverly wouldn't be caught dead here. And yet, here she was, embodying Venus, of all things.

She couldn't be more boorishly transparent if she tried.

"You're here!"

Lips parting in greeting, she turned to a woman she hardly recognized and promptly lost her breath. Ara was clothed in a luscious cream gown that hugged every willowy inch of her body. From the modest display of bosom above the lacy, corseted bodice to the cinched-in waist that flared out to liquid ripples of fabric, she looked like she belonged at a grand ball in Mayfair. Her chaotic curls were clipped in place with jeweled hairpins and a gold feathered mask with strands of pearls covered the top half of her face. That bewitching smile was glossed in pink and quirked with pleasure.

"Aphrodite?" Ara asked with an appreciative look at Margot's costume.

"Close, Roman inspiration not Greek," she rasped through a dry throat. "Venus."

"Well, you're stunning as either," Ara said, eyes shining with approval and something more intense that Margot could not immediately identify. "Marie Antoinette, at your service."

"You..." Margot's voice thickened and trailed off. There was no earthly expression to describe Ara, who simply outshone the French queen she was meant to be by leaps and bounds. Her mouth opened and closed, mind unnervingly blank. Oh, the absolute irony that words would fail the infamous Ice Queen, who wielded them like poison-tipped arrows, was pure comedy. She licked dry lips. "How did you know it was me?"

"I've drawn and painted this body for weeks," Ara said softly. "Do you think I wouldn't recognize the mesmerizing sharpness of this jaw or the elegance of this neck?" Her words were draped in sin and velvet. Then she laughed, the sound rich, low, and full of pleasure, doing inconvenient things to Margot's heart as she tucked her arm in hers. "Come on, let's find some godawful champagne."

Margot stuffed her embarrassment away and let herself be led into the melee. It was fascinating to see this version of Ara from the artist —so radiant and sparkling in a ballgown—and her mind could barely keep up. Margot couldn't help noticing that Ara drew attention wherever she walked, from men and women alike. Or were they looking at *her*? She went rigid, her spine locking with apprehension and feet stumbling on the polished floors.

"What's wrong?" Ara asked, pausing before the refreshments area.

"People are staring," Margot whispered.

"Of course they're staring. You're a goddess in that costume, if you hadn't realized. And that dress, well, I'd bet my entire building that many of them are fantasizing about how it would look on the floor of Mount Olympus."

Margot frowned and then realization dawned. *Oh.* "You're teasing me."

"Only a little, though in that ensemble, you deserve it. I'm certain you only wore that to torture me." Ara leaned in, the familiar scent of toasted vanilla filling her nostrils, eyes brimming with fondness and... blatant interest. The latter made Margot much too flustered. "Relax,

Venus. No one will recognize you. The dress and mask are ideal. Now let me get you some champagne. Stay put."

Shifting closer to one of the wrought iron pillars wrapped in artificial flowers, Margot nodded and swallowed her pointless dread. Ara was right. It was a sea of anonymous faces. The rose-colored, one-shouldered gown, however, was more risqué than anything she would normally wear. Clearly, it had been a stupid choice considering how much attention it garnered, though as Ara had said, it was to her the *woman*, not her, the marchioness.

The bodice dipped nearly to indecency and the corset she wore was several years old. It was a miracle it even fit, but what it did to her décolletage was utterly criminal. Thank God then, for the mask, a concoction of onyx and deep vermillion feathers, which concealed most of her face. It wasn't as though anyone would recognize the *breasts* of the Marchioness of Waverly.

A puff of self-deprecating laughter was expelled. No one had seen her breasts in sixteen years, and even old Waverly had done his conjugal duty in the dark.

"Well, I must say, Margot, Venus suits you."

Clearly, she'd let her guard down much too soon.

Time suspended as her heart climbed and lodged into her throat when she angled her head to the new arrival. For a dreadful moment, she did not immediately identify her best friend in the inventive bat costume, complete with black wings that stretched from her wrists to a matching satin cape. An ornate bat brooch rested over her chest. Margot blinked with delayed recognition, and then relief—was it relief?—sluiced through her.

"Well, wonders will never cease," Honoria drawled. "You said it would be a cold day in hell before you attended one of these parties, no matter how many times I begged, and yet, you insufferable wretch, here you are."

All Margot could manage was a choked noise. "I..."

Goodness. If Honoria recognized her, who else would? She never should have come here. Her reputation would be compromised.

People would talk and gossip. *Percy* would be mortified that she had lowered herself to such tomfoolery.

Hands grasped her trembling shoulders. "I can see the wheels turning in that brain of yours," Honoria said. "Stop it this instant. I only knew it was you because Miss Vaughn told me to make sure you did not run away."

"No, I shouldn't be here." Her mouth opened and snapped shut. She'd done *what*? Good God, every logical sense in her brain had abandoned her. Even the air had the sickly sweet taste of panic. "I must go."

A figure in gold and cream precluded her escape and a flute of champagne was lifted in front of her eyes. "Drink this and breathe," Ara said in a low tone, meant only for her ears, as if she could sense the brewing turmoil. "Lady Rawdon invited me. Us. This is her party. I thought you knew."

Margot fought for breath, hand grasping the stem of the glass as she sipped thirstily, the cool liquid soothing her parched throat. She glanced at her best friend who was watching her with a look of concern, green eyes narrowed behind the simple but stylish diamond-studded mask. Of course Margot hadn't known—Honoria's social life was impossible to keep track of. If she had, she would never have come.

She took another sip and felt her nerves start to settle.

"Miss Vaughn," Honoria said. "It's a pleasant surprise to see you here as well, considering how many times you've also refused my invitations. One wonders why you changed your mind." A coy smirk pulled at her lips as if the answer was obvious. "But now that you're both here, when am I going to see these secret paintings?" Her gaze shifted to Margot. "Unless it's not portraiture you've been sitting for, all these weeks."

"You've been spying on me?" Margot said.

Honoria waved a dismissive arm at the chilly tone that would have made a lesser person quail. "Of course not, I was at the opera house meeting with the director and saw your coachman two weeks in a row.

Do credit me with some modicum of intelligence, darling. And Miss Vaughn's...charm is hard to resist."

The inference was not subtle. "It's not like that," Margot said, unwilling to have their precious time together sullied into something that it wasn't. "I loved the first painting and desired another. The artist was available."

Honoria's stare glimmered with calculated interest. "I really would love to see them sometime. Perhaps you might even consider a showing at my new gallery?"

Margot opened her mouth to decline without insulting her best friend, but Ara nodded graciously and said, "When they're finished, perhaps."

Which would be never. Margot couldn't imagine any of those portraits seeing the light of day beyond the studio. They were openings into her soul, unadorned by nothing but Ara's artistic genius. To show them would be to expose herself, and *that*, Margot would never agree to. Being here was enough of a risk to the life and persona she had built, and she still didn't know what had driven her to agree.

Pleasing Ara.

Margot swallowed, pulse fluttering like a nervous butterfly. That had been the least of it. She'd agonized for hours, and in the end, it had come down to one single, irrefutable thing: for just once, Margot wanted the both of them to be on neutral ground. Silly her.

She watched as a svelte blonde garbed in a form-fitting silver jester costume approached them, and Ara shot Margot an apologetic look before allowing herself to be dragged onto the dancing floor where a rousing Scotch reel was in progress. The hand on Ara's back resting there so familiarly made Margot stiffen for no reason at all.

"That's her former lover," Honoria supplied much too helpfully. "She's an actress at the Covent Garden Theater. A good one, too."

Former lover. Those two words punctured her lungs like bullets.

"Why should I care? It has nothing to do with me," she replied, despite the acid churning in her stomach.

Her friend shot her a skeptical look. "You're not even a little curious as to who she's kept company with? Or who your competition for her attentions might be?"

Was she? Such a thought had never truly entered Margot's mind. Well, it had, but in the context of friendship. *Friends don't feel the way you do.* Nor did friends fantasize in the darkest hours of the night of how Ara's lips might feel against theirs, or dream of long slender feminine thighs intertwined in carnal pleasure, and of whispered moans and sensual sighs.

Setting her jaw, Margot lifted a cool brow. "No. I'm not interested."

The lie tasted like soot in her mouth, and the jealousy that roared its wrath when the pretty jester spun Ara in her arms and kissed her on the mouth at the end of the reel was more than she could bear. Even for the invulnerable Marchioness of Waverly who had ice in her veins. Her lungs squeezed, eyes falling closed, as her stupid chest *ached*.

"Keep fooling yourself." Honoria had always been able to see right through her, but Margot couldn't afford to telegraph the wrong message, no matter what her body felt. She'd always been adept at burying her true emotions and this, too, could be overcome.

Her words emerged like whetted blades. "She's an artist, paid to do a *job*, Honoria. Do not confuse the two."

A hushed gasp was the only signal that Ara had returned just in time to hear the ruthlessly spare sentiment, but perhaps that was for the best. Margot kept her face carefully blank. Rose-colored glasses and girls with smiles brighter than sunlight did not belong in her frozen, barren world.

Chapter Four

What felt like an eternity later but was only really a fortnight, Ara cleaned her brushes for the third time and studied the last of the paintings she'd arranged around the perimeter of the studio. She exhaled as the images of the woman who had obsessed her every waking thought surrounded her from all angles. It was a particular brand of self-inflicted torture, knowing just how out of reach Margot truly was.

Did this version of her even exist?

She's an artist, paid to do a job, Honoria. Do not confuse the two.

The precise diction, the terse snap of each word had sunk into Ara's bones like the warning they'd been. Even now, she could still feel the painful jolt of each. She let out another ragged exhalation. She had hoped that during the party something might finally give between them, but if anything, Margot had become even more distant. Even Lady Rawdon had been taken aback by the marchioness's abrupt departure.

"I'll talk to her," she'd said to Ara. "She's been through a lot."

Ara knew. Or at least she'd guessed because she'd noted it in every infinitesimal flinch, seen it in those mercurial eyes that told their own flawed story, sensed that complex history as the beating, living heart in every single one of these paintings. Ara had likened her to a rose covered in thorns, but what Margot didn't realize was that those very thorns weren't protecting her. They kept things out...but they also kept things *in*. They were strangling her.

Ara had replayed the events a thousand times, and the change in Margot had come after Sandrine, her former partner, had asked her to dance. Despite their turbulent history, they'd ended their ten-month relationship on an amicable note. Sandrine was much too possessive and had used copulation as a form of control, which had never sat well with Ara. But relationships were like puzzle pieces—some people melded better with others—and as far as she knew, Sandrine had moved on happily with lovers who met her needs.

It wasn't even that Ara had permitted the kiss, chaste as it was; Sandrine had just taken it, perhaps in hindsight, to do exactly what she'd meant to do. She'd coyly asked Ara, after all, who her delectable companion was, and Ara, besotted fool that she was, hadn't thought to conceal her feelings.

Had Margot been *jealous*? Still, most people did not shut down and turn into an ice block simply because of a fleeting sentiment. No, if Ara had to guess, Margot had closed herself off because she'd been petrified of whatever she'd discovered *beneath* that feeling...all those raw emotions that were present in every single one of these paintings, even if she wasn't yet ready to acknowledge them herself.

Art had a propensity to reveal.

Then again, they were all created through Ara's eyes.

Bitterness and heartbreak warred with pride as she studied the canvasses. Ara could no more separate Margot from these pieces than she could herself. For better or for worse, they were inextricably connected. Forever bound in oils, if not in actuality. The paintings were arguably Ara's best work, likely because each one had been a love letter to its muse.

To *her*.

It was a series of seven paintings in various poses, whether they were on the chaise or an armchair, but they started with Margot mostly clothed and ended with her without a stitch beneath the robe on that voluptuous body. The seventh was the most sybaritic of all, and Ara sighed softly as she took in the lush lines and the sensual curves of Margot's limbs forever immortalized on the canvas.

With the robe draped completely off her slender shoulders and falling in a cowl just beneath the cleft of her buttocks, she straddled a walnut bedroom chair in reverse. Bare forearms crossed over the back of the chair with her head resting atop them. Her upper body was angled to reveal the sensual curve of a breast under her right arm and her entire back was on display, down to each muscle, each sculpted hollow, and the spattering of freckles along her scapula. The long channel of her spine led to the flare of rounded hips, only half visible above the edge of the dressing gown.

Ara had almost swallowed her tongue when Margot had emerged from behind the screen with the garment untied and bypassed the armchair, saying without inflection that she wanted a different pose, one partially nude and of her choosing. If she'd meant to punish Ara by flaunting what she couldn't have, she'd certainly succeeded. The erotic arrangement, viewed from the back with her legs spread, was etched in Ara's brain. She'd been so aroused she could barely think, much less paint.

As a result, the final sitting for their seventh portrait together had been stilted and tense. Everything about Margot had been impassive to a fault, as though they were nothing but strangers. Her eyes had been gray and wintry, her face unreadable. There'd been no fond words about Percy, no inquiries about the antics of the gossiping washerwomen, no enjoyable banter about the latest fashion or faux pas in the *ton*.

Nothing but silence and an arctic politesse that had chilled the entire room. The entire time Ara had painted, she'd felt like an exposed nerve, and she was sure some of that had been translated to some degree into the final work. It practically vibrated with angst. With wrath. With need. With regret.

Ara didn't care what that said about her; *she* wasn't afraid of her feelings. Falling for Margot had been like falling for the wind, here one moment and gone the next, the only memory of it a whisper of coolness on one's skin.

An evocative, transient memory.

Now that their sessions were done and paid in full—Margot had said on her way out that she didn't care what Ara did with the final pieces—it wasn't as though Ara could go to Mayfair and demand explanations. One, she didn't know where the marchioness lived. And two, why should *she* care? Margot certainly didn't. And Ara wasn't about to behave like some scorned lover, even though the idea was entirely too tempting in her current forlorn state.

With a lump in her throat, she moved the easel out of the way and lay down in the center of the studio on the floor, surrounded by her muse. Bloody hell, she was pathetic. She rubbed a fist against her aching chest, but couldn't bring herself to get up from her prone position. She wanted to wallow in the pain she'd willingly invited upon herself. She'd known exactly who the Marchioness of Waverly was all along.

Ruthless. Heartless. Impervious.

Leopards did not change their spots, no matter how much one might wish them to.

A knock on the door had her leaping up, her heart soaring into her throat. Ara didn't even stop to check her clothing or see if her hair was a snarled rat's nest. She ran to the door and flung it open. "I was hoping you—"

But the face wasn't the one Ara yearned to see. Those blue eyes weren't the right shade, just this side of morning frost. That pale hair didn't absorb the light like the darkest of shadows. This smile was too wide, not stingy and spare and infinitely precious. Her former paramour smirked, oblivious to the cracking sound that was Ara's heart.

"You were hoping I would what?" Sandrine said in a flirtatious tone that was all wrong. It wasn't husky and low, like velvet over gravel. It wasn't *hers*. "I knew I felt a spark between us two weeks ago."

"There was no spark," Ara said.

"Then why have you been pining and looking over at the theater twenty times a day?"

She'd been searching for a particular coach in the street until she'd given up, but Ara was too weary to argue. "What are you doing here, Sandrine?"

"I wanted to see you. I had a break from rehearsal and I brought your favorite," she said, holding up a wrapped parcel. "Fresh, hot crepes with blackberry jam. I thought we could share them."

Sharing anything with anyone was too much. "Sandrine, we are over. Whatever you felt at the masquerade wasn't from me. I told you I need to focus on my art."

Blue eyes flashed, her mouth going flat. "Is that what you've been doing? I saw the way you looked at that woman. Who was she?"

"No one you know," Ara said tiredly, scrubbing a palm over her face. "And besides, it was over before it could even start." Two weeks of silence were a sign that she could no longer ignore. Margot Foxglove was gone. "She's no one."

The silence swelled, and then Sandrine shrugged. "Need a friend then?" she offered. "I'm free for an hour. I could make some tea to go with these. It would be a shame to waste them."

Ara's stomach gave an obnoxious growl and she couldn't remember the last time she'd eaten. "As long as we're clear about where we stand. Friends, nothing more. I mean it, Sandrine."

"Fine, be no fun whatsoever."

With a half-smile at Sandrine's dramatic eye-roll, Ara waved her over the threshold and closed the door behind them. She ushered Sandrine upstairs, bypassing the studio completely. There was nothing in there for her.

Nothing but unnecessary anguish.

∼

Well, then. That was that.

Margot collapsed heavily back on the bench of her carriage and rapped on the ceiling before the coach could come to a stop at Ara's address. A small window near the front opened and the coachman's curious face filled it. "Home, Farrows," she told him. "I've changed my mind."

"As you wish, my lady."

As the coach drove past that familiar red door, Margot blinked, her eyelids stinging with a sharp, unfamiliar burn. Dear Lord, were those *tears*? She hadn't wept in decades and would hardly start doing so now. She was made of much stronger stuff than that! And yet her lungs felt tight, as though she couldn't get enough air and her vision blurred as more of the insufferable wetness gathered.

Clenching her jaw, Margot squeezed her eyes shut, forcing herself to go to that place in her head where she felt nothing. Where no one could touch or hurt her. She hadn't gone there in so long, but it was a needed solace from whatever *this* absurdity was. She needed fortitude.

The sight of Ara's soft smile being bestowed on someone else had cut deeply.

So deeply, she'd felt the slash right in her soul.

But Margot supposed she deserved it. She'd been the one to leave after all, as well as the one to dictate the much-too-cruel terms of their last session, the icy indifference she was known for front and center. Watching Ara at work, trying and failing to hide her desire and confusion, had been torture. Worse, knowing it would be the last time Margot would be there, had felt like peeling stripes off her own heart. And much like she was doing now, she'd resorted to a tried-and-tested version of self-defense to protect herself from pain.

Ara would never hurt you and you know it.

Well, it was clearly much too late to do anything about that now.

The ride back to Mayfair was blessedly quick. Margot didn't want to be left too long with her fractured thoughts. She handed her gloves and coat to the butler, and followed the voices coming from the kitchen. Her mood brightened the moment she recognized the dark mop of hair and the broad-shouldered body of her son. That frame was the only thing he'd inherited besides the marquessate from his father, thank God.

"Percy, love, what are you doing home?" she asked, though her heart was gladdened to see him.

Blue-gray eyes twinkled back at her as he enfolded her in his long arms and kissed the top of her head. It was something she hoped he'd never stop doing, despite warnings from other mothers that *their* sons barely acknowledged them. At only sixteen, he towered over her by several inches. "I should ask you the same question. Every time I've come to visit, Mrs. Hardy tells me the same thing. My lady is out. The marchioness is not at home. Come back tomorrow." He narrowed a mock stare at her. "Do I need to assign you a chaperone? Make sure you aren't causing trouble and demolishing debutants all over town?"

She belted out a laugh. "Hardly." When he stared at her, his mouth dropping comically open, she frowned. Her gaze flew to the housekeeper, who also had a slightly stunned look on her face as well. "Whatever is the matter?"

"You laughed," Percy said. "I haven't heard that sound in an age."

Margot touched her parted lips self-consciously. "I laugh."

"No, Mother dearest. You smile *just so*, exactly one eighth of an inch on either side of your lips every single time. Your cheeks do not move and your eye color does not change. In fact, it is the most precise expression of all expressions, exercised to perfection." She let out a scoffing sound, but Percy wasn't finished, eyes narrowing. "This behavior is new."

"You are being absurd."

"Am I?" He peered down at her with an intense scrutiny that made her want to run and hide. What would he see written all over her? Did lust and seduction sink into one's skin for all and sundry to read? "Where exactly do you go in Covent Garden every Thursday?" he asked.

Margot actually spluttered, her hand rising to her mouth. One look from her, and Mrs. Hardy and the two maids working near the scullery took instant leave of the kitchen as if they were only too happy to escape. "Who says I go there?"

"Farrows told me when I asked, and before you have him immediately sacked, I forced him to tell me so I will simply just rehire him." Percy drew a soft palm down her cheek. "In case you have forgotten, I am the master of this household, and your safety is my greatest concern."

Margot couldn't help it—she burst into tears. And if there was anything worse than a six-foot boy staring down at her for laughing, seeing the same boy in a panic at the sight of her tears was categorically worse. She made to flee, and Percy's hands fluttered like wild birds before banding themselves about her as she proceeded to drench his waistcoat.

"Mama?"

Mortified at her display, she sniffed and stepped back, covering her blotchy, swollen face with her palms. "You haven't called me that since you were a child."

"You haven't cried since I was a child. Here, take this before you get snot all over the floors and we slip everywhere."

A huff of horrified mirth left her, but she nodded with gratitude as Percy handed her a handkerchief from his pocket. "I'm so sorry. That was quite uncalled for. I don't know what came over me."

Percy drew her over to two chairs and made her sit while he fussed over the nearby teapot to prepare her a cup of tea. Margot wanted to bury her face in her hands. "Of course it was called for," he said. "I've never seen you like this, but I do know that this sort of thing is better out than in. I know you've had a lifetime of skill holding things inside, but trust me, it serves no good purpose."

Her jaw slackened. Dear God, how preposterous was it that she was taking advice from a sixteen-year-old, though it was obvious that he had more emotional competence in his little finger than she had in her whole body. "Who are you and what have you done with my son?"

"Your son grew up, Mother. But he was very lucky he had you for a role model." Percy grinned when he brought the cup and saucer over, made just as she liked it with two lumps of sugar. "Though at times, you are rather terrifying to live up to, I must say. The most perfect lady in London."

"I'm not perfect," she said.

He sat opposite her. "Everyone in the *ton* says so. Now tell me what is going on or I shall be forced to go on an interrogation rampage all over Covent Garden for the ne'er-do-well who broke my dear mother's heart."

Margot's eyes widened. "There was no...breaking."

The wretched child actually snorted. "Laughter, tears, emotional bedlam. Your heart is in abject peril, Mother, a fool could see it and you did not raise a fool." With that, he lifted his brows and stared her down with an intense glare that was so like hers that she shook her head in amused surrender.

"No, I raised a miniature tyrant, clearly."

"Stop prevaricating or shall I go fetch Farrows?"

Goodness, was he serious? When he half rose from his seat, she held up a defeated hand. "Very well. There was...someone, but it's finished now."

"How so?" Percy asked.

"I...they're too different for our world, Percy. It would never work. I'm me, and as you well know, practically impossible to love." Her voice gave an abominable quaver on the last. "I have you and that's all that matters."

"You'll always have me." He reached for her hand and squeezed. "But you know that's complete horseshit about you being impossible to love. You are the most wonderful woman I know, even if you pretend to everyone that you're not." Brow furrowed, Percy let out a resolute breath. "Waverly is gone. Don't let him dictate your life and your worth from the grave. You *are* worthy of love."

The bridge of her nose tightened. Oh God, she was going to cry again! "Percy..."

He shook his head, eyes sad but earnest. "He was my father, but that didn't make me blind to his flaws. He was a beast to you, Mother, and you tolerated it for the sake of his name and our reputation." Percy raked a frustrated hand through his hair. "I suppose I do have him to thank for the life lesson on how to *never* treat a woman."

Her heart sank. "I didn't realize you'd witnessed...any of that," she said weakly. "I'm so sorry, I never meant for you to—"

It was his turn to lift his palm. "Don't you dare accept fault for *his* actions. He was in the wrong, not you. Now did this person make you happy?"

She didn't even have to think. "Yes."

"Did he make you smile?" Percy asked.

Margot closed her eyes and thought about all the times Ara had made her smile, so much so that she'd had to hide some of them for fear of developing a condition. Was there such a thing as smiling *too* much? Or being *too* happy? She lifted tremulous eyes to her son. Despite her fears, he was the only one whose opinion she valued. "She did."

Percy blinked in surprise for a slow second and then that brilliant smile Margot so loved took over his face. "Then you have to get her."

"It's too late. She's with someone else."

Her son's eyes flared blue with amusement and so much love that if she hadn't been sitting, her legs would have given out. "Mother, I know this might be news to you, and we're still working on getting that heart of yours functioning, but it's never too late for a good grovel." He grinned with a wink. "Besides, I know just who we can get to help!"

~

ARA LOATHED BIRTHDAYS.

Why, oh why, had she agreed to let Lady Rawdon of all people throw her a party? But the persistent countess was like a runaway carriage when she got an idea into her head, and she'd insisted it would be a way to cheer her up, considering...

Well, considering that Ara's pride and her heart were still equally bruised and showing no signs of recovery. She hadn't left her home or painted in weeks. Her muse had absconded to Mayfair without a backward glance and just the thought of looking at a blank canvas made her stomach roll. Ara had managed to clean her studio, however, but that was as far as she could bring herself near an easel. Thank God, the countess had taken the seven paintings off her hands or she might have started sleeping with them.

Ara could still remember the look on her face when Lady Rawdon had seen them for the first time. "By God," she'd whispered in reverence. "They're...she...magnificent."

I know exactly how you feel, Countess.

The series that Ara had halfheartedly nicknamed *Venus Undone* was a slow seduction, a gradual building of affection as each portrait progressed, and the friendship between them had flourished. As Margot blossomed, Ara had become more infatuated with the woman behind all the icy walls. Her fascination was apparent in each meticulous brush stroke, growing more and more devoted as each consecutive piece reflected more and more of Margot.

A love affair in portraiture...the inevitable fall of the artist for the muse.

God but she was truly a sad cliché.

The art itself was provocative given its racy subject matter. Though one couldn't see Margot's full face in any of the paintings, that didn't take away from the visceral effect they had, especially when viewed in sequence. Symbolically, anyone could read something into the series—a journey of discovery, a descent into carnality, a study in temptation. But that was the beauty of art—it was always open to the viewer's interpretation.

To Ara, however, the series would always embody the deliverance of Margot from her cage of thorns, if ever so briefly, from that very first day to the very last. And that final painting had been Ara's absolute demise—the confident poise, the voluptuous grace, and the bold sensuality had taken it from stunning to spectacular.

It should have been named *The Liberation of Margot.*

And *The Dissolution of Ara.*

No matter. It was all done now. Whatever Lady Rawdon did with the paintings was between her and the marchioness, though what little Ara knew of Margot told her that she'd never put herself on such display for all the fame and fortune in the world. It went against the very grain of who she was...or perhaps who she thought she was. Maybe they would be hidden away in an attic somewhere.

Ara squinted at the clock in the corner of her apartments. Lady Rawdon had said her personal carriage would be coming by at seven o'clock. Could Ara hide? Simply not answer the door? Pretend to be ill? There were so many possibilities. And yet her bleeding heart couldn't go through with any of them. She was never very good at disappointing people.

When the coach eventually arrived and the driver knocked on the door, she put on her cloak without complaint and went.

"Do you know where we are going?" she asked when the driver helped her inside the fancy interior.

He grinned and touched his hat. "The countess said it was a surprise, Miss."

Of course she had. Ara looked around, taking in the plush velvet seats with their embroidered edges. Gold accents adorned the corners and the entire interior screamed of luxury. Lady Rawdon certainly wasn't hurting for money. No doubt Lady Waverly was just as privileged, considering the two shared similar circles. Ara wondered if their paths might cross, but then shook her head. The marchioness had made her position and priorities quite clear.

Don't think about her.

She wouldn't. Not tonight, if she could help it.

Surely this tedious pining would not last forever? One could hope. Ara closed her eyes and made her mind blank until the carriage came to a stop. When the coach door opened and she descended, she recognized the bustling area of Piccadilly and her eyes went to the name of the street in curiosity, New Bond Street.

There were many newer hotels and social rooms about, all upscale given their proximity to Mayfair. Perhaps the party was in one of them. But the coachman offered his arm, and they strolled past several buildings until they came to a shopfront made entirely of glass that was lit from within by colorful lamps. Ara blinked, taking in the details and the name. It was a gallery...an art gallery, to be precise.

And Lady Rawdon stood at the doors, preening like a cat with a full bowl of cream. "Finally! My guest of honor has arrived!"

In a state of disbelief, Ara climbed the steps and entered the large foyer to a thunderous round of cheers and well wishes for her birthday. Some of the faces she recognized—other artists, two of her tenants, a few actors and actresses from the neighboring theater and opera house—including Sandrine, who'd fed her when she'd been too distraught to remember to eat and had turned out to be quite a dependable friend once she realized Ara wasn't remotely interested in reconciliation.

Others Ara didn't recognize, though she expected they were friends of Lady Rawdon's. One gentleman in particular, a tall, vaguely familiar looking young man with dark hair, couldn't stop beaming at her.

How odd.

But then Lady Rawdon clapped her hands, gave a signal and the gaslights went out, much to the delighted whispers of everyone. Ara swung around when a single flickering flame appeared, a path clearing for the person carrying a round cake with a slender candle at its center. But Ara couldn't care less about the cake or the candle when the person bearing the tray in the flickering light was Margot.

Ara's throat dried, her heart kicking wildly in her chest, but she steeled herself. The Marchioness of Waverly was Lady Rawdon's best friend. That was why she was here...certainly not for Ara, even if she ached ever so hopelessly for it to be so. Desperate eyes drank in the sight of her, an impossible knot forming in her throat when Margot stopped inches away and placed the cake on a nearby table.

"Happy birthday," she said in that low husky rasp that never failed to make Ara's knees go weak. "Blow out the candle and make a wish."

Ara was bereft of wishes, but she did it anyway.

When the gallery descended into darkness, the scent of gardenias burned through her senses and the softest pair of lips collided with hers in a kiss so tender that Ara felt it in her bones. *Margot?* Astonishment was followed by a flood of desire as Ara moaned and the slightest parting of her lips on the sound paved the way for a sleek, warm tongue to lick shyly into her mouth. That one honeyed taste was all it took.

"Margot..." she panted against that soft, *soft,* willing mouth.

"Ara."

Within a heartbeat, the kiss went from cautious to heated as Ara slanted her head and sucked Margot's full bottom lip between her teeth. The sweetest answering whimper was her reward. They didn't have much time, Ara knew, before the lights came back on, so she made the most of every blissful second, reveling in the sensual dance of Margot's tongue against hers and the kiss that carried a thousand unsaid words.

And then the gas sizzled and a scant moment before the lights came back on, they broke apart, Margot's lips swollen and eyes so bright they glittered like stars.

"Your eyes are blue," Ara whispered.

Margot nodded, her heart in them. "Sometimes, they turn that color when I'm happy."

Chapter Five

"**N**ow we get to the good stuff," Honoria crowed, her gaze much too knowing as though she could guess exactly what had happened in those fraught seconds that had felt like infinity to Margot. Because heavens above, she'd *kissed* Ara.

In a roomful of people, albeit in the dark.

And it had felt good. *So* good.

The floodgates she'd kept bolted shut on her emotions had finally broken open. Was this what passion felt like? She could barely quell the desire that was rushing around in her veins from a single kiss. Margot almost laughed. That hadn't been a kiss...that had been a meteor crashing right into her. An Ara-sized comet, incinerating everything in its path. And for the first time that she could recall, Margot wanted to burn.

The whole affair had been planned out from beginning to end with Honoria's help. Percy had been right that she was the perfect coconspirator. Margot hadn't planned the kiss when she'd walked out with the cake, but all she'd wanted to do was erase the stark confusion, uncertainty, and flickers of alarm on Ara's expressive face. And in the end, Margot simply hadn't been able to stop herself from laying claim to those parted, trembling lips.

Brow scrunching adorably, Ara glanced in Honoria's direction. "What good stuff?"

"There's more in the restaurant, some magicians and performers, and a supper spread," she told a somewhat dazed Ara, whose lips Margot expected looked as red and ruined as hers.

Would others know? She didn't dare look around for fear of what she would see, but Honoria had carefully organized the party with only friends from their art and theater circles. Even if any of them guessed, they were much more open in their opinions than most of the *ton*.

"Sounds fancy," Ara said.

Margot gave a small nod. "I wanted you to have a memorable birthday."

"I'm honestly happy to leave right now," Ara said, those amber eyes shining and still dilated with pleasure. "There is nothing in the world that can top the past two minutes. I need more of *that*, not whatever else your best friend has up her sleeve." She let out an incredulous laugh, the light of her smile illuminating the room as she leaned in with a whisper, "What in the hell was that, Margot?"

"A birthday kiss?" Margot's lip curled in amusement and a stronger pulse of need throbbed between her thighs at the hungry rasp in Ara's voice and the matching stare in her eyes. No one had ever looked at her like that. "Patience. I promise you'll enjoy it. But first, I want you to meet someone."

"I don't want to meet anyone. I want to leave, get you alone to myself, and tear your clothes off with my teeth."

Margot's gut clenched as every nerve in her body jumped to attention, but tugged on Ara's arm against the flow of people following Honoria. She steered them toward where her son was waiting in a quiet corner, his hands in his pockets. She couldn't read the expression on his face and that made her question her choices yet again. Was it too soon?

For all his energy and impetuous nature, he could be sphinxlike when he chose, too, and right now his handsome face was inscrutable. Margot faltered for a moment. She wanted this—*Ara*—more than anything, but her life had rules and expectations. Could she truly have both?

With each step toward Percy making this real, her stomach inched into her throat. Even now, while claiming such a small piece of happiness for herself, he was ever at the forefront. He'd been her North star for so long that she felt off balance.

"This is my son, Percival, the Marquess of Waverly," she said breathlessly, before she lost her courage. "He's visiting from university and wanted to meet you."

Ara's eyes went wide and Margot was sure she'd bungled it. As if he could sense her awkwardness, Percy pulled her under one arm, despite her muttered protests that they were in public and had to comport themselves accordingly. Her pleas went ignored.

"It's a pleasure to meet you, Miss Vaughn," Percy said kindly. "I've heard so much about you that I feel like I know you already."

Ara's surprise was genuine. "You have?"

Percy smiled. "Yes. I know you're a very talented artist, but all I truly need to know about you is that you've made my mother happier than I've seen her in a very long time, if ever. And I am profoundly grateful to you for that."

"Oh." Her stunned gaze collided with Margot's, whose heart felt like it was already twice its size. "I'm so glad," Ara said softly. "She makes me happy, too."

Margot disentangled herself with a scowl as Percy let out a small laugh. "Good. By the way, I apologize for staring at you like a complete dolt earlier when you arrived. It was just fascinating to me to get a glimpse of the person who could make the unreachable, impervious Marchioness of Waverly,"—the over-the-top, highbrow thespian way he drawled her title made Ara grin—"a mere mortal like the rest of us."

"Percy," Margot chided, but her son wasn't finished.

The soft sincerity in his gaze floored her. "I approve, Mother. Wholeheartedly. Not that you need it." He turned back to Ara, a dimple popping in his cheek. "I'd love to get to know you better, but alas, I have plans. Perhaps we can spend some time together soon. Happy Birthday!"

"Thank you, and I would like that very much."

They both watched as he took his leave, jumping into a nearby hackney on the street, and then it was just the two of them. The foyer was nearly empty as everyone else had headed inside for the rest of the festivities.

"So that was Percy," Ara said. "He's just like you."

Margot let out a scoff. "We are complete opposites."

Ara glanced fondly at her. "You forget I've seen your heart, Margot, and it is the same as your son's. Only he chooses to wear his for the world to see while you tuck yours away." She reached out to run a thumb over Margot's knuckles. "Your reasons are your own and I hope you'll be able to share them with me one day, but you two are more alike than you know. He inherited your eyes, that luminous smile when you choose to use it, your insight, and your kindness."

"No one ever says I'm kind," Margot whispered. "I'm cold and forbidding."

Ara squeezed gently. "No, you're not." Her eyes were so warm, they glowed like honey shot through with pure sunlight. "I know we should stay awhile, or Lady Rawdon will skewer us both, but will you come home with me tonight?"

For once, Margot threw caution to the wind and let her heart reply. "Yes."

~

WAS THIS A DREAM?

Ara didn't dare blink in case it was.

She and Margot did not speak during the drive back to Covent Garden. They held hands tightly, hearts beating in tandem within the dark of the carriage as if a single uttered word would break the magical spell between them. If hands could speak, an entire conversation was being held in each exploratory brush, the soft tangle of knuckles, a whisper-soft graze over a sensitized palm, and the eventual interlacing of bare fingers. By the end of the journey, Ara's entire body reeled on the knife-edge of arousal.

She had never imagined that her birthday would end like this... with the most impossible wish in her heart, fighting like the tiniest ember and refusing to be snuffed out, coming true. Her chest felt so tight that each sip of air was a battle. Honestly, if she did blink, would it turn out to be some fantastical fever dream? Because it was the stuff of fucking fantasies that *Margot* was in the carriage with her. That Margot had kissed her. That she was going home with her.

That she was *here*.

While the evening had not been spent attached at the hip, it had been fraught with enough heated glances across the supper table, from one end of the small ballroom to the other, and anywhere else their eyes crashed together, which was often. The tension had been so thick that the Countess of Rawdon had fanned herself and asked conspiratorially if they required the private apartments above the gallery. Her unequivocal acceptance of what was happening between them, as well as Percival's support, had floored Ara. They both loved Margot and wanted her to be happy.

Ara intended to live up to that expectation.

They entered the building in silence, their interlinked hands the only sign of the heat simmering between them, as Ara led Margot up to her apartments. Inside when the door closed, Margot stood there, that gorgeous blue-gray gaze pooling with affection and so much more.

Ara lifted her hands gently so as not to startle her and skated them over Margot's cheeks into the silky brown tendrils over her ears. With a delicate fingertip, she slowly traced the winged brows she'd painted so many times, slid down the slope of that bold, haughty nose, and grazed the sweeping curves of those delicious lips.

"My beautiful muse," Ara whispered. "So exquisite, so mine. I feel like you've nestled so deeply under my skin, that you're already part of me." Margot's eyelashes fluttered, her throat working at the soft confession. "I've craved you from the first moment you crossed my threshold, all furious frost and winter skies." Ara dragged her thumb across the plush fullness of her lower lip, tugging it down, lust barreling through her as Margot's tongue peeked out to lick the pad of her finger. "Goodness, how you undo me. Are you sure you want this?"

Blue eyes smoldered. "I want *you*."

With a harsh garble of need, Ara replaced her thumb with her tongue, the taste of Margot as intoxicating as the rarest of wines, and when her lips parted so sweetly beneath hers, all pliancy and soft submission, Ara groaned into the embrace.

Her fingers dug into her hair as Margot's hands wound around her neck. She wanted to devour her, but she also didn't want to frighten Margot with her ardor. It hurt to hold herself back, but Margot deserved patience and care. With considerable effort, Ara reined in her eagerness and gentled the kiss only to rear back when a soft chuckle rumbled against her lips.

"I'm not a piece of porcelain, Ara," Margot said, pushing up onto her tiptoes, her fingernails scouring down Ara's back and winding into the fabric of her skirts to anchor her close. "If you're going to kiss me, fucking *kiss* me."

Hearing the oath fall from the cultured lips that never spoke out of turn was like a spark against dry tinder. Ara growled low in her throat, a creature provoked beyond reason, as a bolt of lust almost addled her mind. She reached for restraint one last time. "I was trying to go slow."

"I don't need slow. I need everything you have."

After a searching look at those dilated irises that practically glowed with ice-blue flame, Ara needed no more urging. Grasping Margot's hips, she walked her back, their bodies almost flush but for the skirts between them, and when they hit the wall, she crushed her mouth to Margot's. If the kiss earlier had been unhurried and tentative, this one was all fire and raw hunger. She grasped Margot's chin, angling her head to where she wanted it and slanted her mouth over hers, nipping and sucking, chasing Margot's tongue with hers.

"You taste sublime," she said in a hoarse voice. She tugged Margot's head back with a handful of hair, not enough to hurt, but enough to expose that elegant column to her greedy mouth. She nipped her way down the velvety skin, biting into the juncture of her neck and shoulder, and soliciting a groan of pure pleasure. Ara's tongue edged the lace of Margot's bodice and dipped into the swells of that creamy décolletage. "I want to mark every inch of you."

"Then do it."

Bloody hell, could a person come from the sheer sound of that rasp? Ara was already so wet that her thighs felt slick, the need for friction all-consuming. *Too soon, too soon.* She pressed her legs together as Margot's fingers dug into her scalp while she obligingly nibbled and sucked at the plump curves, leaving a trail of red bites in her wake. The soft moans and kittenish whimpers were music to Ara's ears.

"Quick, unlace me," Margot said in a breathless whisper and twisted around so that she was pressed up against the wall, completely at Ara's mercy. God, the position was so erotic that her knees nearly buckled as Margot's arse rolled back into her pelvis.

She wanted to savor the unveiling of all that smooth skin, to count each and every one of those freckles along her shoulders, but her greedy fingers deftly unlaced the ties at the back of the dress as if they had minds of their own. The heady fragrance of gardenias wafted up as the fabric gaped and pooled around Margot's waist, and it didn't take much more to unfasten the petticoats for those layers to tumble down that superbly formed body.

Ara's mouth dried, her hands faltering on the corset that cinched her waist. Curves on top, curves below, so much *skin*. And her *scent*. Fuck. Ara's brain simply shut down and primal desire took over. Yanking the fabric of the chemise to the side, she sealed her mouth to Margot's nape and ground her hips into hers as she slid her hand around beneath the filmy layers and into Margot's drawers. Her knees nearly gave out at what she found there.

"You're so fucking wet," she moaned, copious amounts of silky arousal coating her fingers, as she licked a hot path up to the sensitive spot beneath Margot's ear and elicited a whole-body shiver.

"Please," Margot whispered, grinding erratically into her palm. "I need..."

"I know what you need," she purred into Margot's ear as her thumb swiped over the bundle of nerves at the top of her sex. The whine that came out of Margot was so deeply carnal that Ara trembled. She slid two fingers inside Margot's hot sheath, knuckle-deep, and they both groaned at the sensation before Ara withdrew and sank back in to the base.

"You feel fucking incredible," she whispered and quickened her thrusts.

They were both so tightly wound that it didn't take long for Margot to detonate, her body seizing and her passage grasping Ara's fingers with each rhythmic pulse. Ara tilted her chin with her free hand and swallowed Margot's helpless cries with her mouth, even as her fingers wrung every last drop of the orgasm from her shuddering body.

"Such perfection," she murmured. "I love feeling you clench so beautifully around my fingers."

Margot gasped. "That was...I've never..."

"Been touched by a woman?"

She shook her head, eyes unfocused with bliss. "Had an orgasm that I didn't give myself."

A satisfied smile curled Ara's lips. "Good, because I'm nowhere near finished." With a purposeful look, she twisted her lover around and wrenched Margot's ruined drawers down. She dropped to her knees and shoved the hem of her chemise up with one hand.

"Look at you," she whispered. "So rosy and glistening for me."

"Ara," Margot said, her cheeks scarlet. "What are you—?"

But the words were torn from Margot's lips as Ara wasted no time in slanting her mouth over the warm, still-throbbing flesh. Her eyes nearly rolled back in her head at the silken ambrosia that met her tongue. She pulled away for a half-second to lift Margot's ankle and toss the discarded pair of drawers out of the way before returning to her task. With a groan of pure need, she spread Margot's thighs wide, exposing every dewy inch.

"Ara?" Margot asked breathily.

"I am going to eat you alive," she promised with a long, slow lick with the flat of her tongue before spearing it deep into Margot's quaking body.

"Oh, my God, that's..." But her lovely muse lost any power of speech when Ara sucked her pulsing flesh into her mouth, her words garbling to nonsensical demands and pleas.

Margot's desperate cries spurred her on, her fingers tangling into Ara's hair as her body writhed against the wall. Ara skillfully brought her to a second climax, this time fucking her with her tongue and teasing her so thoroughly that by the time she lightly scraped the bud at the top of Margot's sex with her teeth, she screamed and shattered anew.

~

MARGOT WAS SEEING STARS.

Her body quivered with the last echoes of the orgasm as a very smug Ara rose and licked her lips before planting her mouth on hers in a ravenous kiss. Curiously, Margot studied the taste of her own arousal on Ara's tongue. It was like nothing she recognized, a tangy, sweetish flavor that inexplicably made her wetter...if that was at all possible.

Because, good God, she was literally a faucet down there. Her knees felt weak, and if there wasn't a wall at her back and an accomplished lover at her front, she would undoubtedly be a puddle on the floor. When they broke apart, Margot wrapped her arms around Ara's waist and flushed. "You're very good at that," she said.

Ara preened, that smile of hers radiant. "That's the beauty of being with a woman. I know what I like and I also know where everything is."

"I suppose that is a clever advantage." They shared a laugh as Ara gently removed the pins from Margot's coiffure, letting the mass tumble loose.

"I love all this luxurious hair of yours," Ara murmured. "Every time you wore it loose, I wanted to bury my face in it. Wind these silky tresses in my fist and have my wicked way with you."

"I'd like that, but later. Now, I have other pressing plans."

"That sounds serious," Ara said with a smile.

Flushing deeper, Margot bit her lip and dragged a purposeful finger over the modest rise of Ara's bosom, drawing a soft hiss from her. More than anything, she wanted to see that long, lean body shivering with desire and witness that sinfully talented mouth begging for release. Her face went hot at the image of Ara with her head thrown back in the throes of pleasure, completely at Margot's mercy. "Will you teach me what you like?"

Ara kissed her lips gently. "We don't have to tonight. We can wait."

"I want to." It wasn't a lie. Between their slow kisses and unhurried caresses, Margot's body had started to heat again, and she wanted nothing more than to please Ara in return. "But first, we need to get rid of all these clothes."

"Are you sure?"

Margot smirked. "Do you require an etiquette handbook on how to disrobe, perhaps?"

"Touché," Ara said with a laugh, clearly also recalling when they'd first met.

They undressed each other hurriedly, laces being unraveled and ties being unthreaded. Stocking and slippers went flying, petticoats and gowns flung in a heap, until they both stood in the altogether, silent and panting and desperate for each other. Margot stared her fill, but her imagination had not done the reality an ounce of justice.

Ara was all sleek lines and sinuous muscle, her body the complete opposite to Margot's. A pair of pert breasts tipped with light brown nipples led down to a flat stomach and long, slender legs. Those endless miles of skin were several mouth-watering shades darker than hers.

Hunger roared in Margot's chest. "God, you're radiant," she whispered.

Warm amber eyes fixed adoringly on her blue gaze after sweeping her from head to toe with undisguised desire. No one had ever seen her the way Ara did...as if she were something precious, something to be savored and treasured for eternity. Margot felt a slow flush warm her flesh, distilling down her neck, over her collarbones to her heavy breasts as a languid heat spread throughout her limbs.

Ara's eyes tracked the pinkening skin, and for a moment, Margot felt a tinge of worry. Was her body as pleasing to Ara as Ara's was to her? The contrasts between them were many, from Margot's curves to Ara's suppler form, from her pallid skin to Ara's much warmer complexion. Where Ara was toned, Margot's body was soft and dimpled. Her breasts were full and her hips wide, marred by silvery streaks from childbirth. In a fit of nerves, she lifted her arms and crossed them over her belly.

"Don't hide from me, you're bloody stunning," Ara whispered and Margot's hands fell reluctantly to her sides. "Now, seeing you like this, I regret not getting you fully undressed before I had my way with you." Ara trailed off, licking her lips as if savoring the taste that lingered there, the voracious look in her stare dispelling Margot's doubts.

"I don't," she confessed with a small shiver. "That was the hottest encounter of my life. But now, I want to go slow. I want to explore you."

A muscle beating wildly in her cheek, Ara grasped her palm and led her over to the bed on the other side of the space. The air smelled like toasted vanilla. Like Ara. "I'm yours," she said simply.

Margot slid her hands through the soft, thick bronze curls, smiling as the ends latched around her fingers. She scraped her nails along Ara's scalp and the sound she made sounded like a contented purr. Those red lips beckoned so she leaned in for a kiss. Unlike the others they'd shared, this one was a sensuous meeting of mouths, a purposeful exploration of tastes and textures. Margot loved when Ara tensed as her tongue teased the roof of her mouth, a low groan rumbling in her chest.

"You like that?" Margot whispered.

"I like anything you do," Ara replied, her breath coming faster when Margot skimmed a teasing fingernail down the center of Ara's chest.

Those pretty brown nipples furled at the touch, and Margot had the biggest urge to caress them with her tongue, so she did. To her delight, Ara's body went as taut as a bowstring, her eyes glazing over when Margot settled her mouth over the sweetly pebbled bud and sucked, her tongue flicking lightly over its tip. Remembering the feel of Ara's teeth on her nether region, she gently bit and was rewarded with a ragged whimper of pleasure.

"Bloody hell," Ara moaned when she switched her attentions to its twin. "You're certain you've never done this before?"

Margot nibbled and licked her way up Ara's chest and claimed her lips in an open-mouthed kiss. "No, but I've always been an excellent student."

With that, Margot shoved her backward until they fell in a breathless tangle of limbs to the bed, their mouths dueling for domination in a slick collision of tongues, teeth, and lips. Nothing had ever felt so good, *so* right. She could kiss this woman for hours. Days. A lifetime.

Ara rolled them so that Margot was straddling her hips, her lower half split so obscenely open that Margot went crimson. The groan that left Ara's lips was positively carnal as strong fingers kneaded her thighs, before skimming up her sides to cup her breasts.

"You're a goddess like this," she said, eyes burning with so much heat that goosebumps broke out over Margot's flesh.

Ara rolled the tightly budded peaks, tugging and pinching them gently, and Margot groaned as pleasure streaked from her breasts to her core. Who knew she was so responsive there? This was a time of discovery for her as well, but perhaps that was simply Ara—everywhere she touched painted heat on Margot's skin.

With a mock scowl, she narrowed her eyes. "Stop trying to take over, it's my turn."

Ara gave an unrepentant grin. "I can't help it. You're too tempting."

"Hands up, grab the headboard," Margot commanded huskily. Amber irises darkened to molten gold, but Ara reluctantly complied. "Good. Don't move until I tell you to."

"Damn, that *voice*."

Laughing softly, Margot shifted to the side and proceeded to drive Ara mad with fluttery touches, from the sweet, upturned breasts Margot couldn't get enough of, down her trim stomach, to the thatch of dark bronze curls at the apex of her thighs. Curious fingers danced over the drenched folds she found there, and Ara's hips canted in desperate need, seeking the friction that Margot delighted in making her chase.

"Stop teasing me," Ara begged, squirming against the bedsheets.

Margot felt satisfaction curl her lips. "But you're so lovely when you beg. I like you like this, at my mercy." Ara's hands slackened. "Don't you dare let go or this stops," Margot warned.

"You're a devil."

Smirking wickedly, Margot dipped her fingers briefly between Ara's legs, feeling the silky glide between her thumb and forefinger, and without letting her gaze leave Ara's, brought them up to her mouth. They both groaned when Margot licked her fingers clean, the earthy-sweet flavor bursting over her tongue, so similar to her own but different all the same.

She sucked her bottom lip with a lascivious moan. "Like nectar."

"Kiss me," Ara begged, and Margot obliged, leaning down to seal their lips together. Her tongue mimicked the actions of her fingers that had returned to the velvet haven between Ara's thighs, by turns featherlight and forceful, delving and retreating, playful and teasing. Margot delighted in wringing every possible sensation from Ara as she could, keeping her right on the cusp of release. When she started to pant and curl her hips, Margot slowed her movements before building her up again, and by the third time, Ara was a writhing mess.

"Margot, for mercy's sake, fuck me!"

Heavens but she loved hearing her name on Ara's lips, that breathy, filthy plea doing unspeakable things to her own enflamed body. When Margot pushed in to the first knuckle with her middle finger, Ara groaned and drove herself down on Margot's hand, chasing the pleasure that had been denied her for too long. A mere handful of thrusts later, she clenched and cried out, her body bucking as the pent-up release crashed through her.

Margot didn't stop. Adding a second finger and maintaining her pace with ruthless persistence, she kept working Ara through the orgasm, even as she sobbed and convulsed on her fingers, claiming that it was too much. Margot was so aroused and in tune with the woman connected to her that every unsteady pulse felt like a jolt to her own body. Searching out her mouth, she lost herself in Ara's honeyed taste, her own core clenching desperately on air.

She was determined to make Ara come at least twice, and she had never failed at anything in her life. This might be her first time with a woman, but Margot hadn't built herself up as the most intimidating lady in London by mere luck. She bent to take Ara's nipple in her mouth, nipping hard enough to make Ara arch and gasp before soothing the small hurt with her tongue.

"I need to touch you, Margot, please," Ara begged, her palms still obediently glued to the headboard. A wave of pride rolled through Margot. Her passionate little artist deserved a reward for such good behavior.

"Then touch me," she said, finding Ara's lips again.

Frantic hands instantly banded around her, nails digging into her arse as Ara's hips moved faster, rolling in a jerky graceless motion, soft cries spilling into Margot's mouth as her pleasure built a second time. Lifting her knee, Margot rocked her pelvis onto Ara's bent thigh, seeking friction for her own mounting excitement. Without warning, Ara's hand snaked between them to touch her right where she needed it most and her legs started to shake.

A single swipe and Margot was dragged under.

"Come with me," she panted, chasing the climax that burned like wildfire through her. Margot wasn't even sure how her body was capable of such a thing, *again*, though clearly it was, with the right partner. Wanting to return the favor, she bit into Ara's soft throat, suckling hard and knowing she'd leave a bruise, right as she added a third finger and pressed down with the heel of her palm.

"Bloody hell!" Ara yelped at the combined stretch and pressure on her clitoris, her entire frame seizing and shuddering as a second orgasm crashed onto the heels of the first. Those pink lips parted on a soundless cry as her head fell back, a sheen of dusky color staining her skin. Her pulse fluttered wildly, abdominal muscles contracting and flexing with the force of her release.

Margot stared in complete reverence. Ara in front of an easel with her face creased in concentration was mesmerizing, but Ara writhing against crumpled bedsheets, spine arched, eyes unfocused, and lost in the throes of bliss was a thing of wonder. Her entire body, wrought in the brilliant hues of pleasure, was a study in the most primal form of art. Heavens but she was the most glorious thing Margot had ever seen. All glowing, sweaty golden-brown skin and sleek, shivering limbs.

"How was that?" she asked when Ara had quieted.

Ara laughed, the rich sound filling the room like music. "Considering you fucked me so hard I'm having trouble seeing straight, I would say rather phenomenal."

Chapter Six

Ara wasn't lying. She hadn't been so well-pleasured in, well, ever.

Then again, this was *Margot*. A thunderstorm in a woman's body.

Said thunderstorm stretched out languorously like a cat beside Ara, all endless limbs and mouthwatering curves. Despite just having come so hard that there were still white spots in her vision, Ara was starving for her again. That lush body of hers was positively sinful, entirely capable of tempting whole civilizations to kneel at her overflowing altar. Fuck, she could still taste her sweetness.

Lazily, she curled herself around Margot's warmth, draping one leg over hers as Ara smiled to herself, her sated core giving a lustful, needy throb. This was the problem with giving in to one's addiction. One could never get enough, and she had the feeling she'd never get enough of Margot. When this ended—and Ara knew it would eventually—the loss would be soul-crushing. But that time wasn't now, and she intended to stay in the moment for as long as she could.

"So, this is where you sleep," Margot murmured, peering curiously around.

"Sleep and other things now," Ara replied cheekily.

A brow arched over passion-blown, blue-gray eyes, making Ara's breath hitch. It was indecent what that one eyebrow could do. Ara sucked in an inhale and told her body to behave.

"Not even with Sandrine?"

The question was so quiet, Ara barely heard it, but the vulnerability there was obvious. "No one but you," Ara said. "She is a friend, nothing more, I promise."

Margot exhaled as if something heavy had left her shoulders. "I like your décor."

Ara glanced around the open space she called home. Considering Margot lived in Mayfair with an army of servants, she was probably used to opulence and excess, while Ara preferred simplicity, comfort, and clean lines. Unlike the artistic chaos in her studio downstairs, the walls here were bare of clutter except for three or four pieces of art that she had collected over the years. A colorful throw lay over the sofa on the far end of the room, opposite the alcove that held her bed, and a handmade tapestry covered one wall. The bathing and dressing rooms took up the other side of the space. As with most houses, the kitchen was in the basement.

"I can't believe I've never been up here after all these weeks," Margot murmured, propping herself up and curious eyes taking in every inch. "It's the opposite of your studio."

Normally Ara didn't enjoy having anyone in her private space, but observing Margot, who seemed to be cataloguing everything with genuine interest, made her inexplicably happy. She liked the idea of Margot knowing who she was, seeing all of her with all her quirks and idiosyncrasies. But most of all, she wanted Margot to let her in, too. To *trust* her with the secrets she carried in that barricaded heart of hers.

Ara rubbed her nose. "Sometimes I need a calm space. This is my haven." She disentangled herself from her embrace and walked naked over to the mantel. "Drink?"

"Water, please," Margot said with another long stretch before she rose, too. Ara hid her smile when she reached for the robe draped over the end of the bed. The mighty Marchioness of Waverly was endearingly bashful. Ara would make sure she lost that shyness in short order. Her body was art in motion, and Ara planned to tell her that as often as she could. "I seem to have a fondness for your robes," Margot said when she noticed Ara watching.

"I like you in them."

Ducking her head to hide her pleased expression, Margot wandered over to the bookcase where her fingers danced over the spines of Ara's favorite novels. She moved on to a figurine of a couple so intertwined there was no way to tell whose body was whose at first glance. "*Infinitely Wound*," she read off the small metal plate at its base. "Did you make this?"

Ara looked up from the pitcher of water. "I did. It was my first foray into sculpture."

"It reminds me of your paintings," Margot said, her palm skimming over the entangled alabaster forms. "So much passion. You never do things by halves, do you?"

"I try not to, but being open to passion means that you also open yourself up to pain."

A curious gaze met hers. "Is it worth it?"

"For art, absolutely." Ara shrugged. "For my heart, however, that remains to be seen." She handed Margot the glass, delighting in the flush when she surreptitiously skimmed Ara's nude body, her pupils dilating with a burst of desire.

"You're so comfortable in your own skin," Margot murmured. "I thought that about you the first day I met you. You love who you are."

"You should be, too. You're a dazzling woman and I'll never tire of telling you that." She sent Margot a glance. "But loving yourself takes work. I wasn't always my best advocate—I let others determine my worth. But we only have one body, and that makes it precious."

"That is wise advice." Margot sighed. "I don't think I'll ever see myself the way you see me, Ara. Everyone else sees tall and daunting."

Ara grinned and winked. "I believe the words you're looking for, my lady, are majestic and statuesque."

"Ah, yes, the ever imposing Ice Queen."

Ara's grin grew teeth as she stalked closer, one fingertip dragging over Margot's hip through the satin robe, sliding tantalizingly close to the crease of her inner thigh. "Speaking of nicknames, I now have it on unimpeachable authority that the misnomer Frost Quim is categorically incorrect." Her knuckles grazed over Margot's mound, drawing a smothered gasp from her. "This perfect cunt shall here-so-forth be dubbed Blazing Quim."

Margot gave a shrill laugh, a violent flush streaking her cheekbones at Ara's vulgar choice of words. "Goodness, you are outrageous."

Oh, how Ara loved to provoke those strict, highbrow sensibilities. Hiding her amusement, she pretended to be thoughtful, tapping her chin. "What do you call it then? The altar of Venus? Cupid's furrow? Cyprian fountain? Pleasure pit?" She giggled at Margot's scandalized expression. "Or maybe even cock lane. Though there're no cocks here." She stuck out her tongue and waggled her fingers lewdly. "Only these, but they're more than capable of fucking you boneless."

"Ara!" Margot's eyes dilated, her pulse flickering. "Now you're just trying to shock me."

Ara took the empty glass of water from her hand and drew her back to the bed. "Yes, my sweet muse. I plan to *shock* you all night long, if you let me. Let the re-education of Margot Foxglove begin!"

"Ara, wait."

While she collapsed in a lazy sprawl of limbs on the sheets, Margot perched primly on the edge of the mattress, her bottom lip rolled between her teeth. Spine straight and chin up, she looked like every inch the frosty marchioness she was—intimidating, icy, and untouchable. One day soon, Ara would persuade her to leave all that rigid propriety behind, but it was so deeply entrenched into her psyche that Margot didn't even realize she was channeling that persona. Ara longed to know what, or who, had shaped her so.

"There's something I need to say before I lose my courage and you deserve to hear it properly from me," Margot said softly, that beautiful face stark but earnest. "I'm so sorry about how I behaved. I was afraid of what my feelings meant, so I took charge as I always do to make sure that I was protected from any vulnerability. I was jealous and I hurt you, and I'm sorry."

Ara's pulse skipped and soared as she propped herself on one elbow. There was a lot in there, but she only heard one thing. "Feelings?"

Margot bit her lip, pink color spilling across those high cheekbones. For someone who never deigned to blush, she was certainly doing quite a bit of it now. That was one small win, at least, in Ara's opinion. "When I married Waverly, I was young. Seventeen. I'd been a sheltered girl who knew my duty was to wed a peer. Like most girls that age, I'd hoped that affection, possibly even love, might come in time." Margot clasped her hands in her lap, her body barely moving. "I was wrong."

"Margot, you don't have to..."

She lifted a delicate wrist. "Let me get this out. I want you to know all of me before you decide to go any further. I'm...complicated, at best." Ara wanted to say that there was nothing Margot could share that would make her change her mind, but she suspected that opening up was somewhat curative for Margot as well. "The marquess was deeply cruel and oftentimes violent. I developed an early aversion to touch, which I know you noticed, and the only place I could go to escape was somewhere deep in my head, especially after he started coming to my bed. Coitus was perfunctory, painful, and degrading, and became a duty I feared."

Ara felt rage fill her veins on Margot's behalf. She reached for a nightrail and pulled it over her head, moving closer to sit near her. Earlier, she'd wanted to know Margot's story, but now she wasn't sure she could bear it. The idea of this strong, invulnerable woman in any kind of pain was unfathomable.

"Eventually, Percy was conceived," Margot went on softly. "And I was left blessedly alone for nine months until his birth. Waverly entertained himself with his mistress for a few months after that. I refused to have a wet nurse, which angered him beyond belief, but Percy was *my* child." A muscle in her jaw flexed, her shoulders starting to shake slightly as they curved inward, sheltering her body from the threat of some phantom memory.

Ara frowned. "Margot, did he *hit* you?"

219

The flinch was involuntary, her hand curling over her abdomen, but it made rage gather in Ara's veins. That craven bastard! As if remembering who she was and who she had been forced to become out of sheer survival, Margot's chin lifted. "Sometimes."

"I'm so fucking sorry," Ara whispered, wanting to hold her and knowing intuitively that she wouldn't want to be touched right then. Too much of her pain was woven into the tapestry of her skin.

"No more than I," Margot said in an emotionless tone that scraped Ara raw. "I should have left him years ago, but I stayed for Percy's sake. If I'd taken my child and run, I would have been robbing him of his birthright, and if I went alone, he would have had to grow up under the thumb of that rotten man. I had no choice." She met Ara's eyes with a grim expression. "So now you understand why he means so much to me. Percy was...is my entire world."

"I know he is," Ara said quietly.

"He's all I ever had." Margot's face pinched. "Your painting of the dog reminded me of one I used to have. They had the same soulful eyes. One day he was there and the next he was gone. It was a message." Her eyes slid closed. "Waverly took everything I had and then some. I was afraid he'd take Percy from me, too, just because he could."

"Did the marquess get worse?" Ara asked.

The only visible signs of Margot's distress were the white-knuckled fists curled in her lap and a slightly hitched intake of breath. After all, Ara knew she'd had nearly two decades of practice in burying her emotions. "Yes. He was a powerful peer in a society that rewards powerful men. When I was unable to fulfill my duty and provide a requisite spare, his abuse behind closed doors worsened. God, the things he would say...the horrid names he would call me." Her voice went so low that Ara could barely hear her. "One would never expect such a respected marquess could ever treat his wife with such contempt, such derision. I was too frigid, too stupid, too barren." She laughed and the sound was heartbreaking. "*Barren* after Percy. No, I made certain that that bastard would never again get me with child."

"Margot."

Her jaw clenched. "Don't you dare feel pity for me, Ara. I *survived*. I taught myself to collect power and influence wherever I could, and eventually, I was able to fly out of his reach. The Marchioness of Waverly rose to unprecedented heights in the *ton*, one even a marquess wouldn't dare assail. My fame reflected on him, you see. Word could not possibly get out that the marquess was hurting his highly regarded wife. I protected my position ruthlessly until the day he died."

"And after he died?"

She exhaled softly. "I went into mourning for the allotted time, I brought Percy home from boarding school, and I sent Waverly's various mistresses each a small settlement." Ara made a surprised noise, and Margot shrugged. "We were all trying to survive. If he could hurt me, his own wife, who knew what he was doing to them behind closed doors?"

Ara couldn't stop herself if she tried. She flung her arms around Margot's unyielding body until she felt her soften in her embrace. "You are the strongest, bravest, kindest, most astonishing soul I know."

"You would be the first to think so." Margot gave a brittle laugh. "There were people aplenty who hated me, too. But I was always careful to only cut those who deserved it. A boat can only rise upon a rising tide if it is not fraught with holes from within. Women are too divided as it is without the caprices of men tearing us apart."

Ara just held her in silence. There were no words that could erase Margot's past, and despite all her secrets, Ara wanted her just as she was. The problem was that Margot had to accept herself first. She might have respected the woman she'd become in the name of surviving a cruel husband, but respect wasn't love.

Eventually, it was no surprise when Margot's body stiffened and she cleared her throat. "It's late," she said faintly. "I should go."

Ara closed her eyes, feeling the woman in her arms shut herself away with every passing heartbeat. Her self-preservation instincts were simply too strong, too ingrained. "Stay."

"I can't." She turned to kiss Ara's cheek. "But I'll see you soon."

That particular battle had already been lost, long before Ara had even come into the picture. The meticulous and ever controlled Marchioness of Waverly bent for no one.

~

"Oh good Lord, Margot, you must help me!" Honoria shrieked, the high-pitched exclamation nearly making Margot clap her hands to her ears. "Honestly, are you just going to sit there and say nothing?"

Why yes, she was.

She'd tuned out her best friend's whining and grumbling for the better part of the last hour. Apparently, from the gist of it, one of Honoria's talented art protégés had up and absconded to Venice, leaving her high and dry for an upcoming show. Margot couldn't understand the dilemma. Artists were a dime a dozen in Honoria's circles. "So hire another. It's not that difficult. Everyone clamors to be shown at your gallery."

Honoria threw a dramatic hand to her chest. "I *cannot* hire someone with such short notice. No one has any pieces worth of showing the prince, for God's sake." If her voice rose anymore, she'd crack windows. Margot blinked. The *prince*? "Yes, in answer to your obvious question, Bertie will be putting in an appearance. So clearly, I cannot just have any artist off the street. Do be helpful, Margot."

"Do you have any old pieces you can reuse from previous exhibitions? Perhaps borrow from the Royal Academy of Arts?"

Honoria gasped in horror and expelled a loud, disdainful groan. "You know how *they* are. Conventional, boring, and tight-arsed. My gallery focuses on including new artists, especially women, and applauding concept, color, and composition. Those myopic rotters would laud it over me for years to come. No, thank you. What a pity that Miss Vaughn had to go to Paris. Is she back yet, do you know?"

Margot sucked in a breath at the name and instantly quelled the visceral effect it had on her. "How should I know? I am not her keeper."

Shooting her a cynical look, Honoria flung herself into a chair with all the dramatics of a professional thespian. "I don't know how you can be so bloody unmoved. My life as a progressive, groundbreaking gallery owner is positively over."

Margot stifled her scoff of amusement as Honoria proceeded to go into a diatribe of the dearth of acceptable substitutes, the single-minded bias of the Royal Academy, and the fact that her poor independent gallery's reputation would be forever tarnished. As much as Margot adored her best friend, she was truly histrionic sometimes and when Honoria got into moods like these, it was best to simply let her fickle temper run its course. A solution would eventually turn up and she would once more be all smiles.

While nodding at the appropriate intervals, Margot allowed her thoughts to run to more pleasurable things. Namely, one nubile artist in particular. She felt her stomach dip at the way Ara had pressed her up against the wall and taken her so thoroughly that her body had been deliciously sore for days afterward. She covertly touched the pad of a finger to her own lips, recalling those passionate kisses and how easily she'd fallen to pieces under Ara's sensual ministrations.

Now *there* was a lover who could use her tongue.

Flushing, Margot bit her lip and wondered if she'd have time to rush down to Covent Garden before the infernal opera she'd committed to attending that very evening. It would be convenient, considering Ara's proximity to the opera house. A rush filled her veins at the thought of seeing her after nearly a week apart.

Six days ago, a message had arrived at Waverly House, the penmanship so whimsical and quirky that Margot had stared at it for a full minute before reading the correspondence. Ara had taken a short trip to Calais with Sandrine to visit her friend's ailing mother and had been due to return yesterday. While the thought of her with her former lover was not pleasant, Margot could not begrudge her for helping a friend in need. Ara was kind to a fault, and that was one of the things Margot admired about her.

Perhaps Margot could surprise her. Her brain was running wild with a slew of heart-palpitating fantasies, each one hotter than the last, and she was in quite a state when she realized that Honoria was practically bellowing her name.

"I beg your pardon?" Margot said, mortified at being caught daydreaming about seducing her lover of all things. Clearly, Ara was a distraction...a *scintillating* distraction who consumed all her thoughts to the point where she couldn't focus. That would not do.

"For God's sake, Margot!" Honoria chided. "What do you think? It's a good idea, no?" An overzealous, worried green stare narrowed on her. "Why are your cheeks so red? Are you ill?"

"No, I'm just a bit hot," she replied quickly and tried to pick through the bits and pieces she'd gleaned in passing. Something about restructuring and possibly including some familiar pieces from earlier shows. "Yes, of course. Inspirational idea as always. You always have the best ones."

"You're certain?" Honoria said, a tiny frown marring the unblemished skin of her brow. "You're not just saying that because you're my best friend and you don't want me to look like a complete ass in front of the prince and the Royal Academy?"

Margot sniffed and lifted her brow in a supercilious expression that tended to put an end to all discussions. "I think it's a marvelous idea, and of course, I support you in any way that I can. What are best friends for?"

Honoria brightened and clapped her hands. "Well, then that's that then. Crisis averted." All smiles again, she flounced over and pressed two kisses on each cheek before glancing at the clock and letting out a shriek. "Goodness, I'm late for my dress fitting. I am ever so sorry to rush off like this. Will I see you tonight at the opera?"

"Yes," Margot said, waving her away with a laugh.

"I adore you, you know!"

Margot rolled her eyes. "I adore you, too."

She spent the rest of the afternoon going over the correspondence and invitations she had ignored for over a month. The stack was nearly a foot high. Anyone who was anyone in the *ton* hoped for the

Marchioness of Waverly to attend their events. With her patronage and stamp of approval, they were practically guaranteed instant success over the season.

But between thoughts of Ara and scandalous reiterations of their night together, Margot could barely concentrate. Instead of running to Covent Garden like a desperately besotted chit, she took a walk in the small gardens of her residence and then a long, leisurely bath to resettle her nerves. Margot would have much preferred to spend a night in than go to the opera, but she had a role to fulfill.

The Royal Opera was crowded with the opening of a brand new performance, and as Margot made the way to her private box, she was greeted by no less than a dozen people in the foyer and surrounded by those hoping for introductions. She was gracious as always, but for some reason, the pretense started to grate on her nerves. None of these people cared about her...they only cared about what she could do for them. Such was the currency of influence.

And a part of her couldn't stop thinking about how easy it would be to slip away and go to Ara whose apartments were a stone's throw away. She had to be back by now, shouldn't she? And if so, why hadn't she contacted Margot? Had she changed her mind? Met someone else? Contempt for her own weakness bloomed on the heels of her qualms.

Oh stop, you are being absurd.

Steeling herself, Margot inhaled briskly and sank into the guise of the marchioness. Power was just as quickly lost as it was gained in these circles, and while Margot no longer needed to insulate herself against her husband, there was still Percy to think about. In a few years, he would be expected to make an excellent match, and such excellence required focus, fortitude, and an absence of scandal. Mothers would be salivating to present their daughters to the young marquess with a very influential mother.

Her box was situated adjacent to Honoria's, though unlike hers, which only she and Percy used on occasion, the countess's box was as always crowded with a hodge-podge of people from aristocratic circles to the demimonde. Insofar as Margot toed the line of propriety,

Honoria scorned it at every turn. Truly, it was a wonder they were as good friends as they were, but perhaps Margot admired Honoria's honesty when it came to being herself. To say that Honoria relished flaunting her less formal connections to the *ton* was an understatement.

Case in point, Margot immediately recognized a famous Italian ballerina who had notorious lovers in the *ton*, several well-known actors, as well as a popular playwright and novelist she'd met before, Mr. Wilde, and his much younger friend and purported lover, Lord Alfred Douglas, known to all as Bosie. The Marquess of Queensberry, Bosie's father, had been a close friend of her late husband's. No surprise considering how similar in temperament both men had been —volatile and vicious. At least Queensberry's former wife Sybil had had the wherewithal to divorce him a handful of years ago for adultery.

If only Margot had been so lucky.

After blowing a kiss to Honoria holding court in her own box, Margot took a seat and scanned the packed hall. Opening nights were always well attended and tonight was no exception. Almost every single seat was taken, and every box filled. There was a small commotion next door as someone else arrived, and greetings began anew, but Margot did not turn. Honoria's box never lacked for company.

"Miss Vaughn, glad you could make it on such short notice," Honoria trilled and Margot froze, her entire body heating and chilling at the name. Honoria went on to make the introductions and then gave a small laugh. "And of course, you've met Lady Waverly, who is just over there."

Margot canted her head, keeping her face vigilantly composed. In a place like this, people were always watching like hawks and waiting for the smallest spatter of gossip. "Miss Vaughn," she greeted politely.

Amber eyes bored into hers, a tiny frown settling between Ara's eyebrows, and Margot flinched at the confusion she saw in that transparent gaze. Guilt sluiced through her. Surely Ara would understand that she could not be as cavalier as Honoria, at least not in such a public venue. She had a reputation to maintain.

"How are you, Lady Waverly?" Ara asked softly.

"Well, thank you." Margot turned away before her eyes could give away the storm of emotions erupting in her belly. Ara was dressed in an emerald gown that made her irises gleam gold. Tendrils of bronze hair curled into her temples as if in defiance of the pins attempting to hold the wayward curls in place. Margot's fingers itched to bury themselves into the silken mass and she clenched them tightly in her lap.

"Perhaps you should join Lady Waverly, Miss Vaughn," Honoria suggested, devilry in her tone. "Since you're already acquainted, and she has so many free seats."

"Alas, Percival and his friends will be joining me shortly," Margot said quickly, nipping that in the bud. "Do enjoy the show, Miss Vaughn."

Honoria's green eyes widened with surprise and not a little disappointment, but Margot pushed her friend's judgment from her mind. She dared not look at Ara, sensing the waves of hurt and bitterness emanating from her. She'd find a way to make it up to her later.

But as the curtains on the stage rose, and the play began, it was almost impossible to concentrate with Ara's eyes boring into her. Even when Percy arrived, fashionably late as usual, her body felt restless and on edge.

Before intermission, she sensed, rather than saw, when Ara stood and slipped out of Honoria's box.

"Excuse me," Margot mumbled and rushed into the corridor in a fit of dismay and desperation, searching for a flash of those emerald-green skirts. Had Ara gone left or right? Chasing the faintest hint of vanilla in the air, Margot went right. But when she rounded the nearest bend, there was no one there.

Suddenly, a hand darted out from a hidden alcove and dragged her into the shadowy space. "Goodness, what on—"

A warm, furious female body pressed her up against the wall, cutting off her breathless words, and that heady scent of toasted vanilla filled her nostrils. "Am I not blue-blooded enough for you, my lady?" Ara asked, palms dragging up handfuls of Margot's hem. Her core clenched on air as those hands delved beneath silk and lace, and climbed. "Am I only good enough for one thing? To paint your portrait and to bring you pleasure where no one else can see?"

"N...no," Margot gasped, but words failed her when slender fingers unerringly found the slit in her drawers and hovered over her damp sex. She'd been wet the minute Ara had arrived.

"Shall I touch you here?" Ara whispered.

"Yes," she gasped. Ara's teeth teased her earlobe, a fingertip penetrating her entrance before curling wickedly in a come-hither motion that made Margot's core clench with desire. Desperate for depth, for friction, for *anything*, she mindlessly shuttled her hips forward. "Please."

"Please what? Is this what you want me for, *Lady Waverly*?" Ara's voice was guttural, hurt and fury saturating her words as two fingers sank into her drenched core. "To be polite and impersonal in public, but fuck you until you can't walk in private?"

Margot's eyes rolled back at Ara's crass words, more liquid warmth flooding her folds. Her hands scrabbled at Ara's shoulders, her knees barely holding her up. She was already so soaked just from Ara's presence that her body offered no resistance when she withdrew and added another finger. They both groaned at the snug fit that toyed with *just* this side of pain.

"God, Ara," Margot said on a strangled sob.

"No *Miss Vaughn* when my fingers are buried knuckle-deep inside of you?" she hissed and covered her lips in a rough open-mouthed kiss that was much too short for Margot's liking. "Fuck, you're so wet for me. Were you sitting there in that box imagining my mouth on you? Imagining my tongue *inside* you? No, don't bother to answer. I *know*."

The noises Margot's body made beneath her skirts as she rode Ara's hand were obscene, and all she could do was hold on for dear life as those fingers stretched her to capacity. If anyone in that theater knew that the Marchioness of Waverly was being ruthlessly fingered in an alcove by a woman ten years her junior, the gossip would be untenable. And yet, she stayed right where she was, rocking her hips and desperate for the release that only Ara could deliver.

Perversely, Ara's movements slowed, fingers pulling out to their very tips, and her tongue swirled around the shell of Margot's ear. "Do you like this? Do you like me taking you in secret? Do you want to come?"

"Y...yes."

Those wicked fingers resumed their slow slide, making her whimper with relief and then frustration as that measured, leisurely pace continued. She bucked her hips to no avail. "Who do you need, Margot?" Ara whispered.

Thighs trembling, she swallowed and threw her head back into the wall. "I need you! Is that what you want to hear?"

With a growl of gratification, Ara relented and gave her what she wanted, working her body into a fever pitch with thrusts of those long fingers, punctuated by maddening swipes of her thumb. When the cataclysm broke, Margot bit her lip so hard to stop from screaming that she tasted blood. Her body slumped as Ara's fingers withdrew from her pulsating center.

Panting, she stared when Ara brought her glistening hand up between them.

"Suck," she commanded, and helplessly, Margot obeyed, taking the wet digits into her mouth and tasting her spent essence on them.

Margot refused to feel an ounce of shame for what Ara was making her do. Perhaps she deserved it. She could barely see Ara's eyes in the gloom, but her ferocity hadn't lessened. In fact, she was still vibrating with it, all biting passion and wrathful lust, a vengeful goddess exacting retribution. Wanting to calm that wild look in Ara's eyes, Margot lapped slowly, imagining her mouth somewhere else... performing a hushed penance there in that small alcove.

With a soft hiss, Ara tugged her hand away and stepped back as if to leave. Margot floundered to explain. "Ara, wait, please. I...you know that I...that Percy..."

They stared at each other in silence. "I know, Lady Waverly. Enjoy your evening."

Chapter Seven

A ra had known exactly what she was getting into. The Marchioness of Waverly had not lied. If the fault lay with anyone, it was with Ara for assuming that her lover and the woman she'd opened her home and heart to would not treat her as though she were nothing more than a stranger in the street. The hurt she'd felt at the opera when Margot had been so excessively cold had brewed and bubbled in her veins until Ara hadn't been able to bear it any longer.

She had known that Margot would follow...but what had happened next in that alcove had been out of both their control.

In hindsight, she shouldn't have done it.

The act of taking Margot so boldly and in a public place had been meant to punish and subdue. She'd made her beg and then clean her own release off Ara's fingers just because she could. Though Margot hadn't complained or protested, Ara felt regret all the same. Intimacy should never be used as a weapon, at least, not without explicit consent. She understood that more than anyone, given her own feelings on the matter. She'd just been so gutted by the callous rejection that she'd reacted badly.

It was no excuse, but Ara was sorry.

So much so that only three days later, she'd fully intended to take a hackney to Mayfair, but out of an abundance of caution given Margot's cagey response at the opera house, had decided to pay one of the street lads to deliver a letter with a written apology instead. Thankfully, she'd had the address from Lady Rawdon for Waverly House before leaving for Paris.

A day had passed, and then two and three, and Ara had despaired of ever getting a response. Until today.

With a ragged exhale, Ara stared down at the reply that had just been delivered. She opened the envelope and her index finger traced the no-nonsense handwriting, a far cry from her own flowery calligraphy. Margot's script was as spare as the meaning in the note.

There's nothing to apologize for. Nothing happened that I did not want. But I think we both knew that this could not work.
~ Cordially, M of W.

WHAT HAD SHE EXPECTED? SWEET NOTHINGS? HEARTFELT confessions? Words of devotion?

The Marchioness of Waverly was capable of none of those things.

And that was who had signed this letter. *Cordially* so.

A tear splashed onto the parchment, followed by another. In a fit of anger, Ara crumpled the correspondence into a ball and threw it in the hearth, watching as it disintegrated to nothing in the flames, just like the pitiful organ behind her ribs. She swiped bitterly at her leaking eyes—that was the downside of being such an intuitive artist —she *felt* everything much too deeply.

Well, so be it. Ara had made her choices, placed her bets, and this was the end result. She could not change someone who did not want to be changed or love someone who had made themselves impervious to emotions.

But as the days turned into weeks, no matter how much it hurt, Ara could not bring herself to regret her time with Margot, even if it was fleeting. She would leave some of the happiest weeks of her life behind with a bruised heart and a brain full of memories. But eventually, the pain would fade and the good hours would eclipse the bad.

Thank God Lady Rawdon had taken all the paintings off Ara's hands a month ago. She could not have borne seeing them. And Lord knew she hadn't been able to go into her studio for weeks without thinking of Margot propped on the chaise with those cool, storm-blue eyes and the miserly, tight-lipped smile that never ceased to make Ara's belly tighten.

She sucked in a sharp breath.

But she had to go back downstairs sometime. And what better way was there to exorcize one's demons or to find a new purpose than with a blank canvas? Before she could change her mind, Ara raced downstairs and flung open the door to her studio. It was just as she'd left it...easel and supplies ready and prepped for whenever her muse would return.

The answer was never, but art didn't always require inspiration.

Sometimes, it required sheer tenacity.

For hours, Ara painted and painted, canvas after canvas, all filled with bold color and brutal slashes. When her paintbrushes started losing bristles from the force of her strokes, she discarded them and painted with her hands. The pieces were a departure from sensory reality, wild slashes of lines, light, and color, nothing but a visual depiction of her battered emotions, but eventually the compositions changed, going from chaotic and angry energy to something spent and much less fraught.

When she had calmed sufficiently, Ara went to her water closet and washed the stripes of color off her hands. Her clothes were a mess, but there was still one more painting inside of her. Searching out a new set of paint brushes from her supplies, she refilled her paints, found a large canvas and got to work. Ara didn't think...she let her hands move, the contours of the painting flowing like a river, moving with her breath and each beat of her heart.

It was a final love letter...a goodbye.

And when she was finished, many hours later—or was it days?—

Ara collapsed into a heap, staring up at the only woman she'd ever loved. The painting was created from memory, and instead of the subject sitting on a chaise or a lounge, she lay on her stomach in bed, turned away from the viewer, the corner of a poppy-red satin sheet draped over the voluptuous arch of her hips.

Brown hair tumbled down the creamy length of her back, those beloved freckles playing peek-a-boo with the glossy strands. Lush, tapered legs, topped by the soft curves of her buttocks just visible from beneath the sheet, were crossed at the ankles. One arm was stretched out over the mattress, fingers extended as though reaching for someone who wasn't in the painting. Wishful thinking on the artist's part, perhaps.

Because the woman in this painting did not need anyone.

"My God, that is outstanding." The soft awe in the exclamation had Ara squinting blearily toward the door, where Lady Rawdon stood with her mouth ajar. She peered past the countess to see if she was accompanied by anyone, disappointment filling her to realize there was no one else there. "I came alone," Lady Rawdon said, as if she could read Ara's expression.

"How is she?" Ara croaked. There was no need to explain who *she* was.

Lady Rawdon smiled sadly. "About the same as you, I suspect, though she has thrown herself into a dozen new charitable endeavors with uncommon vengeance." The countess waved an arm to the rest of the paintings that lined the walls. "She doesn't have this outlet." She frowned and veered past the rags and rubbish that cluttered the floor. "Have you eaten or slept since you started?"

"No. I couldn't stop."

Lady Rawdon nodded. "Why don't you get cleaned up and let me make you something to eat?"

Ara's brows rose. "You know how to cook?"

A wry laugh left the countess. "I'm not completely incapable, you know. I can fend for myself when the need arises. And besides, I wasn't always a countess." She smiled, eyes dancing. "A very long time ago, I was an opera singer."

Ara let herself be led upstairs and watched with some disbelief as said singer-turned-countess drew her a bath and ushered her into it while she disappeared presumably to the kitchen downstairs. The cook Ara employed was recovering from illness, but the parlor maid would help the lady find what she needed. By the time Ara was finished, she was limp and exhausted, but a mouthwatering mushroom omelet lay on a plate at the small table near the window.

She took a tentative bite. "This is delicious."

"Don't sound so surprised," Lady Rawdon said drily.

"Thank you," Ara said, after devouring the simple meal.

The countess leaned back in her chair, green eyes calculating. "I know a way you can thank me, if you like. Allow me to add those new pieces downstairs to my collection. I have a grand concept for the whole series. And before you ask whether I have permission from Margot, I do. She thinks it's a brilliant idea."

Ara frowned—it wasn't as though she *knew* the marchioness. In fact, the last month had proven without a doubt that she didn't, and if Margot wanted those paintings to be seen, who was Ara to argue?

Dear Lord, Margot was going to *die*.

Everywhere she turned, her body was on bold, salacious display, not that anyone truly had any inkling that it was her. *She* knew, however, and the gallery was packed with dozens of eyes scrutinizing every line, every curve, and every *imperfection*.

Oh, she was going to murder Honoria with her bare hands.

The exhibition had opened without a hitch, and yes, Bertie had put in an appearance. Honoria had solved her problem as expected. Only Margot had been in for a complete shock when she'd taken in the special exhibit of a talented new artist.

This entire room was an exposition in itself, devoted to fifteen paintings entitled *The Fall of Venus*. Unlike the Royal Academy, which crammed all artists together, Honoria tended to use the spaces to showcase individual works. All fifteen framed pieces took up space on three of the walls of a private room in the west gallery: seven on one, seven on the opposite, and a lone portrait on the last. The seven on the left Margot knew...she'd sat for every single one.

The seven on the right were new...chaotic and compositional opposites of the portraits they faced.

And the showpiece in the middle...

Good *God*. Her deuced *buttocks* were on display. Again, not that anyone would guess that they were hers. Margot's body felt inexplicably hot and she snapped open her fan. She hadn't posed for that one, but clearly the artist had taken some creative liberty. There was no way in heaven she looked like *that*. While all the other paintings were numbered instead of titled, this piece was simply called M.

"Remarkable, aren't they?" a voice beside her said, and Margot turned to see an older, well-dressed woman she instantly recognized as the Dowager Duchess of Culver. Margot kept her mouth from falling open. She'd never conversed with the woman, but she was known for being a denizen of the *ton* as well as an art connoisseur.

She attempted a shallow curtsy. "Your Grace," she murmured.

The duchess lifted a lorgnette to her eyes. "I do not know this artist, but her portraiture is really quite exquisite, rather Rubenesque in style," she said, peering closer before focusing on the opposite side of the room. "And those over there are so innovative. The stark contrast of such a departure from realism when juxtaposed with the opposing portraits is just prodigious. Lady Rawdon has outdone herself in the story she has told with these pieces."

Margot blinked. Was it a story? She'd been so horrified about the discovery that she hadn't even taken in the meaning behind the new additions, but now that she looked, each of them corresponded to one of the earlier portraits, the wildness of light and color depicting the artist's frame of mind, a symbolic expression of the unconscious.

"Yes, yes, you're quite right, Lady Waverly," the duchess said, making Margot realize she'd murmured the last thought out loud. "It's as though they reflect the descent of the painter into some degree of madness, don't you think?"

Madness or lust. Likely some combination of the two.

"Ah, here is the artist's name," the duchess said, peering into the small pamphlet she carried. "A Miss Ara Vaughn. I daresay I have never heard of her before, but she's certainly someone to be watched with very great interest."

"I agree," Margot said weakly, her mouth going dry at the jarring sound of a name she hadn't heard in weeks. "Please excuse me, Your Grace. Enjoy the rest of the exhibit."

Margot's stomach dipped unsteadily. She'd been so caught up in the subject matter of the paintings that she hadn't thought about their creator. The blood in her veins ran cold. Heavens, was Ara here? Honoria hadn't said so, but then again that sneaky wench hadn't told her about this special exhibit either. Margot hadn't seen Ara in weeks, not for any lack of longing. Her willpower had been weak, and she had found herself being driven to Covent Garden several times before she'd forced Farrows to return home mid-journey.

Ending things so abruptly had nearly killed her, but it had been for the best.

For Percy's sake. Or at least that was what she'd told herself.

Someone behind her jostled her to enter the room, and she moved out of the way. "I heard the artist will be in the dining room later on," a woman said to her friend. "Isn't that lovely? I cannot wait to ask her about her inspiration. Who do you suppose 'M' is?"

"Muse, perhaps," the other replied and then giggled. "Or maybe the name of some scandalous lover."

Margot nearly choked and she hurried out of the room before her infamous composure absolutely failed her. She needed to leave this instant before she did something ridiculous like scream or swoon. But as she rushed toward the gallery exit, she was stalled by the very woman she'd cheerily planned to murder.

"*You!*"

Honoria's green eyes widened in dramatic horror. "What did I do?"

Conscious of not making a scene, Margot dragged her best friend to an unobtrusive corner. "How could you?"

"How could I what?" Honoria repeated with genuine confusion.

Margot pointed in the direction from which she'd come and bit out a furious whisper, "*That.* In the west gallery." She lowered her voice to an inaudible hiss. "*Me.*"

Honoria's eyes rounded comically. "You told me to!"

"I did not!" she shot back.

"I assure you, you did! You said it was a marvelous idea, and you'd always support me. I didn't do this without your permission, Margot. And Miss Vaughn agreed to the others."

They faced off against each other in righteous indignation. "Why on earth would I even agree to such an asinine thing?" But even as Margot bit out the question, the echoes of a conversation came back to her: *marvelous idea, as always.*

She'd been fantasizing about Ara and had pretended that she'd heard whatever it was Honoria had asked.

Fuck, fuck, fuck.

The oaths in her head were like thunderclaps.

"I thought you were talking about something else," Margot whispered lamely. "I didn't... Gracious, not this." Her words started to shake, her body following soon after.

Honoria took hold of her arm. "Margot, breathe," her voice urgent and low. "No one knows that it is you, and surely you must know that Ara would never betray your confidence. She's in—" She broke off and turned away, running a palm over her face. "Look, I can tell one of the footmen to close that room. The paintings will be down by tomorrow, if that's what you wish. You're my best friend, Margot. You're more important to me than any of this. What do you want me to do?"

Did she want that room closed? The answer was an unequivocal yes. But was that her irrational fear speaking? Or was it something deeper? Was it that she hated how free she was in those portraits and it was a freedom that could never, *ever* be hers in this lifetime? Or was it because Ara's chaotic feelings in the surreal, allusive pieces were the exact reflection of hers. The madness wasn't the artist's...it was the muse, who had fallen irrevocably, stupidly in love.

Margot let out a shuddering breath.

She wasn't brave enough to fight for Ara...but she'd be damned if she wouldn't stand up for what those pieces of art represented. A *love story*.

"Leave them," she said softly.

Honoria peered at her with concern. "Are you sure?"

"I've never been more certain of anything in my life."

THE EXHIBITION WAS UNQUESTIONABLY ONE OF HONORIA'S greatest accomplishments for her small, independent gallery, lauded by the public, by her peers, and even Prince Bertie himself, who had proclaimed the identity of *Venus* to be one of his past mistresses because he recognized the hair and the freckles. Margot had laughed quietly into her glass of champagne.

Good thing one could always depend on Bertie's sexual intrigues in a pinch.

She remained in the gallery, perusing the rest of the art when the reception began, knowing that Ara would be there. Honoria had confirmed her attendance, and Margot didn't quite know if her heart could survive a second injury this evening. By the time she'd made the rounds for a third interval, getting something different each time from the pieces on display, most of the guests had already left, but she would stay until the end. Honoria would like that, she knew.

Without realizing it, her feet had led her back to *The Fall of Venus*.

The room was empty except for a tall and very familiar young man, staring at the seven pieces to the right. Margot held her breath for a long second and then exhaled. "Percy," she said, walking toward him. "I didn't know you would be here."

He glanced down fondly at her. "I wanted to support Aunt Honoria."

Nerves flickered in Margot's belly at her son's uncharacteristically pensive silence. He was normally so exuberant, saying the first thing that came to mind. God, had he recognized her as the artist's model? Had he seen that final painting? Should she *tell* him? Her mind was reeling with doubts and indecision. He knew her well enough to guess, and the truth was, she didn't want him to be hurt by any of this. "Percy—"

"Miss Vaughn is very talented, isn't she?" he interrupted softly. "Her use of color and shading is rather exceptional."

Margot swallowed. "It is. She is."

They stood in silence, walking from each of the seven pieces. "I can't imagine ever being in love, and feeling this much," he murmured. "Every one of these paintings makes me feel like I'm intruding on something exceedingly private. Like I'm seeing the inside of a soul."

"She's an evocative artist," Margot said carefully.

"Who loves hard."

For a second, she thought she had misheard the last and heard him say *who loves you*, but then her son was staring right at her. His hands fell gently to her shoulders.

"Mother, I am only going to say this once because you are a stubborn, infuriating, incredibly resilient woman, and I am so proud to call you my mother, but you need to get the hell out of your own way."

She stared up at him. "I beg your pardon?"

Blue-gray eyes glowed with affection. "Life is too short to mince words. But if someone loved me the way this artist loved whomever that is in these paintings, I would not hesitate for a deuced second."

This boy. Her heart felt too big for her chest. "Percy, you don't understand—"

"I'm sixteen, Mother, not ten. I am a man." He grasped her hands and squeezed gently. "And the truth is, I am a man in a society that diminishes women for no good reason...other than stupidity." Her son grinned. "Trust me when I say that I will be fine, no matter what gossip bubbles up in the *ton*. I could gallivant naked through the middle of Mayfair and be forgiven in a week. I will eventually choose a charming partner who loves me for me, which is all anyone can ever ask for." Percy pulled her into an embrace. "And I want that more than anything for you."

"But she's—"

"But nothing. Love is worth every inch of the fight, no matter how bloody you get." Margot hadn't even realized she was crying until she felt gentle fingers swipe the wetness away as her proud, compassionate son gazed gently down at her. "You have to put yourself in the round to even have a chance because if you don't, you've already lost. This is your time, Mother. How will you use it?"

She had an idea...but first, she had to hug her son.

"I love you, Percy," she said, and reached up to embrace him. "You are and will always be the best thing in my life."

He grinned, folding his arms about her. "Love you, too," Percy said, his voice low and full of amusement. "Now, not to ruin a rather pleasant moment, but we might want to think about hiring an excellent alienist to deal with all the emotional suffering that seeing my mother in the nude has wrought."

Her cheeks flamed as he backed away, chuckling, hands in the air.

Oh, she loved him so.

In a daze, Margot sat on the upholstered bench in the middle of the room and let out a sigh. Life certainly had an interesting way of turning out. She'd agreed to do that very first painting to prove that she was living life on her own terms and had spent six more learning about who she was. It had only taken her adolescent son to put things into perspective.

Heart in her eyes, Margot stared up at the last painting of the woman lying in that bed. Any adult with a brain would recognize the state of pure happiness...the delicious laxness of the limbs, the languidness of the pose, the rumpled state of the bed. The woman in question was indisputably *present* in that moment.

Thriving in her own imperfect skin.

And Margot knew exactly *who* that hand was reaching for. She felt her own fingers curl as though wrapping around an imagined palm. Percy wasn't wrong. Love was worth the fight...even at the cost of one's reputation and one's pride. She just had to be brave.

With a soft laugh, she turned and froze at the woman propped against the doorjamb. She was dressed in a pair of trousers and tails, her coat open at the front with a gorgeous silvery blue waistcoat that was designed like a corset on bold display. Hands thrust into her pockets, she looked confident, powerful, and too desirable for words.

Ara.

"Nice waistcoat," Margot said.

"It reminded me of your eyes."

Margot's lashes fluttered at the sound of that sweet, lush voice that wrought havoc on her senses. By God, she was stunning, all lean height, unruly rust-brown curls, and huge amber eyes. She'd lost weight, Margot noticed, and purple shadows congregated beneath her eyes, but she was still the most beautiful woman Margot had ever seen.

This was it. This was *her* time. Suddenly, Margot's chest felt ten sizes too small. She smiled, her lips wobbling as if they could barely do justice to the emotions that brewed within her veins. "You've been busy, I see."

"I have," Ara said. "Do you like them?"

"They're extraordinary." *You're extraordinary.*

Ara shrugged. "They're us."

They stared at each other, only a handful of feet separating them, and yet that paltry distance felt like an ocean. Margot rolled her lower lip between her teeth and Ara's eyes flared, the sunbursts of her irises going dark.

"Were you on your way out?" Ara asked, and Margot exhaled. That wasn't what Ara meant. She was really asking if Margot meant to stay, if she *wanted* to stay.

"No," she whispered. "I was waiting for you."

"Good."

With one foot, Ara kicked the door to the room closed, the latch clicking shut and dousing them in darkness but for the small lamps showcasing each wall. Margot didn't know who moved first, but suddenly, they were in each other's arms, a tangle of limbs and lips glued together as they devoured each other. It felt oddly poetic—with the beginning of their tumultuous story surrounding them, but she didn't care. Ara was in her arms.

Ara was in her arms.

She reared back, panting, lips bruised and soul bright. "I missed you," she said.

"I missed you, too." Ara laughed, eyes glancing around. "As you can tell from the rather rough state of my heart."

Margot's fingers slipped into the curls at Ara's nape, her thumbs grazing the hollows of those lean cheeks and the sensuous curve of her upturned mouth. "I thought what I wrote in that letter was true, that it couldn't work, but I realized only later that I was afraid. I was too much of a coward to *try* to make it work because of what I stood to lose." She exhaled and met that dazzling golden gaze that held so much love and warmth, she almost stumbled. "But what I stand to lose is nothing compared to losing you."

"What about your reputation?" Ara whispered. "The life you've built? Percy?"

"Percy told me to pluck up, in much nicer words." Margot laughed and aligned her mouth with Ara's, kissing each impossibly soft corner before replying. "The only life I'm interested in is one with you. I'm falling in love with you, Ara."

Ara grinned, that beloved smile so radiant that stars glowed in her eyes. "Say that again."

Margot tugged on a curl with affection. "You're supposed to say it back, you know."

"Oh, I intend to," Ara teased, her palms sliding around to Margot's hips. "In fact, if I have my way, in about five minutes flat, I'll be screaming my devotion to the high heavens from my knees."

Her core clenched at the dark promise in those words. "Is that so?"

Ara winked, that stare now full of wickedness. "Ever fucked in a gallery, love?"

"Ara!"

"Bloody hell, I love when you say my name like it's a benediction you simply can't contain." A hot mouth blanketed hers, the taste of Ara like a sip of the most decadent brandy, sweet, tart, and addictive. "Besides, I am the artist, after all, and it's my prerogative to paint." A gloved finger danced over the swells of her décolletage. "On my favorite kind of canvas."

Margot's eyes shot wide as said tongue licked a hot stripe down her throat.

Oh. *Oh.*

"Everyone will know what we are doing in here," she whispered in a scandalized tone, while Ara walked her back until the backs of her knees met the velvet bench at the center. She sat, staring up as Ara removed her gloves with painstaking slowness, the reveal of each slender finger almost an erotic show, because Margot had intimate knowledge of what those clever fingers were capable of. Her mouth went dry at the ravenous, resolute glint in her lover's eyes even as other parts of her went unspeakably wet.

"Almost everyone has already left, but you can be quiet, can't you, Margot?" Ara purred, hands going to her silk cravat. "Or will I have to put this over your mouth?"

Margot's heartbeat thundered between her ears as she gulped. She pressed her thighs together, but there was no hope for it. There wasn't a snowball's chance in hell that she was going to hold a single thing back. Not now. Not ever.

Her lips tipped up into a wicked smile. "Do your worst, I dare you."

Epilogue
ONE YEAR LATER

"Have I told you today how much I idolize you?"

Margot stared fondly at the love of her life, panting in a heap beside her, curls plastered to that beloved face as she stretched fully awake. Morning sunlight from the windows caught Ara's bronze hair and made it shimmer with wine and cinnamon-colored lights. She was growing it out and those titian curls now kissed her dainty collarbones.

"That's because I made you come twice in ten minutes."

"Well, there's that," Ara said with a huff. "But you know that only happens so quickly because of the connection we have, don't you? It isn't like that for *everyone*."

Margot propped herself up to her elbow with a thoughtful look, as though pondering the question. "It isn't? I thought multiple orgasms were the standard. Perhaps I need a broader basis for comparison."

"There will be nothing of the sort, you minx," Ara growled and threw herself over Margot, crushing her to the crumpled sheets. "It absolutely is not the standard and you know it. It's not my fault I'm utterly weak for you." She sighed, hair tumbling down as she lowered her head for a kiss. "Or that you've dragged me under the spell of Blazing Quim."

A choked laugh burst out of Margot. "You did not just call me that."

"I didn't call *you* that." A hand slid between them to brush intimately against her. "I called *this* that."

Giving Ara's bottom lip a playful nip, Margot rolled them over. "Well, if we're going the route of nicknames, then I find it categorically unfair that you don't possess one. It's high time we correct that unacceptable slight." She kissed her way down Ara's sternum, pausing to pay homage to each of her brown-tipped perfect breasts, before continuing down her taut, shivering abdomen until she was settled between her thighs. "Now, what have we here?"

She stroked down the dark bronze tuft with her palm, making Ara's hips jolt. "Responsive Quim? No, much too wordy." She leaned in, inhaling that sweetly seductive fragrance, and blew gently on the damp flesh from her earlier release. "You always smell like toasted vanilla. Perhaps something along those lines?" She kissed the creases on either side, running her nose over the satiny flesh. "Feels like velvet."

"Margot." Her name was a breathless whine.

"Yes, my dove?" Without warning, she licked from the bottom to the top with the tip of her tongue, making Ara start to quiver. Her skin was *so* impossibly soft, so silken and wet and delicious that Margot simply had to do it again. And again. "Succulent, luscious," she whispered. "So many adjectives, not enough time." Margot slid a finger inside and Ara instantly clamped down. "Such a greedy little thing."

Margot glanced up, meeting Ara's dilated golden eyes, her face tight with desire and strain as Margot shuttled in and out. "I'm close," she whimpered. Oh, Margot was aware. She knew Ara's body as well as she knew her own. She hid her grin and shifted down to press slow kisses down her left thigh to her knee. "Margot, where are you going? I said I was close."

"I know, but finding the right name takes focus. I can't have you ruining it *my* creative process because you have a hair-trigger response." She stifled a laugh. "Hair-Trigger Quim?"

Ara gave half growl, half giggle. "No. Absolutely not, you wicked, wicked woman. I have half a mind to finish myself off."

"Do that and face the consequences." Margot hummed. "I don't have to remind you of what happened the last time you defied me?" Ara's body gave a visceral jerk as they both recalled the memory of how Margot had kept her on the edge for what had felt like hours, dragging out her pleasure to such lengths that a sobbing, mindless Ara had soaked the bed linens.

"Fine." Panting, Ara flung an arm over her face. "Only because I need to be able to actually function today. Some of us have to work, you know."

"I do so enjoy being a kept woman," Margot murmured, resuming her journey on the other leg.

As expected, Ara's fame had only grown following Honoria's exhibition. From time to time, she held exhibits of her paintings exclusively at the Rawdon Gallery, and Honoria had become her official art dealer. Her work was always in great demand. Margot had converted an entire wing in the house she'd bought in Essex after the sale of the unentailed Mayfair residence, making sure Ara's studio had the best light. Percy was off on a two-year long Grand Tour and hadn't any need of it.

Their life wasn't an easy one. The gossip mill churned relentlessly, speculating about the Marchioness of Waverly's rapid exit from high society, based mostly on conjecture. She and Ara had giggled at the outlandish theories in the newssheets. One claimed that she had remarried a commoner and couldn't face her former lofty circles because of her diminished status. Another declared she had absconded with a footman to escape the scandal of ruination. A third said she'd been kidnapped by a former debutante whom she'd given the cut direct and was being held for an enormous ransom.

Her personal favorite, however, was that her son, the marquess, had banished her to the country for being so controlling and trying to marry him off to the highest bidder. As if she could stop Percy from falling stupidly in love every ten minutes with someone new. Broken hearts of all persuasions lay in his handsome and much-too-charming wake.

Thankfully, though, the wagging tongues of the *ton* always found some new intrigue to garner their interest, and after a while, the Marchioness of Waverly and her flight from London had become yesterday's news. She and Ara lived happily and quietly, with only eyes for each other, and their love had only grown more with each passing day.

"I love you, you know," Margot said softly.

Ara peered down at her. "I love you, too, but I would absolutely love you more if you weren't such a terrible tease."

Margot snorted at the petulant tone. "You are uncommonly single-minded."

"And you haven't lost your ruthless streak in the least. I want to come."

"How about impatient or irascible?" With a soft chuckle, Margot relented and resumed her efforts at the compelling juncture of Ara's thighs, stoking the embers into an inferno in seconds. She lifted her lips from the wet bliss below her. "Blazing Quim, the second?"

"Margot, for the love of all things holy—!"

Her laughter filled the room and as she brought the love of her life to shuddering, swift completion, she knew exactly what Ara had meant earlier. It was like this between them because of love. Ara knew her heart, knew her body and soul. And vice versa.

Margot crawled back up and gathered a sated, happy Ara into her arms. When she was a little girl, she'd always dreamed of the fairytale... of the handsome prince, magical ponies, and a magnificent castle to call her own. She wanted to love and be loved. She yearned to find that elusive happy ever after. But that was a storied myth, or perhaps it was simply a *story* that had needed a new ending to suit its own singular characters.

Because after a rough start, Margot's wishes had come true, albeit with a few minor adjustments. Instead of a castle, she owned a charming manor house near the shore. Instead of ponies, she discovered paintings held more magic. And instead of a prince, she'd found a stunning, talented, clever, and witty princess who fit her fairytale ending perfectly.

Like the most exquisite glass slipper.

"You're my shoe," she whispered.

Ara snorted and wrapped her arms around her. "Darling, I think my Super Quim has addled your mind."

"That is definitely *not* the name."

"I think it is, and I think you're jealous that yours only has fire powers."

They bickered until Ara silenced her with a kiss, and then after several more heated kisses followed, Margot could only sigh with utter happiness.

Sometime later, Ara stroked her cheek. "Margot?"

"Yes, love."

"You're my shoe, too. We're a matched pair."

Indeed, they were. There would always be room for what they had, for who they were, and what they shared. No one could take that from them. Love, after all, was all-encompassing, inclusive, and infinite. It didn't exist between lines or allowed itself to be defined by narrow social expectations. It didn't exclude or diminish. Love shifted and grew, and became whatever it needed to be. Love made space for everyone.

And this was *theirs*.

HAPPY EVERYONE AFTER
THE END

Author's Note

My heroines are inspired by real LGBTQIA+ people in historical times. Catherine Hilda Duleep Singh, born in 1871, was a Sikh princess who was both a woman of color in Queen Victoria's court as well as a lesbian who lived with her governess and partner until she died. Isadora Duncan, born in 1877 and arguably the trailblazer of interpretive dance, was a dancer and feminist who did not believe in traditional roles for women and was open about her bisexuality as well as the notion of "free love." She had two children out of wedlock.

In England, it was not illegal for women to engage in lesbian or bisexual acts, but in 1885, the Labouchere Amendment criminalized sex acts between men. This act led to the imprisonment of the writer and playwright Oscar Wilde, who was in a relationship with Lord Alfred Douglas, the Marquess of Queensberry's youngest son. Both men make cameos in this story. His father was furious, but Douglas claimed in a letter to his mother, "You cannot do anything against the power of my affection for Oscar Wilde and his for me." Wilde, a popular figure and huge patron of art and literature, was put on trial for "gross indecency" in 1895 and sentenced to 2 years of hard labor, leading to his death in Paris 3 years after he was released. He was only 46. In a more inclusive world, Oscar Wilde might have been spared such a tragic end.

A quick note on Lady Rawdon's gallery, which was inspired by a real gallery of the time called the Grosvenor Gallery, founded in 1877 by Sir Coutts Lindsay and Lady Caroline Blanche Elizabeth Fitzroy and located at 135 New Bond Street in London. The gallery was known for its unique displays as well as its unconventional art, particularly by women. Of over 1000 artists shown during its history (1877-1890), 25% were female. Interestingly enough, Oscar Wilde reviewed the gallery's opening exhibition, and praised its unique arrangement and forward-thinking style.

About the Author

AMALIE HOWARD is a *USA Today* and *Publishers Weekly* bestselling author. *Always Be My Duchess* was one of Cosmopolitan Magazine's 30 Best Romance Books of 2022 and *The Beast of Beswick* was one of Oprah Daily's 24 Best Historical Romance Novels to Read. She is also the author of several critically acclaimed, award-winning young adult novels. Her books have been featured in The Hollywood Reporter, Entertainment Weekly, and Seventeen Magazine. When she's not writing, she can usually be found reading, being the president of her one-woman Harley Davidson motorcycle club, or power-napping. She lives in Colorado with her family.

Visit her at www.amaliehoward.com

Werewolves Save a Kitten

A WERE-GEEKS NOVELLA

KATHY LYONS

CHAPTER 1
It's Raining What?

Yordan Basch had ten seconds warning before alligators started raining from the sky. That wasn't a euphemism but the literal truth. Reptiles up to ten feet long blew through the air from a low-charge grenade shoved into a swamp mound that turned out to be a gator nest.

His warning was Fuse's sly grin. He'd seen that at the same moment he'd watched the man hightail it in the opposite direction from the two-foot-high mound of muck. Thankfully, the idiot wasn't so stupid that he'd endangered their combat pack of five werewolves plus one new puppy. They comprised one of Wulf, Inc.'s seven combat packs, existing to fight paranormal threats throughout the world. Why it fell to the wolves to do the violent work was a question left to the historians. Yordan was more of an it's-fun-to-blow-shit-up kind of guy.

Or rather, it's fun to watch when someone else—in this case, Fuse —lit up a gator mound. Though the moron had picked the wrong mound to make go boom.

Everyone else had been cleaning up camp in preparation for "maneuvers" in the Florida swampland. What they were really doing was seeing how well the pack functioned when swamp goo clogged up their noses and sucked down their paws. But all that planning was destroyed now as big reptiles went flying through the air.

Yordan dove behind the New Guy's (NG) truck, and he couldn't stop a grin. Fuse was from Wyoming and thought he'd just lit up a big mound of nothing. The guy didn't know a gator nest from a termite mound. The look on Fuse's face when he realized he'd sent alligators flying was one Yordan would cherish until the day he died.

Meanwhile, reptiles were dropping everywhere, including into the back of the NG's flatbed. Most of them were stunned, but that didn't last long. The situation was bad enough, but everyone—including Fuse and Yordan—was now covered in a thick layer of swamp tar, and the culprit was laughing so hard, he'd fallen to his knees in the spongy marsh.

Well, both culprits because Yordan might have encouraged the planting of said grenade into someplace surprising. He just hadn't thought Fuse would be stupid enough to put it in a gator nest.

Dumb, dumb, dumb. But it sure was funny as hell, and he might have been laughing too as he leaned against the truck.

A dark hissing sound by his feet silenced his laugh. He could hear it clearly over their alpha's curses, and he turned slowly to see the ten-foot mama gator ready to attack. Most of his pack were the lucky insta-shift guys. Not so for Yordan. He took thirty agonizing seconds to move into his wolf body, and it came with excruciating bone-grinding and muscle-burn like every cell was being lit on fire. It used to take five minutes, but he'd reduced that time considerably. Still, thirty seconds was too long to take in front of a pissed-off gator.

A glance to his side showed him that everyone else was occupied with their own issues. Gummy, their alpha, had just turned his cursing on to two baby gators, each under three feet. That was large enough to take a hunk out of a man—or wolf's—side. Fuse was holding his ribs from his guffaws, and Yordan couldn't see Dreadhead and Error, but he could hear their curses. Even the new, wet-behind-the-ears NG Joey was busy lying ass-upward against a tree. He was groaning as he righted himself, so he was probably okay—but too far away to help.

That meant Yordan was on his own as a human against the gator mama.

First step was to leap out of her way, but he was penned in on the sides, and jumping up into the truck might set him down on the smaller alligator up there. He'd seen it land there after the big boom. Best to back away—

Fuck!

The thing lunged, and it caught his boot. Like two beds of nails slamming down hard. Thank God he had on steel-toed boots or he'd be minus a paw next time he shifted. He screamed and dove forward, slamming his fist straight into the creature's nearest eye. He'd done some research before coming down to the mosquito farm known as the Everglades, and the eyes were the most sensitive spot on a gator.

It worked. The gator cow opened her mouth with a hissing grunt that sounded like gas escaping from hell. He rolled away as fast as he could manage, trailing blood and probably getting infected with whatever lethal plague lived in this crap. Fortunately, Error came around the edge of the truck and got the thing straight between the eyes with a couple handfuls of swamp muck. Error was so named because he always screwed up computers but was a dead shot with a gun. Also with snowballs currently made of sludge.

He nailed the mama gator three more times before she started backing away.

Great, but they weren't out of the swamp disaster yet. Yordan had to go wolf. Yippee for him, the agony in his foot would be drowned out by the agony in his entire body. Error peered at him while he kept a wary eye on whatever was in the truck.

"Go ahead. I'll cover you while you shift."

That was all he needed, and he began shucking clothes covered in swamp shit. Thirty seconds later, he was a whole and healthy timber wolf whose paws sank into the muck. Blech.

Once he was full wolf, he took point in defending his packmates from angry reptiles, big spiders, and whatever else the Everglades threw at them. They managed to corral the gator kids and mama long enough to pack up and head back to base camp.

Everyone was cursing Fuse's name by the time the day was done. Every single one of them ended up shifting into their wolf forms until they looked like four-legged tar elementals. Just the sight alone had him laughing in high yips of amusement.

It was close to midnight before they got back to base, such as it was. One tent next to two tricked-out vans in a seedy campground. All of them were human again except Fuse, who wasn't turning back into a man anytime soon. He knew he was in deep shit, so he was stretched out on the concrete in his wolf form. Funny thing was, even covered in all that shit, his wolf smelled better than the man, so nobody complained.

Yordan was contemplating his sleeping options when Gummy pointed at him and crooked his finger. Yordan put on his best *Who me?* expression before crossing to see what his alpha wanted. As he moved, he pulled up the image of that gator sailing overhead and reminded himself it had been one hell of a sight. Certainly worth the tongue-lashing that was coming his way.

He waited while his alpha chewed on the gummy worm for which he'd been named. Yordan could wait out anything, so he leaned against the side of the van as his gaze took in the stars above. Since they were far enough away from the city lights, the expanse above reminded him of his native Wisconsin, and he felt a surge of nostalgia. At least until Gummy spoke.

"Have you figured it out yet?"

"What?"

"Why you've turned into an asshole?"

Yordan frowned. "What?"

"You think I don't know it was you pushing Fuse to light up a gator mound?"

"I didn't—"

"Spare me. I know you started it. Fuse is great, but he's not going to do something that creative unless someone gives him a push." He jerked the floppy gummy worm in Yordan's direction. "And you were behind those death masks in New Orleans last month and the smoke bomb in the church before that."

"Neither of those was me," he said.

"No, you were the one who poked the others until they blew up in stupid ways."

Well, maybe *that* had been him. Sometimes when he got restless—when that itch started—he scratched at other people. Fuse was an easy target because he had a short fuse and a love of watching things go boom. That always made a guy smile. And while Yordan reflected on his past actions, Gummy kept at him.

"I've always thought of you as the cool head among these yahoos. You keep the team balanced and on track. But lately, you've been a real dick. You poke and poke until someone does something stupid."

That wasn't true...was it?

"It was a harmless prank," he said. "We all have to blow off steam, Fuse most of all."

"Maybe, but this time, you went too far. Any one of us could have been seriously hurt."

"Talk to Fuse, then—"

"I'm talking to you because you're the one who started it. Just like you did last month and the month before that." Gummy popped the last of the candy into his mouth and chewed with loud smacks of his lips. "I don't know what crawled up your ass, but get that shit worked out."

"There isn't jack in my past." Not even a Jill or a John, more's the pity. For a hot, single werewolf, he was annoyingly celibate.

Gummy raised his hands. "I don't need to hear the details. I just need you to work it out."

Yordan echoed his alpha's motions. "There isn't anything to work out. I'm not lying, Gummy. There's nothing wrong except the usual. I'm getting older, the pups are getting younger, and I hate the fucking swamp—"

"Talk to one of the shrinks while you're in Michigan. That's an order."

An ugly chill iced down Yordan's spine. "Michigan. I'm not going back to HQ."

"Yeah, you are. It's almost time for your annual review. They've added a mandatory shrink session, thanks to all that nightmare shit in Wisconsin."

"Oh, hell no. I've had it with the geek pack."

The geeks were the brain trust of Wulf, Inc., and Yordan had been pulled in to help train them. They were nice enough for nerds, but somehow they got the idea that they were supposed to fight as well as think. Talk about a disaster in the making. Those nerds were always tripping over their dicks. Then they started having feelings—not just about how things were done, but about each other. Werewolves were naturally horny, especially at their age, but three of the six recruits had already coupled up, one with the group's alpha. All that lovey-dovey bullshit made Yordan feel old and alone, which was why he'd high-tailed it back to Gummy's pack as soon as he was able.

Meanwhile, his alpha was staring at him thoughtfully. "I thought you liked them."

"I did. Until they started having *feelings* about everything."

"Like getting therapy?"

"Exactly like that. It's whiny and—"

"Yeah, whatever." Gummy folded his arms over his chest. "Maybe being around a bunch of whiny babies will remind you that you're a goddamned adult and you can't take your shit out on the rest of us."

"I don't have any shit—"

"Keep lying to me if you want, but you better damn well work it out or I'm not letting you back after the puppies are housebroken."

Fear did shitty things to a man's gut, and Yordan could feel acid's toxic rise in his belly. Yordan was a career Wulf, Inc. guy. Like so many others, he'd been there since high school and had no job prospects outside the paranormal world. And since he was a werewolf, he worked at Wulf, Inc. or nowhere. There was literally no other job for him, and getting cut from a combat pack was akin to being tossed into the reject pile.

Worse, eighteen months ago, a black hole of death had opened up in Wisconsin. It had taken everything Wulf, Inc. had to stop it, but the disaster had taken its toll. His hometown was now a blighted circle of nada. Which meant he had no one and nothing outside of Wulf, Inc.

Typically, terror made him square his shoulders with a show of bravado. "I'm the best you have, Gummy. I'm the reason we survived in Alaska. I took down that fire-breathing vamp, and if it weren't for me—"

"I'd still be burning to death in Hell." Gummy meant literal Hell, thanks to a devil cult.

"Exactly—"

"So I guess you know how serious I am that you get help." Gummy's eyes softened as his shoulders drooped. "Look, I'm not trying to be an asshole, but I can't watch you pull another idiot stunt. You gotta work your shit out."

"There isn't any shit!"

Gummy's eyebrows went up. They were bushy things, like two thick caterpillars crawling upward on his otherwise bald head. "Are you sure?"

Yordan didn't say anything. The last few years had been brutal. He'd lost good friends when the cataclysm in Wisconsin was followed by an ugly mop-up. For the last eighteen months, Wulf, Inc. had been run ragged, chasing down every monster juiced up by the black hole. Everyone was exhausted, and those who could leave had turned in their resignations in favor of a quiet, mundane life.

That wasn't an option for him, though. He didn't have family in the civilian world. So, he'd toughed out the creeping loneliness and aging body, but apparently he wasn't as cool as he'd thought.

"Everyone's fucked up," he muttered. "I've got it under control."

"Eight flying alligators say you haven't."

Yordan's eyes narrowed. "Eight? I thought there were—"

"Turns out there were two in NG's truck," Gummy said with a snort. "Didn't you hear him squeal?"

He had. "We should name him Squeaker."

Gummy chuckled, the sound warm as it mixed with the hum of the cicadas. And that told Yordan more than anything that Gummy wasn't worried about the prank so much as the problem behind it.

"My shit's clean," he stressed.

"Talk to the shrink anyway." Gummy's eyes hardened, though there was an element of regret in the look. "Or you're not coming back."

It was the regret that made Yordan realize Gummy was serious. But what the hell shit did he have to work out?

He had plenty of time to mull that over as he drove the crap van up to Michigan. Wulf, Inc. had an estate there, complete with a huge mansion where the geeks had been based. All sorts of toys were available up there.

But work was his life—for the moment anyway—so he drove through the night and arrived midmorning to the one thing he hated worse than feelings.

Paperwork.

A huge damn stack of it on a clipboard held by the king of all paper pushers, Kit McNabb, aka The Scot. Not just A Scot. Not a Scotsman. No. He was The Scot because he was big enough, officious enough, and annoying enough to be labeled THE. As in The Biggest Pain in the Ass.

Technically, he was Gummy's boss. He coordinated all seven combat packs and, by all appearances, was fairly good at it. The guy was objectively handsome with his blue-gray eyes and red hair. Some people called him charming with the way he turned on and off his brogue just to get the girls to go "oooh." But what really made him a waste of space was the fact that he was a natural shifter from a whole line of Scottish werewolves. Some of their best fighters had come from the Highland McNabbs, but this guy—the heir to the clan chief—was nothing more than a bureaucrat. Right about when the shit hit the fan in Wisconsin, the great heir to the McNabbs requested a transfer from his combat team and turned into a paper pusher.

Coward.

Unfortunately, he was a coward with authority. And he was waiting for Yordan with the gift of several hours of bureaucratic bullshit.

Too bad Fuse wasn't here. Yordan could use a few flying alligators right now. Especially if one landed right on top of The Scot.

CHAPTER 2

Don't Meet Your Idols. They Remember Every Time Your Offering Sucked

K it didn't have time for this. He had seven different combat teams deployed throughout the country, all trying to clean up the mess left by Wisconsin's black hole of death. The hole itself was gone, but paranormals were acting weird the world over, thanks to leftover voodoo from the black hole. No, it wasn't actually voodoo, but that was what he called whatever was making ghosts start singing karaoke and ghouls take up knitting. Those two were harmless enough, but when the average Barbie doll started acting like Chucky, the mundane world went crazy and Wulf, Inc. had a problem.

He'd been working nonstop for months now, not just to clean up the residual mess but to train his replacement. Or that had been the plan. The last two "replacements" had burned out before they'd made it two weeks. A third hadn't made it a day before flaming out with an "I'd rather live in the death hole than do your job."

At this point, Kit was getting desperate. He had to get home to work his shit out. For eighteen months now, he'd been unable to shift like normal. It was horrible, and no one here could figure out why he was suddenly a freak. He hoped the answer lay in Scotland, but he couldn't abandon seven combat teams without support. They needed someone to do his job ASAP. Which was why he was taking time he didn't have to stand in the motor pool waiting for his secret idol.

Yup. Yordan Basch was his secret werewolf crush. The man was a true badass. He'd seen more field time, defeated more bad guys, and trained more recruits than their semi-mythical founder, Wulfric. But that wasn't what impressed Kit so much. No, what really set Kit's secret heart aflutter was that Yordan treated everyone exactly the same.

It didn't matter how scary, how dangerous, or how stupid the being, Yordan was unfailingly blunt with them all. He said what he thought without holding back, and that was the mark of a true don't-give-a-shit man. He had no need to look smart or prove himself. He did his job and had no patience for those who didn't. He was so badass that his name was his own call sign. No nickname ever stuck. He was Yordan, werewolf legend.

Which, of course, was why he had no time for Kit.

Kit was the man who made him follow seemingly nonsensical protocols, fill out reams of paperwork, and report to their pseudo-shrink, the alien named Gelpack. And now Kit was here to offer the man a lifetime of setting policies, doing reports, and forcing others to check in on their own mental health.

But maybe there was a way Kit could pitch it so Yordan would be interested. There had to be some way to get through to the guy.

He began with a warm smile as Yordan's van turned the corner into the large motor pool lot. The garage was separate from the regular estate, barely paved and treacherous in winter, but necessary given the extent of Wulf, Inc.'s operations. It had been on Kit's list to get the whole area upgraded—potholes were the least of their problems—but life had been one long hop from crisis to crisis since the shit hit the fan in Wisconsin over a year ago.

The van looked like shit. He was used to salt-covered sludge on their cars. They lived in Michigan after all. But this looked like the van belonged in a Swamp Thing movie. Or it *was* the Swamp Thing.

Kit frowned, wondering what the hell had happened, when the daily slip and slide occurred. Yordan's van hit a patch of black ice. They salted or sanded the lot daily, but some things were determined to go disastrous no matter what they did. Apparently, swamp muck and black ice did not go together safely.

In his defense, Yordan came in at a prudent speed, but he'd clearly forgotten that the lot was cursed for one accident a day, no matter the weather. They didn't know the cause, but everyone suspected fairies. They just couldn't figure out who had broken Wulf, Inc.'s prime directive. Don't negotiate with fairies was burned into every new recruit's mind, and yet somehow, people still did it. Everyone thought they could come out ahead with the fae, but the magical assholes always found a way to get you in the end.

And they got Yordan.

The van spun out on a patch of black ice that hadn't been there two minutes ago. Kit saw Yordan try to adjust. The man could drive, that was for sure, but no one could maneuver on fairy ice. Not if it was determined to hurt you.

Like everyone else, Yordan turned the wheels into the spin. That was what you were supposed to do on normal ice. Unfortunately, the minute the wheels were going in the same direction as the spin, the van started spinning faster.

Chunks of muck shot everywhere. It was like putting the vehicle in the spin cycle. Kit ducked. It was a natural instinct, but he didn't run. He'd seen this too many times to be anything more than exhausted by it.

The brake lights kicked on. Yordan was trying to slow down. It didn't work, of course. All around the vehicle, people were putting their hands up in the air. It looked like the motor pool was in a stickup. Even Kit put up his hands in surrender because that was the point.

The only way to stop the spinning was to give up total control. There was nothing Yordan could do to slow the vehicle down. In fact, any attempt to move the wheel or—God forbid—cut the engine, would result in the van becoming a spintop they'd once clocked at 400 rpm, which was enough to make an ice skater hurl.

Fortunately, Yordan was no fool. He threw up his hands, and the car started slowing down. Kit caught his gaze every time the van came around. He knew it was an illusion. There was no way Yordan was seeing anyone in the nauseating spin, but Kit couldn't shake the feeling that Yordan was looking straight at him.

So when the van started to slow down enough that a normal man would think of putting his hands back on the wheel, Kit dropped his clipboard and jammed his hands in the air. "Up! Up! Up!"

That was the last fairy trick. If you tried to reassert yourself before the vehicle came to a full and complete stop, then the thing would speed up for another half hour, and nothing would stop it. Not counter spells, no amount of brute force, nothing. The driver had to be patient until the thing was at a dead stop.

If he or she touched the wheel too early again, that would be a disaster that required medical. The last guy who had been stubborn survived only because he passed out. God willing, Yordan wasn't that stubborn. But just in case, Kit had everyone hold their hands up high as a message.

The van spun around again, nearly stopped, and Kit was horrified to see Yordan's arms start to lower. Kit cried out a sharp command in as powerful a voice as he could manage.

"Hands up!"

Yordan's gaze locked on his, and his arms snapped high enough to press into the roof of the van.

"Stay!"

He saw Yordan's face tighten. No one liked the insulting dog command, but every puppy knew the word and respected it. In a paranormal world, sometimes freezing was your best option. And so, Yordan froze, hands pressed upward, while the van finally stopped with an audible groan.

"Two minutes!" Kit bellowed, keeping his eyes trained on Yordan. "Stay!"

Back when this fairy game had started, they'd made the mistake of opening the van door too soon. That hadn't been good for anyone, so Kit had decided on a two-minute wait time for everything to turn off. It had been long enough so far, but one never knew for sure.

He waited, his arms still stretched upward, while the seconds ticked by. And then, once it was done, he slowly crept forward to the van.

"Don't move until I open the door," he instructed. "Pop the seat belt as fast as you can, then we're both going to dive free. Understand?" He pointed to where a pad was being placed to catch them.

Yordan nodded in a quick, curt jerk of his chin.

This was the part that Kit didn't trust to anyone else. If the van started spinning again, he would have to dive inside or risk being thrown across the lot into any number of hard or pointy things. His particular "issue" when he shifted made him the best candidate to manage the maneuver without massive debilitation. Sometimes the reflexes of a cat were an advantage, even in a roomful of dogs.

Especially in a roomful of dogs.

He locked eyes with Yordan and said, "One, two, three." Then he pulled open the van door while Yordan unbuckled with a speed that impressed Kit. Yordan uncoiled from the seat belt with a fluidity surprising in so big a man, then wrapped his free arm around Kit.

That wasn't at all what Kit expected. People usually just jumped and were surprised when Kit was suddenly not in the way. No one had ever thought ahead to wrap an arm around him such that they sprang together. No one but Yordan.

He felt the man's powerful arm snap around his waist and the press of his biceps as he locked Kit in tight. It was a smart position from which to launch off a moving vehicle, but it was too late. Kit was already mid-shift. Kit had a brief impression of glorious muscles, and then he was a fraction of his former size.

He insta-shifted as he leaped free. He felt himself sail through the air in his feline form. He might look like a goofball as he flew, but small and safe was better than huge and in the way. Unfortunately, Yordan was suddenly gripping an empty dress shirt. Kit had a moment to see the man's eyes widen in shock as he frantically tried to reorient himself mid-leap. Yordan had been expecting to manage the weight of two adult men. Instead, he pushed himself and empty air hard enough to land at the very far edge of the mat.

Nothing he could do about it now. Kit had already landed on four kitty paws, rolled because that was the curse of this body, then tumbled to a stop. An instant later, he was back upright in his human body, naked but less embarrassed than he would be to wander around in his animal body.

Meanwhile, Yordan landed with a heavy thud with Kit's dress clothes flopping heavily on his face. Wow. The man had apparently twisted in the air, planning to land on his back with Kit on top. A heroic move and one that made Kit regret shifting. That would have been a fantasy-come-true to lie, even for a moment, on top of the big guy.

Yordan pulled the clothes off his face with a hard jerk, his gaze efficient as he took in the whole building, from the other workers calmly going back to work, the van no longer moving, to naked Kit leaning down to grab his clothes.

"Where'd you go?" Yordan demanded.

"I shifted," he responded. "Easier for you to get out with me clear."

Yordan grunted as he glared at the van. With Yordan now free, the thing was back under normal physics, and the nearest worker jumped in to drive it to the corner where it would be checked and cleaned.

"What the fuck was that?" Yordan asked, then before Kit could answer, he held up his hand. "Let me guess. Fairies." He spat out the word with a full measure of disgust.

"We don't really know, but yeah, that's our best guess."

Yordan glared at him. "And you just let this crazy shit happen? Put out a landing pad and pray no one dies?"

Had the idiot been asleep for the last year? Of course that's what they were doing! No one had the energy to figure this stuff out after all the craziness. Everyone was living on caffeine and their last frayed nerve.

That's what Kit thought. What he said out loud was, "It's on the list. Next time, call in before you arrive. I'll let you know if it's still happening."

"You knew I was coming," Yordan said, his voice accusing. "You were waiting for me."

"I knew the van was coming." They had trackers on all the company vehicles, not to mention sensors the moment the thing came within a couple miles of the estate. "We didn't know who was in the van." Though, he'd guessed. And hoped.

Yordan looked like he was about to say more, but he didn't get the chance. Kit noticed one of their regular motor pool guys was pale and sweating. Worse, his hand shook like a leaf as he picked up a wrench. Some guys handled the daily spin cycle with boredom. They were living in a paranormal world after all. Other guys didn't manage so well, and clearly, Rowland was one of the not-so-chill guys.

Kit glanced at Yordan. "Can you wait here a second? I've got something to discuss with you." He didn't wait for Yordan to answer but then turned directly back to the shaking mechanic. "Hey Rowland, how's your kid doing?"

Rowland's head shot up and his grip on the wrench abruptly tightened, but he didn't swing. He wasn't the violent type, but frayed nerves made even the mildest people jumpy. "W-what?"

"How's Davy doing? Wasn't that chess tournament last weekend?"

"Oh. Oh yeah." The man brightened. His shoulders went down, and the haunted look faded from his eyes. "He did great, but that's not the big one. That was just a small regional thing."

"So, when's the big one?"

"This weekend in Georgia." He grimaced. "My parents are taking him."

Kit frowned, mentally trying to sort through the lists of tasks for the motor pool. He didn't remember, but it didn't matter. Rowland was in no shape to be working. He'd probably hook the brakes into the air conditioning or something.

"I've got an idea," Kit said. "How about you take the rest of the week off? Go cheer on your kid."

Rowland's eyes widened with hope, but then his expression sagged. "I haven't got the vacation time, and we're short-staffed."

Kit raised his hand. "Let me worry about that. You go and enjoy your kid." He jerked his head at the lockers. "Go on. I'll get someone to cover your work." Even if he had to do it himself.

Rowland didn't need to be told twice. He was out of his coveralls and running for his truck like the hounds of hell were after him. Which, come to think of it, had been last week's fun adventure on the estate.

Of course, now Kit had to square it with the head of the motor pool. That would not go well. Technically, the motor pool wasn't directly in his chain of command, but as the guy in charge of all the combat packs, he outranked the person in charge of all the vehicles. Or he would, if Wulf, Inc. had anything so formal as rank. What they had was a loose structure built on packs with specialties. Since he was in charge of seven combat packs, and the alpha of the motor pool was in charge of just the motor pool, Kit won 7-1.

That didn't mean the command went down easy. The motor pool was short-staffed. Kit had to work to convince the alpha that Rowland really needed to disappear for a while. And by "work," he meant bribe. By the end of the "negotiation," Kit was out $100 and had promised to fix a touchy Oldsmobile himself.

Not his favorite late-night activity, but it was worth it. Especially when a quick glance around the motor pool showed him that everyone else appeared calm as they went about their job. Hopefully, a long weekend off would help Rowland settle back into his job as well.

"I guess I'm going to have to move 'spin cycle motor pool' up to a higher priority problem," he said. "I can't give every nervous Nellie time off when things get weird..." His voice trailed away. In his head, he'd been talking to Yordan, who had waited patiently for him to finish. But of course, Yordan wasn't someone who waited for anyone.

The man was gone, and now Kit had to waste more time searching for him like a lost puppy.

FML.

CHAPTER 3

Some Things Don't Shrink in Water

It wasn't hard to find Yordan. The lingering stench of swamp muck led straight to the showers. The guy probably was desperate for a long, hot soak. He probably hadn't eaten either, so Kit stopped off in the kitchen and reheated some of last night's pot roast. He wasn't supposed to encourage drinking during the workday, but he figured Yordan deserved a beer. The man had driven solo up from the Everglades. So Kit grabbed a local craft brew and wished he could justify taking one for himself. He couldn't. He never drank just one, and if he was going to repair an Oldsmobile tonight, he would need to be sober.

He settled into the bench area of the locker room, the meal tray resting beside him. As long as he was here, he threw a thick towel into the heater and waited. And by "waited," he meant he let the steam wash over him as he imagined what Yordan looked like all wet and ripped underneath a hot spray.

What a joy to sit with his fantasy for a few minutes. He rarely got this kind of time. He'd been yanked from his combat pack when his problem with shifting appeared. They'd given him no choice in the matter, just threw him in an office and labeled it a promotion. Fortunately, he was good at logistics and quickly earned his current role. It helped that Wulf, Inc. was woefully understaffed. Still, coordinating seven combat packs was an all-consuming job and one that no single soul could manage for long.

Thankfully, work was slowing down—finally—after more than a year of mop-up from Wisconsin's black hole of oblivion. And if he sat and dreamed about hot water, soap, and Yordan, then who would blame him except his own blue balls? He'd had fantasies about the guy since the man had taken over training during Kit's first class at Wulf ten years ago. Back then, he'd been a horny teen, but some things never faded with time. And Yordan looked as hot now as he had back then.

Kit was thick and achy when the shower shut off. He let his eyes drift open to see Yordan step out through the steam in all his dripping, naked glory. Broad shoulders, ripped abs, water droplets clinging to flat, tight nipples. Yordan had relatively little body hair, but that only made the dark treasure trail more pronounced. What Kit wouldn't give to lick—

"Luncheon peep show?" Yordan drawled without even bothering to reach for a towel. He knew how gorgeous he looked. Apparently, he didn't care.

"Towel—" Kit had to clear his throat. "There are towels in the heated bin."

The man frowned at him. "Heated towels?" Then he looked around. "What bin?"

"The denim one to your right." Kit smiled while keeping his hands casually relaxed over his groin. No point in advertising what he'd been thinking. "Stratos was testing some old incantations. The only thing she accomplished besides some orange mist and shorting out half the electronics in the house was heating all the denim in the place to near scorching. Ladin suggested making them into towel bins since they're too hot to wear." He grinned and let his brogue slip into his tone. "I like them." Though the seamstress had had to wear silicone gloves to stitch it.

"Denim pants?"

"Something about smokin'-hot cowboy pants. She hadn't meant to get it into the incantation."

"And why the fuck are werewolves doing incantations?"

Kit shrugged. "Why the fuck not? Who says we can't use other magic just because we go hairy?" Apparently, Yordan was one of those purists who thought their whole organization should be restricted to going wolf and beating up on bad guys. "Wulf, Inc. has to adapt or die, Yordan. That means experimenting with new stuff." He watched as the man gingerly pulled out a hot towel from the bin and wrapped it around his waist.

Pity that. Kit had enjoyed looking at the man's long, thick cock. But right then, he was more interested in the way Yordan's expression softened as the hot towel wrapped around his flesh. Sometimes the simple pleasures were the best.

"Not so bad, huh?" Kit taunted.

"How much did it cost to replace all the blown computers?" Yordan retorted. "All for hot towels."

Too much, but sometimes shit happened. That was the nature of experimentation. Especially with magic, so Kit pulled out his canned answer. "They were learning things. It happens."

Unfortunately, one of the things he liked about Yordan was that the man never settled for canned answers. "What they learned is what we already knew. The incantation means nothing. It's all about the power of her belief focused into a result. In this case, we learned that Stratos really loves hot cowboys. As do a lot of other women."

Kit couldn't argue. Magic depended upon belief. Increase the number of people who believed, and the power combined to create every kind of magic ever imagined, from glittery vampires to knife-wielding Chucky dolls. Some, like him, came from ancient mythology. The Scots loved their spooky monsters on the moors. Others, like Yordan, came from way too many B-rated horror flicks. Add in the peculiar random magics from Fairy creatures, and it was a wild, wacky world.

Instead, Kit pulled out another canned answer. "The geek pack follows its own rules. Nero's got it under control." He jerked his chin at Yordan. "You should know that better than anybody. You helped train them."

"And not a damned soul listened to me." He shook his head. "Look at you. What the fuck is that?"

"I thought you'd be hungry after your shower."

He sauntered over, all that big flesh and rippling muscles as he picked up the bottle of beer and curled his lip.

"Craft beer. Of course."

Kit snorted then let his brogue go full force. "What crawled up your ass and died? I was trying to do something nice."

"Nice?" Yordan curled his lip. "You're the combat coordinator for seven packs. You don't do nice. You can't do nice, or they'll walk right over you."

Damn, the guy was grumpy, and Kit wasn't in the mood to keep coddling him. He was trying to be nice, but the gloves were coming off.

"You mean like you did?" he challenged. "Walking away when I specifically told you to wait?"

"Fuck yes," he said as he started drying off. "You ought to assign me to shit work for a week for that."

Grumpy and self-aware. Odd how that combo was really sexy.

"And what would that accomplish?" Kit returned. "I've got puppies for the shit work. You're just spoiling for a fight."

Yordan dropped his hands on his hips. "I'd fucking respect you, that's what. Instead, you brought me lunch and a beer."

Well, that was putting it bluntly. So much for his Yordan fantasy. Kit pushed to his feet. Time to be a hard-ass. But before he could slam the bastard across the room, Yordan kept talking. Apparently, he'd built a whole list of criticisms and was not going to be stopped from letting it fly.

"And what the fuck are you doing giving a guy in the motor pool the rest of the day off? Chess tournament?" He rubbed his face. "Oil Slick runs a tight ship," he said, referring to the motor pool alpha. "I'm surprised you're still standing after undermining his authority that way. You see a problem, you let the alpha deal with it. You don't go around his back and undercut him."

Kit nodded, the heat in his gut rising to a dark simmer. "And did you see Oil Slick in there?"

"Doesn't matter—"

"Oil Slick had a nervous breakdown two months ago. He retired from Wulf before he got out of the hospital. Now he's working for mundanes in Florida, keeping all the old geezers' cars running, and soaking in the sun."

He could see the news caught Yordan by surprise. "Retired? He's younger than I am."

"Yeah, he is. And his hair turned gray one week into the black hole crisis." He jerked his chin at Yordan's short blond crew cut. "How much white you got in among the golden brown there?"

"None of your fucking business," Yordan muttered, though Kit could tell it was reflex rather than attitude. "Who became alpha after Oil Slick?"

"We've had a couple, but it turns out, it's not so easy managing werewolves and big, expensive machinery. Right now, it's Stick."

"Stick! As in Stick up his Ass? Aw, hell—"

"Yes, Stick because we needed the machinery fixed, and he can fix anything mechanical in this whole place."

"He also couldn't see a packmate melt down if he were standing in hot lava!"

Kit tilted his head back and arched a brow.

Yordan huffed. "Which is why he sucks as an alpha. The guy in charge has to understand his people. It's not about getting the job done. It's about getting the people to do the job!"

Kit felt a smirk slip into his expression. Yordan didn't realize it, but he'd just sealed his own fate. And that smirk made Yordan's color rise.

"Which is why you interfered and gave chess dad the weekend off."

"Uh-huh," Kit drawled.

"Why does the motor pool keep losing leaders?"

"A fairy accident a day keeps the leaders away. It's brutal, waiting every day for the disaster hammer to drop."

He heard his brogue seep into his phrasing. Normally, he kept strict control over his accent at the predominately American company. He couldn't eradicate it completely, but he'd mostly gone Midwestern flat in his intonation. Except around Yordan, apparently. Something about bantering with him had Kit relaxing his guard.

"There's an accident every day?" Yordan said, shaking his head. "You oughta stop that."

Kit pushed to his feet. Damn, he was close enough to Yordan that he felt the moist heat of the man roll into his nostrils and fog his brain. Unfortunately, it didn't look like Yordan was the kind of guy to want an illicit bump and grind in the shower, even if Kit could get past the ethical complications of that. So, that meant he was going to have to go hard alpha on the man, which was so not his favorite thing to do.

"That's a great idea, Yordan," he drawled. "Make that your first task."

"What?"

"You're getting a promotion. I was going to go gentle on you." He gestured to the food. "Planned to ply you with a bonnie fine meal and a friendly beer. But that's not how an alpha is supposed to work, is it? Find the right guy, then force him to do the job." Kit's whole stance was one of challenge and dominance.

Yordan didn't take it well. He didn't fight back, though; he evaded.

"I'm not the fucking right guy," Yordan snapped, panic edging into his tone.

"You don't even know what the job is," he retorted. "We'll talk about it as soon as you see Gelpack."

"I don't need a shrink!" More panic. Damn, the guy was on the ragged edge about something. Which made it even more important that he start talking to someone.

"So, you're just fine?" he taunted. "Big macho man who's been around long enough to know what's what. You haven't been affected by the last eighteen months of shit. And any weakling who is needs a good kick in the ass."

"That's not what I said."

"But it's what you're thinking." Kit reached up and poked the man hard in the chest. He wanted to spread his fingers and roll his palms down the gorgeous expanse of muscles. Instead, he used his nail and shoved. "Well, big man, now you've got your chance to put your money where your mouth is. You've got the age and the experience. You know the combat packs better than I do because you've served with or trained every single one." He lifted his hand and patted Yordan's rough-hewn cheek. "So go to it, laddie. Fix what's ailing in Wulf, Inc."

He watched Yordan swallow, his breath short. But in an impressive display of control, he firmed his chin and glared down at Kit.

"Why aren't you doing it? Missed too many golf games lately?"

Was that what Yordan thought of him? That he was hanging out waiting for a tee time? "You've spent too much time in Florida, Swamp Thing. It's winter in Michigan. I'm going on a well-deserved vacation," he lied. "I haven't been back home in a decade, and I need to see my nanna." That was true. She was the only one who might have a clue how to fix his current problem. "So you'll be in charge the minute I take off. Everything you want to do to Wulf, Inc. is yours to command."

"When are you leaving?"

"As soon as you're up to speed."

"For how long?"

"Don't know." He winced. "Got a problem that needs fixing before I can come back."

"And you're putting me in charge?"

"Sure am. Because an alpha doesn't ask what his people want. He just puts 'em where he needs 'em. Right?" Instead of a brogue, he put on a bad Texas accent.

Yordan's jaw worked furiously. He wanted to fight. He wanted to rail. He was a man who perennially avoided command, and Kit wanted to know why. But instead of talking, he just stood there and took it.

Which meant Kit had to push.

"Unless you want to sit down and eat your meal. Maybe drink that craft beer that is pretty damned good. Then you can stop belly-aching about all the things I'm doing wrong and talk to me about what the fuck is going on with you."

Yordan's gaze slid to the floor. "Nothing. There's nothing wrong with me, and I've got nothing to say to you or that alien plastic bag Gelpack."

Kit sighed. For some people, taking on the hardest job in the entire organization was easier than facing their feelings. "Then congratulations. You're now my understudy."

CHAPTER 4

Why Do Aliens Care about Assholes?

W TF had just happened?

Yordan watched the Scotsman stride out of the locker room like a god finished with his mortal acolytes. He spun on his heel and walked his cute ass straight out before Yordan could even think to shut his mouth.

He shouldn't have found that sexy. Damn it, everything about the bureaucrat ought to disgust him. But the man had brought him food and beer and had somehow turned Yordan's arrogant posturing into a put-up-or-shut-up promotion.

And he was perverted enough to find that sexy as hell. The man had sat here with a hard-on—yes, he'd noticed that despite the clever placement of Kit's hands—and listened to Yordan's blathering criticism. He'd let Yordan go on and then showed him exactly how much of an idiot he was. And then he'd nailed Yordan with more work and more responsibility. Put up or shut up. The perfect, no-nonsense response to a blowhard.

Hard not to respect that in a man. And given the man's broad Scottish good looks, intelligent green eyes, and pert rear end... Well, now Yordan was the one sporting a hard-on.

He leaned down and took a swig of the beer. Damn, it was good. And the meat casserole? Fantastic.

He dropped down onto the bench where McHottie had been sitting and picked up the plate. The food was welcome, the beer warming by the second, but he didn't care. Compared to the swill they'd had in the Everglades, this was ambrosia. He leaned back as he chewed, his mind quieting as his food settled. He was clean, warm, and now fed.

This was contentment, so long as he didn't think too deeply about anything but being clean, warm, and fed.

"It is time for your appointment now," a sibilant voice said.

Yordan's eyes jerked open as a translucent alien walked in. The man (creature?) was naked and see-through, except for the remains of his last meal floating somewhere around his right calf. There wasn't a lot that grossed Yordan out, but that was downright unsettling.

Gelpack worked as Wulf, Inc.'s shrink, though he had no official credentials. The alien had shown up one day like the Silver Surfer, and the higher-ups had given him an office on the second floor. Yordan did his best to avoid the alien, but his opportunity to duck away was lost.

Served him right for loitering naked in the locker room with lunch and a beer. Still, he did his best to escape.

"Crap, Gelpack. Get out of here. Let me get dressed, and we can meet in your office like civilized people."

"Your appointment time is now," Gelpack answered. His voice held no inflection. None of the usual cues to help a man read his opponent. Gelpack was a fluid outline of a body with fried chicken in his leg. And he wasn't going anywhere.

"Fine," Yordan grumbled. "What do you want?" He stuffed a huge bite of casserole into his mouth so he wouldn't be able to answer whatever question came at him.

God, this casserole was delicious.

"What behaviors make an asshole?"

"Wha—?" The word was cut off as he swallowed his food. "What?"

"This word is used often by you and others. There are synonyms if you would prefer to define one of those. Dickhead. Asswipe. Prick.

The linguistic obsession with anatomy proximal to the pelvis is well-documented."

"I know the synonyms," he grumbled. Then, as a way to delay, he fumbled through a closet in the corner. It was filled with Wulf, Inc. attire, and Yordan pulled on a pair of sweatpants. The clothes he'd worn here would have to be burned unless he wanted the Swamp Thing moniker to stick. Which he didn't.

Once he was dressed, he paused a moment and pondered his options. He could find some excuse to delay, but Gelpack was well-known for following recalcitrant people everywhere. The bathroom, the bedroom, the middle of a fucking battle. He'd stand exactly one foot away day and night until the "subject" broke. One stupidly stubborn werewolf had started punching the creature. But beating on a thing made of gel was worse than useless. Gelpack absorbed all blows, sealed up all cuts as if they'd never been, and worse, his residue ate like acid on the skin. Fire didn't even seem to harm him.

Which meant Yordan's choices were to give in to the creature's questions or live with a gel shadow forever. Unless distraction worked.

"Did McBastard send you in here?"

"Who is McBastard?"

"McNabb. He just left. Did he send you to me?"

"Alpha Gummy put you on my calendar."

Oh yeah. Gummy had said he was going to do that. "And he called me an asshole?"

Silence.

"What did he say about me?"

Silence.

Fuck it. He knew this game. He'd used it many times on new puppies. You stood there while they twisted in the wind with delay after evasion. Eventually, they got tired and answered the question.

Which was what Yordan was going to have to do.

"Fine. What do you want to know?"

"Please define the behaviors that make an asshole."

There were a lot of smart-ass responses he could make, but once again, Gelpack could out-patience a rock. Yordan decided to give the question a serious answer.

"Anything that intentionally hurts or endangers another person." And he wasn't so sure on the intentional part.

"How many such actions are necessary to become an asshole?"

Again, there was no emotion in the question. It could have been asked by a computer. Maybe that was what Gelpack was. Either way, Yordan had no answer.

"How the fuck do I know? It depends on how often and on how serious the asinine things are."

Gelpack didn't respond, but then again, he didn't really need to. The next question was obvious. Had Yordan done things without regard to other people's feelings or the injuries that might occur? Of course, yes. Had he intended for Joey to get thrown into a tree? No. But he'd lit a fuse when he'd poked at Fuse. And never had a guy's handle been more accurate. Then he'd sat back and laughed as Joey had landed hard against a tree and their day's work had turned into fighting gators in a swamp.

And that was the most recent example of him being a dick.

All during the long drive up from Florida, Yordan had stewed on what he'd been doing. Gummy was right. He'd never been this reckless before, and yet the last three months had seen him becoming increasingly obnoxious.

The question was, why?

"I've been feeling twitchy lately," he finally confessed. "Like an itch right at the base of my brain. Don't ask me why because I don't know. I just keep thinking about everyone who has died."

They'd lost so many in the past eighteen months. Not all of them died. In fact, most of them opted out after facing ghouls and psycho fairies, monsters of every ilk and mundanes who thought up every stupid excuse not to see what was right in front of their noses. So many of their fighting forces had simply thrown up their hands and called it quits. They wanted to settle down, have families, and not risk their lives on the latest demon doll that caught the public consciousness. Thanks to the internet, new scary monsters were popping up everywhere, and whack-a-demigod got old really fast.

Yordan had considered stopping as well, but unlike the others, he had no one to go home to, no family outside of Wulf, Inc. His mother and older brother were long dead, both from overdoses. He'd never known his father. Even the town he'd grown up in had been sucked into the Wisconsin dead zone. The best thing that had ever happened to him was getting bit by a preteen werewolf who'd thrown himself into horror flicks until he'd become one.

Both of them had been scooped up into Wulf, Inc., and suddenly, Yordan and Coffee (real name Dwayne) had an entire werewolf family. They'd both thrived here, and while Yordan had worked with Gummy, Coffee had joined Nero's elite pack.

Coffee died a few weeks before the Wisconsin black hole of death appeared. Which meant Yordan had no close friends left except Gummy, who was now calling him an asshole.

Hell, was he a loser or what?

"I'm not going to be a dick anymore, okay?" He didn't exactly know what he was going to do or how he was going to apologize to Gummy, but he wasn't going to continue like this. Twitchy, acting out, and never thinking beyond the boom in the next gator mound. He was too old to be acting like a moody teenager.

But what was he going to do? He felt so alone sometimes that causing an adrenaline rush—even a stupid one—was the only way to fill the emptiness.

He finished off the last of the beer. Maybe figuring out what fairy bullshit was going on at the motor pool would distract him for a bit. And while he was doing that, he was going to decide whether it was time to quit Wulf and find a gay bar somewhere. Maybe one in Scotland with a whole bunch of redheads with pert behinds.

He looked back at Gelpack. "Any other questions?"

"Thank you for your time. I will let you know if I require more definitions."

Oh joy.

CHAPTER 5

And the Winner of the Wet T Is...

Yordan moved quickly upstairs, feeling like he'd been beaten to hell and back. He was too young to feel an all-nighter like this. He really didn't want to talk to anyone, so he avoided the kitchen and living spaces, heading to the bedroom wing without seeing anyone. He'd lived here for almost two years ages back, and so he went for his usual room, second to last on the left. But in order to get there, he had to pass down a long hallway of emotional land mines.

Nero's combat pack lived here, and they'd taken the nearest rooms for their own. But before Nero commanded the geek squad, he'd had the slickest, best pack in Wulf history. Or so they'd claimed. And then they'd died in a hideous demon hunt gone wrong.

Yordan had known them, most when they'd come to HQ for initial training. Shit, every inch of the mansion held memories, but the bedroom wing was a barrage of things that were lost, people who were gone, and opportunities that would never come again.

He touched Mother's door first. That was her handle because she loved to say, "I'm not your mother. Clean up your own shit." She was badass through and through and could shoot the wings off a fly with her Beretta, but she had a secret love of all things dragon that he'd discovered on her second day in training. Dragon mythology, dragon tattoos, Dungeons & Dragons, and even dragonflies.

His lips curved in memory at how he'd teased her about her obsession, and out of reflex or nostalgia, he tried her doorknob. The door opened easily, and he braced himself to see someone else's things inside. Any of the new geek recruits, maybe. Or just the bland sameness of a basic guest room.

He winced. This room was occupied by a *Star Trek* geek, by the look of things. Not to mention the large pile of MCU graphic novels in the corner. Yordan shut the door before he accidentally smashed a cardboard model *Enterprise*.

He should have just gone on then. Straight to his bedroom and oblivion, but instead, he found himself looking into each bedroom door, to every single member of Nero's team that had died. He'd known these people, trained and gotten drunk with them. It was only the luck of the draw that he'd been with Gummy's team instead of with them when a psycho demon had wiped them from the planet.

Pauly's room was next. He'd been the prankster with a love of magic and mischief. His room was also occupied by a new recruit. At least this guy was a neat one. Freakishly so, by the looks of things.

Across from his room were the adjoining bedrooms for Cream and Coffee. The two had paired up in training and were like one single mind split into two bodies. Cream had been the playboy, and his handle was as gross a joke as any horndog could make. Coffee had been the gambler with so much energy to burn that everyone said they needed a cup of coffee after spending five minutes with the guy. He could be that exhausting. He also had a computer-like brain for statistics and weird facts. Yordan had learned early never to play trivia games unless Coffee was on his team because the guy never lost.

Yordan twisted the doorknob to no avail. When had the puppies been allowed to lock their doors? Then he remembered that Coffee had a magic twist to his door. Yordan didn't know if it was a mechanical tweak the guy had added or just a freak of door engineering. In order to open it, Yordan had to lift at a diagonal angle and then wiggle the knob in the right way. It took him a moment to remember the exact pattern, but he got it.

And then, like magic, the door swung open like normal. Which was to say it opened halfway because it was blocked by a dropped bag of rocks, of all things.

Yup, the place was Coffee's usual disaster. The guy could have the room spotless for inspection, but five minutes later, everything went every which way. Coffee carried things with him when he needed them and dropped them when he didn't. Shorts, tablet, his glasses, or his coffee mug—they ended up wherever they landed, and he'd find them eventually when he next needed to unearth them from the piles.

Yordan stepped in, his heart in his throat. Why hadn't the room been cleaned?

He looked around at a year and a half's worth of dust and felt his breath choke off. But underneath the dust were wave after wave of emotion. Coffee had been his oldest friend. They'd woken up together in the Wulf cages down below. That was where they put all the new, out-of-control puppies. Together, they'd found a way to control their animal and had become good men. Not just good fighters for Wulf, but good men.

And now, here was everything they had of Coffee, layered in dust and abandoned like a deserted cabin the woods. It was horrifying, and yet, it felt so damned familiar. Without even thinking, he stepped into the room. There on the dresser was the only clear spot in the room. Coffee called it his payment box for every bet he'd ever made.

The guy once said he had to make a bet once a day or be turned to goo. As of the moment Coffee died, Yordan was $182 in the hole. They never paid up, but they carried the tally into the next challenge, the next bet, or the next drinking game. Except there would never be another because Coffee was gone. Burned to ash, and the pain of that cut like a razor down the spine. Coffee had been the one with endless energy. Coffee was going to outrun, outwork, and outlive them all. He'd even tried to get them to bet on it, but no one would agree. They all thought he'd outlast everyone.

Until a demon had burned all but Nero to ash, and now Yordan had to pay up. Without any idea of what else to do, Yordan rooted blindly in his backpack and pulled out his wallet. He jerked out the bills, pretending to count but too shaky to care. He placed bills one by one on the dresser, while memories of drinking games, midnight drills, and tussling together as wolves burned through his mind. He couldn't see through his tears, and still, he pulled out bills.

He leaned hard against the dresser because he couldn't hold himself upright anymore. And when his wallet was empty, he slapped the entire billfold down on the dresser and laid his head down on the pile and sobbed. Loud, gasping heaves that drowned out everything but the sound of his grief.

He tried to keep it muffled. He buried his head in his arm and pressed his forearm to his mouth, but it didn't stop the pain. His friend was gone. And not just one friend but four.

He didn't know how long he struggled. One minute? One thousand? Every breath was wretched; every exhale was ragged. And then he felt a hand on his shoulder.

He stiffened immediately, trying to cut off the display. It ended up choking him. He wanted to straighten up, but instead, someone shoved a T-shirt into his hand. He used it to wipe his face. And then he heard words spoken in a low brogue.

"Grief is an honorable emotion. There is no need to hide it."

The Scottish asshole speaking some fortune-cookie platitude. Yordan wanted to dismiss it, but the words sank in anyway. And once inside, he felt the meaning of them soothe him. There was nothing shameful about mourning his friends, and fuck anyone who looked down on him because he was weeping like a child. He'd gotten the news the day before his pack had taken on an evil witch coven. There'd been no time to properly mourn then, and afterward, he and Gummy had gotten rip-roaring drunk. That had been more about burying the pain instead of feeling it.

Now, he'd somehow ended up sitting on Coffee's unmade bed, and he couldn't stop himself. The tears wouldn't stop flowing.

"We're alone," The Scot said, his hand squeezing tighter. "No one will see."

The Scot was seeing, but it was too late to prevent that. So Yordan let the grief flow. He knew it was an open wound that needed to bleed. He stopped fighting it and breathed into the cotton tee while the tears seeped into the fabric. McNabb remained at his side through it all, eventually sitting beside him and drawing him close with his large body, warm and comforting.

Yordan sobbed like a child for a very long time. It wasn't just because he grieved Coffee and Mother and all the others who had died in the last two years. He grieved for himself, the survivor who had to go on somehow with a gaping hole in his life where his friends once stood.

He'd managed to do it for a while. For eighteen fucking months while he filled his life with postapocalypse cleanup and poking at his packmates. But here, now, he saw what was wrong with his life.

He missed his friends. He missed Coffee, who was more of a brother to him than anyone else. And he missed the innocent belief that as trained combat werewolves, they could face down anything and win.

Sometimes surviving sucked. And with that realization came a fresh wave of tears. Fortunately, these felt like cleansing tears. And in time, they faded to nothing. Eventually, he could breathe again without shuddering. And while he used the tee to mop up his face, The Scot finally asked a question that had obviously been weighing on his mind.

"How'd you get into the room?"

"What?"

"We've been trying from the beginning. Couldn't get into his room or Cream's."

"I just opened it."

"But—"

"There's a trick to it. On both their doors."

"Oh." A long pause followed as the man leaned back against the wall. "What kind of trick?"

Yordan sighed, wondering why this was so fucking important. "It's a way you lift and twist it. Takes half a second to learn."

"And would this trick make the door unbreakable?"

"What? Of course not." The doors on the bedrooms were plywood. A hard sneeze could break them. Unless... He frowned at The Scot. "You couldn't get the doors open?"

McNabb pointed to the closed adjoining door to Cream's room. "Neither one."

"What did you try?"

"A locksmith. A chainsaw. A sledgehammer."

What?

"Then it became—"

Yordan was smart enough to finish the sentence for him. "Another thing on the list."

"Yup."

The two of them stared at each other for a long moment. For the first time, Yordan noticed how tired the Scotsman looked. A haunted exhaustion lurked beneath all those ruddy good looks. And a sharp mind.

Fortunately, Yordan could be pretty sharp himself. "How many things are on this list? Things like doors that won't open and sudden spinning vans in the motor pool?"

"Dozens."

"And do they all feel like—"

"Fairy tricks? Yeah, they do. Any idea who might have forgotten the Wulf, Inc. motto?"

Never make a deal with a fairy.

"Ummm."

McNabb straightened with a scowl on his face. "Are you fucking kidding me?"

"Not me!" Yordan rushed to say. "But, um, Coffee used to say he had a Get out of Dead Free card."

The Scot jolted. "What? How?"

"I don't know!" Yordan rubbed a hand over his face. The conversation had happened years ago when they were both shit-faced. "I didn't even remember it until this second."

"Think hard."

He was trying! "Cream would know." But of course, Cream died at the exact same instant as Coffee had. "And maybe the others on his team." His voice was subdued.

"Nero?"

Nero was the alpha of the team and the only one who had survived the mission. "Um, no. Nero had a healthy fear of the fairies."

"With good reason!"

Couldn't argue with that.

The Scot ran a hand over his face. "So, what—exactly—was this fairy deal?"

"I don't know that he had one. We were drunk. He was laughing about his Get out of Dead Free card..." His voice trailed away. They both knew that fairies were the only ones who could give something like that. And they always, always held some sort of trap.

"How can we find out?" McNabb pressed.

Yordan looked around. "There would have to be some sort of clue. Some record or something. And it would be—"

"Here. In his personal things."

"That have been locked behind an impenetrable wall for nearly two years?" He glared at McNabb. "How could you let it go this long?"

"It's a really long fucking list!"

Yordan pushed to his feet, his exhaustion fading beneath a desperate need to search every inch of Coffee's room. And if the bastard really was alive somewhere in fairy heaven, then he was going to grab the asshole by the collar and...and... He'd kill him for real. Or kiss him. Or both, probably.

"Damned asshole," Yordan muttered. He went to Coffee's desk as The Scot started on the closet. "You don't have to help me look."

"The hell I don't. If he's alive somewhere, we have to find him."

"What if it's fairy heaven and he's sunning himself on a beach somewhere?"

The Scot shot him a hard look. "You know any fairies who have reason to treat werewolves with that kind of kindness?"

No. No. And hell no.

"Then we better get to work."

CHAPTER 6

Deal? What Deal? Did Someone Make a Deal?

K it felt his gut clench in panic. Fairy deals were slippery, ticking time bombs, and if Coffee really had died with a deal in place, any number of existence-ending disasters could be now on the horizon. Most people made expedient deals. Get me out of this problem, and I'll give you my firstborn child. Those were personal disasters. Not so fun, but really not his problem. But a get-out-of-dead deal was something bigger. It was long-standing, and it messed with reality. Coffee would have had to give up something big in return. Like the nuclear codes kind of big. No, not like that. Fairies always wanted something weird. Turn people into donkeys weird or spin straw into gold.

Wait, he was mixing stories. He took a deep breath and tried to focus. What kind of fairy deal could Coffee have made? Best guess came down to—save me from death, and I'll be your servant.

Given that Coffee was privy to a lot of Wulf, Inc. secrets, that could mean havoc on the organization. And it could explain all the weird disasters going on around HQ. Maybe.

Bottom line, they had to find out the details. But Coffee's room was a disorganized mess of clutter and dust. Five minutes of searching told him that they needed a systematic search.

He looked at Yordan and realized the man was calmly moving in an organized pattern through Coffee's desk area. It was reassuring, really, and it helped Kit clear his emotions away enough to breathe. Or he did until Yordan looked up at him.

"You're panicked."

"No. Maybe. Well, yes. I'm thinking about all the possibilities. Some of them are—"

"Horrifying. I know. But the only way to get more information is to find it." Yordan clenched his hands into fists. "What the fuck was he thinking?"

"Now who's panicking?" Kit shot back. It helped to banter a bit. "But randomly going through this disaster area will take hours. We'll have to do it, but there has to be a better way. You knew him better than I did. Where would Coffee keep something important?"

"The man was a random collection of impulses and trivia. Look around. This was as organized as he got."

Both their gazes landed on Yordan's stack of bills. It was the one clear place in the entire room. They both had the same thought as they stepped closer to it.

"Why did you put the money there?" Kit asked.

"It's where people paid their debts. Always. He had a ritual where they had to—"

"Come to his room to settle their bets. I remember."

Yordan's gaze cut to him. "You had a running bet with him, too?"

"Not a running one. Just one, but..." Oh God. It couldn't be.

Kit felt the blood drain from his face. Holy shit, could that be the source of his problem? All this time, it was a fucking bet with a dead man?

Yordan caught his elbow as he swayed. It was just the contact he needed to find his focus again. But damn it, panic was half a breath away.

"You had a bet," Yordan confirmed. "Did you pay it off?"

"It wasn't that kind of bet."

"It was always that kind of bet."

Yes, it was. And it explained Kit's horrifying, debilitating problem. The one that had begun days after Coffee had died. God, he was such an idiot for not thinking of that before. But damn it, who remembered drunken bets?

Meanwhile, Yordan shot him a look that promised to poke deeper into that little problem. Wow, that was going to be painful. But for the moment, Kit was able to distract him.

"If this is the only clean place in the room, then it stands to reason that—"

"He'd keep whatever was vital right here," Yordan said as he began opening drawers on the dresser. It was the usual collection of underwear, sweats, and novelty T-shirts from every random place Coffee had ever been in. And he'd been in a lot.

"This is just his T-shirt collection," Kit said. That was the man's favorite bet with new puppies. How many novelty tees are in my dresser? True or false, I have a tee shirt from a dive bar named Titty Galore Gives Blue Balls. (True.) There was an endless supply of humor surrounding his T-shirts, and he never failed to bring them up with new puppies.

"I know, I know," Yordan muttered as he systematically searched through the drawers. He pressed into the back and the top, looking for secret compartments or hidden folders. Nada. "It wasn't that he was chaotic, you know," he said. "He was a creative thinker, always coming up with random facts and the like."

Kit nodded as he looked around. "As if he had an organization that isn't obvious to a logical mind." Which meant Yordan wouldn't be able to figure it out. The man was a straight shooter. His room probably had his clothing stacked in precise piles and his shoes had the toes flush with an invisible straight line.

Kit frowned, trying to imagine the situation. "When puppies came in to pay up, where would Coffee sit? What was his ritual?"

"You never saw it?"

Kit shook his head. He'd been in a different combat pack and only rarely coincided with Nero's pack.

Yordan pointed to the office chair. "He'd sit in his office chair like a king on a throne. The puppies would stand there, holding their cash or whatever. Coffee had a lecture he'd give about always paying debts and then make them set down the money, one bill at a time right there."

Just like Yordan had been doing a few minutes ago.

"And then what?"

"He'd ask if they wanted to try double or nothing, and eventually, everyone learned to say no."

Kit nodded. He'd heard of double-or-nothing bets that ended up in the thousands of dollars range.

"When it was done, the puppies would have to say 'I've learned my lesson' and leave."

"That's it?"

Yordan nodded. "That's it."

Kit went over to the desk and sat down exactly as Coffee would have. He opened the desk drawers. Nothing.

"I already looked there," Yordan said.

Yes, but Yordan was organized. Coffee was *creatively* organized. Which was to say, where would Kit put something secret and important that he could grab right from this seat? His gaze landed on the tiny bedside table just close enough to reach if one were as tall as Coffee. The table had a drawer filled with random shit and a few condoms. Kit knew because it was half open and he could see inside. But what wasn't immediately visible was the back of the table.

He reached behind, fiddled around blind for a second to find the hidden latch, and then popped it open. He pulled out several thin notebooks and what looked like a kid's diary.

"I would have found that eventually," Yordan said without heat. "But I never would have thought my way there."

"Wulf, Inc. has a lot of employees. I've learned some require more flexibility of thought when working with them."

Yordan grunted. "Which is why I don't work with them," he said as he took the diary from Kit. "This kind of shit drives me crazy. Without discipline, everything falls apart."

"Werewolves aren't exactly known for their discipline."

"Which is why we need it even more."

"And just how disciplined was it when you poked Fuse into blowing up a gator mound?"

Yordan flushed and looked away. "I fucked up. I admit it. And that's why I don't deserve a promotion. You don't reward fuckups."

No, but you did move them to where they would be most valuable to the company after—theoretically—ending the screw-ups. That was what he was thinking. What he said, however, was even more important.

He touched Yordan's arm, squeezing it until the man met his eyes.

"No one thinks you're a fuckup, least of all me."

"Then why haven't I ever been given a combat pack of my own?"

"Because you never wanted one!" The need to deal with Coffee's screw-up burned in Kit's gut, but nothing would stop him from finally having an honest conversation with Yordan. "I know your file word for word." In fact, he'd developed an unhealthy obsession with it. "You never push for alpha, you always take the beta role. You dole out the discipline with an even, fierce hand, and you're great with new recruits. There's not an alpha here that doesn't want you in his pack."

"Gummy does just fine for me."

"Why? Why do you always accept the beta role?" He shook his head. "It's not a lack of confidence. You know your worth."

"I do," Yordan agreed. "And I know what I'm not." He glanced back at the secret compartment behind the table. "I'm not flexible."

"But—"

Yordan cut him off. "Priorities, Scot." He opened the first page of the diary, but Kit grabbed his arm.

"You're just as much a priority as this."

Yordan snorted. "Fairy-created Armageddon?"

"Let's just say that you're very high up on my list."

Yordan visibly gaped at him. "Because Fuse blew up a gator mound?"

"Because you're not a beta. And after the last eighteen months, we need you to get over your shit and start leading."

He saw the weight of his words hit Yordan. He watched as the man's eyes widened and his shoulders stiffened as if he were being threatened. And maybe he was. Wulf, Inc. was massively understaffed. It needed all its people stepping up like never before. Whatever the deal was with Yordan, Kit had made it his mission to figure out.

"You don't know a damned thing about me," Yordan countered, his tone angry.

"Maybe not, but I want to." Understatement of the year.

"Uh-uh. Leave that to the shrink."

"Uh-uh. This is not something I'm going to delegate."

Kit stared hard at the man, making sure his intentions were absolutely clear. Yordan was not going to hide from him. Wulf, Inc. needed him desperately, but more than that, Kit wanted to find out what drove the man. What were his secrets? What were his loves?

And then, maybe, he would know if his obsession with the guy was built on fantasy or something a lot more interesting.

CHAPTER 7

When Is a Diary Not a Diary?

This was fucking crazy.

Coffee could be alive, thanks to some fairy deal. Odds were he was in some fairy prison helping a psycho fae cause havoc on the human world. That's what fairies did after all. And yet, all Yordan could do was stare at The Scot and ache.

The man wanted to know him. He had just declared his intention to rip into Yordan's guts to figure out what was holding him back, what was screwing him up, and what was making him want. And Yordan was so damn lonely and confused that that sounded good to him. At least someone cared to look, right?

No one thinks you're a fuckup, least of all me.

McNabb was his boss's boss. If this had been a simple dressing down by a superior, then Yordan could handle it. It wasn't the first time the higher-ups had wanted to chew his ass out for one thing or another. But The Scot was a different kind of higher-up.

Apparently, The Scot cared.

No one thinks you're a fuckup, least of all me.

Yordan shouldn't need that kind of reassurance. It shouldn't slide into his gut and make him want to roll belly up, but it did. Not just because of the words but because McNabb had said it.

It was his eyes that clinched the deal. To feel the man's focused attention was like a strobe light aimed straight at his soul. Yordan wanted it. Damn it, he craved it. But it also left him feeling exposed and so vulnerable that he wanted to run. He knew he had skills above the usual meathead, but damn it, he'd also screwed up. He was much better at pointing out the flaws in other people's plans than crafting the plan in the first place.

All those thoughts ran through his head while he stood there locking gazes with The Scot. His heart lurched, his lips tingled, and his cock thickened until it was a distracting throb.

He watched the man's eyes widen as the biological message got through. He saw his nostrils flare as he swallowed. Just how big was The Scot's dick? Inquiring minds wanted to know. And hands and mouths and ...

He slammed the cage door on all those thoughts so loud he felt the clang. Discipline! Order! It was the only way to survive, and damn it, thinking about banging your boss's boss was not the way to a successful career. And given that Yordan was nothing without Wulf, Inc., he was not in a position to toy with any of the thoughts that were spinning in his brain. Or suggested by his dick.

And yet, he wasn't the first one to look away. The Scot suddenly seemed awkward as he lifted the stack of spiral-bound notebooks up between them and tried to speak.

"I'll read—" His voice came out rusty enough that he had to clear his throat. "Um, these. You—"

"The diary. Yeah. Right."

Back to business. He should feel relieved. It was what he wanted, right? No.

He dropped down onto Coffee's unmade bed and tried to focus his thoughts. Fairy deals could have world-ending consequences, right? So he had to get to work. He opened the journal and immediately saw a child's immature handwriting, complete with jerky words and bad spelling. The first sentence was, *This is my birthday dairy.*

Yordan forced himself to focus, skimming with increasing speed as he settled into the mind of twelve-year-old Dwayne. Apparently, Dwayne was a spaz—his own word, though the jerky handwriting bore that out. Born to a family of natural werewolves, he was the only one who'd failed to shift. It hadn't been a problem until his twelfth birthday when his younger brother had his first shift, which was proof positive that poor Dwayne was a retard—again, his word.

His mother, a therapist for paranormals, suggested that whenever Dwayne felt too emotional to handle things, he should write things down in this dairy [sic], and it would help him deal with his feelings. So, the boy did—in huge, emotional swaths of words—before going silent again for weeks. Yordan skimmed through fury at a missed monster truck rally, several fights with his brother the werewolf dick (young Dwayne was not good with clever nicknames), and then the absolute despair when his younger sister went puppy at a sleepover with her best friend.

It legitimately looked like Dwayne was a mundane in a family deeply embedded in werewolf culture. This was a difficult position for any kid, but lots of people found their way. Hell, half of Wulf's support staff were mundanes who knew about their world without being able to shift. The other half were older werewolves who just didn't feel like getting feisty anymore.

So young Dwayne went about his own rocky path to acceptance of being less doggy than the rest of his friends and family. Until one day he met a fairy. And not just any kind of fae, but one who apparently loved gambling. Gamfae, according to the really-not-that-clever-with-nicknames Dwayne.

This was where Yordan slowed down his skimming. There was no indication of how the two met. Either one could have sought the other out. But suddenly, young Dwayne was working out the details of a fairy bet. Like everyone else, the kid knew that fairies were tricky creatures, but this one bet seemed like a no-brainer. A simple either-or.

According to the bet, Gamfay (he changed the spelling of the name for some unknown reason) bet that Dwayne would shift in a week's time; Dwayne bet he wouldn't. If he didn't, then the fairy would make the kid into a werewolf.

From Dwayne's perspective, it was a win-win. No matter what happened, he got to go furry.

Great, but what did the fairy get if the kid shifted on his own? Meaning, what happened if the fairy won the bet?

The now-fifteen Dwayne wasn't so focused on that information, but he finally got there. If Gamfay won the bet, he got an acolyte. (Dwayne had needed to look up the word. Good thing, because Yordan wasn't so sure about it either. It meant an assistant or follower.) What it meant in reality was that if Dwayne shifted naturally, he would lose the bet and become a Gamfay slave on Earth.

Yordan shuddered. That didn't sound good at all, but the young Dwayne didn't think it was so bad.

Gamfay's driving addiction was gambling. He'd bet on anything and everything. Didn't care if he won or lost; he just liked the bet. And he really loved watching mortals gamble. So as Gamfay's Earth acolyte, Dwayne would make bets with his friends, his family, with everyone and everything. One a day, every day, with allowances for illness.

And then on Dwayne's death, all outstanding bets would revert to Gamfay. Anything that wasn't settled fell under fairy terms, which basically meant the fairy got to screw with you until the debt was paid.

Well, shit. No wonder Yordan's life had been chaos for the last eighteen months. He'd had an outstanding cash debt with Coffee, which then reverted to Gamfay. Was that why he'd been an asshole? He'd have to think about that more later. Right now, the important thing was that his debt was paid. Yordan kept reading, his mind spinning out scenarios even as young Dwayne was caught. The kid took the bet and lost. Not because he made a bad bet. He did not shift naturally the way the rest of his family did. Nope. Dwayne got bit by a lycanthrope an hour before the end of the bet, and poof, he became a werewolf with all the instabilities of lycanthropy.

Yippee. Two years later, Dwayne bit Yordan, and they both ended up in Wulf.

So now they knew the specifics of the fairy bet. Thankfully, Dwayne had been meticulous in recording the bargain with Gamfay.

What he hadn't been was clear on the exact *name* of the fairy. And names were really, really, really important, especially if one wanted to end the angsty teenager stupidity.

The Scot looked up from his reading. "Got an answer?" he rasped.

"Yup. Fairy deal. Got a fairy name in your books?"

"No. Just a detailed list of outstanding debts."

"All of which shifted to Gamfay on Coffee's death."

"Gamfay?"

"Nickname. Don't ask. It's dumb."

The Scot nodded. "So how is that a Get out of Dead Free card?"

Good question. Yordan held up the diary. "This covers the initial terms between Gamfay and teenage Dwayne. It doesn't say anything about keeping him from dying."

Without a word of discussion, the two of them switched notebooks. Yordan got five spiral notebooks (the ones The Scot hadn't looked at yet). And the boss's boss got the diary. Ten minutes later, McNabb sighed.

"What?"

"What happens if Coffee misses on his acolyte promise?"

"What?"

"What happens if Coffee didn't make a bet? What if he forgot or he couldn't because he was trapped in ice?"

Yordan thought back, a sinking pit in his stomach. "Wasn't he in ice for a couple days? Conscious but frozen in—"

"Magical ice. Yes."

"He thawed out okay. We called him Captain America for a bit until he got too obnoxious calling himself one of the hot Hollywood Chrises."

The Scot's lips quirked. "I remember that." Then he sobered. "But he couldn't have made any bets while frozen."

"Shit."

"Yup."

Together, they started flipping through the spiral notebook dated the year Coffee had been turned into an ice cube. They found it quickly enough. It was a single bet on an otherwise pristine page.

"Double or nothing bet. Dwayne bets Gamfay that the fairy can't find the Big Tits Bar tee in ten minutes of looking at human speed. If Dwayne wins, all missed bet consequences are gone, *plus* he gets a single Death Save. If Dwayne loses, Gamfay gets a Lost Love."

McNabb frowned. "What's a Lost Love?"

"No clue. You?"

"Nada." Yordan pointed. "But it looks like it didn't matter. He must have won. Had to have if he claimed he had a Get out of Dead Free card."

"That's g—" The Scot started to say but then caught his breath. Yordan, too, as dark, flourishing words appeared on the formerly white page.

Unless Dwayne cheated, in which case, all penalties and benefits are enacted at my whim. And I have a lot of

WHIMSY

The last word was writ large and with expanding lines of flourish until it ended in a grinning smiley face that kept winking at them.

"Oh shit," Yordan muttered. When what he actually wanted to do was scream, *What the fuck, you fucking idiot?* at Coffee. But that would be undisciplined and completely unhelpful.

Meanwhile, The Scot proved that he was a quick thinker by grabbing a pen and scribbling his next words onto the page.

What's your name? We want to make a deal.

Yordan gasped. "No! No, we don't! That always makes it worse!"

The Scot sucked in a breath and nodded. "You're right," he muttered. So he carefully scratched out the word "We" and replaced it with "I."

"Don't be an idiot," Yordan grumbled, though it was too late. The Scot was already well on his way to repeating the same mistake that had created Wulf, Inc.'s special habit of insanity. Apparently, "Never Make Fairy Deals" actually meant "We Always Make Fairy Deals When We're Desperate."

"It's my risk alone," McNabb grumbled.

"I'm sure that's exactly what Coffee thought. And Nero. And Bruce." He continued listing off the wolves he knew who had made simple, clean, desperate fairy deals and ended up nearly destroying the world several times over.

But it didn't matter because Gamfay was answering.

Prove you're worth my time first.

"Fuck you," Yordan answered just as McNabb scrawled.

How?

Collect the rest of my debts. Then we can wager on Dwayne's continued existence.

Yordan's breath caught. "He's alive?"

Apparently the fairy didn't need the words to be written out because he answered.

He isn't dead.

Which didn't necessarily mean he was alive either, but it was a glimmer of hope. And that was all Yordan needed. He snatched the book from McNabb's hand. The Scotsman was way too important to Wulf, Inc. to risk himself. Whereas Yordan could get screwed over by a fairy deal and no one would care.

Deal, he wrote. Then he signed his own name to it and felt the weight of the magic settle on his shoulders. Only to have The Scot grab his hand.

"Are you fucking crazy?" he demanded.

No. Just desperate. Just really fucking desperate for a reason he couldn't even name.

"Uh-uh," McNabb said as he snatched the journal back. "As your superior officer, this lands on me." Then he scrawled his own name at the bottom and went to draw a big, dark line through Yordan's name.

Except, true to the fact of all fairies being assholes, the pen abruptly stopped working. Both their names were now writ big and bold right at the bottom of the page.

"Fuck," McNabb muttered. "That's not what I intended at all."

Which was what always happened whenever some idiot made a fairy deal.

CHAPTER 8
Werewolf Captain America?

K it groaned when he saw both their names in bold letters at the bottom of the page. He'd meant to spare Yordan this task. He knew how close Yordan and Coffee were. Hadn't he just walked in on the guy sobbing out grief that had been churning inside him for nearly two years? It was not Yordan's task to fix Coffee's screw-up. It was Kit's as head of all the combat packs.

But now, they were both tied into this disaster, and they had better start working on it now.

Fortunately, he knew just the person to help. If he ever needed something to be handled super quick, he called on Pee. Her name was actually Serena Chin. She was a Chinese werewolf whose magic somehow made her work at twice normal human speed. And that was on a slow day. She'd picked the name Speedy Gonzales, which her friends shortened to Pee because packmates could be obnoxious.

He grabbed his cell phone and typed his first email to her. The second went company-wide, saying that any debts to Coffee were now held by a fairy. All forfeits must be dispatched immediately to Pee or suffer the consequences. He didn't bother to spell out the threat. Everyone knew that fairies could be real assholes.

Serena was in the room before he hit send on the second email. Her eyes were bright, her expression calm. One might even call her inscrutable if it weren't for her mouth that perpetually quirked into a half smile. As if she knew something funny but wasn't going to share. Which she probably did. Also, because she was busy, not inscrutable.

He shoved the diary at her without a word. Yordan was already going through the spiral notebooks. They had to figure out who owed what and get all debts resolved ASAP.

It took Pee all of two minutes before she looked up and said, "You two are idiots."

Yordan snapped back, "Opinions like that waste time."

At the exact same moment, Kit tossed her the rest of the spiral notebooks. "Organize and start collection. Meanwhile..."

Meanwhile, what? He swallowed and tried to think through things clearly. There was too much. Flexible thinking was no help when the task was so big his mind shorted out.

Worse, he kept remembering his own bet with Coffee. Why the hell hadn't he realized it long before now? Here was the cause of his "shifting problem." One night of drinking with Coffee and... Fuck! A drunken confession turned into a challenge, which led to a stupid bet. He hadn't even remembered that night until he'd seen the bet written dark and bold in the spiral notebook.

Well, at least he didn't have to go to Scotland now. The cause of his freakish debilitation was now clear.

"I can't think..." he murmured. Fortunately, Yordan was able to help cut through the chaos.

"Focus on the alphas first. If they have a debt, that'll screw up the whole pack."

Only one pack was on a mission right that second. All the others were resting or en route to one. "Oh shit. It's a puppy pack facing their first monster."

He punched a number into his phone and spoke for everyone's benefit. "I'm taking the helicopter to Torch Lake. I'll be in there in ten. Who have we got who's combat ready?"

Pee frowned. "Torch Lake?" She got it a second later. "Fuck."

Again, Yordan kept them on track. "Not helpful."

"Right," said Pee. "But there's no one available."

"I'll go," Yordan said. "What's at Torch Lake?"

Kit shook his head. "You haven't slept in thirty-six hours. A shower doesn't make you rested, and I don't allow stupid macho shit." He thought about his options. "I'll fly up there. Hopefully in time. Pee, you organize this shit and recall Gummy's pack." He glared at Yordan. "You get some sleep."

Yordan arched his brows, a look that had no right to be so sexy on him, then he crossed to the back corner of Coffee's closet. He tossed aside a pile of clothes to uncover a safe. He punched in the code—a not so clever 7734 which spelled hELL upside down—then pulled out a paper envelope.

Both Kit and Pee watched with interest.

"What is that?" Kit asked. "And why didn't you tell me he had a safe?"

"Because I know what's in here. We all did." He lifted out small plastic container filled with colorful somethings.

"And what's that?" Kit asked as Yordan ripped it open and pulled out a long, thin, and very gross gummy worm.

"A week's sleep," he said as he stuffed the whole thing into his mouth and started chewing.

"Bullshit."

"Truth," Yordan said between bites. "Not all his fairy bets were moronic."

"But—" Kit's eyes widened. "Is that what Gummy eats all the fucking time?"

Yordan shook his head. Apparently the worms were really chewy. "Nah," he said as he worked the worm in his mouth. "His are mundane candy store stuff. But this is how he got the taste for them."

Kit sighed. Clearly, Yordan was privy to a whole world of combat secrets. "No way does magic work as well as a good night's sleep."

"Course not," Yordan agreed. "But I'm not letting you go up to Torch Lake without backup."

Kit wanted to argue, but he didn't have any good options and time was running out. He couldn't get Marsha on the phone. She was the one leading a pack of new puppies against the Torch Lake monster. For all he knew, he was already too late.

Damn it. He couldn't think straight. Yordan wasn't the only one who was operating with too little sleep. With a groan, he held out his hand. "Give me one."

Meanwhile, Pee was already halfway through the first notebook, but she had enough presence of mind to shoot him a long, hard look of fear.

"I had no idea," she said.

"What?"

"That there was so much stupidity here." Her gaze included the spiral notebooks and Kit.

Yordan swallowed the last of his worm. "You people in the home office have no idea."

Kit had started on his own gummy worm, and the thing was like chewing warm tar. But it tasted great, which was a contradiction, but somehow made sense.

"That's exactly why you've been promoted," he said as he headed out the door.

Yordan shot him a look of pure hatred, and Kit had the gall to laugh. "Welcome to my world," he quipped, then he abruptly sobered as he pointed to Pee. "Stupid we may be, but you need to keep these bets in absolute confidence."

She nodded. She wasn't there yet, but eventually, she'd find out his bet, and damn it, he shuddered to think how her opinion of him would plummet. But he hadn't the time to be discreet.

Thankfully, she understood. Meanwhile, he jerked his head toward the helicopter pad. "It should already have our gear," he said to Yordan. They were halfway down the hall when his scattered thoughts popped up a new horror. "Run back and keep that door open," he said to Pee. "Last thing I want is to lose the bedroom again!"

She was gone before he finished speaking. He turned his attention to updating Yordan as they walked. It helped that whatever fairy magic was in those gummy worms was slipping through his body like ten hours of sleep followed by a massage and a nap. Hell, he hadn't felt this good in years.

"Where did he get those worms?" he asked, a renewed strength filling his voice and his step.

"There's a downside," Yordan warned.

Wasn't there always? "What?"

"When it runs out, it'll hit you like a ton of bricks."

"Great."

"Tell me what's in Torch Lake, besides the usual?"

"You ever meet Marsha?" She was named after the famous *Brady Bunch* kid because she'd spent her puppy year caught between two obsessive wolves who had eventually killed each other. Not every werewolf was stable, and she'd gotten the attention of two bad ones.

"The weirdly smart one?"

Kit chuckled. Marsha saw patterns others missed and usually tried to point them out. When she'd first started training, she'd come up with the strangest conspiracy theory bullshit based on random evidence. Most of the time, her ideas had been totally wrong, but as she'd matured, she'd honed that skill. She'd learned to do research—and not the ten minutes on Google kind. And she'd gotten a ton of experience. Her last alpha had warned Kit to never ignore her. Never take her on blind faith either, but take her concerns seriously.

So what had he done? He'd ignored her. Or rather, he'd put her concerns on his list. Way, way, way down at the bottom of the list.

"Marsha told me that her missions were getting more dangerous. Always worse than expected. Always a bit weirder too, and the issue was accelerating."

Yordan nodded. "That's probably because of the black hole of death in Wisconsin. It should be easing off now."

"That's what I said."

Yordan frowned. "But you took her off combat and set her on a training run to Torch Lake just to prove her wrong?"

Kit nodded, pleased that Yordan understood what he wasn't saying. Torch Lake had a lake monster created by a camp counselor and immortalized into song by a folk singer. It was also on a nexus of energy lines, which meant that every few years, the Torch Lake monster manifested. All that energy going into scaring little kids created exactly what they feared.

It wasn't a big deal. In fact, it was the perfect training ground for new recruits. Entice the serpent creature out of the water, then kill it. Everyone came out covered in slime, but victorious.

"Why is this bad?" Yordan pressed. "What did she bet?"

"It wasn't a bet. It was a curse phrased as a bet."

They'd made it to the helipad in record time. Their gear was just being tossed in the back, and they both pulled on helmets and strapped in like the pros they were. And if Kit snuck a peek at Yordan's ripple of muscles, broad shoulders, and tight ass, then who was to blame him? He couldn't be all panic all the time.

Two minutes later, they were in the air. Kit had started flying helicopters when he was a boy in Scotland. Putting this one into the air was a sweet joy, even if the thing was a little rickety and desperately needed a few dozen replacement parts. That was why it was the only one available. The others were already deployed.

Meanwhile, Yordan brought him back to business. "What was the curse?"

"That Marsha would face increasingly hard monsters until she admitted to Coffee that he was cute."

Yordan groaned. "She'd never say that."

"Exactly. She bet him that he didn't have the strength of will to make a curse stick. Which we now know he did because Coffee was backed by fairy magic."

"So, Marsha's taken a bunch of puppies up north to fight—"

"The Torch Lake monster."

"Do we know which monster it is?"

"Nope." The Torch Lake monster had two manifestations—a huge, slimy, lizard dragon or a huge, slimy, panther dragon. The difference was in the face and sometimes in how the creature attacked. The lizard spewed scalding water out of its mouth. The panther used claws to trap before biting off the victim's head. It was all part of the fun of monster manifestations.

Yordan's fingers tapped nervously on his thigh. He was either thinking hard or a nervous flyer. Or both.

"How good are the puppies?"

Kit shot a look of mea culpa at Yordan. "They're new geeks. This was supposed to be their one and only mission before setting up in research and development."

Yordan took a moment to absorb that, but far from the fury or condemnation Kit expected, he flashed an excited grin.

"I loved my Torch Lake mission. Glad I get to go back."

And wasn't that Yordan to a T? No condemnation. No worry. Simple process of the basics. *Here's the problem; let's go fix it.* If Kit weren't already half in love with Yordan, this would have tipped him straight over the edge.

Kit might be a flexible thinker, but that meant he often got lost in the weeds. He might see all the possibilities, but he quickly got overwhelmed by the magnitude of all the variables. Then he castigated himself for not being able to focus.

Yordan didn't waste time on blame. He attacked the problem head on without emotions, and that was a godsend right now. Kit wanted to say something mushy then. Something that was grateful and hinted at deeper feelings.

But now wasn't the time. Especially since he had a confession to make and it was better done not watching Yordan's reaction. So he focused on flying as he oh-so casually mentioned his personal problem.

"So, um, I've got to warn you. I'll be using a gun in this fight. I'm a pretty good shot—"

"A gun?" Yordan snapped. "With puppies around? Unless you're a dead shot, that's fucking stupid."

"I won't be much use otherwise—"

"Bullshit. I don't care if you're frightened. Don't care if your blood runs cold at the sight of big fangs. Whatever the problem is, these puppies are your responsibility. What the hell happened to you? You used to be one of the badass fighters. Whatever made you go bureaucrat, get over it. We don't have the time for it."

Kit felt his gut twist. He knew there were rumors about why he'd suddenly been thrown into a noncombat position. Most people thought he'd gotten an injury—which was close to the truth—but without a visible limp or missing limb, people thought he was off in the head. Apparently, Yordan thought he'd turned coward, and that hurt.

"Shut up and listen. I can't shift like normal, so I'll be using a gun."

Yordan stared at him, and Kit returned the glare. A moment later, Yordan flushed and looked away. "Sorry. I shouldn't judge. I don't know—"

"You're damn right you don't know. You think I wanted to leave my pack?"

"I thought you asked for the transfer."

"I did." Damn the guy for being so well-informed, but not well-informed *enough*. "Because I wasn't going to endanger anyone else."

Yordan nodded. "So you'll use a gun."

"Yes."

"It better be a goddamned missile launcher, then," Yordan said as he pointed outside. While they'd been talking, the campground had come into view. Kit hadn't seen it at first. He'd been busy flying the helo while trying not to throttle Yordan. But now that he banked around, he finally got a good look at the campground.

Holy shit. They were so screwed.

CHAPTER 9

One for the Money, Two for the... Holy Hell, What's That?

T he Torch Lake monster was a lot bigger than Yordan remembered. When his puppy pack had taken on the thing, it had been the size of a cement mixer with equally hard skin. Its mismatched eyes were big, glowing targets, though, and once they'd managed to blind the thing, it had roared in agony. That opened its mouth wide enough for several well-placed bullets to fly up into its brain.

Not exactly easy, but exhilarating, nonetheless.

Today's incarnation of the lake monster was three times the size and shot slime acid straight from its gullet.

How did Yordan know it was slime acid? Because right when the helicopter banked to come close to the battle zone, the thing shot a big green goober straight at them. Yordan didn't have to see the melting windshield to know what was happening. He could hear the sizzle as electronics fried, not to mention The Scot's curse as he fought with the controls.

Yordan had never learned how to pilot anything. Aeronautics were not his strong suit, so all he could do was clutch his seat and pray while the copter seemed to roil in the air.

The Scot's calm voice steadied him, though, even as his words were, "Hold on. We're going down." At least he was speaking in his full Scottish brogue, which was somehow reassuring.

The rapid rise of the horizon, however, was not reassuring. Going down was right. And not just down, but into the water down.

Actually, that might be a good thing, Yordan tried to tell himself. Better than going splat on the blacktop. Except a moment later, The Scot's steady voice cut through the beeping alarms.

"When I say go, jump."

Jump? Like, into the freezing water jump? Half the lake was still frozen over. It was one of Yordan's nightmares to be trapped under hard ice and unable to break through.

"Sure," he said, though his heart was beating like a panicked hamster's.

"Go wolf. It'll keep you warmer."

But it'd seriously cut down on his swimming capability. Though it was probably better not to be frozen. Wolf it was. Unfortunately, since he was a slow shifter, he had to begin the shift ASAP. He unbuckled and reached to unhook McNabb.

"Don't bother. Go." The Scot's brogue was in full force now, but not even that could blunt the terror of what he said.

Still, first things first. And that meant unhooking McNabb. Yordan could already tell The Scot was aiming the helo straight at the acid-spewing monster. Hopefully the blades would be whole enough to chop the thing in half as it went down. Either way, there was no reason for McNabb to go down with the ship.

Without a word, he unhooked McNabb and shoved hard. He would have dragged the guy with him, but he didn't have leverage. Then it was all he could do to fling himself backward out his side.

Too late. There hadn't been time.

He crashed into the monster with all the screaming terror of dying machinery and slime monster. Fortunately, he had his own secret weapon.

No one understood the magic of a lycanthropic werewolf. Only that it took thirty seconds of agonizing pain as his body twisted and reshaped itself to a wolf. Thanks to his extensive career fighting scary shit, he knew that he could be broken in half during a shift and his body would still reshape itself according to the rules of a wolf. Which meant his screaming body could take a great deal of abuse and end up whole in the end.

That was exactly what happened. If he hadn't been practicing these last twenty years, he wouldn't have had any control during the shift. Turned out that if he focused on using the last of his strength to throw himself out the side of a helicopter, he could get whopped by chunks of decapitated monster and buried in burning acid and yet still reform whole and complete underwater.

The acid was mostly washed away—he was sure he'd have thin furry parts until the next shift—and his bones were solid as he kicked free of the last of his clothes and began doggy-paddling to shore. Even if it was in water cold enough to freeze a man's balls off.

Where the hell was McNabb?

Yordan lifted his head, searching left and right while still paddling. The decapitated monster was sinking down—crap, that thing was huge—and would quickly dissolve into nothing. That was the thing about monsters created from campfire songs. Every summer, they renewed themselves. And when you killed them, they just dissolved—acid phlegm and all—as if they had never been. That was because the folk song never talked about the thing's demise, only about it rising from the depths of Torch Lake to eat unsuspecting campers.

So that worry was gone. Acid was disappearing fast under the half-frozen lake. Which meant he ought to see McNabb's wolf paddling quickly toward the lake's edge. He ought to see it right now...

Right there...

Right...

Nothing. Damn it, he was sure he'd thrown McNabb clear. He'd shoved the man out with all his strength. There'd been no monster on his side to grab him and no spinning helicopter parts. Or so Yordan had thought.

He looked to the shore where the puppies were gathering. They were all worse for wear but not dead. And there, running along the shore, was Marsha in her slender gray wolf form. She sounded like she was yipping something, but hell if he could hear it.

Didn't matter. He saw her plunge into the freezing cold water after something. That meant it was important enough for him to go help.

He wanted to change into his human form. God knew he could cover more ground that way, but his naked human body would get hypothermia in ten seconds or less. Best keep with the dog-paddle.

Then he saw where he was headed and had to blink the water out of his eyes to make sure he was seeing clearly. It couldn't be. McNabb wasn't that stupid.

Except, apparently, he was.

There was the idiot turning blue in the water, already stupid from hypothermia. He was a naked human man, and he was sinking fast.

Yordan put on a burst of speed. No way was Marsha going to get to him in time. For one thing, there was too much helicopter debris in her way. For another, she wasn't as strong a wolf as he was, and it took all his strength to get there. Thankfully, he had the help of a dissolving monster leg and a piece of helicopter to provide some momentary traction. And then he was there, diving under McNabb while the guy sank into oblivion.

If he had a human mouth, he would have said something. Probably a long string of curses. As it was, he got underneath The Scot's body and pushed up. He prayed that the man had enough consciousness to wrap his arms around Yordan. If not, then they were both screwed because he had no way to save the man, short of chomping down on McNabb's arm and dragging him out of the water.

They'd both have hypothermia if that happened because even timber wolves couldn't handle the cold forever.

Damn, it was hard to swim like this. He felt McNabb's arm slip off his shoulder, and he let out a growl. It was the only thing he could think of that might wake the guy up.

Come on!

He tried again to settle the man's weight on his back. It was difficult and unsteady, but he managed it for a moment. Long enough for Marsha to finally get to them.

She couldn't shift to human any more than he could, but she could brace The Scot on the other side. Keep him on Yordan's back as much as possible.

Thank God. That might work.

And then, miracle of miracles, he felt McNabb's arms tighten. He had some consciousness left. It might be clumsy, but it was all they needed to get him headed to the shore.

Why the fuck wasn't the guy shifting? What the hell was wrong with him that he couldn't? All questions that needed answering ASAP.

Fortunately, they had even more help. The puppies were on the shore, half of them in human form. Those were the ones ready with warming blankets and towels, so that when Yordan finally cleared the deep part of the lake, they were there grabbing The Scot and wrapping him up. Naked Guy Hypothermia 101. They knew what to do even though every single one of them was thinking the same thing.

Why wasn't McNabb shifting?

Yordan dug through his memories of everything he knew about The Scot. Wasn't he an insta-shift wolf? At least six times a day. Yordan was limited to twice back and forth unless it was a full moon.

The puppies were doing all the right things. Wrapping The Scot up, chafing his skin, and generally trying to wake him enough to get him to shift.

"Come on, dude," one kept saying. "Just shift, and this'll all be over. You'll be fine. Go wolf."

That was exactly what Yordan was thinking, though he added a ton of curses to his train of thought. He was about to go human just so he could slap some sense into The Scot, when life got infinitely worse.

They all heard it at the same time. It was the yowl of a pissed-off cat. A panther, to be exact, and it was coming from the lake behind them.

Oh shit. Oh shit. Apparently one lake monster wasn't enough. There were two.

The helo had taken out the acid-shooting lizard asshole. Now they were faced with the scaly panther. And everybody had been so focused on The Scot, they'd forgotten to look around.

Good news. This one incarnation was easier to kill. Its skin was more like beaver fur than hard scales.

Yordan gave Marsha a sharp, high yip and jerked his chin upward. They didn't have the benefit of long association, but some commands were universal among the packs.

Step one: Draw the predator away from the puppies. He and Marsha agreed on a direction with a simple jerk of the head, and the two of them went barking and yipping down the edge of the lake toward the empty youth camp.

Better to zip and swerve between campfire pits than smash up boats and houses on the private property that surrounded the rest of the lake.

Step two: Once they grabbed the panther's attention, they started dashing toward the water and back, forward and back, trying to draw the thing out of the water. Once it climbed up, the plan was to do running attacks that slowly sliced up the monster. It wasn't glorious work, but it was the standard wolf pack method of taking down a larger creature. Hamstring it and, when it topples over, take out the throat.

But that was hard to do with just two of them. Which was why Yordan was grateful when two of the puppies joined them. But even four wolves yipping into the lake and back were not enough to hold the panther's attention.

Well, hell. For whatever reason, it seemed intent on where the two human puppies were trying to warm up McNabb.

Yordan cursed loudly—which came out as an angry, growling bark —then dashed forward. Why, oh why weren't the geeks running away? Sure, they thought they were being heroic, staying next to the possibly dying McNabb, but if they would just dash away, the creature wouldn't do more than ignore The Scot as so much driftwood.

That was the nature of predator cats. They saw movement, not downed Popsicles.

See me! yipped Yordan. *Over here! Look at me!*

He made as much noise and commotion as he could, but the panther was stalking closer to the puppies.

"Run, you fucking idiots!" Marsha bellowed.

Yordan glanced back. She was on her hands and knees as a naked woman, slowly climbing to her feet. Well, hell. That was one less wolf. He had no idea how soon she could shift back to canine, but he had to assume not anytime soon.

Then he looked back at the human puppies. They were dragging The Scot away from the water's edge. They weren't naturally strong humans, and McNabb wasn't exactly small. It took the both of them, and now they presented a single, slow-moving target to the panther.

God save him from puppies.

"Leave him!" Marsha screamed, but apparently they were the stubborn kind of heroic. So that meant it was going to be a tooth and claw fight.

Fine. It was his job to stand between monsters and idiots, and Yordan embraced his mission as holy law. He was running full tilt toward the puppies and intended to leap into the breach, when the panther readied his attack. The puppies didn't see it coming, but the panther was starting that clicking noise that cats made. And its butt was twitching. It was about to make a killing strike.

Then the absolute worst thing happened. McNabb started to wake. He'd probably been shivering for a while, but Yordan was too far away to see it. Now the guy curled into himself and moaned.

Not good! Not good!

"Stay still!" Marsha bellowed. She was running on two feet but was much too far away to do anything.

Then the panther lunged. Yordan had no idea how so large a body could leap out of water so easily, but it did. It was one of the crazy things about magical monsters. They didn't obey the laws of physics.

That was okay. He was used to impossible monsters, and he timed his leap perfectly.

He caught the panther's face just as it came down. Scaly lizard legs landed on the sand with an oomph, enough to knock the puppies back. But Yordan caught the panther's face with what was essentially a headbutt.

And—hallelujah—the panther was now laser focused on him. Cool. He could fight a cat any day. Even one twice as large as he was.

The cat lunged again, Yordan dashed away and tried for a side swipe. No go. It wasn't that the skin was too tough. Nope, his claws would slice it right open. But the cat was so damned fast, he missed by a few key inches.

Next time. *Nope.*

Next time. *Shit.*

His peripheral vision showed him that McNabb was waking, coming back to full consciousness. Good. Maybe the guy could shift and help in this fight. Another trained wolf would be a godsend. Yordan was good, but he was getting tired. Magical gummy aside, no one could keep this up for long.

To the other side, Marsha was organizing the puppies, and pretty soon he had slower, stupider wolves dashing in and out. It helped. Gave him a breather and all, but it wasn't enough.

And then. Sweet heaven, thank you. He saw the telltale shimmer around The Scot. Good. The guy was finally going wolf—

Fuck!

He'd been distracted watching The Scot and had missed an attack. Got a panther paw rake against his flank.

It wasn't fatal, but it stung like a bitch. That leg was going to be slow now.

On the upside, the strike had pulled the panther into perfect position for wolfy McNabb to leap and sink his teeth straight into the creature's neck.

Like right now.

Now!

Where the fuck was The Scot?

"Merowwwww! Mew, mew. Whimper. Meow!"

What was that?

Yordan wasn't the only one looking. The panther reacted as any feline mother should. It sniffed, cocked its ears, and turned its whole head to where wolf McNabb should be standing right now. Except there wasn't a wolf there. Instead, Yordan saw a large kitten squatting miserably in the sand.

What the fuck?

Not only was it a kitten, but it was one of those Scottish floppy-eared things. It wasn't even a proper cat! Was that The Scot?

Couldn't be. He'd never fought directly with McNabb before, but he'd heard the tales. The guy was a big gray wolf. He was sure of it.

Except right now, he was a mewling, pitiful gray kitten. He had big, limpid eyes and ears that fell in adorable little folds. If Yordan weren't so shocked, he'd be laughing his ass off. Or cursing because the damned kitten was about to get eaten.

The panther dashed forward, dropping its head down as it sniffed then opened its mouth.

No!

Yordan and every wolf on the beach started barking, trying to distract the creature, to no avail.

With a grumbling kind of purr, the panther put its mouth around McNabb's neck and lifted the kitten up by his scruff. Well, hell.

The Scot dangled from the panther's mouth like a naughty kitten with his feet hanging down and his shoulders up around his folded ears.

Talk about a sight Yordan would remember for the rest of his life. It was downright hysterical until he realized the panther was taking the kitten back to its lair or den or wherever mamma cats took their kittens.

Too bad this cat was a lake monster. Its home might very well be under the freezing water. That was not going to work for The Folded-Eared Scot. But what the hell was Yordan going to do about it? And what the fuck was McNabb doing? Was he in pain? Was he trying to wriggle free?

It looked like The Scot was swinging back and forth, harder and harder. Enough to make the panther slow down as she tried to fight his momentum.

Weird.

And then Yordan watched the cleverest use of insta-shift he'd ever seen in action. Right at the moment of farthest arc, the kitten was covered in the golden glow of a shift. McNabb was shifting back to human with all the change in weight and dimension that entailed.

It never would have worked for Yordan. He took too long to change. But the insta-shift meant that the panther was abruptly carrying the weight of a full-grown man, who looped an arm around the creature's neck rather than go flying back out into the half-frozen lake.

The panther toppled sideways onto the sand with its neck stretched out from the pull of McNabb's human weight. And bam, there was a perfect target for Yordan and any puppy within reach.

Perfect, if one ignored the fact that The Scot's back was ripped open by the creature's teeth. McNabb's kitten scruff had become human flesh. God willing, it had been McNabb's back and not his neck.

Either way, Yordan couldn't deal with it now. He took the opportunity McNabb had sacrificed his back for and attacked.

Success.

He ripped out the monster's neck, and just as the creature's lifeblood began to drain away, the thing splintered into a thousand pinpoints of light and disappeared.

Gone. Back into the lore that created it.

In its place lay The Scot, who was a bloody, shivering mess.

Marsha got there before Yordan did. He needed to shift back to human before he could help. And honestly, he was supposed to stay wolf just in case the lake decided to throw a third monster at them.

But the discipline was hard. McNabb was on the ground with blood staining the sand like sick ink, and there was nothing a wolf could do to stop it.

Yordan made room for Marsha, splitting his attention between watching the surrounding area and seeing if The Scot was in his death throes.

"Are you all right?" Marsha gasped. "What do you need?"

The Scot opened his mouth to answer, but no sound came out. Instead, there was the telltale shimmer as he turned back into a kitten in all his bedraggled, floppy-eared glory.

"Meow."

Never had a kitten sounded more disgruntled with his life. A single, short meow as it sat there and pouted. Apparently, he couldn't shift back to human yet. Insta-shifts often had a lag time between changes. That meant The Scot had to stay kitten for what was going to feel like a humiliatingly long amount of time.

Fortunately, the kitten looked fine. The Scot would live. And Yordan knew just what to do. No stranger to humiliating antics, he padded over and gently, carefully picked up his boss's boss by the scruff of his neck and carried him back to base camp.

And if he drooled a bit on the kitten head, then who could complain? Wolves weren't exactly neat when carrying itty-bitty, fluff-ball kitties.

CHAPTER 10
Warm Kitty, Soft Kitty, Little Ball of Fur

K it didn't mind the drool. It was a lot better than the kitty litter and catnip jokes that he knew were coming. And frankly, it would be deeply painful to receive that kind of humiliation from Yordan, so he delayed it as long as possible by remaining feline.

It helped that he'd shifted far more than usual today, not to mention the icy swim. He doubted he had the stamina to shift, despite the magic gummy.

Truthfully, he was more worried about Yordan. He could smell the blood dripping from his wound, and he was deeply afraid for the man.

He needn't have worried. Yordan was responsible enough to see everyone got safely back to base camp before making the gut-wrenching shift back to human. Lord, Kit didn't know how lycan-thropic wolves willingly went through that much pain. He watched every bone-grinding second as the man turned from wounded wolf to healthy man.

Healthy, *naked* man, and even in his kitten state, Kit wasn't above a little lustful looking.

Then, still fully naked, Yordan squatted down in front of Kit.

When he spoke, his voice was level and serious, but Kit was eye to eye with the twinkle of amusement that lingered in the guy's expression.

"My guess is the only reason you're not human right now is that you've burned through your shifts for the day."

He paused as if waiting for a response, so Kit nodded as best he could, given that he was stretched out with his chin on his front paws.

"Now don't sulk. You're too purrrrty for it."

Kit looked up and hissed. It only made Yordan grin.

"I'm going to get the puppies squared away. I know Marsha has them well in hand, but someone's got to report the crashed copter. They'll send the other one eventually. Or a van, but you and I, we're going to have a conversation before then. Might as well be here after the puppies leave."

Didn't the idiot realize Kit was his boss? Yordan was acting like he was in charge, which, come to think of it, he was. Kit had already promoted him, which meant that when Kit was out of commission, Yordan was the boss instead.

"Don't worry about a thing," Yordan continued. "Marsha and I are old hands at this."

That was the understatement of the year.

"Is there anything else you need while I'm doing your job?"

Kit was sorely tempted to just curl up and die, but he had responsibilities he couldn't abandon. He'd left in a rush and crashed the helicopter. Best if he reported it himself.

So he mewed at the computer set up across the room. Given that Torch Lake was a common monster zone, Wulf, Inc. had purchased a small cottage next to the kids' camp. It was home base for all sorts of training maneuvers off-season and a vacation retreat during the summer. That meant it was kitted out with medical supplies, up-to-date computer equipment, and a stocked kitchen for a full werewolf pack. Kit had no excuse for remaining out of contact when he was here.

Yordan frowned. "Really? You can't be away from the office for ten minutes? When are you going to sleep?"

Kit croaked a cranky mew, which was as intelligible as what he would normally say to a question like that. He had seven combat packs under his direction. If the shit hit the fan, then he needed to know.

Yordan grunted his response—equally unintelligible—then he picked up kitten Kit and dumped him in front of the computer. He even obliged by setting the keyboard in such a way as it could be used —awkwardly—by kitten paws.

"That all?" he asked as he turned the thing on.

Kit mewed his best thank you, and Yordan chuckled.

"That's fucking adorable."

And Kit nearly died right there of embarrassment. Thankfully, Yordan sauntered out, his tight butt swinging saucily as he moved. The cottage was outfitted with spare clothing, but apparently Yordan preferred showing off his glorious physique.

An hour later, Kit was ready to claw the computer to shreds. Typing with kitty paws was incredibly difficult, but every time he tried to shift back to human, all he got was a pounding headache. This might be the rebound from the gummies or the sheer frustration of pecking at a keyboard with his very flat nose. He could kill Coffee. Why the hell hadn't he realized that one drunken night with the werewolf was the cause of this curse? Coffee had actually said, "If you lose, everyone will know you're just an itty-bitty Scottish kitty."

Arggggh!

Fortunately, Pee had things under control back home. She'd already emailed him a neat spreadsheet of the bets in Coffee's book, categorized as money, silly, screw-ups, and world-ending. Thankfully, there wasn't anything outstanding under "world-ending," though one never knew with fairy bets. That left the silly and the screw-ups as worrisome, and he was only partially amused to see his bet listed under both.

The door popped open as Yordan strode back in, and Kit was able to hastily change the page on the spreadsheet. It wouldn't save him from Yordan's snooping, but it would at least delay the situation for a bit.

"Still too tired to go human?" Yordan asked as he strolled in. He wore low-slung sweats on his narrow hips and nothing else. Even his bare feet were sexy as he crossed to look at the screen. "Email? Need help?"

He wiggled his fingers over the keyboard, then at the last minute, tickled Kit under the chin.

"Unless you'd like a little rubbin', swubbin'?"

Kit twisted and managed to bite down on his finger in response. Yordan only laughed harder.

"Don't be a cwanky kitty. Big daddy-o is here to help his little wubbins."

Kit wished he'd drawn blood. He hadn't. The man's human skin was as thick as wolf fur. No kitten jaw was going to pierce that.

"What have we got here? Email?"

Kit responded with a hard meow and a firm jerk of his chin at the main house. Yordan correctly interpreted that as a question about everyone else.

"Oh, right. The puppies are okay. Some basic first aid and a stern talking-to about thinking calmly during a battle. They'll probably need to talk to someone about what happened. This was pretty traumatic for a first mission, but they'll be all right."

Kit absorbed that and meowed a short question. Again, Yordan seemed to understand.

"Marsha will settle her outstanding debt to Coffee. She's cool." He glanced at Kit's twitching tail and grinned. "But I'd expect kitty litter as your Christmas gift for years to come."

Yeah. He'd already figured that out.

"They're all gone, by the way. We'll take the van."

What van? Kit looked up with a cat frown.

"Yeah, you don't know about that. And you still don't. Because Nero would never hide a sweet conversion van in a garage near here. One that is tricked out as a geek's paradise sex van whenever they train up here."

Kit croaked a slow meow of irritation. No wonder Nero's pack loved training missions here.

"Have I covered all the questions?" Yordan asked.

Kit grunted and looked back at the screen. There were a few things that needed handling by a person with fingers. Might as well get them done now.

Yordan nodded and then started tapping. The problem was that it was awkward with them both trying to see the screen. Kit kept peering around the keyboard and blocking Yordan's view. In the end, the guy cursed and picked up Kit by the scruff of his neck.

"This is going to take forever if we don't work together," the man grumbled.

Then he put Kit on his shoulder. Kit was a big kitten, large enough to dwarf someone else's shoulder, but not Yordan's. After an indignant yowl at the manhandling, he settled on the guy's shoulder with a huff.

"Keep those claws contained," Yordan grumbled.

Kit did. And in a moment, he allowed himself to lean into Yordan's neck. Lord, it was warm and comfy here, and pretty soon, the two of them settled into a rhythm, moving through Kit's work with surprising speed.

They developed a shorthand of yeses and nos by his meows. Yordan guessed at what should be said in responses—with fairly good accuracy—and typed it in his usual straightforward language. Typically Kit would be more circumspect, but Yordan's bluntness had its advantages. When Kit would normally offer an explanation, Yordan typed, *No*. Or, *Never*. And once, *Dream on, sucker*, but that was to Nero, so he got away with it.

The important tasks were finished quickly, and Yordan settled in to see the breadth and depth of Coffee's outstanding bets.

By that point, Kit's exhaustion was creeping in. The warmth of Yordan's body, the gentle rocking of his breathing, and even the low chuckle as he commented on the more stupid bets had Kit's eyes drifting closed.

"So Gummy bet that he'd be surrounded by numbnuts for the rest of his life. Which means the flying gators weren't my fault."

Not exactly accurate, but close enough. Kit responded with a low purr.

Yordan lifted his shoulder and nuzzled Kit's back.

"Getting sleepy?"

Kit couldn't deny it.

"Me too," Yordan said with a loud yawn. "Guess the gummy worm has worn off. I think the rest of this can wait for now."

Kit's response was a low purr. Honestly, he wasn't fully aware of making the sound except that it felt so good to let it rumble through his body. This was something cats had over dogs, and he'd never appreciated it until now.

Yordan stood up, still carrying Kit, and headed up the stairs to the bedrooms. There were several there. Plenty to pick from, but of course Yordan headed for the master. It had the biggest bed and a gargantuan attached bath. And somewhere between the door and the bed, Kit fell fast asleep.

CHAPTER 11

I Thought I Saw a Pussy Cat

Yordan had never had a pet, even before he was part of Wulf, Inc. And if he had lived in one place long enough to get one, it wouldn't have been a rumbly kitten with ears that looked broken. Yet he couldn't deny the visceral joy of stirring awake to the feel of a fluffball curled up against his chest. He was a side sleeper—usually naked—and the feel of that ultrasoft fur against his chest was almost as delightful as the low, purring motor that was The Scot.

Lord, he'd never woken with such a deep contentment before, and he found himself scratching the kitten behind the ears before he truly remembered it was his boss.

And then he watched in delight as the big, bad Scotsman stretched out his tiny little paws with needle-sharp claws and wriggled like a powder puff of cuteness. Yordan couldn't help but chuckle. He was already tickling the kitten under his chin, the furball motor purring with pleasure.

All shifters did that to one extent or another. Just as they woke, they were often more animal than human, and you could catch grown men squirming ecstatically with their backs in the dirt or tiny kittens purring right before a jaw-cracking yawn.

Then McNabb woke up.

He froze in mid-yawn, half choking as he snapped his jaw shut.

Then he hopped up onto all four paws, his adorable mismatched eyes blinking with fury at being caught being so cute.

"It's okay," Yordan said with a laugh. "I don't really want people to know that I snuggled a kitten in my sleep either."

The Scot dropped down on his butt as he stared at Yordan. There was a question in his gaze, though he didn't make a sound, and Yordan glanced to the bedside table.

"It's a little after three a.m." They'd fallen asleep about six p.m., so that made sense. "We both needed the sleep. You feel up to shifting?"

The Scot hopped back up to all four paws, then frowned hard. It was adorable for about a half second. Then the kitten was surrounded in a bright glow, the air got suddenly chilly enough for Yordan's nipples to tighten, and then bam, there was a full-grown Scotsman about to tumble off the side of the bed.

Oh shit!

Yordan reacted without thought, grabbing the guy and hauling him back onto the bed until he had a naked Scotsman sprawled sideways and face up on his chest. And not too surprisingly, little Yordan perked up in interest.

Even worse was the smell of the man. Something feline and masculine that should have repulsed Yordan, but instead had him inhaling deeply as one of his hands tightened around McNabb's thick bicep.

Wow, The Scot was big. And sexy. And little Yordan was ready to rumble.

"Oh shit," McNabb murmured as he tried to readjust. His voice was husky in that just woken-up way (or just shifted to human way), and Yordan didn't want to let him go.

He did, of course, while sliding over to the side to give Kit more room on the bed. The resulting maneuvering had Yordan's heart racing and his dick throbbing.

And then their gazes locked. There was no mistaking the expansion of McNabb's nostrils as he, too, inhaled. His eyes went hungry, and his lips curled back as he locked on Yordan.

The hunger was obvious—in both of them—but a smart man

would think about this. A smart man would not fuck his boss's boss. And right now, Yordan was trying to be a smart man.

He swallowed. "You had a bet with Coffee," he rasped out. "I saw it in the spreadsheet."

"Yeah," McNabb answered. "I think it's why I turn into a kitten now."

Really?

"So, can you fix it?"

"Trying to."

What? Crouching naked on the bed next to Yordan wasn't exactly him trying to pay off some debt.

"Um, Yordan," The Scot said slowly. "Is that just morning wood or, um..."

"Do I want to mount you like an alpha dog and fuck your brains out?"

"Yeah."

"The second."

Blink. Blink. "Okay. I'd like that."

Yordan's dick surged enough that his hips lifted slightly off the bed. But that was all he did. He didn't grab McNabb or leap. He didn't even reach up to kiss the guy, though he had to curl his fingers into the sheets to keep himself still.

Then after a moment, he said, "We're coworkers, you know."

"It's worse than that. I'm in your direct chain of command." The Scot's expression turned bleak. "This could be considered sexual harassment."

Yordan nodded. "But I don't feel harassed. I don't feel forced at all."

The Scot flashed a sexy grin. "You can be on top." Oh hell, his brogue was back, and that never failed to feel like soft hands stroking his dick.

"I don't want this to screw with my job. It's not..." Fuck, it was hard to think with McNabb looking all come-hither. "There're all sorts of reasons not to do this at work."

The Scot didn't disagree. His voice was light and his eyes languid as he said a cheerful, "Yup."

"Right now, I don't care."

"As the supervisor, I need to care." McNabb's expression turned wistful. "But I've wanted this for so long, I don't think I can stop you."

It took a moment for Yordan's brain to process that through his fog of lust. But when the words filtered in, he found himself smiling. "A long time, huh?"

The Scot adjusted himself on the bed, shifting so that their bodies were aligned, touching but not grinding. Yet.

"Do you remember the day we met?"

Yordan shook his head. They were already face-to-face, so it was easy to let his hand stroke up and down McNabb's flank. The man flexed with the touch, and he heard a for-real purr—a very manly one —underneath his next words.

"It was after my first mission," he said. His eyes darted to the side to indicate the lake. "Here, actually. We were already back at the mansion, and I was bragging about how badass we were. Well, how badass I was. But we were all—"

"I remember," Yordan said. The pack had been high on their own success, halfway to drunk, and steeped in glory. Just like every puppy after a first mission. But Yordan had been back from a hard one. His pack had survived—barely—and there had been civilian casualties. He remembered getting angrier and angrier as McNabb had glorified the wrong things. Then he'd gone on to pitying the mundanes, and Yordan lost control of his temper. "I shouldn't have reamed you out," he said softly. "It wasn't my place, and I was too raw from my own shit."

The Scot shrugged, his expression too guarded to read. "You told us—well, you told me—that every soul has a power and a purpose. Obviously, we'd been given strength, but if we didn't start looking for the power in every living soul, then we were short on smarts."

Yordan winced. "I sound like a pompous ass." What right had he had to piss on anyone's first mission? They deserved the high.

"You were right. I'd never thought of it that way before. It's so easy to glory in our abilities, but if we don't see that other people have value and their own kind of power, then we miss the whole point of this life." His expression grew soft. "I learned that from you, and it's been a guiding principle of my life."

Yordan gaped at him. "Bullshit."

"Not shit. It took me a couple years for the truth of it to really sink in, but you planted the seed."

Yordan shifted, uncomfortable with being seen so clearly. "I was steeped in my own shit. I shouldn't have rained on your parade."

"I've wanted you ever since."

"Because I spouted some bitter—"

"Because you have a wisdom that nobody else seems to see. It guides your life and, damn it, is so quietly impressive that I've followed your career, read every single mission report about you, and..." He shrugged. "I've been stalkery crazy about you."

Wow. "I didn't know."

Worse, he didn't know what to do about it. It felt vulnerable to be so seen by this man. Everyone tended to dismiss him as a quiet jarhead. Himself included. But in the quiet of the dark nights, Yordan thought about this kind of stuff. About what every living creature brought to the planet. About how he was here to protect the weaker ones, the ones who made art, the ones who had families, the ones who led nations, as well as the ones who took care of sick kids. He was here to protect them.

But he was also here to protect the assholes. It wasn't his job to judge what they did with their power. It was his job to protect them until they figured it out. And sometimes, he got full of himself, and he lectured new puppies.

"I, um, I don't know what to say," Yordan said.

"You don't have to say or do anything. I kind of sprung this on you."

Maybe. Maybe not. After all, he'd followed McNabb's career, too. He'd heard about The Scot's missions and strong leadership style.

That was why he'd been so disappointed when the guy had turned coward and moved into management.

How idiotic that thought was now. First, the guy wasn't a coward. No man turned himself into a kitten just to distract a panther that could have easily eaten him. Second, he'd seen all of McNabb's emails. Shit, the guy juggled a ton. Management was not a coward's way out of responsibility.

Besides, if Yordan's werewolf had suddenly turned into a tiny kitten, then he'd be the first to demand a transfer out of his combat pack. A fluffball could not pull his weight in a combat pack, no matter how cute.

"I shouldn't have called you a coward. I shouldn't have even thought it."

"You aren't the only one." McNabb shrugged. "Maybe I shouldn't have hidden my, um, feline affliction."

Yordan grinned and thunked himself on the forehead. "Kit. Your name is Kit. Oh my god, that's funny."

"Yeah, yeah, yuk it up."

The banter had lightened the mood, but they were still two naked men pressed together on the bed. Not full flush, but enough that their bodies brushed erotically against each other with every chuckle.

It didn't take long for hunger to thicken the air. And parts that were not rock hard.

"I'm not going to touch you, Yordan," Kit said, his voice husky. "But if you want to..." He cleared his throat. "If you want something with me, then I'm all in. No pressure. And no career repercussions, I swear."

That was like spreading out a banquet in front of a suddenly hungry wolf. Yordan felt himself respond body and soul.

"Anything I want with you. This night only?"

Kit's chin jerked down. "No questions asked. I'm saying yes."

Yordan grinned. This night, this second, he couldn't think beyond that anyway. But before he indulged half the things in his mind right then, he had a few things that needed to be said.

"Oh, there are going to be questions," he growled as he levered himself up on one elbow. "First, I'm clean. You?"

"Yes." The word came out strangled as Kit understood what was about to happen.

"Good. Second question, do you like it rough?"

The Scot grinned. "Oh aye, laddie," he drawled in his best brogue.

Damn, that turned Yordan on.

"Me too."

Then Kit held up a hand. "Third, there are condoms in the bathroom. We should use them."

Yordan frowned. "Since when?"

"Nero made me do it a few years back. Puppies will be puppies, and safe is better than sorry." He winked at Yordan. "I'll get them."

Kit rolled off the bed, landing on his toes like a cat. A big, sleek, Scottish killer cat. Yordan admired his cut form, his tight buttocks and broad shoulders, not to mention the hard, thick thrust of his cock. The Scot wasn't quite as tall as Yordan, but he made up for it in compact power. Plus, he had a grace that Yordan would never achieve.

Kit found the condoms quickly, but while he was gone, Yordan arranged himself on the bed for maximum effect. He lay on his side, one knee up with his cock thick and heavy, thrusting forward. He was probably grinning as he imagined just what he was going to do to his boss's boss. And he arched a brow in challenge when McNabb slowed his steps as he approached the bed.

"Now that's a bonnie sight."

"Okay, kitty cat," Yordan growled. "Given that you've put me in charge, here's what you're going to do."

McNabb's cock bobbed at that, and his expression lifted into a delighted grin. Of course, his words belied that.

"Oh really?" he challenged. "And what am I going to do? Be exact."

"You're going to put that condom on me, and then you're going to return to that kitty cat position right on the bed. You're going to be on all fours while I mount you like the dog I am. What do you think of that, pussy cat?"

He didn't have to ask. He could see the come pearling on the end of McNabb's cock. The man wanted it as much as Yordan did.

Yordan arched a brow. "What are you waiting for?"

"Just wanted to see if there were any other commands."

"Nope."

McNabb grinned. "Good. Because it sounds like I get to take my time on the way to my 'position.'"

Yordan arched his brows, but he didn't have time to do anything more than that. Kit leaped onto the bed, and though he was a big man, he landed precisely atop Yordan. Suddenly, The Scot had made a cage around Yordan enough that their cocks bumped wildly together.

And while Yordan was recovering from the lightning shock of that, Kit started kissing Yordan with hungry abandon. He could feel every minute of the man's pent-up desire. It was there in the way he gripped Yordan's head, the way he thrust powerfully into Yordan's mouth, and the way—in a shock that had Yordan stiffening in pleasure—he twisted Yordan's right nipple.

"Even a kitten has claws," Kit growled. "Tell me if it's too rough."

Two could play at that game, and Yordan was there scratching a nail across McNabb's tight nubs.

"Bring it, putty tat."

Then it was on. Nails were the least of the things they used to learn about each other's bodies. Teeth and tongue, hands and feet. They were both strong, big men, and the wrestling they shared tore up the bed in the most pleasurable of ways.

Eventually, the condom went on. In time, Kit was down on all fours while Yordan stroked his hard cock with a grip that would have made a lesser man whimper. Not Kit, though. He arched into the stroke and spread wide when Yordan mounted.

Then they moved together. A hard thrust with a steady pull that grew wilder and hotter with each passing ecstatic second.

Tight and wet.

Strong. Hard.

He'd never timed it so well or felt more in sync with anyone.

Again and again

Yes!

When it was all done, they collapsed sideways together, lying there in ecstatic breathlessness. Yordan had never felt so good.

It was a long time before Kit stirred. When he did, it was to kiss Yordan's nose. Or maybe it was a kittenish lick. Hard to tell. Then he leaned down and purred words that slipped straight into Yordan's mind and down to this thickening cock.

"My turn now, puppy pie."

CHAPTER 12

Wild Thing, You Make Me Sing

The sun was trying to burn away the lake ice when Kit finally opened his eyes. The bed was in shambles, but someone—Yordan—had thrown a blanket over him.

He stretched out stiff muscles, felt aches that made him smile, and searched for Yordan all in one long dance of muscles. Lord, he felt so good. Or he did until he found Yordan sitting across the room and frowning at the laptop in the corner.

That couldn't be good.

"What're ya doing over there?" he asked, too lazy to soften his brogue.

"Reading your email."

Kit sat up fast enough that his head swam a bit. "What's going on?"

"Nothing. You said I was your understudy. I'm studying."

True. "Okay. What's the word in my email?"

"You're in deep shit for wrecking the helo."

He sighed as he fell back onto the bed. Yeah, he'd already guessed that.

"But they're glad you're alive. They already have another one on order."

"Aye, but that was to replace the one that got trashed a month ago in Hawaii."

Yordan frowned at him. "Was that from Godzilla's baby?"

Kit stretched his neck and shoulders as he answered. "That was in Japan."

"Kracken?"

Again, Yordan surprised him by being so well-informed. But he was still wrong. "That was near Guatemala."

"Oh. So what did this?"

Honestly, it took a moment for Kit to remember. Oh yeah. "Hawaiian fever dream made manifest. Think spider monkey that burps acid."

Yordan grunted. "What is it with the acid monsters lately? They're ripping the hell out of our machines."

Didn't he know it. Kit stood up and headed for the bathroom while Yordan kept talking.

"Anyway, you're forgiven and all that. So long as you find a way to cut costs somewhere else to cover the price of a new helicopter."

"Not going to happen."

"I told them that."

Oh shit. Kit poked his head out of the bathroom. "Um, I was going to ease the brass over to that conclusion. Sweet-talk them with delays and pretend cuts—"

Yordan cut him off. "I said, 'No fucking way.' Signed it as Acting Commander me, so it'll blow my way, not yours."

Not part of the plan. Kit wanted Yordan in management, not getting bounced out early because he had no tolerance for bullshit. His next question came out tentative.

"So...is there blowback?"

"Nothing so far." Yordan looked back at Kit. "Apparently they're all jonesing for you to get more help. They seem thrilled that you've roped me into it."

He nodded. "Everyone likes and respects you. They want you at the home office with more responsibilities."

Yordan snorted. "I don't think they realize what they're asking."

He looked back at the screen. "But they're getting an idea now. I've answered a few more of your emails. If they don't like blunt and a little crude, then they'll have to demote me."

Kit got the feeling Yordan was hoping for that exact result. So maybe it was Yordan who didn't realize what was happening. No one was going to demote him. At least, not if Kit had anything to do with it.

Kit turned back to the bathroom, already knowing the answer to the question but asking it anyway.

"So, are all the fires out for now?"

"Yup. Pee has most of the money collected. I've sent a nyah-nyah email to Gummy, telling him the gators were on him this time. And the rest seems to be cleaning up pretty quick. Funny how a fairy debt gets paid off ASAP."

"Funny that." Kit chuckled as he started shaving. Damn, this was pleasant. Bantering over morning email. "Any more spin cycles at the motor pool?"

"Not since all eleven of the guys and girls there paid their debts. Coffee's sister is going to get a sweet sum of money when this is over."

Kit lifted his chin to shave his neck. He knew from the paperwork that Coffee's sister was the designated beneficiary. At least until Coffee returned from Fairyland or wherever the hell he might be. He continued shaving, humming a bit as he relived some of the best parts of last night. It took him a moment to realize that Yordan had left the computer to lean against the frame of the bathroom door.

Kit finished with the shaver and turned, his expression softening as he enjoyed the sight of the man lounging so casually with his torso bare and his sweats slung low.

"Hey there," he said in his best come-hither voice.

Yordan's hard expression didn't crack. Instead, he folded his arms over his chest, making his biceps bulge. "So, about your debt," he began.

Fuck, fuck, fuck, fuck.

"It's not important now," Kit said airily as he turned back to the sink and started cleaning out the electric shaver.

"Really?" Yordan challenged. "Let me see if I have the timing right. You're climbing the ranks as a badass werewolf. Became alpha of your pack within a few months. Several successful missions later, the brass is grinning, and Gummy's pack is cursing your name for getting the juiciest missions."

Kit flashed a pleased grin. "You guys cursed me? How sweet."

"Not actual curses, just the usual, 'Fuck you, asshole' shit."

Kit nodded. He knew exactly what that meant. "We said the same things about you—"

"Then suddenly," Yordan interrupted, staying with the hard tone. "The big bad happens in Wisconsin. Instead of helping out up north like every other combat werewolf, you suddenly turn coward and take a desk job."

Kit stiffened, even though he'd heard the rumor before. "Is that what you think?" he challenged. "That I went into management because I was afraid?"

"I did. The timing was too coincidental, and you gave no other explanation."

Now his blood was heating as he leaned back against the sink, consciously mimicking Yordan's pose.

"We've already talked about this. I wasn't being a coward."

"It was this kitten thing, right? You left your pack in the lurch. They were already one down, and you made it two. In fact, you gave all the signs of someone who had lost his nerve since you refused to shift."

Kit winced. "I didn't lose my nerve," he said, his voice tight with pain.

"But you made it look that way. You gave up leadership of your clan, too. Or future leadership, right? The new McNabb will be your sister."

Now that was striking close to home. And fuck Yordan for being so well-informed and yet not understanding a damn thing. Tired of standing there naked while Yordan grilled him about things he knew nothing about, Kit pushed off the sink and shouldered his way through the door. All the rooms were stocked with sweats, and he was quick to grab a pair, yanking them on with barely suppressed fury.

"Kit—" Yordan's voice was gentle, which made everything worse.

"My sister is the better leader. She's been living there while I've been off fighting monsters here. She deserves it."

"Maybe," Yordan said. "Or maybe you lost a bet to Coffee. That's why you change into a kitten, isn't it? And not just any kitten, but a Scottish Fold kitten. That matches his sense of humor."

Yeah, it did. And he was an idiot for not realizing that at the time. But with Wisconsin being the flash point to world-ending disaster, he'd had bigger things on his mind than why he was suddenly unable to go wolf.

Still, the whole situation had ripped out his heart. Losing his combat status, stepping away as the McNabb heir. As if everything he did, everything he was, was tied up in going wolf. Except that was bullshit! He was a hell of a lot more than a kitten or dog, as everyone who had a disability or career-ending injury knew.

Everyone, that is, except his entire family. Or the brass at Wulf, Inc.

"Kit..."

"Drop it, Yordan."

"What was the bet?" Like a dog with a bone.

Kit turned to glare at Yordan. "You asking as my lover or as my understudy?"

Yordan's brows rose, but he didn't answer.

"Because if it's as my understudy," Kit continued, "your boss just told you to drop it."

"I've got a problem with authority. All my evals say that."

"No, they don't." He knew because he'd read them. "You have a problem with stupid authority." Yordan had always walked a very fine line. He only defied orders when things had gone well beyond questionable into really dumb. But once he refused a direct order, he did not waver from his conviction. It was one of the things Kit adored about him.

Until that defiance stomped forward and challenged him eye to eye. Damn it, Yordan was using a dominance tactic in a test Kit couldn't afford to lose. Not as Yordan's boss and not as his lover either. He didn't want their relationship to be one of alpha/beta. That was not ever going to work for either of them.

So he stood his ground. He didn't flinch, and he didn't back away. Kit met Yordan with his chin raised and his hackles up.

"We need to be very clear here, Yordan," he said, his voice hard. "Last night was fun. Last night was better than I'd ever imagined. But since we've left the afterglow behind, I need to know what the plan is."

Yordan frowned. "What plan?"

"Are we lovers? Is this continuing? Because I'd really like to talk to my lover right now. But if we're just coworkers, then you can fuck all the way off. I've told you everything you need to know."

He watched as the man chewed on that. It was as if he could see the gears churning in Yordan's mind. What did he want? What did he feel? And damn the man for not speaking his thoughts out loud. He didn't. He just stayed silent while expressions almost settled on his face before twitching away.

Until Kit couldn't stand it anymore.

"Yord—umph."

The man kissed him. And not just any kiss, but a deep, thrusting, hungry demand.

Well, he could match that. In fact, he did. Suddenly, he was thrusting and grabbing with the same fervor until together they fell together onto the bed. Not so much fell as started mounting each other as they ripped off their sweats.

Kit won that round, pinning Yordan's shoulders face-to-face as he settled heavily between the man's knees. But he didn't thrust yet. Instead, he paused while he tried to control his thudding heart.

"Yordan—"

"Lovers, you asshole," Yordan snapped. Then he gripped Kit's ass and impaled himself. He pulled Kit straight inside.

Lovers, then. Worked for him.

He started moving, thrusting a steady rhythm while Yordan writhed beneath him.

"Coffee called me—a fucking pussy cat—a Scottish kitten."

"Why?"

Kit thrust extra hard, embedding himself fully even as he reached down to stroke Yordan. The man moaned beneath him, squeezing Kit enough to make his eyes roll back with pleasure. But it didn't stop his words. He needed to say this now while Yordan was spread open and getting stroked by Kit.

"I had a month," Kit said. "To tell my secret crush how I felt."

Yordan blinked, his quick mind catching the meaning quickly. But he still made Kit say it.

"Secret crush? As in—"

He rolled his hips just to make Yordan squirm.

"As in you," Kit said. "I had to tell you how I feel."

Yordan bit his lip, his back arching to seat Kit even deeper. "Me?" he said, his voice rasping. "You wanted me." He sounded amazed, even though Kit had said as much last night.

"Yes, you." His tempo was speeding up. He couldn't help it. "I. Want. You."

Yordan bared his teeth in a wide grin. "I want you."

"Good."

"Nah. It's great."

And that was the end of the talking. There was a great deal more said in the way of bodies. In gasps and moans, in thrusts and squeezes, and yes, yes, yes as they pounded together.

Lovers.

Yes!

CHAPTER 13
Who's on Top?

Yordan had never had a lover per se. He'd had hookups, of course—with women as well as men—but he never stuck around long enough to move it into a real relationship. The closest he'd come was a friends-with-benefits arrangement a decade ago with a girl who was now married with three kids. And since he thought office romances were a terrible idea—and he was always working—that left him thinking he would be alone for the rest of his life.

Instead, he and his boss were now lovers. He ought to be appalled, but instead, he felt a bone-deep contentment that startled him. When he was with McNabb, he felt seen. As if Kit—his lover's name was Kit —saw things in him he didn't even know were there. And if Kit saw that, then he saw the messy stuff too, and that made everything okay.

Yordan wasn't stupid. He still thought office romances were a terrible idea, but damn it, if he could feel this safe with another soul, he didn't care who it was with. He was going to hang on and do whatever it took to keep them together.

He stroked a hand down Kit's flank, loving the way he stretched into the gesture. Like a damned cat, he thought with a smile. Yordan leaned in.

"Purr for me, kitty cat," he whispered.

"I think I already did," Kit answered. Then he shot a look at Yordan. "So did you."

Yes, he had. Yordan pressed a kiss to the Scotsman's shoulder. "You've told me everything? About your bet with Coffee?"

"Yeah. Why?"

"So why haven't you shifted? Go wolf."

He watched Kit's eyes widen with understanding. His expression flitted between hope and fear with a healthy side of worry.

"Don't think about it, just shift. You'll never know until—" His voice cut off. Kit was already glowing as he initiated the change. The air turned cold, and Yordan rolled out of bed. Last thing he needed was a full-grown wolf landing on top of him while he was a naked human. Scratches in the wrong place hurt! By the time he was on his feet beside the bed, Kit had fully manifested as...

"*Meow.*"

...a disappointed kitten who dropped his head on his paws and looked as depressed as his floppy ears.

Okay, so that didn't work.

"Did we miss anything? This had to be Coffee, right? There's no other reason you suddenly went kitten...right?"

Kit looked up and nodded. Then he dropped his head back on his paws.

Fuck.

"When I was in school, I learned Spanish. Did pretty well at it." Yordan was thinking out loud, trying to twist his mind around something that wasn't filled with massive disappointment. "Then I tried to learn Chinese. Don't ask me why. It had something to do with those martial arts films." He shrugged. "Anyway, it was a hell of a lot harder than I thought it'd be. Not just because it's a totally different kind of language with all those tonal things, but because my brain was English and Other. Whenever I went to a language that wasn't English, I ended up in Spanish. Then I had to consciously shift to Chinese."

The kitten huffed out a breath. Kit didn't even lift his head.

"Don't you get it? When you change to a wolf, are you really thinking wolf? Or are you just thinking 'change'?"

Kit lifted his head slowly, cocking it to the side. It was freaking adorable, and Yordan really wanted to scratch the puss under the chin. But he refrained.

"Remember when I said, 'Don't think'? What if you thought about going wolf? Like, actually becoming a wolf. All the little bits about being canine..."

He stopped talking because the temperature was dropping again, and the Scottish Fold kitten was surrounded in a golden glow.

Yordan held his breath. Kit probably did too.

And then, right in the center of the bed, stood a full-grown gray wolf. The creature was huge, his jaw was large, and he was abruptly dancing around and yipping like a puppy. Or a very happy Scotsman turned wolf.

Yordan threw himself enthusiastically into the joy. Nothing compared to moments like this where man and wolf could play together in absolute delight. If he were an insta-shift wolf, he would have joined Kit in canine play, but this was equally great. They played for a time until both of them dropped onto the floor in happy exhaustion.

And then Yordan sobered.

"You've got both the kitten and the wolf," he said, a twinge of envy in his voice. "You lucky shit." That could be a huge advantage. There were plenty of times when a huge wolf wouldn't work. Just about any mission in a town or city. But a cute little kitten? "You can go anywhere and fit in."

Kit leaned his whole canine body against Yordan and purred. Or at least attempted a purr. Wolf bodies didn't really do that like cats could, and the resulting sound was funny as shit. Yordan laughed as he dug his fingers into Kit's ruff.

"So, now you're back, better than ever." He took a breath. "And Pee said she could have all the bets collected by now. That leaves only one thing."

He glanced down at Kit to see the canine face looking at him. The expression was serious, as was the slow dip of his chin as he shimmered back to human. A second later, Yordan had his arm resting on Kit's naked back.

"We can't go yet," Kit said, his voice starting gravelly but stabilizing within seconds. Then he stood up and crossed naked to the computer. The man was in work mode now, and his entire body went from giddy enthusiasm to focused leader as he quickly pulled up his email. "You're right," he said after a moment, though Yordan hadn't said a word. He was too busy admiring the man's lean body. "The debts are all handled now, even Marsha's. Plus, Pee says there hasn't been a spin cycle in over a day. That tells us we're on the right track."

Yordan looked up. "Right track? We know—"

"We never know anything for sure with fairies."

True enough.

"But all the other glitches seem to be gone too." He tapped a few more keys. "Even our Hawaiian fever dream helo seems to be miraculously fixed." He glanced out the window. "Looks like I'm not in hot water after all for losing that one."

Yordan straightened up to his feet. "Bonus."

"Yeah, but..." Kit continued tapping on the keys. "Recovery crew is coming up tomorrow to get the pieces. Nero's pack finished their mission and is heading home." He started listing off what every combat pack was doing and what they would need in the next few weeks while Yordan watched, amazed.

He'd never really thought deeply about the sheer logistical challenge of managing seven combat packs. Kit seemed to know what every piece of Wulf, Inc. was up to and how each person supported the whole. It was impressive as hell, and he began to realize that Kit couldn't leave everything to chase a fairy. He was too important.

Which meant it had to be him.

"It's all right, Kit," he said as the man continued flipping through things on the computer. Wow, Yordan could barely process the spreadsheets Kit clicked through in a rapid tap-tap-tap. "I'll go."

"Not without me, you won't." It wasn't a growl or even a threat. It was a simple statement when Yordan wasn't even sure Kit was listening. "Both our names are on that page," he continued.

"But you don't need to. I can handle it, and frankly, you're way more—"

"If you say I'm more important than you, I swear I'm going to deck you." Kit stopped typing and looked straight at Yordan. "You're thinking hierarchically," he stated. "You need to think laterally. Or holistically. Or like my fucking lover."

Yordan held up his hand. "You're my boss. That's a fact."

Kit shrugged. "Every piece in the organization is important. Every combat wolf—that's you and Coffee—supports the whole structure. Every nerve that coordinates the wolves is important. That's what I do. And you, too, if I have anything to say about it."

Yordan rolled his eyes. "Let's leave my future employment out of this."

"Let's not." Kit stood up. "I can't keep doing this job alone. It's killing me. I'm exhausted all the time, and frankly, I'm not growing any younger."

"What are you? Twenty-two?"

"Thirty-two and still pretty." Kit grinned. "Just two years younger than you, and some mornings, I feel every mission I've ever been on. You've got to feel the same."

He did. That was part of why he'd been struggling lately. He knew he couldn't keep going in a combat pack. Eventually, his body was going to give out, and people were going to die. The younger wolves were faster, stronger, but they weren't smarter. Smarts came with experience, and that Yordan had in spades.

"Come on, Yordan. Why don't you want to lead?"

He didn't think about his answer. Words spilled out that shocked him to the core. And once said, he gaped at himself in the mirror.

"Because it's lonely at the top."

"What?"

Wait, what?

Yordan's mind was reeling, but once started, he couldn't stop talking.

"When was the last time you had beers with the guys? When do you sit around a campfire and laugh about gators soaring through the air? Who do you talk to at the end of the day?"

And when the fuck had he cared about friends? He knew the answer even as he mentally asked the question.

He'd always cared about friends. He'd had no one as a kid, and on the street, loners usually died. The camaraderie he'd found in Wulf, Inc. meant everything to him. And the idea of leaving any of the packs he'd been part of to sit at HQ was akin to death. Even the lure of calling the shots as alpha had been too frightening for him. Leaders didn't get to pal around with the grunts.

And so, he'd sabotaged every effort to move up the pack ladder. Except now he wasn't one of the regular grunts either. He was the old guy trying to be as stupid as the twentysomethings. It didn't work, and with Coffee's death or disappearance, his last connection to true friendship had broken.

Until Kit.

"I don't want to be alone," he said, ashamed of the weakness. "But I don't fit in with the regular guys anymore. So I guess I turned into an ass." Damn it, now he was going to have to apologize to Gummy.

Kit touched Yordan's face, drawing it toward his in a long, tender kiss. And when they separated, he smiled. "What do you think about working together, then? Why not share beers with me every night?"

"And ordering the cubs around during the day?"

"Yeah. We could share the load together."

Not to mention what they could share every night.

Yordan took a moment to think about it. What he visualized made his heart sing. "I could do that," he said, his voice thick. "I want to do that."

"So do I." Kit grinned. Then he leaned forward for another kiss, but Yordan held back.

"But I have to get Coffee back first. If I can."

Kit nodded. "I know. I've already let Pee know that we're going to bargain with Gamfay for Coffee's freedom. But we have to find him first."

Yordan flinched. "Did you have to—"

"Let the brass know what we're doing? Yes. But we're going to have to move quickly before they stop us."

That worked. "Okay. So we call Coffee as if he's a fairy? Just say his name three times?" That usually worked with fairies, except Coffee wasn't one of the fae. He was a wolf trapped in Fairyland.

Kit wrinkled his nose. "Want to guess how many times people say, 'Coffee, coffee, coffee?' If he hasn't appeared by now, that's not going to work."

"We could try his real name. Dwayne, Dwayne, and my other brother Dwayne." He paused.

Nada.

"We've got to call—"

Kit interrupted. "Gamfay, Gamfay—"

Yordan took up the call, repeating the fairy's name a third time with Kit. "Gamfay. Let's talk."

"It's about fucking time," muttered a voice behind them.

Yordan spun around, Coffee's real name bursting from his lips. "Dwayne!"

There was Coffee, standing in a ridiculous elf costume. He looked gaunt and miserable, especially with the thin green leash around his neck. And there, holding on to the leash, was a bright, tuxedo-wearing game show host, complete with a microphone and a shit-eating grin.

"Hello, boys," he chuckled. "Place your bets. Daddy's ready to make a new deal."

CHAPTER 14
Bob Barker Did It Better

D amn, Kit really wished he'd taken the time to get dressed. Naked while negotiating with a fairy was just embarrassing. But no time for that now, especially as Yordan was already going aggressive.

"You're a fucking idiot, you know that, Dwayne?"

"Duh," his friend shot back. "You think I'm wearing this because I'm a Mensa candidate?"

Gamfay rocked back on his heels, while somewhere canned laughter filtered into the room. And now game shows were officially ruined for the rest of Kit's life.

"Let's get down to business," he interrupted. "We want Coffee back. Er, Dwayne. What's that going to take?"

Gamfay heaved a mighty sigh. "Exactly what you think it will. You've got to win a bet." He grinned. "Easy as eating a mince pie."

Yordan snorted. "I don't even know what that is."

"Meat pie," Coffee said. "Tastes like shit."

Gamfay rolled his eyes. "Yours tastes like shit. My pies—"

"Aren't important right now," Kit interrupted. "And my nanna's mince pies are to die for."

Damn it, he would have preferred a little more preparation before going into negotiations, but that was a vain wish. There was no way to really prepare for something like this, so they might as well get to it now.

"What is important is getting Coffee back. So, what are the exact details of his bargain with you?"

Gamfay gave a low chuckle. "His is unbreakable, but honestly, his whining is getting annoying."

Coffee perked up. "Good to know."

"You two, on the other hand, are a lot more interesting."

Kit shook his head. "Actually, we're really boring."

Gamfay wasn't having any of it. He walked about the room, touching the rumpled bed and making a show of sniffing the air. "Now this is really interesting," he drawled. Then he batted his eyes at the two of them. "Is it twue wuv?"

"None of your business," Yordan growled. He had moved next to Coffee, where he was tugging at the clasp of the leash. It looked like it ought to break with a sharp tug, but Kit wasn't surprised when it held fast.

"*Au contraire*, my growly friend," Creepy Game Show Host continued. "What if we wagered on the strength of your wuv?"

"No," said Kit at the same moment as Yordan said, "Why not?"

"What?"

"What?"

Kit couldn't believe Yordan would want to wager on their love. Their relationship was an hour old. Nothing was assured, but Yordan shrugged.

"Relationships are tricky, vague things," Yordan said. "We can twist it as much as he can."

Which made it a terrible thing to wager on, but Yordan looked supremely unconcerned.

"Our relationship is something *we* control," he continued. "Not him. That's the best bet there is."

Gamfay clapped his hands together and rubbed them greedily. "I smell a bet."

Meanwhile, Coffee squeezed Yordan's arm. "Be careful," he murmured. "He's a slippery bastard."

Thank you, Mr. Obvious. All fairies were slippery, but that didn't slow down this train. The fairy rocked back on his heels and looked at them with a merry smile. "I like you guys and I'm in a generous mood, so I'll make it simple. I'll bet that I can end your happily ever after together with one true statement. If I can't, you get Dwayne here, free and clear. But if I do..." He waggled his eyebrows and held up two more leashes. "You're mine."

"No—" Kit returned. He was not going to let Yordan risk enslavement, but Yordan didn't give him the chance.

"I agree, but you get me alone, not Kit."

"For God's sake, Yordan! Would you slow down?"

The man didn't answer. He was too busy squaring off with the evil game show host. "One for one is fair."

"But the question is about the two of you."

"Don't care. You get me or nothing."

"Hmmm," said Gamfay as he looked at Kit. "I'll go with nothing." Then he and Coffee winked out.

Shit, shit, shit. "Yordan, you have got to get a grip. We either work together on this or not at all."

Yordan shook his head. "I'm not risking you on some fucking fairy—"

"Both our names are on that page," Kit nearly screamed. "Both of us are in this relationship. You've got to stop going it alone, or this is never going to work." And by "this," he meant their relationship, the fairy deal, and their working together. "You aren't alone anymore. Unless you make it that way."

He saw that information filter in. He watched Yordan's stubborn shoulders slide down as his expression softened. "I'm trying to protect you," he finally murmured.

"And I want to protect you, but you know it doesn't work that way. We've got to take the risk together. Especially if we're risking our relationship."

"Listen, it's an easy bet," Yordan said. "He can't change the way I feel about you. There's not a damn thing that I'd believe out of his lying mouth. So if you feel good about us—"

"Of course I do." That was a rash thing to say after less than a day of honest communication between them, but Kit was certain how he felt. After all, he'd been feeling it for years.

"Then we're good. We win," Yordan said.

Too easy. This was too fucking easy for a fairy bet. But they didn't have any other options.

"We've got to do it together," Kit said firmly, and he waited until Yordan finally agreed.

"Fine. Together." Then he leaned over to kiss Kit, but before their mouths could touch, Coffee and Gamfay were back. They blinked in with a hearty ho, ho, ho that made both of them jump.

"Do we have a deal, then?" Gamfay asked.

Kit dropped his hands on his hips. "Give me the particulars. Slowly."

Gamfay chuckled. "Dwayne, show your friends the game, shall we?"

They turned and saw Coffee prancing about, this time dressed as a game show girl, long skirt, bright lipstick, and all. He set down a podium with a large red button on it. Above it hung an arrow pointing straight up between TRUTH on one side and FALSE on the other.

"It's simple," Coffee growled, clearly annoyed with playing Vanna. "He says something, and the arrow goes to Truth. You then say something, and it slides to False."

"Now, now," interrupted Gamfay. "That's not exactly correct, is it? This is a lie detector, gentlemen. If what you say is the true, then it'll point to true."

Yordan rolled his eyes. "According to you. It's a fairy game. It'll point to whatever you want it to."

Gamfay held up his hand. "Upon my life, it will answer honestly."

"How can it?" Kit challenged. "Truth is too complicated for any machine to effectively judge it. Especially if it's about feelings."

The fairy stroked his tie. "True, true. But the machine measures if you think you're lying or not. Not the actual truth of the matter. If you actually believe Coffee is my sweet baby boo, then it'll read true. If you don't but say he is, then it'll know you're lying." He grinned as he pointed to the big red button. "Go ahead. You can test it, if you want. You don't even need to say the words out loud. It'll know."

Yordan stepped up immediately, putting his hand on the big red button. He thought for a moment, then pressed the button down. The arrow swung straight to TRUE. Next press went to FALSE. And then a couple more landed somewhere in the middle to indicate sort of true or sort of false.

He stepped back and looked at Kit.

"It works well enough now. Don't know if we can trust it in the moment."

Coffee shook his head. "Not his style. He's a prick, to be sure, but he'll play by the rules. He figures we're weak enough to keep playing. Eventually, we'll overextend and lose. It's the nature of gamblers."

Kit frowned. "Is that what happened with you?"

Coffee grimaced. "Get me out of this, and I'll join Gambler's Anonymous. I swear."

He was going to do more than that, but first things first. Kit tested out the true/false machine. He thought about simple stuff like whether he'd eaten breakfast this morning or not, then more complicated things like how he desperately wanted to retire (mostly false) and how he was going to get blamed for losing the helo (mostly true) but that he wasn't going to get penalized for it (straight up in the middle because he really didn't know). And then, just to be sure, he tried out this silently.

I love Yordan. It's still early, but I'm sure we can make it work.

The arrow pointed right at TRUE.

Okay, then. Given that he wouldn't trust a single thing Gamfay said—and he was sure Yordan wouldn't either—they should be fine. He looked back at Yordan.

"I'm ready to risk it. You?"

"Yup," Yordan said. Then they stepped together, shoulder to shoulder, and faced the creepy elf.

Kit summarized. "You get to say one thing, and then we'll say that our love hasn't died. Once that's done, Coffee is free."

"Assuming," Gamfay corrected, "that your love hasn't died. If what I say ends it..." He held up the two empty leashes. "Then you're mine forever."

"Nope," Yordan said. "You get us as slaves for a day."

"Forever," Gamfay countered.

"Bullshit," Kit said. "A week."

"Are you telling me your love is worth a week? Come on." Then he waggled his bushy eyebrows. "A fairy week."

"Never," Yordan snapped.

"Very well," Gamfay said with a dramatic sigh. "A human year."

Coffee spoke up. "He can make that feel like an eternity."

"Whine, whine," Gamfay mocked as he tugged on Coffee's leash. "It'll feel like a human year, all right? Can we get on with this now? I'm growing bored."

"No, you're not," Coffee shot back. As if for proof, he pointed at the arrow which, weirdly, had been moving back and forth without their hands on the button. And right now, it pointed straight to FALSE.

Gamfay chuckled. "Clever wolf. Now, are the parameters set? We have a deal?"

Yordan opened his mouth to answer, but he abruptly waited as he turned to look at Kit. "Ready?" he mouthed.

"Yeah. You?"

He nodded. Then together, they looked back at Gamfay.

"Let's have it. What's your big reveal?"

Gamfay grinned. He clearly relished his moment. He moved to the big red button and put his gloved hand on it. "Here it is, kiddies. There's a love spell on your HQ. That's why you've had people falling in love left and right. Nero and Josh, Laddin and Bruce, Walter and Bai." He pointed a long, fat finger at them. "You two." He grinned. "Love spell."

Then he pressed down on the button. The arrow banged straight over to the TRUTH side with a much too cheerful *Ding!*

Kit nearly snorted at the ridiculousness of the statement. It was obviously bullshit, no matter what the arrow pointed at. What Kit felt for Yordan wasn't induced by any fairy spell.

But then logic started slipping through his thoughts. He started listing in his head the number of couples that he knew about. The number was dauntingly high. Not just the three Gamfay had listed, but others, both likely and unlikely. In fact, Pee had made that joke the other day when two of the motor pool crew had been caught making out. She'd even said, "Geez, is there a love potion in the water or something?"

Not a love potion. A fairy spell. That made sense.

Fuck. That made a lot of sense.

He looked at Yordan and saw the same thoughts flitting through his expression. Oh damn. Oh hell. He felt his heart sinking fast.

"Wait," he said as much to himself as to Yordan. "Let's think this through."

"How many couples can you name?" Yordan countered. "Just in the last year?"

A ton. "But that doesn't mean anything. We're wolves. We're horny. Sex happens."

"But how many of them are love matches? Married, happily ever after, until death do us part?" Yordan didn't wait for him to answer. "Nero was never going to fall in love, ever. And yeah, Laddin is a forever kind of guy, but Bruce? Have you met him? He doesn't believe in the shit right in front of his eyes. And yet there they went, hand in hand, in love."

"People do fall in love," Kit said, hating the note of desperation in his voice. "*We* are in love."

"Are we?" Yordan challenged in his customarily blunt way. "I never thought I would."

"I did," Kit snapped back. "I've loved you for years. Long before Coffee made his bullshit fairy bets."

"You don't know that. Coffee made his alliance here as an adolescent."

"But I didn't make a bet with him until just before his death. You saw the book. The bet was about me telling my feelings to you." Kit lifted his chin. "My feelings for you are real, Yordan." He was sure of it. "They existed long before any of this nonsense."

Yordan nodded, his expression turning bleak. He didn't need to speak the words for Kit to know what he was thinking, but Yordan was never one to hold back something he thought was obvious. Sure enough, he spoke, and every word hurt.

"But I didn't. I didn't know about how you felt."

"But you knew me. You noticed me." He'd said that...right?

Yordan nodded. "Of course I noticed you. I was impressed by you until you quit your pack right when the going got tough in Wisconsin. Then I thought you were a total coward."

"But you know now that wasn't true. You know why I quit." He clenched Yordan's arm. "I was taken out of the pack! Because a kitten can't do shit against a lych, and that's what we were about to fight."

"Yeah," Yordan said, though his tone made it clear it didn't make a difference. "I understand now, but that's not enough to fall in love with you."

Oh fuck, fuck, fuck. Yordan had already given up. It didn't matter if the fairy love spell was a lie. Gamfay had sown enough doubt that Yordan didn't believe his own feelings. Now what?

"Kit," Yordan said, his voice strangled. And when Kit looked into his eyes, he saw a bleak despair that shook him down to his toes. He'd lost Yordan.

"Damn it, how can you believe that?"

Yordan didn't answer. His gaze flickered to the arrow pointed straight at TRUTH. In his mind, everything he felt for Kit was a fairy lie.

"Wait—" Coffee said as he stepped forward. But before he could say anything else, Gamfay jerked hard on his leash. Suddenly, the collar was choking him, and he wheezed as he struggled to breathe.

"Now, now," Gamfay admonished. "No interference from the peanut gallery."

Kit jerked forward, grabbing hold of the choking Coffee. "That wasn't part of the rules!"

"You're right," the fairy conceded. "That wasn't part of your bet, but it was part of his. And I control when my slave talks and when he doesn't."

Kit saw misery in Coffee's eyes and felt his heart lurch. There was nothing he could do right then to help. Nothing but win his current bet.

"Okay, okay," he said to Gamfay. "But don't kill him. It'll really tank the game show ratings, don't you think?"

"Hmmm," Gamfay said, clearly unconvinced.

"Pat Sajak never choked his assistant."

"Fine," Gamfay said as he held up the leash.

It slowly loosened, and Coffee managed a shuddering breath. Fine. That was something, but it was clear there'd be no more help from Dwayne. Except, there had been something, right? He'd been trying to tell them something.

Kit turned to Yordan, who was on the same page.

"There's a loophole," Yordan said. "Something we haven't figured out."

"Always," Kit said. It was a fairy bargain after all. "So, what is it?"

He tried to remember everything there was to know about fairy deals and love spells. There was a lot, and all of it might or might not apply to this situation. It was so much that he pressed his hands to his temples as he tried to force himself to focus.

It didn't work. He needed a sounding board. He needed Yordan.

"What do we know about love spells?"

"That they're stupid," Yordan grumbled.

"What?"

"They're stupid. They never work." He waved his hand. "The genie in *Aladdin* even says he won't do them. He does stuff to make Aladdin more attractive to Jasmine, but he can't force anyone to love another."

"Right. Right!" Kit's eyes widened.

"But that was in a movie," Yordan countered. "Who knows how they work here? Nero and Josh are stupidly in love. And don't get me started on—"

"No, you're right. Love spells are stupid. They can't actually make us fall in love."

"But—"

"Let's say a spell can create a hard-on. Maybe it can make me tingle every time I see you. Maybe it puts humping thoughts into my head, but that's not love."

Yordan wrinkled his nose. "It feels like love."

"Maybe. But it's not going to give me that feeling of safety whenever I'm with you. It's not going to make me crave talking to you or change the joy of figuring out hard stuff with you." He gripped Yordan's arm. "It wasn't any spell that made me hold you when you were grieving Coffee, and it sure as hell wasn't any fairy spell that had me wanting you at the very beginning. I like being with you. I'm impressed by who you are. And I feel wonderful when we're together because you make me happy. That's not some fairy spell. That's love."

He could feel the truth of his words as he spoke. He knew it was true even as he saw Yordan's expression soften into hope. He was listening. He saw the possibility.

"I don't know if we're going to live happily ever after, but I can damn well tell you that whatever bullshit he's spouting—" he jerked his head at Gamfay "—doesn't change how I feel about you one damn bit."

Just to prove it, he slammed his hand down on the big red button. Right on cue, the arrow dinged loudly as it pointed straight at TRUTH.

"I love you," Kit said. He knew it in his bones to be true.

Now it was Yordan's turn, but the doubt was still tight on his face, and Kit's heart sank. Even if Kit had been secretly in love with Yordan for years, that wasn't true the other way around. This was too new for Yordan, and the man wasn't very experienced with this kind of emotion.

Which meant Kit had to explain it to him as bluntly as he knew how.

"A fairy can make you horny," Kit said. "I'm cute as a button, and I've got a great ass. A fairy can make you want to drill me all day and night, but it can't make you feel safe in my presence. It can't make you want to talk with me, watch me as I'm sleeping, or call me on my bullshit."

"I want to call everyone on their bullshit," Yordan countered.

True. It was one of the reasons Kit loved him. "You told me secrets about yourself. Intimate things. You let me hold you when you cried. You even let me dominate you in bed. That's not something a fairy spell can make you do. That's not a tingle in your dick. That's love in your heart."

Yordan looked at him, his expression shifting all over the place, the emotions too rapid for Kit to label. But in the end, all he saw was doubt. Yordan doubted, and that was going to kill their happily ever after.

"It's okay to doubt that this is going to last," he said. "We're less than twenty-four hours into our relationship. Of course we should doubt that. But it's not going to fail because of some fairy spell. No game show host can change what I think of you deep inside. What I *feel* for you. So, forget the sex, ignore the tingle and all the other physical stuff. What do you feel for me inside? In that place where no fairy can touch?"

He watched as Yordan settled into himself. It was as if he could see the man mentally strip away all the fun stuff and land in that place of self that was quiet and wholly one's own.

"Do you want to spend time with me?" Kit asked. "No sex, no tingle, do you want to hang out?"

"Yes." The word was whispered at first. And then it came out stronger. "Yes."

"Did you want to do that before we banged?"

"Yes."

"Do you want to keep doing it after this? Every night? Every day? As much as we can?"

"Yes!" Then with a quick twist, Yordan slammed his hand down on the red button. "You didn't change a damn thing. I love him." He looked at Gamfay. "And you're an asshole."

Ding.

TRUTH.

Kit launched himself into Yordan's arms, and the big man caught him in a hard embrace. To the side, Coffee cheered as his leash disappeared, and even Gamfay ho, ho, ho'd as if he hadn't just lost a slave. But Kit barely registered that as he and Yordan kissed. It was deep, it was sweet, and it was the happily-ever-after kind of kiss.

It was love.

Hallelujah!

When they finally separated, Gamfay was gone and a free Coffee was there, still in his Vanna costume.

"I'm free," he said as he spun around fast enough to make his skirt flare. "I'm free!"

Yeah, he was. And Kit and Yordan were in love.

Epilogue – Why Business Trips are the Best

ONE YEAR LATER

"No, no, no! Gummy's pack needs to go to Upstate NY. They'll have no problem with the tunnels under Albany." Yordan poked at screen to digitally move the green dot to NY. His hand shook a bit with the magnitude of what he was about to do, but he didn't think Kit noticed.

"Of course they'll have no problem with the tunnel ghoul," Kit returned. "That's a cakewalk better suited to one of the less-able packs. It's more important that they go help in Europe where the—"

Yordan cut him off. "No, it's not. Gummy's from Brooklyn, remember? This will let the whole pack visit his mom. That woman can cook, and it's like a week of R&R put into a single meal. Trust me, Gummy's pack needs to go there."

Kit leaned back, his desk chair adjusting to his shift in weight as he stared across his desk to where Yordan sat at his. Between them was a combined work space of mammoth proportions, but it suited them fine. They were both big guys after all, easily able to reach the map that lay between them.

"Why is your hand shaking?"

Damn. Kit noticed everything. It was one of the things he adored about the man.

"What?" he returned, his voice sounding much too innocent.

Kit's feet dropped to the floor as his seat returned to upright. He leaned forward with narrowed eyes. "Out with it. What's going on?"

Yordan considered covering with a half-truth, but he always felt like a schmuck when he did that with Kit. In a year of being together, he'd never lied to the man. No reason to start now.

"Well," Yordan finally confessed. "I'm a little nervous."

"Nervous? About what?" Kit's gaze swept the office, touching on maps and paper piles and all the debris of their shared work life managing Wulf, Inc.'s growing number of combat packs. It was too big a job for one person, and early this year, the company had made it official. Yordan's "understudy" position was now of equal rank and authority as Kit's. It might not work for anyone else in their situation, but it worked for them. And if the two ever disagreed, Captain M had the final say.

But in a year of working together, they'd never needed someone else to make the decision. They'd disagreed plenty but had always been able to work it out.

Yordan came out of his chair and walked to Kit's desk side. "I think we need to go to Europe for the conference."

Kit's eyes narrowed. "You hate conferencing. You said you'd rather be fed to a swamp monster than set foot in—"

"I think we should have Wulf, Inc. pay for our trip to Europe and then head on to Scotland to get married." So saying, he pulled a box out from his pocket and offered it to Kit with a shaking hand.

The love of his life stared at the box then up at Yordan. "Are you proposing to me?" His voice was hollow with shock as he slowly opened the box. Inside lay a polished metal ring nestled in velvet.

"Yeah, I am," Yordan said, his voice low. "I can't believe I ever thought what I feel for you is a fairy lie. It's love, Kit. I love you, and I want us to be together forever."

Kit shook his head as he looked up at Yordan towering above him. "You know, that is not how a man proposes to the love of his life," he drawled, his brogue heavy and sweet.

"Fuck you, kitten," Yordan said. "That's how I propose."

"Obviously." Kit got out of his chair, one hand shoved into his pants pocket. "But the way you're supposed to propose is on one knee." With those words, he dropped down before Yordan and held up a velvet box. "I love you, Yordan. Please say you'll be mine forever." Then he arched his brows. "Now that's how a man proposes to the love of his life."

Yordan reached down and popped open the box to see a polished wooden ring. He pulled it out and slid it on. It fit perfectly. Of course it did. As did Kit's when he slid on his gleaming metal ring. Then they both held up their hands until the rings clicked against each other.

"So I guess that's a yes, huh?" said Kit, his voice ringing with happiness.

"I guess so."

"And you want to get married in Scotland?"

"Why not? Don't you want your clan all around you?"

Kit rocked back on his heels, apparently considering. "Yeah," he said softly, "I do. But all I really care about is seeing you in a kilt as we say I do."

Yordan snorted while happiness bubbled up inside him. "Not going to happen, kitten."

"Wanna bet?"

"No. Never. Not going to do that again."

Kit laughed. "Agreed."

"But maybe, if you put on your short, tight, little skirt—"

"It's called a kilt, you Neanderthal."

"Then maybe, I'll take it off you."

Kit melted forward just as Yordan did the same. They met in the middle—as always—and the kiss was so magical it made everything else disappear.

"But," Kit finally said as he pulled back, "what does this have to do with Gummy's pack?"

"It's so he can be close if there's a problem here while we're checking out your kilt."

"New York isn't that close—"

"Yeah, it is. Because after a night of his mother's pasta, Gummy will be in a great mood and will happily come back here and train the new recruits."

Kit frowned. "He will? That's a six-week job." And one that he and Yordan usually did.

"Never underestimate the power of pasta."

That had to be some pasta. But it would be an even better honeymoon.

Kit waggled his eyebrows. "I can't wait to introduce you to haggis."

Yordan groaned. "It's a good thing I love you."

"Yeah," Kit agreed, his voice thick with that brogue Yordan found so sexy. "Because you'd be lost without me, my sweet, bonnie love."

He was right, and Yordan didn't mind one bit.

About the Author

Kathy Lyons is the wild, adventurous half of USA TODAY bestselling author Jade Lee. A lover of all things fantastical, Kathy spent much of her childhood in Narnia, Middle Earth, Amber, and Earthsea, just to name a few. Her love of comedy came later as she began to see the ridiculousness in life. Winner of several industry awards including the Prism—Best of the Best, Romantic Times Reviewer's Choice, and Fresh Fiction's Steamiest Read, Kathy has published over 60 romance novels and is still going strong.

Her hobbies include racquetball, rollerblading, and tv/movie watching with her husband. She's a big fan of the Big Bang Theory (even though it's over) and her favorite movie is The Avengers because she loves everything created by Joss Whedon. She's usually found at the loudest table in the coffee shop or next to the dessert bar. To keep up with all things Lyons/Lee, sign up for her newsletter at www.KathyLyons.com You'll get early peeks, fresh news, chances to meet her in person, plus prizes and geeky gifts.

Potential New Girlfriend

SARA NEY

Prologue

The black luxury vehicle slowly pulls under the covered portico, coming to a full stop in front of the stately cement steps, it's driver climbing out and coming around to the back passenger side.

Opens the door and steps aside as one glossy high heel hits the pavement, followed by the other.

Sleek.

Sexy.

They're hot pink heels—not exactly appropriate for the occasion, *if I'm judging*—shining in the warm, southern sun, attached to a pair of long legs that go on for miles.

I watch behind the veil of a sheer curtain and out of view as the young woman steps all the way out.

I can't see her face; it's hidden beneath a wide brim hat, one with a pink ribbon that matches her shoes, but at least she's wearing gloves and a relatively modest dress.

Her hands clutch a designer matching handbag for dear life as her feet propel her forward, car pulling away slowly away.

Click click click.

I can hear the sharp stilettos clicking against the concrete steps from my spot in the crying room overlooking the portico and front lawn; watch intently for our guest of honor to finally make her way to the door, where she'll then find her seat amongst the other visitors, my mouth bending into a pleased smile.

Everything has been going according to plan.

Excellent.

I let the curtain fall back into place, humming happily to myself as I descend the limestone stairs, mentally counting the cash I'll make for this side-hustle all the way back to the nave.

This is shaping up to be a wonderful day, indeed.

Chapter One

MIRIAM

"... **A**nd as we gather to pay respects to Grandfather, we cannot do so without remembering his witty sense of humor and how he loved and doted on his grandchildren."

Palmer Leland Winchester Darling the fourth plucks at the periwinkle pocket square, removing it from his suit coat and dramatically dabs at one eye, then the other.

Sniffs sorrowfully before folding the cotton tissue neatly, tucking it back inside his pocket.

Resuming his speech from the pulpit of the church, Our Holy Immaculate Lady of God, I'm almost certain Palmer's family is not only *not* a member of the congregation but probably haven't attended a service of any kind in decades, if my presence here is any indication of Palmers *ethics.*

But whatever.

This family's moral compass is not my problem.

On the pulpit, Palmer continues. *"I recall the time Grandfather bought me a polo pony for my birthday even after my father told him I couldn't have one—well, a new one, anyway, cuz I already had two."*

He chuckles into the microphone, regaling the tale, amused at his own quip.

New polo pony, ha!

What a lark!

When the crowd chuckles, too—as if polo ponies are *gafaw gafaw giggle giggle* humorous—I roll my eyes and stifle a yawn, reading from the prepared note cards in my hands to keep Palmer's momentum moving forward.

"*...How furious were my parents when Grandfather had Citation— that was my pony—delivered to the house only a few days later, scattering all over the lawn the day of my party?*" More chortling bemusement. "*But no one was about to tell Palmer Darling the Second what to do.*"

Wow. What a dick move by Grandpa.

The crowd chuckles again.

I barely muster the enthusiasm to recite the words (I myself have written) with a straight face, glancing down at the notecards from time to time, speaking softly into the tiny mouthpiece hidden in the fussy collar of my black dress shirt.

The dress shirt isn't my usual style, but I had to blend in with these folks; the dress is also a great disguise for the technology secreted in my neckline—a small black wire that doesn't quite match my dark brown hair, but close enough.

In my ear is an ear piece, one that matches Palmer's.

I press my finger against it as I speak the following instructions. "Now when you remove the tissue from your pants pocket, carefully dab it below your nose," I tell him, watching when he reaches for the tissue in the pocket of his slacks like he's been told, wiping below his nose.

It takes several moments, but then...

...tears begin forming in his dry eyes.

He goes to dab at them with the— "Use the pocket square from your suit coat to dry your eyes! Do *not* use the cotton tissue again." I hiss quietly, holding the ear piece with one hand and throw the elderly man walking past me a peace sign and a toothy grin.

A peace sign, Miriam?

Seriously?

You're at a freaking funeral.

Up front, I watch in horror as Palmer confuses the two handker-chiefs; watch as the dumbass uses the white cotton disposable tissue to pat at his misty eyes, which only makes him cry more.

I cringe, gut clenching with sympathy pain when he begins rubbing his eyes with balled up fists, doing his best to wipe the tears from his eyes.

Shit, that's gotta hurt.

But honestly, the silver lining here: Palmer looks way more bereft than he actually is, which is what he's paying me for.

"Fuck, Miri, this stings," he whimpers through the micro-micro-phone hidden in the collar of his dress shirt, speaker disguised as his tie clip.

"Dude, are you trying to look like you've lost your mind in front of the church?" The guy needs to chill out.

"Fuck, fuck, fuck."

I grimace. "Word of advice? Maybe lay off the F Bombs until you're off the pulpit.

"I'm trying, but fuck!" he whimpers again, acting like a total pussy, as if someone squirted him in the eye with bear spray or mace and blinded him.

He's loud enough to wake the dead.

"No offence, Grandpa," I silently pray, making the sign of the cross. *"Amen, thanks be to God, yada, yada."*

"Meet me in the vestry," I order, already headed in that direction.

"The what?" he whispers.

At the front of the church he squints, hands fumbling in the air, feeling for things that are not there.

"The vestry. The antechamber." I sigh heavily, frustrated. "The room behind you," *Jackass,* I want to add, but don't because he's paying me to help, not to verbally assault him. "Do you see the door? Go through it."

"I can't see shit," he grumbles.

My ballet flats tap against the stone floor as I hasten toward the front of the church—not as loudly as a stiletto or a pump would click, but it's audible enough that I begin a fast-paced tip-toe toward the anti-chamber behind the pulpit, giving the fancy blonde a quick once-over on my way past.

She sticks out like a sore thumb, pretty in pink and swimming in a sea of black and navy blue; I wonder if she'd gotten the memo that it's considered appropriate to wear dark colors to a funeral and not hot pink?

Then again, this is Palmer Darling we're talking about. Palmer, who is more than likely taking this young woman for cute lunch once he's done pretending to mourn, or at least fucking her in the backseat of his vintage Rolls Royce.

Next, I creep past Palmer's parents, a stuffy looking couple in the front row, neither of them crying the same way Palmer had, stoic in every way.

Bit of how I'd imagine the royals to be at a funeral, only not as posh.

I shove the ornately carved wooden door; it weighs a ton and takes a bit of effort. When it creeks on its hinges I cringe again, falling against it after it closes.

Phew.

"I can't see!" Palmer is flailing, feeling around the room for something to rub on his face, hands grappling at the discovery of a decanter of holy water placed on a nearby table. "Get this off me!"

I snatch it out of his reach before he can douse himself with it. "You can't use holy water to clean your eyes, dude—what the hell!"

Ugh.

This guy, I swear.

Calmly and rationally, I remove a wet wipe from the fanny pack around my waist. Tear it open and shake it out so it resembles a teeny, tiny bed sheet, then begin wiping beneath his nose.

Palmer flounders when I try handing him the wipe so he can clean his face. "My eyes—get my eyes." His hand pushes mine away. "You do it for me." He pauses. "Please."

He is such a baby.

"You need to calm down for the love of God, it was just a bit of Menthol and Vapor Rub."

We might not be in the church right now but he's loud enough that the funeral-goers present, paying their respects, can undoubtedly hear his whining.

I chuckle to myself at the irony. Here we are, putting on a show in the house of the Lord, lying to the man's entire family on a lark, while his dead grandfather lays in a casket just outside the door.

"It fucking stings! I can't see!" His fingers try to grab at the wet wipe but I swat them away. "Where's that water carafe I found before?"

The fact that he continues calling it a water carafe...

"I'm not letting you wash your face with holy water! No. Over my dead body." Shit, that was a classless joke considering his grandfather lies in wake in the very next room, but it rolled off my tongue before I could stop it same as the other one had.

"Stop crying, Palmer, you're fine. The stinging will go away in a few minutes, chill."

I pause, studying his face now that he has his eyes squeezed shut.

Palmer isn't unattractive looking—if you're into the buttoned up type, which I am not. Slicked back hair. Clean shaven. Long sleeve button down shirt, navy suit jacket, matching slacks, expensive brown dress shoes.

I bet he wears socks and a bow tie when he has sex.

"I'm trying. It hurts."

"You sure whine a lot." I can't stop myself from adding.

Palmer scowls. "You didn't tell me this was going to *burn*, Miriam."

"Yes, well—if I had told you, you wouldn't have done it and you wanted to get emotional, remember? This whole thing was your idea."

"The Vapor Rub wasn't." He sounds petulant and pouty, the way I would expect a spoiled silver-spooner to sound. "All I said was I wanted to sound emotional so Gemma would see my softer side. I don't need her to see me looking as if I'd been stung by a bee and had an allergic reaction."

His softer side?

At a funeral?

How is this guy for real?

How is he best friends with my brother, Winston?

Winston is nothing like this. My brother is cool and chill and spends most of his time in jeans and flannel shirts. Definitely always has a baseball hat on, sometimes he wears it backwards.

I mean, okay—in all fairness, Win and Palmer *were* fraternity brothers in college, which is how I met Palmer to begin with. But in my wildest stretch of the imagination when he messaged me and said, '*Miriam, I need a favor and Win said you're the only one who can help me*,' I had no idea we'd end up at a funeral with his pretty, blonde date in one of the pews.

Guess there's a first time for everything.

I dab gently at his eye, wiping it free from menthol gel. "I still can't believe you invited a date to your Grandfathers funeral."

Honestly, who does that?

Palmer smiles, lids fluttering slightly. "Isn't she hot?"

He sniffles as tears drip from the corner of his eyes in an unflattering way.

"Uh, I hadn't noticed. I was too busy trying to be incognito at the back of the church." The last thing I need is his mother or father, or aunt or uncle, catching me reading him the lines to his eloquent eulogy—which Palmer had paid me a nice chunk of change to spoon feed him. "You really think you're clever, don't you?"

"It's brilliant, actually." He drawls lazily, sounding a bit British. "Gemma gets to see two sides of me; the classy, casual side and today, she gets to see my sensitive side. Shows her I can get emotional."

"Couldn't you have just gone to the Humane Society and pet the kittens?"

Palmer pulls a face. "Cats? From the *Humane* Society?"

"Oh, that's right, I forgot: you prefer purebreds." I roll my eyes. "You don't think it will bother her that this is all so...fake?"

"So? She doesn't know that."

I'm not going to argue that point—he's convinced this was a great idea and nothing will convince him otherwise, and I'm not being paid to give him my opinion.

I'm being paid to make him look good.

"Did you actually tell her she'd be walking into a funeral or did she think y'all had plans to do something else today?"

"She knew." He yawns as I wipe up the last of the gunk and toss the wet wipe in the trash. "I told her it wouldn't take long—we plan on skipping the memorial cocktail hour."

I pause mid wipe. "The memorial *cocktail* hour?"

"Yeah, Gan Gan is hosting a cocktail hour at the Club for a few hours, you know how it is—shrimp, hors d'oeuvres, probably a prime rib station. Nothing fancy."

The level of self-control I'm exercising right now is unparalleled because the level at which I want to snort and roll my eyes is off-the-charts. I want to pat myself on the back for keeping a straight face if only for the simple fact he calls his grandmother Gan Gan.

As if she were the Queen of England.

"So, what are you going to do instead?" It's none of my business but it kind of is, since funerals are so personal and I'm slightly invested.

Palmer shrugs. "Take her to a cozy lunch at the Ivy—play a game of strip backgammon and hopefully fuck, not necessarily in that order." He walks to the mirror and studies himself, squinting as he readjusts his bowtie, straightening it. "Wouldn't mind getting to know her first, my mom has been on my ass to settle down."

He shrugs.

"I mean, any woman who sticks around after you bring her to a funeral for a date sounds like a keeper."

Palmer beams at me. "You think?"

"Oh, for sure." I zip up my fanny pack and give it two pats for good measure. "Now. *About the payment for my services...*"

Chapter Two

MIRIAM

L et's just get this out of the way, shall we?

I, Miriam Bennington, am broke.

Like—broke ass, not that anyone asked. But I mention it to illustrate the reason I'd help a cad like Palmer Darling, despite the simple fact he's my brothers college buddy.

That aside, I need the side-jobs.

Why?

A girl's gotta do what a girl's gotta do when she's staring her own business.

Yup, my one and only sole motivation for participating in the ridiculously *absurd* exercise that was playing puppet master for a spoiled rich kid...

Money.

Gross, I know.

I should be ashamed of myself, blah blah blah, yes, yes, I'm well aware.

But I digress.

Walking up the steps to my rented duplex, I pull the house key out of my pocket and smile at Ravioli—my most handsomest pug in the whole wide world—when he shoves his smashed face against the front window.

"Hey little buddy! Give me one second!" I stab my key into the hole, turn, and brace myself for the onslaught of pug.

Ravioli, bless his little heart, goes bananas when I enter the tiny little foyer, jumping all over like Tigger as I try to remove my shoes and dump my keys into the bowl next to the door.

I bend, giving him a cursory scratch behind his ears. "I know, I know—you've been cooped up all day and have to pee." I rise, still talking to the dog. "You wouldn't believe what I did today—babysat some rich kid so he could put the moves on a woman at a funeral! Can you believe that shit?" I say. Ravioli cocks his head as if he can understand me as he follows me down the hall. "Trust me, I didn't want to but I needed the money, and besides, he's friends with Uncle Winston."

We reach my small kitchen.

"I can't believe no one noticed me loitering—I wasn't even sitting down." I take a grape from a bowl and pop it on my tongue. "No one said a word."

And if they did, they most likely assumed I was a photographer or an employee working for the funeral parlor, or possibly a nun without her habit?

Don't nuns hang out in churches?

I certainly looked like one with my black blouse and its prim lace collar, tucked into black dress pants, hair falling down my back in a dark curtain.

"A nun without a habit," I chuckle to the dog, who has lost interest in me and has gone to stand next to the treat canister, panting and batting his bulging, beady eyes.

I tsk. "Dude, you have to go outside first. I don't want any accidents on the floor."

He's two years old but every once in a while, the little guy can't hold it in.

Opening the door I let Ravioli outside, into the fenced in backyard where he takes off like a shot—or at least, as fast as a fat pug can go.

Naturally he gets the zoomies, forgetting that he has a job to do. And that job is peeing so he's not peeing on the kitchen floor when he comes back inside.

I leave him there to play; leave the back door open since it's gorgeous outside, sliding my feet into slippers and brewing myself a cuppa tea.

Sigh.

Catfishing and puppeteering is *not at all* how I want to spend my weekends—but unfortunately for me, that's what's paying the bills; every side hustle counts and keeps the electricity on so I can spend as much time as I can building my business.

No, strike that—I wouldn't consider myself a catfish, not by any stretch of the imagination—at least not the kind you see on television. It's more like... I'm a people person helping people when and where I can, in exchange for the capitol (aka: money) I need to build my business full time.

One half mercenary, one half community service.

And if the universe is on my side, there will be a day I will not have to have a side-hustle.

But that day is not today.

Water steaming hot, I add a tea bag, leaving it in the mug so it can steep, watching the steam rise as I lean my hip against the counter. Behind me in the back yard, Ravioli zooms in circles burning off all his pent up doggo energy.

"Good, get good and tired," I tell him out loud though he can't hear me. "I have shit to get done later and don't need you trying to climb into my lap and lick my face because you want attention."

My phone buzzes, still on vibrate, startling me.

Skips around the counter until I grab it, looking at the screen.

UNKNOWN CALLER.

Nothing new there, plenty of telemarketers call during the day, scammers too.

I hit decline and let it go to voicemail.

∼

IT'S HOURS LATER BEFORE I CHECK MY MESSAGES, TAKING the rest of the afternoon to check emails, do some marketing, design a few banners and graphics for social media to promote my business.

Checking my bank account, I audibly moan when the balance pops up and I click, click, click on the ENTER bar because surely there are some numbers missing from the total?

"That cannot be right." I squint at the piddly number, a pit forming in my stomach. "WHY GOD WHY! I don't want to keep having to do these dumb side jobs for quick cash!"

Ugh!

College educated. Funny.

Motivated.

Self-stater, I was able to get a great job out of college but realized pretty quickly that the corporate culture wasn't for me. So, I left with a decent nest egg, determined to 'strike out on my own.' Everyone else was doing it, why shouldn't i?

Social media was buzzing, influencers were taking the world by storm, I knew there was a niche in there for me, too.

But this balance in my bank account keeps dwindling, rent sucking up most of it with not enough contract work to go around, it seemed. Or maybe I wasn't looking hard enough?

I shut my lap top and rise from my desk, determined not to check it until after my check from Palmer was deposited.

Yes. Yes, I need to get to the bank, stat, with his money.

"That will help," I nod into the mirror as the water pours into the tub, step out of my robe once it's halfway up the side, cringing when it stings my ass as I sink into it. "Hot, hot, hot."

I run some cold water, just a smidge.

Toe sticking out my bubble bath, wine glass in one hand, I thumb through my phone before realizing one of the phone calls I'd declined earlier in the day had left me a voicemail.

I sip and swipe.

Transcribe the voicemail so I can read it rather than listen, mouth puckered as I swig from my glass.

"Miriam? Hi, my name is Decker. I'm, um, a friend of Palmer Darling's? He gave me your number, I hope that's okay. Listen, he told me what you've done for him and I...might need your help, too? So, if you could give me a call back, that would be great. Um, this is Decker."

I stare at the transcribed message, then hit PLAY, lifting the phone to my ear so I can hear the sound of Decker's voice.

Decker?

What the hell kind of a name is that?

The name of a guy who probably grew up with a guy named Palmer, whose name is as pompous; stuffy and stuck up as a polo pony but with plenty of cash to fund my social media marketing business.

"...Miriam? Hi, my name is Decker. I'm, um, a friend of Palmer Darling's?"

I sit up straighter in the tub at the sound of his deep voice.

Dang, Decker—for someone coming off as super needy, you sure have a sexy voice.

My toe fiddles with the bubbles at the edge of the tub, and I watch as a sudsy blob falls from my foot and lands in the water.

I listen again.

Then once more, because why not, the guy has an incredible voice.

".... he told me what you've done for him and I...might need your help, too?"

Ugh, flipping Palmer, blabbing to strangers about my services.

The last thing I need is another yuppie for another funeral, or worse, a *wedding*. I do a lot of those, too, in case you didn't know—incognito speeches at the back of the reception hall, an easy in and out job kind of like in that movie The Wedding Planner.

If there's a hiccup involving me, it usually includes ear pieces, WiFi, or trying to communicate with a drunken groomsmen.

The last thing I want to do is entertain another errant playboy and his need to impress some random date, regardless of the circumstances.

Still.

I'm broke, remember?

Beggars can't be choosers.

"Should I give him a call back, Rav?" I'm a few thousand bucks short of the new computer I need, not to mention: rent, food, utilities.

I need a computer desperately, the one I have is old, outdated, and every so often shuts down on me while I'm in the middle of designing something.

Ravioli blinks which is all the confirmation I need.

"Okay fine, I'll call him back. The least I can do is see what he wants."

Perfectly rational.

If Decker is the kind of guy that can cough up the same dough that Palmer did, I'll be closer to my goal and better off for it.

I hit CALL BACK and listen while the phone rings.

It rings.

And rings.

And just when I'm expecting the outgoing voice message to kick on, a male voice answers.

"Decker Dunham speaking."

Decker *Dun*ham?

Stop it.

The voice on the other end of the line is masculine and rich. Hesitant—almost as if he were uncertain he answered his cell on purpose.

"Decker?" I repeat the name like an idiot, unsure of what else to say.

He clears his throat. "This is he."

"Hi Decker, this is Miriam Bennington. You called and left a message?"

I say no more.

He is the one who cold called me, not the other way around.

"Oh! Yes. Yes, sorry, I'm—hold on for one second, would you? I have to close my office door."

"Sure."

Bubbles float around my body, slowly bursting and dissipating the longer I linger here.

I sip my wine; it's a grocery store vintage I'd found on the endcap and taken three bottles of; I'm not one to balk at inexpensive alcoholic grapes.

I am good and buzzed...

"I'm back." He says, the sound of a desk chair squeaking in the background. "Thanks for returning my call."

"Of course." I stare down my body at the bubbles covering my boobs, the cold air from the bathroom causing my nipples to go hard. "You mentioned being a friend of Palmer's? I figured it couldn't hurt to call you back."

"Did I say *friend*?" He amends, clearing his throat. "I meant we work together at the same law firm. Collogues?" He babbles. "He gave me your number after cornering me in the supply room when I was grabbing loose leaf paper." Decker chuckles as if that were an amusing fun fact. "After you worked his grandfather's funeral earlier today."

"Already? I thought he was taking Gemma on a date?"

Dude works freakishly fast.

"He was. He did. He stopped in because apparently he forgot his wallet in is desk. Popped in to say hello and gave me the rundown."

I wince. "Worked his grandfather's funeral?" I laugh. "Please tell me that's not how he's describing it to people."

"Sorry, no—that's just how *I'm* describing it, it seemed apropos. He uh—we uh, got into a conversation about who his date was, he was still dressed up, and I asked how it went, expressed my condolences." Decker clears his throat again. "He told me you were the driving force between his match with Gemma."

I was the driving force behind his match? "That's a stretch, but go on."

I want to hear all the details about how amazing I am.

"While I think it's bizarre that he brought a date to his grandfather's funeral—"

"Oh my god!" I sit up in the bathtub, water sloshing every which way. "I'm so glad you think so too. Weird, right? Who does that?"

"There are no words to describe Palmer Darling," Decker laughs.

"I bet if you gave me a few minutes, I could come up with a list..."

Decker chuckles. "In any event, after he and Gemma left, it got me to thinking."

Okay—here it comes. "Don't tell me, let me guess; you're the best man at a college friend's wedding and you need me to feed you your speech so you don't biff it."

"Uh..."

Oh, so that's not it? Hmmm. "Okay what about this one; you need me to help you through an awkward interview so there are no awkward silences?"

No, that wouldn't make sense. He already said he was a lawyer, which means he probably hasn't had to interview for a job in years.

"You're taking your company public and you don't want to use a teleprompter during the big speech."

Hmm. That doesn't sound right either.

My brain does a mental rundown of the possible suspects, the usual things I'm contracted for because my communication skills are so on-point, my price at a premium that only men like Decker and Palmer can afford.

"Uh, no." He manages to insert himself back into the conversation.

He waits to see if I'll keep talking and I clamp my mouth shut to stop myself from interrupting him again.

"I seem to find myself in a place in my life where I..." He hesitates uncomfortably; I can hear him shifting in his chair. "I work long hours but I've been cutting back and I find myself...avoiding going home."

Eh?

What's this now? What this talk about him not wanting to go home and being overworked?

It sounds like Decker is spilling his guts and I have no idea why.

Most of my contacts don't start their spiel like this and for once, I have no idea where this conversation is leading.

"You avoid going home? Why?"

Is his wife unbearable? Is he a hoarder? Does he live in a five story walk up and can't physically tolerate it? I have so many questions.

"It's too lonely. I've decided now is the time to get serious about dating."

Oh shit. He does want me to crash an event with him. He wants me to—

"I need a matchmaker."

What's this now?

My brow furrows out of confusion. "How does this concern me."

"You. I need you as my matchmaker."

My face resumes it's normal expression as I relax back into the tub. "I'm sorry to say this Decker, but you've got the wrong gal. I'm not a matchmaker."

Don't know what gave him that idea.

"What *is* your job then?"

"My job is social media marketing?" Why am I asking it like it's a question.

I clear my throat. "I'm in social media marketing."

There.

Firm.

Assured.

"Maybe you're a matchmaker and you don't even realize it— some people have gifts and they don't tap into their fullest potential."

I snort. "Not me. I'm good with graphics and creatives but not people."

That's probably not true—I am good with people. I just have no desire to schlepp around some guy and find him a mate based on zero information. Not that I would if I had information but...

"Why not just hire a professional? Or go on dating apps?"

"I have no desire to put my face on an app where thousands of random woman can see it. What if I work with some of them? What if I bump into one in the break room?"

"Wouldn't that be a good thing?" I muse into my empty glass. "Then you would know who was single in your office and who wasn't. The app literally shows you the distance between singles, it's kind of great."

I've done dating apps a time or two myself and I'm familiar with how they work.

"I don't want to date someone in my office and I don't want anyone in my office knowing I'm on a dating app. I work long hours, I don't mix business with pleasure. I'm *private*."

"Then how do you expect to meet anyone?"

"That's why I called you."

"Well." I wave my hand through the bathwater. "I'm not a match-maker, so...."

"I'll pay you."

Duh, obviously he'd be paying me if I let him hire me.

But I'm not for hire.

Plus, he probably has no idea how much professional match-makers actually cost, which can be thousands. Or more.

"I appreciate that, Decker, but I'm not for hire."

"Palmer said you needed the money."

Wow. Okay.

Not Palmer out there airing my personal business amongst his colleagues.

Freaking Palmer and his loud, yuppie, blabbing mouth. I take a deep steadying breath before delivering my next words. "I am the least qualified person to help you. I'm sorry but I think you should contact Love Beans—they're a matchmaking service in the city."

I've seen or heard their commercials over and over. They always have my eyes rolling and my mouth cringing.

"Love Beans?" Decker scoffs. "On what planet am I ever going to contact a company that refers to themselves as Love Beans. What does that even mean?"

Good question.

One I've asked myself plenty of times.

"Google it."

It's not my job to educate some random dude who cold called me out of the blue while I'm trying to unwind and enjoy some quiet time. Today was long, though easy, and mentally draining. The last thing I want is to continue this conversation, especially when my bathwater grows colder by the second.

"Is that your final answer?" Decker asks quietly.

"That's my final answer." I nod definitively even though he cannot see me. "Thanks for the offer—I appreciate it, but will not be accepting it."

He goes silent a few seconds, then, "Sounds good. Thanks for hearing me out."

"Yup. Best of luck to you."

I end the call, staring at the phone number before setting the phone on the edge of the porcelain tub.

Chapter Three

MIRIAM

I'm charging this bride fifteen hundred dollars for me to deliver the Best Man his speech.

Exorbitant, I know.

Still, her father can afford it and she was desperate, and considering working a wedding the weekend after I worked a funeral?

This is the last place I want to be.

She wanted her father to sound articulate and the Best Man to sound brilliant and not like the drunken mess he actually is.

Fidgeting with the tiny speaker lodged in my left ear, I give it a little tweak so it's nice and snug, locate an inconspicuous spot in an alcove at the back of the room, and watch as the wedding processional strides into the reception room.

It's a gorgeous space with parquet floors and large, round tables filled with champagne flutes, wine and water glasses, and silver charging plates.

I watch as guests take their seats.

Lift my chin when numerous members of the bridal party put their hands to their ears, too, and adjust the speaker there.

"Miriam to Mister Stadler. Mister Stadler, can you hear me?"

At the front of the room, Steven Sadler—our lovely Bride's father—nods. He may be the CEO of a successful company, but the man is terrified of public speaking and hadn't wanted to make a speech, and, with failing eyesight, he wasn't confident enough to use a teleprompter or cue cards.

"Whenever you're ready to say the prayer before the meal, just nod your head again, Sir."

A nod was our signal.

It takes Steve Sadler a good five or seven minutes before he gives me the go ahead to get the ball rolling.

"Ladies and gentleman," I say as quietly as I can to still be heard over the noise. "Can I please have your attention." Obediently, Mister Sadler repeats after me. I mean—this is what I've been hired by his daughter to do; feed her father and a few others their lines.

She did not want anyone botching these moments; not with so many guests, photographers, and the media in attendance capturing it for all posterity.

"Before we start serving the meal, in lieu of a toast, I'd like to say a few words of Grace." I watch from the back as he bows his head.

"Dear Lord, we gather in this beautiful ballroom tonight in the spirit of celebration and gratitude. Thank you for the blessing of bringing Janelle and Evander together in marriage today. We ask you to bless their marriage, their future family, and all of their relationships with all of you." He is speaking particularly and at an excellent pace. *"Help them stay strong through adversity, and to treasure and protect the joy of marriage. May we, as their family and friends, commit to uphold and encourage them to the best of our ability."* I instruct him to have everyone raise their glass. *"Janelle's mother and I ask that you, Lord, please bless this food we are about to receive. Amen."*

The bride's father shoulders visibly sag when he passes the microphone to the wedding coordinator, Liz, and scurries back to his seat, duty done.

Liz turns to find me and winks, nodding toward the Best Man.

Peter.

"Miriam to Peter; can you hear me?"

"Roger that, Mir Mir." He hiccups. "Is it whiskey time to tango?"

Whiskey time to tango?

Jeezuz.

It's not my problem if he's sauced; I mean—the groomsman usually start drinking long before the reception, so I wouldn't have been shocked if he'd been tipsy. But I'm being paid for him to repeat me so he doesn't say anything embarrassing, implicate the groom in any past transgressions, or make jokes no one else will think are funny.

It won't be easy if he's drunk.

From my chat with Liz, it didn't sound as if the bride, Janelle, was a Bridezilla—hallelujah—but she was clear about her expectations and wanted zero over the top wedding drama, some of which can begin and end with a groomsman toast.

It's basic science.

Patiently I wait in my cozy little nook, watching as the servers come around, setting plates at the front table, then the round ones, neatly and efficiently—thank god. The last thing I want to do is hide here all night.

As soon as I'm done feeding Old Petey his speech, the rest of the evening is mine.

"Peter, Peter, Peter—I hope you're ready to get through this. After everyone starts eating, I'll give you the cue to stand and raise your glass, okay? It should only be a few short minutes before we can begin."

A server walks by and catches my eye, see's that I'm speaking to absolutely no one, and raises their brows.

What! Plenty of people walk around weddings talking into mini-microphones!

"Peter, you ready?"

"Ten-Four Merry Go Round."

Oh lord. He's given me yet another nickname...

You're making one thousand dollars to be here, you're making one thousand dollars to be here, you're making one thousand dollars...

"Alright." I am all business. "I'll say the line and you repeat it. Understand?"

"I know dude, we've been over this."

I had popped into the wedding's rehearsal dinner last night and quickly prepped Peter and Mister Stadler on how this all works. Showed them the equipment, fitted them for the mic and ear piece, did a practice run.

"Can you stand up for me so Liz, the wedding planner, can bring you the microphone?"

Peter pops up from his seat a little too quickly; wobbles a bit but readily takes the microphone Liz offers him. Taps on the top of it even though last night I'd specifically told him *not* to.

As predicted, the mic produces a screeching sound, half the weddings guests in the room cringe from the feedback it causes. Particularly the older folks in the crowd.

Without me instructing him to, he raises the mic to his mouth.

"Testing, testing, uno, dos, tres. Can I have your attention por favor?"

He's loud as hell.

And also: not Spanish.

"A bit more quietly, please. You don't have to shout," I instruct through gritted teeth. "Thank you all for coming tonight—I know some of you traveled especially far. We have family of Janelle's here from Poland." He pauses so everyone can politely applauded the Polish cousins. "And if there's anybody here tonight that's feeling tense, exhausted and queasy at the thought of what lies ahead for Evander and Janelle, it's probably because you're already married."

Everyone laughs.

I smile.

Still got the magic touch...

"My name is Peter Hansen and I've known Evander since we were in junior high school together and trust me folks, you don't know how much I was looking forward to this day. This *moment.*" I pause so Peter pauses. "After all years I've been friends with Evander he has finally admitted that I am in fact the BEST man."

More laughter.

Peter grins from ear to ear as if the idiot himself had anything to do with the witty words coming out of his mouth.

"When my best friend met Janelle, we were in college; we didn't think the relationship would last because let's face it—there were many drunken nights, missed classes, and not many opportunities to be romantic because Evander isn't a guy who drops his buddies because he'd met the love of his life. Janelle is a one of a kind woman that we all adore."

Smiles all around the room, especially from the Bride, who sits prettily on her satin draped throne as if she had no idea her grooms Frat boy of a best friend could be so eloquent.

As if she weren't paying me to be his puppet master.

When Peter teeters a bit and holds the back of his chair for support, her cool demeanor falls along with her grin.

Shit.

"Well folks. I don't believe in roasting the groom on his special day. Therefore, this speech won't contain anything embarrassing or controversial about Evander, like ex-girlfriends or embarrassing moments. Instead, I'll only give my speech about the kind, funny sides of his character—so thank you and goodnight."

The room erupts into cheers, a few whistles in the back.

Another day, another deposit in the bank.

Grinning like a Cheshire Cat because *this is way too easy*—I back up a few feet, ready to retreat to the bar for a glass of white wine (compliments of the bride and groom, of course), bumping into a solid pillar.

A warm, solid pillar.

"Well done," The pillar has a deep voice and speaks in my ear. "You are truly brilliant."

Startled, I turn.

A man is standing there; one that's tall, with sandy brown hair, a smooth face, and dimple in his right cheek.

"Are you certain you're not willing to become my matchmaker?"

Chapter Four

MIRIAM

"Are you certain you're not willing to become my matchmaker?"

Oh shit.

I may not have met this guy in person but I would know that voice anywhere.

My eyes narrow.

"Decker Dunham," I whisper as if this were a showdown in the middle of a dirt road, giving him the longest cursory glance I've ever graced on someone's person. Starting at his feet and working my way up, I would be offended if he were doing the same to me and remember myself, finally forcing myself to meet his gaze.

Mouth in an amused purse, he gives me a mock bow. "At your service."

There's a tidy red bow-tie at his throat winking in my direction with tiny white polka dots that looks quite dapper with the navy blue suit, his tan dress shoes polished to a shine.

Oh la la, Decker Dunham is fancy.

Mister Fancy Pants.

Decker also looks like the type of guy who spends way too much time at the office, holed up behind his desk. Dude hasn't had the sun shining on his skin in years.

Freckles dot the bridge of his nose.

He's cute, that's for sure.

His voice doesn't match the vision of him I had in my head, but still, he's a pleasant surprise.

"You must be Miriam."

"At your service." I repeat his words, extending my arm for a handshake then pull it back in. Too formal and unnecessary, this is a wedding reception not a business meeting.

It would be a business meeting if you were letting him hire you...

But you're not.

So, it isn't.

"How did you know it was me?"

Instead of answering, Decker crosses the stone patio and walks to the bar, which was my intended destination, pulling out a bar stool and offering it up to me like a gentleman, and despite myself, I blush a little.

Clear my throat and move toward it, sliding onto the metal seat and get comfortable, my purse on the countertop in front of me.

Decker orders for the both of us—wine for me and a Manhattan for him—then turns his attention to me, his big, brown eyes wide. Dark sooty lashes that have no business being on a man when I spend so much money on extensions and serums.

Ugh.

"So" I say. I know he's going to plead his case again. "How did you know it was me?"

He shrugs. "How many people do you know who work events and feed people their lines? A modern day Cyrano De Bergerac."

"Cyrano de who?"

Decker laughs. "You don't know who Cyrano is?"

The bartender sets down my wine glass and I waste no time taking a swig.

I mean—sip.

"It's a famous story about a man—Cyrano—who was in love with a woman named Roxane. But because he thought his was unattractive and his nose was too big, he didn't have the confidence to woo her."

I have no idea where this story is heading, or how it's even close to what I'm doing.

"He begins to send Roxane love letters. She believes they are from another man, a man who then has Cyrano continue writing them. He hides in the shadows while Christian woes her beneath the balcony, feeding him sweet words to use on Roxane from the shadows."

Ahh. That makes more sense to me.

"Well, Decker, what I'm doing doesn't exactly have a romantic element." I wave my hand through the air airily.

"How can you say there isn't a romantic element to what you do? It's all very mysterious, which makes it sexy, which makes it romantic, don't you think?"

"That's a reach, but sure. Whatever you say, me lurking in a corner and feeding the drunken groom his dinner toast is romantic." I roll my eyes. "Okay."

Decker leans against the bar, cocktail glass in his hand, studying me. "Are you not a romantic, Miriam?"

"Of course, I'm a romantic."

"But you have no interest in helping me." His brows are raised and I notice one of them has a small scar through it.

I wonder how it got there but don't ask.

"Pardon me for saying so, but you hardly seem like the kind of gentleman that needs help from someone like me."

"Based on what?"

His appearance. The sound of his voice.

I shrug. "You don't seem to lack confidence, why don't you go out and meet someone?"

He hesitates. "As I explained on the phone, I work a lot and typically spent a lot of time in the office so I didn't have the ti—"

I cut him off with a laugh. "You're going to sit there and tell me you don't have the time and don't leave the office? Then why on earth would I want to help you find a girlfriend when you don't have time for one?" I sip from my glass. "That's horrible. I would never set someone up like that; for a relationship you have no time for."

"Are you going to let me finish?"

I huff, a puff of air coming out my nose. "Fine. Finish."

"I typically spent a lot of time at work. I don't anymore. And it feels like I was underwater and finally came up for air and now I'm looking around," Decker looks around. "With no idea where to go from here. I have no idea how to go about it."

"Most people start with the dating apps."

Jeez, does this guy know nothing?

"I did that."

"That's a good thing." I pause. "*And?*"

"And... it's not great."

"What do you mean, it's not great?"

"I don't know half of what anything means. LTR? FWB? What even is that?"

Blankly I stare, not sure if he's being serious or not. "LTR," I repeat. "Means *long term relationship*. FWB means *friends with benefits.*"

I assumed most people knew this but Decker's eyes grow wide, mouth opening. Closing.

"Oh... okay, that makes sense." He reaches up and scratches his head, then uses those same fingers to readjust the smart red bow-tie beneath his chin. Seems to loosen it a tad. "I had a few theories about what those meant and neither of those were on the list."

"You could have googled it on the internet." I laugh.

His face blanches humorously as if looking the acronyms online had never occurred to him and I laugh again, damn near spitting the wine out of my mouth.

He looks so goofy I soften.

"Would you mind showing me your dating profile? Not because I want to help you—I'm suddenly curious."

I might not be on dating apps but I know how important they are in attracting the right people—or, rather, the kind of people you want to attract.

Decker blushes. "Do I have to?"

I shrug. "No—you don't *have* to. But if you can't show me your profile, how would you expect me play matchmaker and find you a girlfriend?"

"But you haven't agreed to be my matchmaker. Ergo, showing you my dating profile puts me in a vulnerable position."

Hmm. Guess he's right about that, it kind of does put him in a vulnerable position? Still, I'm nothing if not curious, more so now that he's admitting he does not know the most basic of online dating terms.

"Based on how pathetic it is, it could be a determining factor."

He pulls a face. "I offered to pay you a shit ton of money and you didn't bite. How is me showing you this profile more of a determining factor than cash?"

I rub my chin in thought. "Did you actually offer to pay me a shit ton of money? No. I only recall you saying you'd pay me—then adding a bit about Palmer saying I needed money." I nod toward his phone, palm out, fingers wiggling. "Show me the profile and I'll see how badly you need my help."

He's holding it in his hand, cradling it in a rather large palm.

Obviously I can't help but notice.

I am female after all, and one who happens to notice details, regardless of whose body they're attached to.

Le Sigh.

The first thing I do when Decker hands over his phone is read his BIO.

DECKER, 37

Work hard, play hard. Successful businessman looking for his partner-in-crime.

"My god you did not say partner in crime." I groan. "So cliché."

I read on as he sputters and tries to get his phone back.

I hold it out of his reach and side-eye him. "Do you seriously *play* hard? You just got done telling me you have no time to date."

He shrugs. "It just felt like the appropriate thing to say, I can't very well say I work long hours and have neglected my personal life."

I mean.

He could.

I read on. "*Looking for a long-term commitment. Not looking to play games. Love dogs and red wine. Quiet nights in and volunteering for at risk youth. Cooking in my gourmet kitchen.*"

I snort. "Cooking in my gourmet kitchen? Do you even have groceries?"

Decker grapples for the phone again. "Must you read that out loud?"

I must. "*Must love dogs.*" I look at him. "Do you even have a dog?"

He shakes his head, face flushing. "No but someday I'd like one."

Not the same thing but whatever.

"Okay well. if you don't mind I'm going to sneak a gander at the conversations you've been having."

He groans loudly, taking a healthy chug of his cocktail. A really, really healthy chug.

Decker, it seems, has matched with a decent number of women and has already started dialogues with most of them—most, but not all.

I scan the small, round thumbnail photographs and poke on a a blonde named Trishell, her face popping up larger at the top of the screen.

She begins the convo with a *Hey!* And a waving emoji, then asks how his day is going.

Decker: *Good.*

Good? Surely he knows better than that, a one worded reply with no follow up is literally the kiss of death when it comes to dating app etiquette. Everyone knows that!

Everyone except Decker.

Trishell: *That's good. How are the dating apps treating you?*

Decker: *They're alright. I haven't been on them long.*

"Decker. No offence but aren't you a lawyer? You've supposed to be good with words. Your communication with this woman is..." Let's see, how do I put this? "Horrible."

He blanches. "Is it that bad?"

"Yeah, sort of. She's clearly gotten bored. I'm shocked she hasn't unmatched with you yet."

"On to the next one."

I poke on a woman named Ari. Dark hair, blue eyes, cute dimples, the woman is adorable—and totally my type, if I had a type.

They say you can tell a lot from a photograph and pictures don't lie, and Ari's give off a 'I'm the kind of girl you can bring home to mom, but also light a fire under your ass.'

Ari: *Hello, hello, Decker! I love that name, so unique! Just wanted to be the first one to say hi. You look like a nice guy. Must love dogs!? I agree. I have the rudest dachshund named Prince Louise—what about you?*

Decker: *I don't actually have a dog, I just really like them though haha*

The back and forth goes on for several more sentences before Ari gives up and ignores him, most likely on to bigger, better flirting.

Honestly, Decker has to be the world's most cringe conversationalist and if there was anyone who needed me—it's him.

I set down the phone and slide it to him.

Stare blankly, giving my head a shake. "No words."

"That bad?" He's cringing.

"On a scale of one to 'you're never getting laid again,' I say it's a nine."

He leans back in his chair. "What am I supposed to do? It's not like I can get better overnight."

"You actually could if you spent more time trying. Haven't you ever heard the phrase 'Effort is sexy?'"

"No."

I toss my hair. "That's because I made it up."

He laughs. "So, what are we going to do?"

I shoot him another once over—not that I'm completely mercenary but let's be real here: I'm not in the business of charitable causes. Someday perhaps I'll have that luxury, but that day is not today.

"How much did you say you were willing to pay me to be your matchmaker?"

"Ten grand."

My eyes almost bug out of my skull. "Are you for real? You're going to pay me ten grand to be you on a dating app?" How lazy is this guy?

And, can I realistically pull the wool over a woman's eyes pretending to be a dude?

Ten grand.

So many bills to pay.

Debt up to my eyeballs.

Slowly, I nod.

Slowly, I extend my hand.

"It's a deal."

Chapter Five

ARI

"Hello Ari—long time no speak. Let me start by apologizing for my sub-par showing when we first started chatting..."
I stare at the message on my phone from Decker D, a man I'd all but written off as boring, dull, basic. It takes him forever to reply and when he does, it's not at all exciting.

Let's be real: Decker doesn't seem to be much different than his male counterparts, but it was a disappointment nonetheless when he dropped the ball on follow-through.

I want exciting!

I want entertaining!

I want sexy!

And he wasn't serving it...

Oh well. There are plenty of fish in the sea I'm swimming in.

I stare, debating. Did I want to bother messaging him back? This new message was more words than he'd spoken combined so already that was a nice change.

But.

Still.

Sighing, I send a short reply because it's not as if I had any great prospects on the horizon; a few one hit wonders but nothing to call home to my sister about.

Me to Decker: *Well, well, well, look what the cat dragged in. What made you come sniffing back around? Bored at the office?*

I can't help my wee bit of sarcasm—blame it on the coffee or blame it on the bitter taste of being let-down by men. I don't know.

Decker: *Nothing like that. Truth bomb coming your way: when I first started on the apps I wasn't fully committed to the task and wasn't giving it the attention it deserved.*

Me: *And now you are?*

Decker: *And now I am. Scouts honor.*

Me: *Were you ACTUALLY a scout of are you just saying that to win my approval? lol*

Decker: *Okay fine I wasn't actually a Scout, but I did always admire their uniform.*

Me: *Is that so?*

Decker: *Not really. LOL*

Decker: *So anyway, here I am. Thanks for replying, I wasn't sure you would.*

Me: *I wasn't sure I would, either, but I figured—why not. I have nothing else going on tonight.*

Decker: *What are you up to this weekend?*

Me: *Took a run around the park, now I'm doing laundry and laying on the couch in a robe, flipping through reality TV. You?*

Decker: *Sort of the same, minus the running part, minus the laundry part, minus the robe part....*

Me: *LOL*

Decker: *Mostly just the part about the TV*

Me: *Very cute*

Decker: *I try.*

I bite down on my bottom lip, thinking of ways to keep the convo clipping away, then do an internet search on the 'best questions to ask your date.'

Me: *If you were in prison, what's the last meal you would eat?*

Decker: *Well, I HAVE been in prison and I really like the mash potatoes...*

My eyes bug out.

Me: *Wait. Are you being serious???*

Decker: *NO. LOL. My last meal would be steak, a good red wine, and cheesecake. You??*

Me: *Yum....! I think something similar but maybe throw a lobster tail on top of that steak, give me some kind of potato on the side, a vegetable, hollandaise sauce.*

Decker: *Uh. It sounds like you've given your prison meal a lot of thought. Is there something I should know about you?*

Me: *LOL only that I love food? No prison record, never gotten into any trouble if you don't count trying to get my friends out of trouble in college.*

Decker: *Yeah, no—I don't think that counts as trouble.*

Me: *What about yourself, have you ever found yourself in hot water?*

Decker: *Not that I can think of. I'll let you know if something comes to me.*

Me: *Please do.*

Decker: *So, Ari—what are you looking for in a partner?*

Me: *Probably the same things you are; a person who enjoys going out —and staying in. I love dressing up and wearing heels. I'd love to date someone who can travel, who has some flexibility... obviously my dog must approve*

Decker: *A person? Not a man specifically? Ha ha*

I cock my head, studying the sentence and the question, curious that of all the things I mention in that small paragraph, he would pull that one simple detail out.

Me: *No, not a man specifically.*

Decker: *Ahh.*

Ahh? What does *that* mean?

For the moment I decide to ignore it and move the conversation along, not needing to bother explaining myself to a man I haven't met in person and may never.

I don't owe him an explanation.

Me: *What are you looking for in a partner?*

Decker: *Someone who is just as comfortable in a dress as she is in sweatpants.*

Ugh. How cliché.

I roll my eyes. Literally every single guys says that.

Literally.

My phone pings again.

Decker: *Did that make you gag? I bet every guy says that.*

Me: *As a matter of fact...they do LOL but that doesn't make it any less true.*

Me: *If you're a lawyer I imagine you need someone who can go to dinners and fundraisers with you, who likes to dress up.*

Decker: *I do! LOL. Comes with the territory unfortunately. And it's not as glamorous as some people think it is; work is work is work, even if I'm wearing lipstick.*

Decker: *Even if YOU are wearing lipstick—I didn't mean me*

Me: *Hey, no judging if you were*

I'm an equal opportunity lover.

Decker: *Phew, what a relief**wink wink***

I haven't been on a date with a decent guy in months, though not for lack of trying. It seems like every match has been a fail, or the guy has been married and lying about it, or he's way more into me than I am of him.

The curse of having ones shit together...

Decker seems like a keeper—and if he's as charismatic in person as he is in the dating app, then whoa baby, I would twirl in circles and be doing the happy dance.

Not really my type physically, although to be fair, I'm not sure what my type is. It varies, if I'm being honest. Big burly. Tall. Clean shaven but also: bearded. Dark hair. Hairy. Not hairy. Shaggy hair or well groomed—my type is all over the place. Not only that, I've toyed with the idea of widening my search to include everyone, not just men.

Love is love and all that, and if I still haven't found what I'm looking for—why not?

And since we're on the subject, I have a little secret to spill about the time I went to the dentist and accidentally hit on her. She was working on my teeth and as you know, having a conversation while you're sitting in the chair isn't easy.

It's damn near impossible.

My dentist is beautiful. Funny. Big, bright smile.

She always has a story ripped from the headlines and makes small-talk about it, wanting to know my opinion about this or that as she's drilling away in my mouth. While she drills, I study her face; hair. Eyes. Teeth.

The bridge of her nose, which is always visible above her surgical mask.

I shouldn't have a crush on her but I do.

Anyway, one day when she was doing an impression of my top teeth, patiently doing the work herself because her assistant had to go see another patient, she asked me a question and good-naturedly, I waited to answer until the metal mold was out of my mouth.

"We should continue this conversation over coffee," I joked. "I can never answer with gunk in my mouth."

The doctor swiveled on her stool, busying herself with writing my name on the impression mold, expression neutral.

Oh shit.

Had she thought I was hitting on her?

Was I?

It felt like it—but that's not at all what my intention was.

I don't think.

Couldn't have been...

My phone pings again, putting an end to my woolgathering.

Decker: *This might be sudden since we've only been talking for a few hours but would you want to meet for a drink this weekend?*

By no stretch of the imagination do I consider this sudden. My style is ripping off the band-aid and finding out whether we're a match so I can move on and match with someone new if we're not.

Me: *Let's do it.*

Chapter Six

MIRIAM

"Hi." I rise from my seat and cross the bar, hand extended as Ari glances around searching for a man who is *not* showing up tonight.

Her date.

I'm here instead, vetting her to save my client time and also: he has a last minute meeting with the partners in his firm that he could not miss. I mean, what was he supposed to tell them? Sorry boys, I can't make your meeting because I'm meeting a woman I've never met for a drink at the Rugby Lounge?

Not likely.

Not Decker.

Instead, we decided that I would do just fine—I just have to convince Ari that I'm a suitable replacement, as unconventional as this is.

"Ari?"

She nods, confused, still glancing around the bar.

"Decker isn't coming," I blurt out.

I've never done this before—gone on a date in someone's stead, least of all not a man's. Dating by Proxy.

I'm surprised when Ari extends her hand, letting it slide into mine.

"Decker isn't coming?" Ari's head is tilted to the side, her long wavy hair moving along with it. "Who are you?" She breaths. "And please do not say his wife."

"Oh god, no—I'm not wife." I laugh. "I assure you, Decker is very single. I'm his matchmaker."

"You could have led with that," she says, chin tilted up. "Do you have any idea how many married men are on these hideous dating apps?"

Ari already has her purse off her shoulder, ass sliding onto a bar stool, signaling the bartender.

"Too many?"

She nods. "Exactly. Too many."

"Sorry to spring this on you—he's a busy guy. The partners in his firm called a meeting this afternoon; sprung it on him, actually, and he didn't want to cancel."

"So, he sent a representative?" Her laugh is sardonic. "How kind of him."

I set my purse next to hers on the bar top and take a seat next to her. "It's more than most guys would have done."

Another laugh.

"Uh, no. This isn't normal. If you can't show up, you can't show up. You make up am excuse and beg for forgiveness than schedule another date, which you may or may not also cancel."

I steal an olive out of a glass that's full of them across the bar. Pop it in my mouth.

"Ordinarily I would agree with you, but Decker is an entirely different species of male."

"Hmm." Is all Ari says, her lips pursed. Turns to peruse me. "Do you usually get this dressed up when you show up to break a date?"

"I couldn't help it—I don't get out much," I joke, blushing

despite myself as her eyes run down the front of my blouse. My hair. My hips, thighs. "Any excuse to get dolled up."

Her hair tosses. "I like that top."

I run a hand down the silky fabric. "Thanks."

"Do you want a drink?"

"Yes." I swallow. "I've never done this before, I could use one."

Ari and I both order drinks—two glasses of wine, which cannot be poured quick enough.

"Never done what?"

"I've never been a matchmaker and I've never gone on a date for a client before." I pause, not sure how much to tell her. "This isn't my normal routine, and this isn't actually my job. So, it's a little nerve-wracking."

I pull a face, sticking out my tongue.

"What is your job?"

"Social media marketing." I take the glass that's set down in front of me and sip from it. Then sip again, relishing the liquid pouring in my throat. The liquid courage I need to get through these next few minutes, although to be fair, Ari has been pretty darn cool so far.

Decker is one lucky guy.

Ari is beautiful. Smart.

Confident.

She seems unbothered by the turn of events, taking it in stride that I'm here for the ride and not her date.

Decker who?

"What about you?" I ask Ari as the wine slides down my throat a little too easily.

"Very boring," she takes a drink out of her glass. "Nurse practitioner."

"Ohhh." I should have known; should have asked while I was pretending to be Decker, but I didn't. Too busy bantering and trying to make him seem interesting.

Whoops.

"What kind of nurse practitioner?"

"The gynecological kind." She laughs.

I want to make a wise crack about how she must really know her way around a vagina, but clamp my lips shut. Not at all inappropriate; I hardly know this woman and I'm here on a mission, not to flirt or make jokes.

Ari fiddles with the napkin laid out on the bar top. "So. Your day job is social media marketing and your side-gig is matchmaking? How did all that come about?"

I consider my answer, not wanting to sound like a money-grubber but also: I am one.

"Decker found me through a co-worker that had hired me to do a side-job. Sought me out, I said no. Then we bumped into each other at a wedding last weekend and long story short, he is very convincing."

"Convincing? How so?"

"He's just really nice. Like—a super guy. Otherwise, I would have told him to piss off and be on his way."

I clamp my lips shut. Here I am trying to be *classy*, throwing out phrases like 'piss off.' What am I going to do next, drop a few F Bombs?

Ari crosses—then uncrosses her legs. "What kind of side-job? Like posting for them on social media or..." her voice trails off.

Shit.

Do I actually tell her I fed a man lines at a funeral so he could scam his way into a woman's' heart? When I say the words in my head it sounds worse than it was. Or was it as bad as it sounds?

"Not exactly." I take a healthy chug of the wine in my glass then motion for the bartender to pour another.

I have a feeling I'm going to need it, and probably some actual food, too, so I don't get tipsy.

But tipsy isn't always a bad thing...

"How exactly?" She pins me with a stare I imagine she uses on male counterparts when she's trying to make a point, or get the upper hand. I don't blame her, considering that Decker and I pulled a bait and switch.

I lean back against the back of the barstool I'm sitting on, wine glass in one hand, the other waving about the air as I begin my story.

"It's actually really funny. My brother is friends with this guy named Palmer—who works with Decker. Palmer knew I was freelancing." What a nice way for me to say I'm broke and needed money. "Anyway. Palmer had a loss in the family and one of his fears is public speaking—he hired me to talk him through the eulogy."

It takes Ari a few seconds to make sense of all this in her brain before the questions catch up.

"Wait. What do you mean, he hired you to talk him through the eulogy? Were you like, consoling him on the sidelines?"

"No. I was literally telling him what to say in his ear."

And making him cry, the insensitive bastard, by putting menthol in his eyes.

"Telling him what to say?"

I nod. "Yes, feeding him the lines."

Her lips part. "But...couldn't he just write a speech like a normal person would?"

One would think. "I think he wanted to look like he was winging it and had a way with words."

"At a funeral." Ari deadpans. "That makes no sense."

Ya think?

"Who was this guy?"

I shrug. "A friend of my brothers. Total prep, spoiled rich kid, wanted to impress his new girlfriend."

"Pause." Ari holds a hand up. "Wanted to impress his new girlfriend?" Silence. "At a funeral?"

I nod.

"Impress her how?"

Let me see, how do I put this? "Erm. By pretending to be sensitive and emotional, I guess?"

"He needed you to make him look sensitive and emotional?"

"I guess so."

"How the hell do you make someone look sensitive and emotional?"

I consider my next works. "By making him cry."

Ari's eyes are wide as saucers. "Make him cry? Why did he need you to do that—you were at a funeral for pities sake."

"He, uh, wasn't all that close to his grandfather? But wanted to make it look like he was."

So complicated and so weird, if not a tad unethical.

"So. How'd you do it?"

I tilt my head in her direction. "Are you sure you really want to know?"

She nods enthusiastically. "Hell yes."

"Vapor rub."

"Vapor rub." She repeats. "Where?"

"Under his nose. He also accidentally rubbed it in his eyes, which practically blinded him."

Not really but it sounds dramatic, and has Ari cackling.

"Oh my god, stop it." Her laugh is loud, head thrown back.

I watch the curve of her smooth neck and swallow, forcing my eyes up to her face so I'm not staring at her cleavage.

When she's done giggling she asks, "How much did he pay you?"

I finish the last of my wine. "Not nearly enough."

Ari pushes her glass toward where the bartender is standing until it touches mine.

"What a douche."

I shake my head. "Agree."

"See, Miriam." She gives me a nudge on the thigh with the tap of her finger. "This is why I hate online dating. No one is ever who they appear to be. You can pay someone these days to help you lie to a woman." She pokes me again. "You're the perfect example. Decker posted photos of himself as a successful, young attorney—but it turns out, he's actually an attractive, funny young woman."

Chapter Seven

ARI

I was not expecting to be attracted to Miriam.

Obviously.

I came here tonight to meet a man, not a woman, except I'm enjoying our time together and do not miss the fact that I'm missing out on a first date.

This feels like one.

Is that weird?

"...but it turns out, he's actually an attractive, funny young woman."

I'm not flirting with her, I'm not.

Can't be.

I came to meet a man.

One she is here to champion, talk him up, make him look good.

I could care less.

Miriam is far more interesting.

Nonetheless, I suppose it would look strange if I didn't at least pretend to be somewhat interested in her client.

"And Decker is a friend of this Palmer characters?"

She makes a face. "Eh, I'd say they were more co-workers than friends. Palmer is an acquired taste."

That's good to hear because it sounds like this Palmer guy is a real piece of work. You know what they say, you are the company you keep! Or something like that...

It would suck if Decker had idiot friends.

"Why do you think Decker is single?" That's an okay question to ask, right? He sounds successful, looks handsome and put together.

"He's a workaholic." Miriam blurts out before she can stop herself, then cringes, realizing her mistake. WRONG THING TO SAY. "That's not what I meant."

Clearly it was.

I gesture around. "If he wasn't a workaholic, he would be here now, wouldn't he?"

She cringes again. "Good point."

"It hardly matters." I tell her. "Honestly. It's not as if I were emotionally invested, he and I only chatted for a few hours." Although. "It's too bad because he's so funny." I pause. "Is he as funny in person as he is in a chat?"

Miriam is taking the two new glasses of wine from the bartender and sliding one over to my spot, then pulls the bread and dipping oil that got ordered somewhere along the way over, too.

"You think he's funny?"

"Yes. Or I wouldn't be here." Why is she being coy? "I think you can tell a lot about a person by how they communicate online."

She laughs. "Do you?"

"Sure. Don't you?"

Her shoulders shrug and I let my eyes rest on her long, brown hair. It's down, and wavy, and kissing her exposed shoulder where the shoulder of her dress hangs off ever-so-slightly.

The skin there is luminous and I wonder for a second if she's wearing an iridescent powder or lotion, then I wonder what it smells like.

When I lean forward for my glass, I give the air a little whiff, as discrete as possible.

"I do think you can learn about a person by how they communicate online. But. Since we're being honest here I should tell you..." Her voice trails off.

I hold up a hand. "Wait. Don't tell me—let me guess." My teeth bite down on my bottom lip. "That was you I was chatting with, wasn't it?"

Slowly, Miriam nods.

I lean back, crossing my arms. "I should have known. Decker was a real pill the first time we chatted."

She blushes. "Sorry." Hesitates. "He is a great guy though. He really, truly is—so nice. Kind. Not a mean bone in his body."

I narrow my eyes. "Be honest: does he wear bow ties."

That makes her laugh. "Yes."

"Dammit!"

"Do you not like bow ties?"

"I mean—they're fine, but they don't get me wet."

My eyes get wide at the admission, I hadn't meant to say anything sexual—at least not within earshot of other people, like the dude sitting next to me or the bartenders behind the counter.

And.

I hadn't meant to say *wet* the way I said *wet.*

Miriam isn't bothered by it in the least. "Bow ties are not for everyone."

Hmm.

Is she actually talking about bow-ties or does she mean something else or am I just overthinking her raised brows and flushed cheeks?

Dang it Ari, get your mind out of the gutter. She is his matchmaker! She's not thinking about sex right now, she's trying to find the guy a girlfriend. He is paying her!

"No, bow ties are not for everyone." Not all of the time, and only on certain occasions, apparently.

Miriam has her legs crossed at the ankles and I wonder why she got so dressed up tonight when essentially, she was here to entertain me, not wine and dine me. Were I in her place, I might have worn jeans and a cute blouse, not a form-fitting dress that shows off my curves.

"So, what about you?" She has her own story to tell. "Are you single?"

Miriam nods. "Yes, I'm single. I would ask if you are but I already know the answer." She leans forward and narrows her eyes. "You are single, aren't you?"

"Ha." I tease. "Yes, of course."

"Good. Because I wouldn't want to set my client up with a woman who's not."

The sentence hangs in the air the same way her perfume does—and mine—lingering. Tempting me to rebut it. Tempting me to tell her I'm already bored with the idea of dating Decker, he and I won't have the same chemistry she and I have.

Sorry not sorry.

Guess he should have shown up when he had the chance.

His loss.

I busy myself by pulling off a hunk of bread, then dip it in the olive oil and vinegar, chewing slowly while Miriam watches me, neutral expression on her face.

It's obvious I'm older than she is by at least eight years, not that age matters. And it's obvious there are thoughts going through her head she isn't likely to share; at least, not tonight.

"Do you have any pets?" I ask.

"Yes, actually. I have a pug named Ravioli."

I grin. I love pugs. "That's the cutest name."

"Thanks, but—he's a monster. Kind of like your dachshund."

Ahh, she remembered, of course she did, considering it was her on the other end of the conversation and not Decker.

"What else are you into? As far as hobbies go."

"Hmm. I don't know, to be honest. I work a lot because I'm trying to quit all my side-hustles to focus on my day dream. Sometimes I feel like I'm running around like a chicken with my head cut off."

"Well, you're young. You have plenty of time." I hope that didn't come out wrong, I'm trying not to sound bossy or superior.

I touch her shoulder as a sign of compassion.

Her eyes follow the same way they had when I touched her leg and I pull back, not wanting to overstep. What the hell has gotten into me? I'm not overly touchy, especially with people I'm not dating or romantically involved with let alone women.

What an odd predicament to be in, this weird buzzing with whatever this tension is....

Chapter Eight

MIRIAM

Is Ari flirting with me?

It's so hard to tell.

How the hell is a person to supposed to know?

The leg touching. The lingering stares. The way her eyes track my movements—the same way my eyes track hers.

There's a new static in the air that has nothing to do with my fabric softener, a tension that wasn't there when we arrived. When she was here to meet a man and nothing more.

But my attempts to bring the conversation back to Decker seem to go rebuffed, Ari no longer having any interest in discussing him.

Shit.

How am I going to explain this turn of events to him?

Sending me tonight was his idea—he thought it was brilliant, and thoughtful and considerate. "She's going through all that trouble to get dressed up and put on make-up, I don't want it to go to waste."

He'd wanted me to pick up a dozen roses on my way over but that's where I drew the line.

I wasn't her date, why the hell would I bring her flowers?! It was strange enough that I'm sitting here in his stead to begin with.

"What are your hobbies?" I ask her, though I know some of them already; riding bikes. Hiking. Walking along the lake.

"I love going to my parents cabin. It's quiet there and the WiFi is terrible so it's a great place to unwind and recharge."

"I love the sound of that."

"Haven't been there in months—you know how busy the health-care industry has been." She shrugs. "I'll have to take some time off."

"Yeah, same. I knew starting a business would be hard but I didn't think it would be this hard. Or that I'd have no free time because when someone calls, I go running." I drink more of my wine. "My motto has become '*Has laptop, will travel.*' Working anywhere has its perks—and it drawbacks."

I'm never not working and I'm never not strategizing.

Exhausting.

"Clearly you have a high work ethic or you would have told Decker to fly a kite when he asked you to come here tonight."

She's not wrong.

"Guilty as charged." Though not nearly as hard-core as he is, breaking a date for a meeting. I'm sure I would have done the same if I were in his position—the boss is the boss and his job is important. Still, the first impression he's making is less than ideal.

How pissed would I be if some dude this to me?

Oh my god. So pissed.

I wouldn't still be sitting here chatting with his lackey, that's for damn sure.

"I have to give you credit—I personally wouldn't still be sitting here if I were in your shoes." I give a low whistle. "I would have been out the door the second you told me Decker wasn't coming."

She smiles. "Trust me, I thought about it."

My brows raise. "You did? What stopped you?"

Her smile turns coy. "I don't know. You?"

I swear my breath catches, damned if it doesn't. What's up with that by the way, this is a work appointment? So what if we've been drinking wine and she's touched me twice and I can't stop the heat rising into my cheeks.

I'm not blushing, you are.

Ugh.

She is into guys.

She is not into me.

Decker.

Not you.

Your client.

Get that through your head and stop thinking with your tingling body parts.

I'm no better than a dude!

"Me?" I say with a laugh, not sure if I want her to laugh, too.

She doesn't.

Ari only tilts her shoulder up in a cute little shrug, the way she's done a few times already.

"Sure. You. Don't you love a girls night out sometimes? I know we just met but it feels good to just have girl talk and not the pressure of impressing a man." She signals to the bartender to bring us the check. "I'm over it."

"I don't blame you. This is why I haven't dated in ages."

She doesn't look as if she believes me and when the bill comes, we argue over who is going to pay it. I assure her that Decker has given me enough cash to have paid for an entire meal, let alone four glasses of wine and a sub-par appetizer.

Reluctantly I slide off the bar stool and remove our purses from the bar top, handing Ari hers before nodding our good-byes to the staff who'd been serving us.

A breeze that wasn't there when I walked in earlier greets us at the door, my hair whipping before settling back onto my shoulders.

It must be a mess.

"This was nice. Even though I was stood up." Ari shifts on her heels, adjusting the strap of her purse.

I roll my eyes; I cannot help myself. "You weren't stood up."

She shrugs. "Doesn't matter."

"Of course, it matters, I don't want you to feel bad he—"

"That's not what I meant. I meant that it doesn't matter if he was here or not. I told you, I could care less. I had fun." She pauses. "Probably way more fun than I would have had with him, let's be honest. You can stop acting like he and I would have had chemistry."

Slowly, I nod. "Chemistry is important. You never know when you're going to find it."

She is so beautiful.

"Indeed." Ari is nodding slowly, a small smile playing at her glossy lips.

I clear my throat, taking my eyes off her mouth. "Where did you park?"

God I am so bad at this...whatever this is.

"Across the street in the parking lot—I managed to get a spot. I hate paying the ten dollars for valet."

Same. "I actually took an Uber. I don't live far, so I thought it would be easier."

Her brows go up. "Then I'm giving you a ride home."

Together we cross the road, the usually busy street feeling empty, almost deserted. Quiet.

Calm.

Calmer than I feel, my stomach in knots, all the dormant butterflies coming to life.

We chatter the entire car ride to my house, the directions I'm giving her coming almost too late; she missed my street because I wasn't paying attention—I was studying her profile like a weirdo.

"Are you staring at me?" Ari laughs when we pull up to my tiny duplex, grinning as she puts the car in park at the curb.

"Do people admit if they're staring or not?"

"That depends on whether you were—or not."

"Mmm." I hum. "That doesn't help me decide how to answer."

We both laugh, the car idling so quiet I can barely hear the engine. If I didn't know better I would have assumed it wasn't running.

The house beyond us has one window illuminated—I leave a light on for Ravioli, and the television sometimes so he doesn't get lonely. Is that weird? From the street it would be hard to gauge if anyone was home.

"You don't have any roommates?" Ari is glancing around me at the house.

"No, just the dog." Who is probably already waiting at the back window for a treat and his evening bathroom break.

"What a cute place."

"Thanks. I would invite you in but I don't want the dog jumping all over your dress, scratching at your bare legs, or slobbering on you with his obnoxious jowls." I groan. "Seriously, he has no manners. I've tried so hard to train him—it's like he has a mind of his own."

"Try training a wiener dog."

"Anyway, any other night of the week and I'd have you in. I just don't think..."

The legs.

The heels.

Ari nods. "I'll definitely take you up on that."

My hand is on the door handle, ready to push.

Hesitating.

Unsure.

"Let me walk you to your door." Ari is out her door before I can open mine, coming around to my side, heels sinking into the soft ground when she steps off the sidewalk.

Our heels click on the concrete.

Click when we climb the three steps to my small, front porch.

The air is electric.

"Thanks for the drinks."

I nod, turning to face her and pressing my back to the door. "You're so welcome. Thanks for not getting...you know, pissed off that I wasn't your date."

"This was way better."

Way better. In what way? I want to ask, words caught in my throat.

She already told you she was sick of dating and loved having the girl chat—do you need her to keep repeating it?

No, I want her to explain away this feeling—the tingles in my stomach and the nerves that have my legs a little unsteady.

Ari smiles.

I smile.

It's awkward and at the same time, the tension makes it all the better.

"Alright. Well." Her voice is a low whisper, as if the neighbors would be able to hear her if she spoke any louder.

"It was good meeting you."

Don't leave, don't leave, don't leave...

"You too."

I want to invite her inside at the same time I don't.

Nerves.

Fear.

Then.

She's leaning in or I'm leaning in—not sure who does what first—our lips tentatively touching and *I've never kissed a girl before.* A woman.

It's soft.

Gentle.

Tentative like you see in the movies, my hands stuck at my sides while Ari's reach for my waist, palms skimming my hips.

Oh shit...

She's barely touching me and my entire body tingles.

Lips press against mine; mine against hers.

Finally, I lift my hand to brush the hair out of her face, the long strands sticking to my gloss, a problem I've never had kissing before.

Her boobs press against mine and I want to run my hands up her stomach, over the silky fabric of her dress just to see what breasts feel like when they're not my own.

Next time, my brain tells me.

Next time.

Epilogue

"Pardon me—what did you just say?" Decker Duhman's eyes are wider than any one human's eyes that I've ever seen, his head shaking in disbelief.

I arrived at his office a few minutes ago, wanting to give him the news in person.

"The meeting with Ari went really well, but not the way you might have hoped."

I can barely get the words out without my face turning crimson, heat radiating up my chest, to my cheeks, to my hairline.

This is so embarrassing.

I not only hijacked his date, I also stole her right from under him.

The only detail not making me feel like a piece of shit friend is the fact that he hadn't met her yet. Barely knows what she looks like. Has never heard the sound of her voice.

"She isn't interested in dating you because...she wants to date me."

Decker still sits stoically at his desk. The pink bowtie at his chin matches the color of his face, which matches the color of mine.

"We've been on two dates already."

His eyes get huge; round as saucers. "What?"

"I'm sorry. I wanted to come and tell you in person." I bite down on my bottom lip; the same way Ari had flirtatiously bitten down on it when we were kissing goodnight last week.

Now is not the time, Miriam.

"It was a dick move and I'm sorry—I don't know what else to say. We obviously weren't planning it, neither of us have ever dated women before. But we're going to give it a shot."

"A shot." He repeats.

I nod.

"That doesn't mean I can't keep looking. For you. Um. For a match."

I stop talking, the fishbowl that is his glass office has me hyper-aware that we're surrounded by men and women in cubicles, some of them curiously peering over the tops of the gray walls of their cubbies.

Decker presses his index fingers to his temples. "I need a minute." He pauses. "Actually, no—I need a lot of minutes." He raises his head to look at me. "How about I get in touch after I've processed this information?"

I nod. "Yes." Certainly. "Of course."

Who could blame him.

I *stole* his potential new girlfriend.

Ari would argue that no one can steal a person from someone, least of all someone they have never met—so technically I've done nothing wrong. But obviously, because Decker is my client and paying me to make matches for him, this has the potential to be a huge problem.

Not to make this about money but... I need it. And if this gets back to my brother before I have a chance to explain that I met someone and that someone doesn't look or sound like the match he envisioned for me? The whole reveal is going to be so dramatic.

As dramatic as Palmer Darling's funeral extravaganza.

I buckle my seatbelt once I'm in my car and text Ari, a smile already returning to my face.

She makes me so happy. Ridiculously so. I have no idea what will happen between us; if this will work out, if we'll continue exploring our romantic connection or part as friends—but I'm excited to see where this takes us.

Me: *Well. That went better than I'd hoped.*

Ari: *Really? That's good news!*

Me: *Actually NO—it was worse. He looked stunned and now I feel terribly guilty.*

Ari: *We knew it wasn't going to be easy telling him but I'm proud of you for marching in there and getting that out of the way.*

Ari: *Are you relieved?*

Me: *Yes. It's been stressing me out.*

Ari: *I know it has. And I'm glad it done. This thing with Decker will work itself out, I'm confident of that.*

Me: *I agree. I just have to give it time.*

Ari: *Should we get a drink later to talk about it in person, or do you want to wait until our date tomorrow?*

Our date tomorrow, our date tomorrow.

I stare at that sentence, biting down on my bottom lip happily.

I have a date tomorrow with a gorgeous, fun, smart woman and I don't want to wait to see her.

Me: *Let's get a drink.*

Ari: *I was hoping you would say that.*

Ari: *I don't think I can wait to see you.*

Same.

THE END

This may be the end of this novella, but it's just the beginning for Miriam and Ari....

About the Author

Sara Ney is the USA Today Bestselling Author of the How to Date a Douchebag series, best known for her sexy, laugh-out-loud sports and contemporary romances. Among her favorite vices, she includes: traveling, historical architecture and nerding out on all things Victorian. She's a "cool mom" living in the Midwest who loves antique malls, resale clothing shops, and once carried a vintage copper sink through the airport as her carry-on because it didn't fit in her suitcase.

For more information, a list of cities/venues where Sara will be signing, or to purchase signed books, please visit her website at www.authorsaraney.com.

Caelan: Guards of Clan Ross

HILDIE MCQUEEN

Rejection is second nature to Archer, Caelan, and yet hope springs after a tryst with warrior, Lachland. That he could ever aspire to more with the handsome man was a huge mistake. Heartbroken, Caelan decides to become stronger without the need of anyone by his side.

Lachland accepts that he is attracted to other men, yet he refuses to allow deep emotional ties between himself and another man. That is until meeting Caelan, who brings out a side of him, he's never known. However, there is no room in their world for love between men, and he will assure, above all, not to be found out.

Only love can push past obstacles and make a way.

Chapter One

ISLE OF UIST, HEBRIDES 1703

The morning mist added to the allure of the moment. Caelan's boots crunched the dried leaves, the noise loud in the quiet forest. Despite every instinct telling him not to, he walked in the direction the muscled warrior Lachland had gone.

Perhaps it was all in his head, the idea that the man had signaled to him to do so. Yes. He was mistaken, the warrior probably went to relieve himself and here he was following behind, desperate for what he'd perceived as an invitation.

An invitation to what, Caelan wasn't sure.

The breeze blew against his arms, like a velvety caress across his overly sensitive skin.

This was a mistake. He'd never once acted on his impulses. Always maintaining the demeanor of a young inexperienced man. Which, in actuality he was. Caelan had never been with either a man or a woman, for that matter.

Never had he felt such a strong pull to another man than when first laying eyes on Lachland Cameron. Not that the warrior had ever shown any interest in him. If anything, the warrior had always been aloof, almost unfriendly toward him.

And yet, now here he was walking through trees hoping to find out what would happen next.

"Ye came?" Lachland seemed to appear out of nowhere. The man stood beside a tree, his green gaze pinning him, his handsome face without emotion. "I am surprised."

"I-I was nae sure if ye wished for me to come," Caelan replied, fighting the urge to turn on his heel and leave.

"Come closer," Lachland said. Still no expression. It could be the man wished to either kill him or fuck him. Either way, one would expect some sort of hint.

Nonetheless, Caelan's attraction was strong, and he walked and stood next to the same tree. "What is it?"

Lachland pushed him against the tree, the back of Caelan's head hitting the hard wood. If not for the crashing of Lachland's mouth over his, he would have punched the man.

The kiss was possessive, not asking, but demanding. At the same time, Lachland did not hold him in place, the option was there for Caelan to disengage and leave.

Even strong horses would not be able to drag him away. Instead he grabbed the warriors' broad shoulders, and kissed him back, swallowing his taste.

Lachland broke the kiss, moving back, his chest heaving. With a stoic expression he searched Caelan's face. "Have ye ever had a man take ye?"

Ignoring the fact, his legs went weak, Caelan reached for Lachland. He had to have more of him. Another kiss.

Now that it was obvious that the man desired him, he wanted more. This moment was more than he could have dreamed of. "I want ye."

He would not admit to never being with a man. It could make Lachland change his mind. No, not after months of wanting this, wanting Lachland so badly, he'd often pictured the warrior when taking himself in hand until coming.

"I want ye to take me." Caelan repeated. Unlike Lachland, he was sure his face was easy to read. Want, desire and desperation intertwined with hope. He wondered how he looked to Lachland at the moment.

The warrior neared, his face so close, Caelan could see the golden flecks in his eyes. "Good." Once again, he took Caelan's mouth, this time no different than before. It was almost a savage kiss, one of possession of claiming.

"Turn around," Lachland instructed, taking him by the shoulders and turning him to face the tree.

Caelan's hands shook so bad, he could barely untie his belt. Lachland barely waited for him to do so before yanking his trews down below his buttocks.

The cool breeze across his bared arse brought awareness of what was about to happen, and Caelan moaned, a deep guttural sound.

"Ye are anxious for my cock," Lachland's voice was at his right ear, the warmth of his breath tantalizing. "Good. Spread for me."

Unsure what exactly to do, Caelan went with instinct, reaching back and grabbing each orb, spreading himself.

"Perfect," Lachland said, his voice husky. Liquid slid between his bottom, and he looked over his shoulder, but couldn't see what Lachland did.

"Oil," Lachland said. "Hold still."

It proved impossible when Lachland's oiled fingers slid down the center and prodded at his hole. Caelan jerked at the invasion, unsure what to do or think.

"Yes," he urged.

"Be quiet," Lachland hissed. "Someone can hear us."

"Hold yerself open for me," he instructed again.

The thick head of Lachland's cock pushed in slowly, allowing for Caelan to adjust to it. Then inch by inch, he thrust in. Each movement making Caelan want to scream with pleasure. Instead he bit down, squeezed his eyes shut and swallowed the sounds.

"Hold on to the tree," Lachland said, once fully seated inside.

He'd never felt so full, so taken as in that moment as he held onto the tree.

"I'm going to fuck ye Caelan."

Sliding out, Lachland drove back in, then repeated each movement. When Caelan's arms trembled, Lachland grabbed him by the hips and continued driving into him. The sound of their flesh slapping, the feel of Lachland's sack on his upper thigh was more than he could withstand.

Caelan pushed back to meet Lachland's thrusts, searching for the special place that when hit sent sensations like nothing he'd ever experienced through every inch of his body.

"More," Caelan grunted out.

Lachland withdrew and over his shoulder, Caelan watched as he oiled his thick cock. The man was well endowed.

Lachland's flat gaze met his as he took him by the hips and once again thrust into him. "Ye feel good. Tight."

Each thrust was followed by another, faster and harder. Caelan wasn't sure he could hold on to his release, his breathing now coming in gasps.

Just then Lachland reached around and took Caelan's cock, sliding his oiled hand just twice before Caelan came with force.

"Now my turn," Lachland said, pushing in deeper, withdrawing almost completely before once again delving.

Somehow the warrior managed to crest with barely a sound, only a low growl that vibrated through Caelan's' body.

Lachland withdrew and turned away. He walked a short distance to another tree and grabbing a cloth from his horse, cleaned himself.

Unsure what to do next, Caelan lifted his trews and belted them. When he turned to face Lachland, the man was already walking away in the direction of the guard camp.

His breathing sounded like gasps as he fought to regain normality. It was as if his entire body was aflame.

He wanted to be relieved to finally know what it was like to have his fantasy fulfilled. Already he wanted Lachland again. It had to happen again.

The path was empty now, only the light mist hovering, hiding the retreating warrior from his view.

. . .

Upon heading back to the guard camp, Caelan stopped after a few steps, the soreness something he'd expected, but now that it was very much real, a constant reminder of what had occurred.

Shoulders straight, with a flat expression, he walked to where a group of archers stood in line waiting to be fed. "We were just going to go look for ye," one said.

His stomach clenched. "For what?"

"Ye are on patrol with Brock today," he motioned to a stocky man who sat at a table eating.

"I did nae forget."

Upon seating, he ensured not to fidget, purposely keeping his gaze away from where Lachland usually sat. Within moments, he lost the battle and glanced only to find that the warrior was in a deep conversation with one of the leaders. Lachland seemed at ease, one elbow on the table, listening intently to whatever was said.

Patrol that day was dull. There hadn't been much activity to worry about since they'd fought and beat the abusive council in the nearby village.

Caelan dismounted at the creek, his partner, Brock, doing the same. The warrior looked to the sky. "I am going to ask permission to visit my family. My mother is ailing."

The idea of not knowing how his own family fared made Caelan's stomach clench. "I hope ye get to go."

"Our duty is to patrol, not to stand around gossiping." Lachland glowered in their direction from atop his horse. "If ye decide to stop, first ye let someone know. I had to come looking for ye."

"We've only just now stopped," Caelan's companion replied.

"So ye say," Lachland replied, his flat gaze meeting Caelan's. "There is no room for lazy men in our ranks."

Caelan's hand clenched. "Go on yer way. Ye are not our leader. If anyone is lacking in their duties it is ye. This is our area."

Before he could utter another word, Lachland dismounted and

stalked to him stopping only when they were nose-to-nose. "Do not speak to me... boy."

The man was goading him. If he thought him a weakling, he was about to be surprised. Caelan's eyes narrowed. "Move back."

"Or?" Lachland's voice was a low growl

Caelan shoved him back, at the same time punching him in the throat.

Lachland coughed and charged forward, which Caelan expected, he deftly moved sideways punching the back of his opponent's nape.

The momentum too much, Lachland lost his balance and fell to all fours. Now he was furious. He scrambled to stand, planted his feet and held up both fists. "Fight fair, coward."

Obviously the man outweighed him by a couple stone, so Caelan had to use cunning to best him. When Lachland swung, he punched him in the ribs. Unfortunately, Lachland landed a couple punches, sending him reeling. At the next punch, Caelan bent to avoid the hit and sunk his right fist into Lachland's stomach.

"Enough!" Torac, one of the leaders had arrived. It distracted Lachland enough that Caelan could tackle him to the ground.

"Whore's son!" Lachland growled.

"Do not speak of yer mother thusly," Caelan replied.

Warriors hurried over to pulled them apart. Caelan glared at Lachland while wiping blood from his bottom lip. "Whatever ye are trying to prove, ye are still who ye are."

Lachland's eyes narrowed, and he turned away.

Chapter Two

THREE MONTHS LATER

The ax flew handle over blade, the progress too fast to see until it was impaled onto the target several feet away. Just shy of the center, enough to lose a competition.

Lachland cursed under his breath. His aim was off that morning, every throw worse than the last.

On the sidelines, several villagers stood watching. A pair of women doing everything in their power to distract him and the other men who practiced.

He'd not paid them much attention, not interested in anything they had to offer. Instead, he was distracted by the sharp pain on his lower left side. This was the wrong time for any kind of ailment. Rotating side to side helped relieve some of the pressure and he let out a long breath.

"Tense? Ye should have gone with us last night," a guard called Tate shouted as he threw his ax. The damn thing landed almost perfectly in the center. Tate grinned. "Can nae be tense when tossing the ax. The ax knows."

"Yer face knows ye are an annoyance when my fist hits it." Lachland stalked to the target to pick up his axes.

"Ye are usually the best. We can nae lose tomorrow," Tate said holding his ax while waiting for Lachland to get out of the way.

"We will win," Lachland replied. "Even if I have to take two women to bed tonight."

Those who overheard chuckled.

The competition field was set up near the guard camp, which was on the outskirts of Taernsby, near the southern shore. It was a short walk to the guard quarters.

One last throw and Lachland would quit. The first ax flew and hit the target almost dead center. He lifted the second and as he threw it, pain cut down his left side, from under his arm to his waist. The searing pain so deep, he fell to his knees.

Tate hurried over. "What happened?"

"I pulled something," Lachland grunted. He accepted the other warrior's hand and stood, stifling the need to groan loudly at his side protesting the movement.

"Best go see Alpena," another warrior suggested, his expression taut. "We need ye tomorrow."

While sparring a few days earlier, he'd taken a hit to the side with a wayward battle ax. The hit had sent him flying sideways from the impact. Now, the entire area was bruised, ugly colors of purple and blue with yellowing edges. Since, his side throbbed non-stop, hard pain when he turned.

HOBBLING THROUGH THE FRONT DOOR, LACHLAND looked around for the cook, who was quite adept at healing. "Alpena!"

"What happened?" Alpena, the cook asked, her shrewd gaze taking him in when he stretched out on his cot. "'Tis not like ye to be lying about."

"My side hurts," Lachland grumbled. "The left side."

The cook hurried over, gave him a sharp look. "I told ye to rest before the competition. Men are all like young lads, do nae listen." She made a tsking sound. "Take yer tunic off. Roll onto yer right side."

Moments later, salve was being massaged onto the spot he'd

motioned to. Lachland gritted when her hands pushed into the sore spot. "Are ye trying to cripple me?" he complained.

"It will feel better on the morrow. Today, remain abed."

He started to argue but groaned instead when the older woman seemed to put all her weight into the next rub.

A young man, who helped in the kitchen was called over to help wrap him around the waist and finally he was left to sleep.

He let out a breath as warmth from whatever herbs Alpena had used seeped into his body, the balm seeming to grow hotter all the while soothing.

SOUNDS OF ACTIVITY OUTSIDE WOKE LACHLAND. HE'D awakened to eat last meal the night before, then promptly fallen into a deep slumber. Despite the morning's activities, he'd remained in his small room, enjoying the fact he could sleep without pain for the first time in days.

"The others arrive from Welland." Tate stood at the doorway.

At the comment, Lachland rolled over and sat up. The pain in his side returned, a dull throb. "I know them all and have no doubt we will beat them easily."

Tate gave a one shoulder shrug. The good-natured warrior always gave the impression of being without a care. However, in battle, he transformed into an unrestrainable beast.

"I hear the archers Torac and Caelan are unbeatable."

As soon as Tate said the second name, a picture formed in Lachland's mind. The lithe archer bent at the waist, hands pulling his buttocks apart, eager for him.

"No one is unbeatable."

He stood and dressed with care.

THE NEWLY ARRIVED GUARDS WERE ASSIGNED A SPACE TO put their belongings and most made their way to the tables, to either eat or rest.

Lachland was glad to see the men he'd served with at either the other camp or the keep, and he spoke to several. Most of the guard goaded one another about the upcoming competition, which made for expectation of a good event.

He'd not noticed Caelan, perhaps because he didn't search for him. It was best to keep any kind of assignation with another man secret. Besides, he was sure Caelan held nothing but contempt for him.

It mattered not that he'd often thought about their interlude and craved for it to happen again. It had been one time, but it had been one of the most satisfying experiences of his life.

Needing to prove himself to the others, he'd fucked women, many women. Often he and other guards paid whores to attend to their needs, the women servicing more than one of them. Admittedly, he'd enjoyed such interludes. However, unlike time with the women, the time with Caelan was one he'd not been able to leave behind.

When he'd been with others, often the archer would come to mind, and damn him, the release was more satisfying when he pictured Caelan bent at the waist taking all of him.

As if conjured by his thoughts, the lithe archer walked to the doorway from outside, the light behind him outlining his body. With smooth graceful strides, he walked into the guardhouse, hesitating for a moment to sweep his blond hair away from his angelic face.

Caelan didn't study the room, instead he held a conversation with another man who walked beside him. When the man said something, Caelan laughed, the sound traveling over the space.

The archers' leader, Struan walked to greet the duo, obviously pleased to see them.

When Caelan's lips curved, Lachland could not look away. He'd kissed those lips, had covered them with his own. Plump and pink, inviting a man like him to taste, to linger.

Just then Caelan turned to look in his direction, his blue gaze meeting Lachland's for only a second. Instantly, the younger man's expression hardened. A slight curl to his upper lip showing his displeasure at seeing him. If looks could kill, Lachland would be dead.

It was but an instant, and yet it was enough that Lachland lost his breath and his cock twitched in recognition.

He looked to the men to his left and right wondering if anyone witnessed the exchange. By the continuing conversation no one did. When he looked back to Caelan, the archer had assumed a relaxed expression, continuing in his conversation with the other archers.

"How long are they going to stay?" Lachland asked the man to his right.

The warrior looked up and around, shrugging. "Hopefully no longer than a sennight. It will be quite crowded in here."

A sennight. He would have to avoid Caelan for seven days. It should be easy as they competed at very different events.

THE COMPETITION WOULD BE THE NEXT DAY. LACHLAND, along with two others would be competing against men from the keep. One last opportunity to practice.

He stood at the line and concentrated on the target. He held the ax in his right hand, focused and lifted it. The ax fell to the ground just a foot from Lachland, again searing pain cut through his side.

Not wishing to give up, he did his best to work past the pain. He picked up the ax and threw it. The ax missed the entire target.

Breathing heavily, sweat pouring down his face, he managed to make it to a bench. Cursing under his breath, Lachland refused to look at anyone.

"Ye are not competing tomorrow," his leader, Gavin, said, peering down at him. "Ye will instead judge the archery competition."

"I do not wish to..."

"I am not giving ye a choice. Ye are one of my best warriors. I will not allow ye to injure yerself further over a game. Now, go watch the archers." Gavin placed a hand on his shoulder. "I need ye battle-ready. A competition is not as important as saving lives."

It was true, however his pride was injured, as he was sure to place, if not win the ax throwing contest.

He'd also signed up for the caber toss. Now he'd be a spectator, no worse. He'd be judging the archery competition. It would be impossible to avoid Caelan now.

For a long while, Lachland didn't move, instead sat and waited until the painful throbbing ebbed.

Across the field, where the targets had been placed on hay bales, he spotted the archers walking up to practice.

The men seemed in good spirits, most of them friends, enjoying the break from the daily monotony of patrols and practice.

Already villagers had set up tables, tents and started fires for cooking. The next few days would be enjoyable. There would be food, drink and music.

Lachland stood and stopped at spotting Caelan. Once again, he was accompanied by the same man who'd walked into the tent with him that morning. The man was tall and muscular, more a warrior than an archer's build. However, he had a bow strapped across his back and a quiver hung from his left shoulder.

The man placed a hand on Caelan's upper arm, stopping him from taking a step further and said something. Caelan shook his head. They continued walking.

Was there more than met the eye between the two? Lachland watched the men and they continued to walk closer to the target area. They seemed comfortable in each other's company. If they fought together and trained together, then of course they had to be friends.

Suddenly the archery practice became interesting.

Lachland had to know if Caelan had a lover.

Damn him for wanting to know.

Chapter Three

To Caelan it was comical to see Brock compete. Other archers watched perplexed as Brock walked past to where Caelan stood.

The muscled warrior was his closest friend and had taken up archery, stating he wished to be able to fight for the clan in different ways.

Even before turning, Caelan sensed Lachland. Out of the corner of his eye, he caught sight of the brawny warrior who stood with arms crossed over his chest to watch.

Glancing toward the area where the ax throwing competition would happen, there were men practicing. Why was Lachland not there?

"Men," Lachland called out clapping his hands to get their attention. "I, along with Struan," he pointed to the head archer, will be judging the archery competition."

Caelan narrowed his eyes. Interesting.

"Yer no archer," Brock called out and laughed. "The arrows are quite different from yer wee ax."

Other archers joined in laughing and asking questions, while Lachland took it all with humor, even chuckling at some of their barbs.

"Brock, Calum, Jamie, Caelan, yer first," Struan called out. "Line up and shoot three arrows."

Doing his best to avoid eye contact with Lachland, Caelan walked forward turning to face the target. He studied the distance, the wind and lastly the soil under his boots. Then holding up his bow, he pulled back on the taut string to ensure all was well. Of course, it was. He spent hours working with the weapon, always ensuring it to be in pristine condition. After all, his life depended on it.

When he notched the arrow, Caelan then concentrated on his breathing, each movement calculated as he pulled back, let out his breath, focused on the target and released, aiming a bit higher and to the left of the center.

The arrow sunk just a bit to the right of center. It was a good shot and he grinned with satisfaction.

"How the bloody hell do ye do it?" Brock asked shaking his head. Brock's arrow had missed the center altogether.

"Study the wind flow," Caelan said preparing to shoot a second time. "Every archer knows that."

Brock walked closer to him and glowered. "I know that. Just made a comment that's all."

Unable to keep from it, Caelan laughed. "Ye need to breathe, then."

His friend shrugged, his wide shoulders moving up and down as he went back to his spot. Caelan admired the man's ability to remain in good spirits. If it wasn't that Brock very obviously preferred women, Caelan would have liked to pursue more than just a friendship. He was however very glad to have Brock as a close friend.

Sensing something, he turned to where Lachland and Struan had been. Struan had gone to speak to an archer, whilst Lachland remained rooted to the spot. He met Caelan's gaze for an instant. The man looked to Brock and then his right eyebrow lifted in question.

Caelan pretended not to notice. He wasn't going to give the idiot the satisfaction of a reply. If he wished to know something, he could ask. Not that it was any of Lachland's business what he did.

When he'd shot his last arrow, Lachland walked over and after ensuring everyone else was done, motioned to Caelan to walk to the target with him.

It was annoying that his stomach tightened when he went closer, and they moved to the target. Lachland met his gaze. "Ye are a bit off."

Caelan looked over to the other archers. "I shot the best. I am the best archer of the four."

"Ye were very good from what I remember," The double meaning of the comment brought memories of Lachland's breath on the back of his neck, of the warmth of his lips on his nape.

He blew out a breath and met Lachland's gaze. "Why are ye judging and not throwing?"

"What do ye think?" Brock walked up and motioned to his target. "I may just beat ye, Caelan."

Lachland ignored Brock for a long moment, his gaze flitting between them. Finally, he turned to Brock's target.

The one arrow had missed the center altogether, but the other two were right next to each other just to the right of the center.

"If ye study the wind before shooting, then aye, ye have a good chance," Lachland replied.

As Lachland walked past to go speak to another archer, he bumped Caelan's shoulder hard. "Prepare to shoot again."

Brock's eyebrows rose. "Ye best hope it's not up to him who wins if things get close. He's not forgotten the time ye and he fought."

"He's a ripe bastard," Caelan replied yanking the arrows from the target. "Aye, he will nae be fair to me."

After shooting another three, this time Struan was the one who walked up to the target and discussed their aims. Caelan admired the man, more than most of the guard. Struan was a strong and fair leader whom he'd served with for many years. Now Struan lived with his wife near Taernsby, still serving as head archer for the laird.

"The laird will arrive in the morn," Struan informed the archers who gathered. Lachland was noticeably missing. "Once the competition starts, do yer best. This is an opportunity to make yerself known, to allow the laird to gauge yer capabilities for who will be chosen for head archers in the future."

The men murmured in agreeance. Then they were dismissed to rest and watch the others compete.

The ax throwers were also done, giving room for those who wished to practice with the stone throw, battle ax and wrestling.

Those competing in the caber toss did not practice, choosing to save their energy for the next day instead. It was a wise idea.

CAELAN WENT TO THE GUARD HOUSE, ATE AND THEN found his mount. He rode the horse to the seashore and dismounted. The salty air combined with the soothing sounds of the waves lapping on the shore was, in his opinion, the perfect way to rest. He'd grown up on the southwestern shore of Uist, running up and down the shore as a child, hunting for imaginary treasures that had been dumped from pirate ships that he and his brother made up.

Once, when a ship had actually wrecked somewhere north of their home, they'd been delighted to find plenty of things that washed up. Their parents had joined them in the hunt, ultimately returning home exhausted but with armloads of blankets, clothes, wooden jewelry boxes and other items.

It had been one of the most enjoyable moments of his life. Now, following the trek of a small dingy as it made its way across toward where fishermen's other boats bobbed in the water, he took in the familiar view.

Gulls flew in circles where men cleaned fish, some swooping down hoping for a morsel.

"I will judge ye fairly," Lachland's voice shook him. He swung around shocked to find the man so close behind.

"I-I didnae hear ye approach." Caelan wanted to curse at his obvious comment and ensured a flat expression. "We will see."

"Ye hate me."

It was a statement that did not warrant a reply, so he remained quiet and turned away from the green with gold speckled gaze.

"Men like us..."

"Do not speak of whatever ye consider that we have in common. I do not wish to hear it." Caelan cut him off. "I came here to rest my mind to prepare for the morrow."

When Lachland chuckled, Caelan fought the urge to punch him square in the face. Instead he kept his gaze on the small boat that had made it to the shoreline. The fisherman jumped out and pulled it onto the sand.

"Have ye thought of how it felt to have my cock inside ye?" Lachland said, instantly causing Caelan's breath to catch. "I do. I remember what it felt to fuck ye."

Unsure why, Caelan turned to look toward the tree line. Immediately regretting it when Lachland touched his arm. "I see ye do."

"I wish to be alone."

"Aye so do I."

When he turned, Lachland walked toward the trees, his stride sure atop the sandy surface that would have most men struggling to keep their balance over the sandy and rocky terrain. Not Lachland. It was as if he walked on a grassy surface as he turned away from the trees and headed toward the guard house.

Caelan let out a long breath and closed his eyes. Whatever it took, he would ensure not to be alone. The intimate time with Lachland was etched in his mind and each time he saw the man all he could think of was being touched, taken and kissed by him.

The pads of his fingers slid over where Lachland had touched him on the lower arm. Just the light touch had sent awareness through him.

THAT NIGHT, THE FULL MOON GAVE PLENTY OF LIGHT FOR walking outside next to the guardhouse.

A privy of sorts had been set up, with a hole dug in between three walls for the guards to relieve themselves.

Caelan was exiting from one upon noticing movement between trees. It was an instant before recognizing the large body that emerged from the shadows. It was Lachland.

Just as he was about to turn away, Caelan changed his mind. He wasn't going to act as if the man intimidated him.

Lachland approached. "Looking for me?"

"Nae. I was not."

The male had the nerve to grin, the smile not reaching his eyes. Then he shoved Caelan back against a tree. Before he could react, Lachland's mouth was over his. The kiss was raw, without emotion, proprietary. And so very good.

Just as Caelan was to reach for Lachland, to pull him closer, he realized it was best not to give in to the arrogant man. Instead, Caelan shoved him backward.

Their chests heaved, but it was Caelan who regained control first. "Never do that again." He turned and stalked away.

Chapter Four

The buzz of excitement was in the air. From what Caelan heard, there hadn't been a celebration in Taernsby in months and the people were more than ready.

Overnight tents with colorful banners had been added to the few from the day before. Spectator stands had been erected for those who wished to watch the competition from a short distance.

On a grassy hillside, families and children sat or lay on blankets, the mothers doing their best to keep up with the bairns who used any opportunity to escape.

Stables for those competing on horseback were set up behind tents where competitors could keep any items they didn't wish to carry. Outside the flap, a guard was posted to ensure nothing was stolen.

Along with Brock, Caelan arrived and went to the tent to deposit their bows and quivers. It would be a few hours before they had to compete.

"I see a lass I know." Brock stuck out his chest and hurried away in the direction where two young women sat on a blanket.

Caelan chuckled at his friend's obvious attempt to impress the women.

"I thought ye and he were more than friends," Lachland's deep voice fell over him like a bucket of ice water.

Turning to face him, Caelan ensured a flat expression. "I hoped, but no. He prefers the lasses. I hear ye do as well now."

Lachland slid a look to where a pair of warriors stood. "I would prefer to fuck ye." The darkened gaze moved to his mouth. "Have ye been with any one since me?"

At the bold words, Caelan cleared his throat. "I will see ye at the competition." Walking away, he could feel Lachland watching him. He may as well have been touching Caelan's skin by the way it affected him.

"Watch where ye go," a warrior snapped when bumped into him. The man's thick hand grabbing him by the arm. "For an archer ye seem unable to see clearly."

It was Struan, the head archer there at Taernsby, whom he'd run into. "I was thinking," Caelan explained.

Struan looked past him. "Ye and Lachland need to stay away from one another. Nothing good can come of it. Ye are aware?"

Heat rose from Caelan's throat, and he was sure his face turned red. "I know."

"Come," Struan walked in the direction of the archery range and Caelan fell into step beside him.

"What do ye feel toward him?" The head archer asked.

Needing to confide in someone, Caelan spoke freely. "I am not sure. I hate him one moment and want to be with him the next. I wish I'd never met him."

Struan stopped and gave him a quizzical look, then his expression softened. "Ye are in love."

"That is the worst thing that could happen," Caelan admitted.

"Aye for so many reasons. People do not understand that kind of love. Two men." Struan spoke softly so no one could hear. "There can be ways to stay hidden, but I would not wish that on anyone. To hide yer entire life."

Caelan let out a long breath. "Neither would I." He looked into the man's eyes. "What can I do?"

"Talk. 'Tis better than the ongoing animosity between ye." Struan shrugged. "Anything more, I cannot advise."

"Thank ye."

Struan placed a hand on his shoulder. "Love does strange things to a person. However, there is nothing more powerful."

~

LACHLAND LOOKED ON AS THE ARCHERS GATHERED TO draw their lots. The sun was high in the sky, the breeze light, which was beneficial to the competitors.

One by one, they pulled a wooden token that had a number etched on it between one and four. Each group would compete and then the top archers would fight for first place. The laird brought bags of coins to be given as prizes for those who place first and second in each game, an enticing prize.

When Caelan and Brock drew their numbers, they banged chests in celebration and Lachland hated the pang of jealousy. It was obvious the two got along well. Did Caelan confess to Brock about his sexual preferences?

He studied the man. Brock was dark haired with a rugged face. He had a muscular build and easy-going personality.

Just then a horn sounded, calling for the competition to begin.

Despite his disappointment at being unable to compete, soon Lachland lost himself judging the archers. The men congratulated each other, then argued moments later about who should gain points.

All in all, the competition was close, most of Clan Ross' archers being exceptional marksmen. Several times, he and Struan had to measure arrow placements with their fingernail because some were so close in aim.

"I am not competing," Struan told him as they walked toward the targets. "It would not be fair."

"The archers are hopeful to beat ye," Lachland replied.

"I will shoot against the winner," Struan said. "It will be entertaining."

They arrived at the targets. "I spoke to Caelan earlier," Struan began. "Ye need to talk to him. I grow tired of the ongoing animosity between ye."

Lachland swallowed, a cold terror at being discovered filling him. "I can just stay away from the bastard."

"And yet ye have not." Struan looked around, then his gaze met Lachland's.

The man knew. Somehow he knew.

"Ye can say it is not for me to intercede. However, when something affects one of my archers, then it is my concern. Ye and Caelan may not ever be together, however, do ye not think it is better to at least be friends? If ye care for someone, why not have good moments instead of bad?"

Lachland's blood went cold. "I do not know what ye think ye know, but..."

"I saw ye," Struan interrupted. "Months ago in the forest." The man held a hand up. "Do nae worry. Erik and Torac are also aware. But have ye noticed a change in how any of us have acted toward ye? Nay. That is because ye are both good warriors and part of the guard."

Lachland was frozen in place. That his preference toward men was known by the leaders was not something he'd ever expected. He'd been careless. Stupid.

"I can leave."

"Do not be daft," Struan replied. "Have ye not heard a word I said? Who ye prefer to fuck does not affect our respect for ye as a warrior."

"And as a man?"

Struan chuckled. "Well if anything, by the bit I saw. I was impressed."

Despite the situation a bark of laughter escaped and with it all the tension eased. "I am not sure what to say. Thank ye."

They turned to study the target, both still chuckling.

. . .

CAELAN WON SECOND PLACE. IT SEEMED MOST OF THE archers were not surprised surrounding him to congratulate and slap him on the back. A wide grin on his face, he graciously accepted the bag of coin and much deserved praise from the laird.

Once the sun sank below the horizon, campfires filled the air with light and smoke. People danced to lively music and most of the men sat drinking ale, hoping to avoid being yanked onto the dance floor by mothers, aunts or wives.

Caelan approached Lachland who'd walked to where ale was being poured. "Moment?"

"Aye," Lachland replied, his heart racing. He wanted to look around and see if anyone watched, but he'd learned long ago, when someone did that, it drew more attention.

"What is it?" Lachland stood with a tankard in one hand, the other arm to his side.

"The inn at the village. Second floor, first room on the right." Caelan said, his expression not changing. Then he walked to the man serving ale, refilled his tankard and walked away.

THERE WERE ONLY TWO MEN AT THE TAVERN WHEN Lachland walked in. The owner was gone to the competition, leaving an old man at the bar, who was too drunk to mind the place properly. A second man, also older, sat at a table, head thrown back, snores erupting.

Lachland slipped past and up the stairs to the first room. The door was slightly open. He slipped inside and closed it.

Caelan sat in a chair removing his boots and looked up as he entered.

"This is dangerous," Lachland said. "Not a good idea."

"Then why are ye here?" Caelan remarked tugging at his boot, pulling it free and tossing it to the side.

"Because we should talk," Lachland said lowering to the chair opposite. "We have to change how we are around each other. Someone has taken notice."

Caelan chuckled. "I doubt anyone other than perhaps Torac and Struan know anything."

"How can ye be so indifferent about it. Men who fuck other men are beaten, killed."

There was a bit of silence, and he studied the flames in the fireplace.

Caelan met his gaze. "We should agree to stop the hostility and even if we're not friends at least not fight all the time."

"I am not sure I will ever be yer friend," Lachland leaned back into the soft chair suddenly feeling tired.

"Ye hate me," Caelan stated. "If I am to be honest there is little I like about ye."

His eyes flew wide. "Is that what ye think? That I detest ye?"

Standing he stalked to where the younger man sat, placed hands on the arms of the chair caging him in. "I do not detest ye. I desire ye. Every damn day. It is my feelings for ye that I abhor."

It was as if a rope squeezed around Caelan's chest. "Sometimes, we cannot help how we feel about others."

Reaching to cradle the back of Caelan's head, Lachland covered his mouth to his. There was no resistance, neither did Caelan kiss him back. Instead he allowed it.

"I'd best go." Lachland straightened. "I give ye my word to be civil, if ever we come across each other."

They stared into each other's eyes for a long moment, then Lachland went to the door.

As he reached for the door handle, the press of Caelan's hand on his back stopped him. "Stay."

There was no hesitation, Lachland whirled around and pulled Caelan against himself. The younger man's body slender and perfect against him.

Their mouths collided, this time with hunger and need that was like an all-consuming fire.

Tearing at each other, their clothing was done away with in a matter of moments, and they fell to the bed and tangle of limbs, each touching, feeling and caressing as much as they could.

Rolling him to his back, Caelan gripped Lachland's cock, the hand firmly moving up and down making him so rock hard that he had to grit his teeth to keep from spilling.

"No. I-I have to be inside ye," Lachland stuttered, the words sounding breathless.

"I want ye," Caelan said as he slid his hand up Lachland's stomach to his chest. "I have wanted this for so long."

The room seemed to spin and Lachland had to blow out several breaths to settle and keep from taking Caelan without constraint, savagely. "Do ye have any oil?"

Caelan pressed his lips to Lachland's throat. "Aye. I hoped we would need it." Sliding across him, the lithe body bringing every inch of his to life.

Just a moment later, Caelan lifted a small vial. "Perfumed oil."

"Roll over," Lachland commanded. Yes perhaps he should wait, allow them more time, but he needed to take him. He needed to know Caelan was his, even if for a few moments.

If Caelan found his request brusque, he didn't show it. Instead he rolled onto his stomach and then lifted to his knees.

Lachland was struck speechless. He wasn't sure to have ever seen someone so perfect. An image he hoped to burn into his memory, never to forget.

Taking the oil from the vial, he stroked himself, oiling his shaft and then poured a few droplets onto his finger.

He then pushed his finger between the pale round orbs of Caelan's arse finding the perfect place then slipped it in.

Caelan gasped, turning to look at him. The blue pools were dark with desire, his lips parted in a soft moan when Lachland pushed his finger in deeper ensuring to oil him properly.

Without needing to be told, Caelan reached around and pulled himself apart in invitation.

He slid in easily, the tightness of Caelan gripping him in a way that made it almost impossible to keep control. Lachland took his time, sliding out and driving back in, the pace slow as he savored every sensation.

When his thrusts became harder, Caelan gripped the bedding, his face turning red as he was fighting not to cry out. Instead he pushed his mouth into the bedding to muffle the exclamations.

Deeper and deeper, Lachland thrust until fully inside. Then he rocked in and out, their sacks slapping together. Every single movement brought spikes of passion, until Lachland lost all control.

Taking Caelan by the hips, he thrust harder, faster, each drive deeper than the last. The bed shook with the movement, but he didn't care. He had to take him, had to do all the things he'd fantasized about.

CAELAN WAS DRENCHED IN SWEAT, NOT ONLY FROM BEING taken, but from his face buried into the bedding. Already he'd spilled onto the bed, unable to keep from coming as soon as Lachland thrust into him.

Now as the man continued the wonderful assault, he was hardening again.

"Roll onto yer back," Lachland said, abruptly pulling out.

When Caelan did so, Lachland pushed his legs open. "Hold yerself like this." He guided Caelan to hook his arms around his knees, thighs parted.

He watched enraptured as Lachland oiled his thickness. The cock glistening in the lamplight.

Then he met his gaze as the thick head prodded at his entrance. "Have ye ever been taken like this?" Lachland asked.

Caelan shook his head. "No."

Lachland pushed in slowly, this time allowing for Caelan to relax at the intrusion. The thickness of the man's cock stretching him to his limits. It was a wonderful pain being stretched so wide.

"Ahhh," Caelan moaned as the head of Lachland's cock hit a special place inside that sent his eyes to roll back. "Ohhh," he exclaimed when he hit the precise place again and again until Caelan could not keep from crying out.

To quiet him, Lachland kissed him, driving his tongue deep into

Caelan's throat swallowing his cries of passion. The primal act all he needed to come a second time.

Lachland moaned into his mouth, the warrior's solid body shuddering as he came with so much force it spilled out and between his bottom cheeks. The warrior collapsed on him, the weight of him perfect.

For a long moment, they held each other. Both were struck speechless, unable to utter words, or to breath evenly. There was so much tumbling around them. Questions, sensations, rawness and more than anything, a sense they'd never forget this moment.

It was moments later, that Lachland rolled from him and both lay side to side, shoulders touching.

Caelan turned to study Lachland. Thick curls wet from perspiration framed his handsome face and arm up over his head, he was the picture of perfection.

"I cannot promise ye anything," Lachland said, not looking at him. "I do not wish for any..."

There it was the rejection he'd been dreading. He interrupted quickly. "I expect nothing from ye."

It was the truth. Although his hoped Lachland would feel as strongly, it was obvious all he wanted was what happened in the moment.

"I leave tomorrow," Caelan said before rolling to face the wall. "Stay and sleep if ye wish."

Sometime during the night Lachland left.

Chapter Five

I t was interesting to Caelan how quickly life went back to normal. Although in the first days since returning from Taernsby he'd often thought about the night with Lachland, he'd somehow managed to push it farther from his mind. Now two months later, he was glad to have experienced something so pleasurable. One day he'd be with a man again and he accepted it would not be Lachland.

On patrol, it was a blustery day, and he was glad for the wind on his face. It smelled of nature and freshness.

Brock motioned toward a gathering of trees. "Someone is there, perhaps more than one. They hide."

Pulling their steeds to a slower pace, they went toward the grouping of trees.

"Who is there!" Brock called out.

Instantly men raced away on horseback. They were no match for the archer's huge war horses and soon they were able to catch them and pull them from their mounts.

"What were ye doing back there?" Brock screamed at the one he held by the scruff of his tunic.

The other man sat on the ground looking defeated. "We did nae mean to hurt her."

Instantly Caelan tied the man on the ground up and jumped to his horse heading back to where they'd spotted the men.

On the ground was a woman, her clothes had been torn and she was curled into a ball, seeming to be lifeless. He jumped from his horse and hurried to her.

Her eyes were expressionless, staring past him to the sky. "I want to die." Her voice was faint, but he heard her despair loudly.

"Ye will nae die." Caelan wrapped her in his tartan and lifted her to his horse. With the woman in his arms, he raced to the camp.

Thankfully other warriors saw him, and they went to go help Brock, while he continued to the guard house. The entire time, the woman was still, her head bent.

MOMENTS LATER, WHEN HE WALKED INTO THE AREA behind a hastily hung blanket to serve as divider, the woman lay on a cot, her bruised face had been cleaned and her wounds seen to. He felt sickened that his kind would so something to a woman just because they were weaker.

"How do ye fare?"

Her pale eyes met his. "I cannot say. I should thank ye, I suppose." She sniffed, a single tear trailing down her cheek. "My betrothed will nae have me now. I am unsure what my future holds."

"Yer family?"

"Someone went to fetch my parents." She sighed. "I live in Welland."

As if conjured, a couple hurried around the blanket. Instantly the woman went to the bed, kissing the younger one's face. "Thank God ye are alive."

The father was less forthcoming, but it was obvious he fought to keep his emotions in check.

Caelan stood and went to leave but the young woman stopped him. "He is who saved me."

The father hurried to him, shaking his hand. "Thank ye. I do nae know what I would do without my lass."

He left to give the family time and went to find Brock. The two who'd been caught had been taken to Welland. The constable would see to their punishment, although Caelan suspected the beating they'd gotten from the guards would be the worst of it.

"We do not have patrol on the morrow," Brock said at seeing him. "We can go to the village. To the tavern."

IT WAS LATE MORNING THE NEXT DAY WHEN THEY RODE TO Welland, enjoying the warmth of the sun on their backs as they headed to the village. Neither of them really drank overly much but leaving the camp was a good way to spend time among others.

"Did ye hear that we are to get new guards sometime today?" Brock asked.

Caelan shrugged. "Aye and some who've been here are leaving. I prefer to remain here. I like this post."

"I do as well," Brock agreed. "The area is large, so it keeps us busy."

The village was bustling with activity, the warm weather inviting the people to come out and gather.

People called out from the market stalls, whilst women hurried from one place to the other, filling their baskets with purchases. The men lingered on the sides, some sitting at tables sharing ale and whatever stories they could share.

Noting a young woman who looked familiar, Caelan hesitated. When she turned, her eyes widened in recognition, she dropped her basket and ran to him.

"Brother." She threw herself into his arms. "I heard ye were nearby and had hoped to come and find ye," Galena was seven years younger than him, making her ten and six now. She'd blossomed into a beauty.

"Who is this?" Brock neared, studying his sister with interest.

"My sister and ye do best to keep yer distance."

Unfortunately, Galena had other ideas. She grabbed a startled

Brock's hand. "Ye must come and sit with us. I wish to hear all about my brother."

Noting his pointed look where their hands were clasped, Brock extricated his. "I will return in a moment after ye both have time to talk."

"Let us get yer basket," Caelan said walking with her to where she'd dropped it. "Did ye come alone?"

Galena shook her head. "I came with our parents. They are over at the meat pie shop right now."

It had been five long years since he'd left home. His father standing at the door watching as he lifted a sack of clothes and walked away. A word had not been spoken, but the message clear. There was no room him, for someone with his tendencies in the family.

His father had caught him kissing a lad in the stables. When he'd stumbled away in shock, he'd knocked over a shovel, alerting them of his presence.

Caelan would never forget the look of disappointment. The lack of words, his father standing by mutely as he'd packed. Meanwhile, his mother had asked why he was leaving, all he'd said was that it was time for him to find his place in the world.

"I best go. I am glad ye are well. Ye look good, sister," Caelan hugged Galena. "Be with care and hug father and mother for me."

"Ye can do it yerself. Come, speak to them. They do miss ye terribly." Galena grasped his hand with her free one. "Please."

"I cannot." Caelan pressed a kiss to the center of her forehead and walked away.

Moments later, he leaned against a post, waiting to catch sight of Brock to tell him he was returning to camp. He bit a chunk out of an apple he'd purchased, chewing thoughtfully.

Where he stood, it would be hard for his family to spot him as he was out of sight but could see the goings on clearly.

When someone tugged at his tunic, he turned prepared to hand a street urchin coin only to lose his breath at his family.

"Caelan," his mother's voice shook. She took a tentative step forward and he closed the distance hugging her tightly. It was hard to swallow past the huge lump that formed in his throat.

It took all his courage, and yet he could not lift his gaze to his father. Shame filled him and he wished with all his heart that he could change himself. More than anything to be the man a father could be proud of.

"Son," his father's voice was gruff. "I hear ye are a great archer."

It was then he finally met his father's gaze and to his astonishment saw pride.

"I would not say great," he said, his voice cracking.

"Please come to the house for a visit," his mother said wiping tears with the edge of her sleeve. "I have missed ye so. Yer brother would be happy to see ye."

His brother, just a year older was the gruff type, who would rather spend his time tending to the livestock than being around people.

Caelan looked to his father for confirmation, that he was indeed welcome. "I keep quite busy with guard duties…"

"I am sure the laird gives ye time to see family," Galena protested. "If not, I will write him and ask in yer behalf."

"Ye will come and visit," his father said, with meaning, then closed the distance between them and placed a hand on his shoulder. "Ye are my son and will always have a place at the table."

Like his older brother, his father was not one for demonstrating emotion. That he'd touched him in public was shocking not just to him, but to his mother and sister who gawked.

"It is settled then," his mother said and looked him up and down. "I will purchase fabric, ye are in dire need of new clothes."

Just then he spotted Brock walking toward him. "I best go. I will visit in a pair of days. I will have no duty then."

His father nodded. "Good."

THE RIDE BACK TO THE CAMP WAS SO VERY DIFFERENT. Caelan's heart was light, and he talked non-stop, telling Brock how it was the first time seeing his family in years and how they'd invited him to come to visit.

"Why have ye not gone to visit. They do not live far?" Brock asked.

Caelan sighed. "Father and I had a disagreement."

"About?"

Despite Brock being his closest friend, Caelan would never divulge the truth about himself. The fewer people knew the better. "Something stupid I did. I was young and without thought."

His friend studied him for a moment. "Ye should have gone back sooner and spoken to yer father. By his expression, he has missed ye."

"Aye, mayhap."

They continued for a while longer, the camp coming into view.

"I must say something," Brock said slowing his steed. "I know ye prefer men to women. I want ye to know it does not change our friendship."

Caelan squeezed his eyes shut. "How do ye know?"

Was it so obvious about him that people could tell. What if more guards figured it out? He could be killed in battle by his own side.

"Lachland confronted me, told me to watch over ye and keep ye safe in battle. Most men would never do that unless there was a reason." Brock chuckled. "I believe he is jealous of me. I assured him ye and I are only friends and I prefer a lass' legs around my waist."

If not for his instincts, Caelan would have fallen off his horse in shock.

"When was this?"

"Just before we left to come here." Brock let out bark of laughter. "Is that him?"

Caelan's eyes widened at seeing a group of guards standing at the camp, Lachland standing out, taller that those around him.

"Do not say or do anything," Caelan warned Brock, who grinned widely while wagging his eyebrows.

"Brock..."

"What?" His friend made kissing motion, his lips pursing comically. "I am so glad I didn't stay at the tavern."

Chapter Six

After checking on his horse, in the stables, Lachland stalked to where the others were lined up for last meal.

So far Caelan had managed to avoid him, which was admirable given the small size of the camp. He'd seen him ride toward the camp earlier that day with his friend Brock. Then he'd gone to stable the horse and effectively disappeared since.

Like the quarters at Taernsby, each man had an assigned cot with a divider made out of wood and fabric. Other than that, there was little privacy.

The entire way from his last assignment, he'd wondered how it would be possible to have a relationship with Caelan, without anyone suspecting. It would be impossible.

"Yer back." It was Brock who spoke, meeting his gaze. "Need new scenery?"

Despite himself, Lachland liked the gruff red-haired man. "Aye. Ye could say that."

"Hmm," Brock replied, then walked away with his overfilled plate.

It was moments later, after he lowered to an empty seat at one of the tables that he saw Caelan. The man sat on the ground under a tree, next to him a pair of dogs with whom he shared his meal.

When one of them sat on its hunches, holding up both paws, he threw his head back in laughter. It was a beautiful sight.

The next time he looked over, all three dozed, Caelan with his head leaned against the tree and the dogs, one with its head on the man's leg, the other sprawled next to them on the grass.

Caelan seemed at peace, almost as if a burden had been lifted off his shoulders.

"He saw his family today," Brock said walking next to Lachland as they moved from placing their plates in a basket for washing. "They invited him to visit."

"That is good," Lachland replied. "Do they live near?"

"Aye, but he'd not seen them in five years," Brock shared scratching his beard. "I'm off for a swim." He sniffed under his arms. "I stink." The man sauntered away, whistling.

THE MOON WAS HIGH AND BRIGHT. CAELAN LOOKED UP studying it, still at the tree. He would wait until most were abed before going inside. This was definitely a day of mixed emotions, he considered standing and stretching. The dogs had gone, knowing the cook would offer scraps while cleaning up.

When a man emerged from the building and walked toward him, Caelan stood and steeled himself. Nothing good could come from Lachland coming there. Why had he?

"Why are ye out here?" Lachland asked, his voice gruff. "Is it because I am here?"

"Nay," Caelan lied. "I wanted time alone to think."

Lachland walked closer, his gaze piercing. "I came because of ye. I find it hard not to see ye. It does nae mean I expect anything from ye. Just that I cannot deny how strongly I feel for ye any longer."

The thundering of his heart was so loud, Caelan wondered if Lachland could hear it. "What are ye saying?" He had to hear it, had to know exactly what Lachland meant.

Lachland looked to the tent, then took him by the upper arm and guided him around to the other side of the tree and out of sight. "That I love ye."

"We cannot. What I mean is-it is impossible. I-I..."

"Do ye love me?" For the first time Lachland seemed vulnerable. "If ye do, I want to be with ye. To find a way."

"I do," Caelan whispered. "I do Lachland."

It seemed an eternity before their mouths collided, and Caelan grabbed Lachland around the shoulders, not wanting the kiss to ever end. Lachland did not disappoint, he kissed him with fervor, until making Caelan's legs weak.

"We will be together, I promise," Lachland said pressing his forehead against his. "I want to have a life with ye."

It was an impossible dream, which Caelan allowed himself to believe for the moment.

"Kiss me again."

FOUR MONTHS LATER...

"And we have been overtaken and slaughtered whilst ye wait to shoot yer arrow," Brock commented with annoyance. "Get yer head out of the clouds."

Caelan chuckled. "I am about to beat ye. I would not be so keen on pushing me to hurry." He loosed the arrow and it hit dead center of the target, to the right of Brock's which had missed the center.

"Ye owe two drinks at the tavern," Caelan said. "One more?"

"Nay," Brock replied with a sneer. "We do nae have to patrol tomorrow, are ye going to the village?"

Caelan shook his head. "I am going to visit family."

THE NEXT DAY, ONCE THE LAST ORDERS OF THE DAY WERE given, Lachland rode away, not bothering to make any excuses. Caelan on the other hand headed in the directions of his family home.

Usually, Lachland went directly to the cottage, while Caelan went to the village or to spend time with his family prior to going to the cottage.

In truth they'd found a small cottage where they could spend time together regularly. The widow who owned the small plot of land with two cottages, was thankful for the rent they paid. Being the woman was so old, she rarely went anywhere and was happy that Caelan stopped at the village to get her food items.

The fire in the hearth could not compete with the inferno within as Lachland pushed deeper into Caelan, every ounce of his being begging for more and more. Grabbing Caelan's hips, he held him in place pulling out and then driving in, over and over until he could not keep from losing his hold on reality.

Caelan's took himself in hand, working his own length shuddering in release just as Lachland pulled out spilling onto his lover's backside. The view of Caelan's opening glistening was a sight he dreamed off on the nights they slept apart.

Caelan collapsed onto the blankets, eyes closed, lips parted, breathing ragged. "Ye are so good."

A chuckle escaped his lips, the sound become more normal to his own ears. "Only because it is ye."

Lachland rolled his lover onto his back and lay next to him. "I love ye. Never forget it."

"How can I. Ye say it often."

It wasn't often they spent time at the cottage, once a sennight perhaps, but it was worth keeping the cottage. They did not know what the future held, for now, they lived in the moment, enjoying the times together.

"What are ye thinking?" Lachland asked lazily.

Lifting up, Caelan hovered over him. "That I wish for ye to kiss me again."

THE END.

About the Author

ENTICING. ENGAGING. ROMANCE.

If you like strong alpha heroes and feisty heroines, you will love USA Today Best-selling author Hildie McQueen's writing.

Army Veteran Hildie McQueen grew up in California and has lived in S. Carolina, Germany, Texas, Hawaii, and now resides in Sunny Georgia USA.

Her obsession for all things pink and Paris can only be beaten by her love for dogs. Thanks to her super hero husband Kurt, she can write full time with her constant companions, the trio of fearless doglets, Lola, Pippa and Harley.

Get to know Hildie better, sign up for her
monthly newsletter
Visit her website at www.hildiemcqueen.com

Her Princess at Midnight

ERICA RIDLEY

Chapter One

Miss Cynthia Talbott's muscles ached from spending the hours since dawn down on her hands and knees, scrubbing the floor spotless whilst her stepmother and stepsisters lay abed.

Task complete—for now—Cynthia hurried to the scullery to begin the preparations for their breakfast. The sun was rising high, and the sleeping ladies usually awoke by noon. No two of them ever wanted the same dish, causing even more work in the kitchen to keep them from berating her or flinging the unwanted delicacies to the floor. Again.

Cynthia had never dreamt she should one day be an exhausted, bedraggled maid-of-all-work in her childhood home. As a young girl, she had never even wondered how their French chef created his masterful sauces and marvelous *pâte à choux*. She certainly hadn't imagined that after the death of her beloved, humble-born mother five years prior, Father would remarry a widowed lady with expensive tastes and two daughters of her own... Or that the following year, after Father's subsequent death, the three women would spend every penny of his life savings with breathtaking speed, until every servant had gone elsewhere and Cynthia was forced to become a scullion in her own home.

She would have left without hesitation if she had any money to her name—and if she could bear to abandon her parents' home and the remaining memory-imbued furnishings and keepsakes to the careless hands of her stepmother and stepsisters.

"Cynthia, you snail!" screamed a voice from the dining room. "Where are my eggs?"

That was Dorothea, the elder of Cynthia's two stepsisters and impossible to please—making her the darling of her mother. The screaming was often more to appease Lady Tremaine than to torture Cynthia, although it generated the same result. Had the eggs and kippers been ready five minutes earlier, Dorothea would have pronounced them "old" and "too cold" and sent Cynthia to begin all over again.

"Coming!" she called out as she hurried the heavy tray into the dining room.

Stasia was seated at the table as well, her pale face propped up by both hands, and her red curls awry. The sisters had spent the past night at a ball, and Stasia appeared the worse for wear. Perhaps the provided supper had not agreed with her. Their mother, Lady Tremaine, appeared to still be abed.

A small blessing. As was the trio's absence from home the evening before. As much as Cynthia dreamed of attending a fancy ball one day, dressed like a princess, a few stolen hours of peace and quiet in which to catch up on her work and take a much-needed nap felt like a gift from the heavens.

She served generous portions onto the sisters' pre-warmed plates. "Here everything is, hot and fresh, as you like it."

Dorothea poked at her eggs with her fork, testing their consistency for some failing to report back to her mother—who always asked for the latest ways Cynthia had failed to live up to expectations.

Stasia simply groaned and dropped her face lower into her hands, ignoring the repast altogether.

Cynthia's stomach growled as she set the remaining dishes on the sideboard, though she knew better than to take a seat at the table.

Dorothea's black cat, Morningstar, darted out from beneath the sideboard.

"*Rowr!*" he screeched, clawing at Cynthia's slipper as he passed.

"Leave Morningstar alone!" Dorothea scolded Cynthia, despite her not having stepped anywhere near his paws or tail, scooping the demon feline onto her lap in order to feed him bits of her kippers.

"Please scream at her *quietly*," Stasia mumbled into her palms.

The sound of trumpets blaring at a distance startled Cynthia from arranging the dishes. "What was that?"

Dorothea rolled her eyes. "The royal parade."

"How dare they," Stasia moaned. "It's barely past noon."

"How dare who?" Cynthia asked, befuddled. "The Prince Regent?"

"Not Prinny, you featherwit. The visiting royalty from Italy. Prince Azzurro's hunt for an English bride is the only thing anyone has been talking about for months."

Cynthia was no featherwit. She had once boasted the finest tutors in London. It was not her fault that once the staff had been dismissed, there was no one left for Cynthia to chat with. Her only interaction with the outside world came from reading scraps of discarded newspapers and overhearing snippets of gossip between her stepmother and stepsisters.

"Come on, Stasia." Dorothea threw a bun at her sister. "We cannot miss him!"

"Cynthia didn't brush my hair," Stasia protested, lifting her face from her hands.

"Put on a bonnet," Dorothea snapped. "Or stay here with her, whilst the prince falls in love with *me*."

"Is he meant to select his bride this afternoon?" Cynthia asked.

"At tonight's grand ball, unless he falls in love beforehand." Dorothea dragged her sister out through the front door to the street, where a crowd was already forming.

Cynthia followed, careful to stay a few feet behind, lest the duo notice her presence and send her back into the kitchens.

Luckily, Dorothea and Stasia—like the rest of the gathering crowd

—were too busy jostling each other and raising up on tiptoes to notice a scullery maid in a patched and tattered blue-and-brown dress lagging shyly behind.

Soldiers and musicians marched by first, followed by eight white stallions pulling an enormous, gilded open carriage. The crowd roared its approval at their first glimpse of the royal passengers. Several women shrieked in excitement. A few young ladies swooned at the sight of the Italian prince.

Even Cynthia's mouth fell open in awe.

"Who is *that*?" she blurted, slack-jawed and blushing.

"Prince Azzurro," a young woman to her right breathed dreamily. "He's come to select a bride from the best England has to offer. I hope he chooses me. Have you ever seen eyes so blue, hair so black, and shoulders so wide?"

"Not *him*." Cynthia pointed as surreptitiously as she could. "There, seated *next* to him."

"That's his spinster sister, Princess Ammalia. She's here to help him find his match."

Dorothea spun about and caught Cynthia staring. "Don't think for a second that his royal highness will spare a glance for the likes of you. At that ball, either Stasia or I will win the hand of the prince. *You* won't even leave the scullery."

Cynthia couldn't care less about the prince. Her eyes dazzled and her stomach filled with butterflies at the sight of the resplendent Princess Ammalia...

Whose black-lashed, bright blue gaze had just locked with Cynthia's.

Chapter Two

The horses, like Princess Ammalia's heart, came to a sudden stop.

She did not know what had impeded the progress of the royal stallions this time, but she did know exactly what had caused her own heart to fail, then to burst back into motion, beating twice as swiftly as before. She gazed out of the carriage in wonder.

Thousands of onlookers flooded the streets in the hopes of glimpsing visiting royalty. The teeming masses were what had clogged the escape path—er, parade route—the horses had been following. But it wasn't fear of a surging crowd that set Ammalia's blood pumping faster.

It was a woman.

She was toward the back of the throng, half-hidden from view. It didn't matter. She had the sort of ethereal beauty that could be *felt* from yards away and in the pitch black of night, if necessary.

It wasn't the golden blond hair or the plump rose-petal pink lips that had caught Ammalia's eye. It wasn't even the high cheekbones or the becoming flush of color rising up her peaches-and-cream skin.

It was the wide blue eyes that had latched onto Ammalia's own, as if this woman, too, had felt the connection between them as strong as a thick metal chain capable of hauling a ship back to shore.

Anchored in place by eyes like those, Ammalia couldn't dream of going anywhere else. If the mass of jostling onlookers parted enough to let the horses trot anew, Ammalia would throw herself down from this carriage and elbow her way through the crowd until she reached—

"What are you looking at?" her brother Zurri asked with interest.

"Nothing," Ammalia said quickly.

But she could no more tear her enthralled eyes from this captivating woman than she could rip her pounding heart free from her chest.

Zurri followed the direction of his sister's gaze. "Who? Where?"

She didn't answer.

Their father, the king, was in the carriage behind theirs, no doubt watching his children closely. Not because he feared scandal—this entire spectacle was because the king loved to be the center of attention, at any cost. The bigger the drama, the better.

Nor did his majesty worry about the future of his only daughter, whom he'd given up caring about at the disappointing moment of her birth. Neither Ammalia nor her theoretical children were of import. It was the male line that counted. Her brother was the future king. Rather than arrange a political alliance, Father was even allowing Zurri to select the most beautiful bride in all of England and align the two nations that way.

Ammalia, as the elder sibling and worthless female, was supposed to be finding this enviable match for her brother.

Zurri was, as always, the center of attention—just as he liked it. He needn't even be charming. Being a prince was more than enough for women everywhere to fall in love on sight.

"I don't care to know who's caught your eye," Zurri said petulantly, as though he were a child of six years, rather than a man of six-and-twenty. "I don't want anything or anyone that pleases *you*. You have terrible taste."

That was the rumor, anyway. Ammalia wouldn't have had to be the twenty-seven-year-old spinster sister, if she'd bothered to accept any of the many offers for her hand that cropped up repeatedly over the years, often from highly sought-after gentlemen.

Duke of this, Lord of that, His Royal Highness such-and-such. Ammalia was bored by them all, no matter how handsome and wealthy and well-connected they were. She didn't *like* men, and never had. Fortunately, as a royal princess, the one concession afforded her by her father was that she needn't marry any man against her will.

Of course, what Ammalia *willed* was to marry the woman of her dreams. This scenario was not a thing that existed—a publicly condoned Sapphic royal match wasn't even the stuff of fairy tales—but that hadn't stopped her from wanting it viscerally. She longed for love. To find a happy-ever-after with a woman who made her feel not unlike the one whose celestial gaze was still locked on Ammalia's.

Outside of her family, however, no one knew about her preferences. Although a princess could get away with almost anything, Father had warned her not to embroil the family in gossip or to draw attention away from her brother until after Zurri was safely wed, and the alliance with England secure.

Until then, Ammalia's wishes didn't come second—they didn't matter at all.

"All right, I give up," Zurri groused. "*Please* tell me who it is you cannot look away from."

Because her brother had said please, Ammalia gestured in the general direction of her mystery woman. Not too precisely, of course. With luck, one of the other screaming young ladies flanking her should catch Zurri's eye.

Unfortunately, Ammalia was not in luck.

"The one with the handkerchief tied to her head and the smudge of dirt on her face?" he asked in disbelief. "I suppose she'd be halfway passable, if she weren't dressed in rags."

To be honest, Ammalia hadn't noticed the smudge or the hand-kerchief or the patched and tattered gown. Even now, after Zurri had so uncharitably pointed it out, Ammalia could not make herself care about such inconsequential details. She wanted to know all the things that *did* matter. Like, what was this woman's name? Was she spoken for? Did she like good wine and ocean sunsets and focaccia fresh from the oven and the smooth feel of cold mosaic tiles beneath one's bare feet on a warm summer's day? Would she like to experience all those things with Ammalia?

"Maybe your pauper is just the trick to add sparkle to my image," he mused thoughtfully. "A pet project, for the public's sake. Like the time I adopted that dog."

"*I* adopted the dog. You held that Pomeranian in your lap long enough to get your portrait painted, and then never gave the poor wretch another glance."

Zurri's stunt had generated the desired effect: young ladies all over the Parmenza region of Italy purchased penny copies of that portrait, and acquired Pomeranians of their own out of solidarity with the prince.

"It was furry," her brother protested. "I don't like things with fur. I might not mind—"

"No," Ammalia said firmly. "That woman is a person, not a Pomeranian. She's not to become your pet, even for a moment."

Zurri was not listening to her. His head was cocked to one side, his eyes narrowing with calculation. "She does have good bones, does she not? Perhaps with a bath and a better dress, she might become the English rose I've been looking for."

"No," Ammalia said again, the word coming out strangled.

Her relationship with Zurri was like this. Though they loved each other, he and Ammalia had sniped and fought with each other for so long, they didn't know any other way to interact. If Zurri saw something his sister wanted, he took it from her. Ammalia didn't even *have* this woman, and already her brother was plotting how to take possession.

Interest from her brother could only spell disaster. For the poor young woman, who would either be leg-shackled to a spoilt brat—or publicly discarded by him in front of all her peers, with no more thought than he'd given the Pomeranian.

Ammalia wouldn't be able to gather the gorgeous woman up and take her home. Not after a public rejection by the prince. Instead, Ammalia would be forced to leave her behind...

Or else watch her become Parmenza's next princess and future queen. Living under the same roof, yet untouchable. For the rest of Ammalia's life.

Chapter Three

"He's looking at us!" Stasia squealed. "The prince is looking right at us!"

Cynthia didn't even flick a glance in his direction. She couldn't have moved if she tried. It was as though she and Princess Ammalia stood at opposite ends of a glass tunnel. The rest of the world was still out there, muffled and distorted, but the only object of perfect clarity was off in front of her, tantalizing and out of reach.

Longing shot through Cynthia, sharp enough to steal her breath. She swayed forward toward Princess Ammalia's piercing blue gaze.

"It's me." Dorothea flipped her long brown hair with confidence. "He's looking at *me*."

The crowd surged closer, squeezing around Cynthia and her stepsisters like a human boa constrictor, each vertebra made up of unwed young women, desperate to insert themselves in view of the prince's gaze.

With a jerk, the carriage moved forward once again. The prince grabbed his sister's elbow, forcibly turning the princess to face him.

Her attention lost, the spell was broken. The glass tunnel, shattered. Cynthia's unsteady limbs wobbled adrift without the incessant swell of the crowd to prop her up.

"When is the grand ball?" she gasped, once she could draw breath.

"Tonight," Dorothea replied absently, still waving her arms at the retreating prince. "Nine o'clock."

Cynthia could see no more of Princess Ammalia but the back of her glossy black chignon as the eight white horses pulled the gilded carriage out of view.

This could not be Cynthia's last sight of her. It could *not*.

She spun toward her stepsisters. "You have invitations to the ball?"

Dorothea rolled her eyes. "Unnecessary. *All* unmarried young women are invited, at the prince's bequest. How is he supposed to select the prettiest flower if his garden is incomplete?"

"Where are the festivities to be held? At the assembly rooms down the street?" Excitement bubbled in Cynthia's veins. "That's walking distance from our house."

"Stasia and I won't be *walking*," Dorothea snapped. "Obviously we'll hire a carriage."

A carriage! A grand ball! That magnificent princess!

"I'm going with you," Cynthia whispered.

That got both sisters' attention.

Dorothea wrinkled her nose as though Cynthia were something rancid found on the bottom of her shoe.

Stasia's pitying expression was not much better. "Dressed in... rags?"

"One of you could loan me a gown," Cynthia said in a burst of inspiration. "Any gown at all, no matter how unfashionable, so long as it hasn't any holes or—"

"No," Stasia said flatly, and turned toward the house. "Mother would never allow it."

"Unthinkable," Dorothea agreed with a haughty sniff. Her nose lifted into the air as she strode away from the crowd. "I won't have your dirty hands grubbying my silk. Even one I never intend to wear again."

Cynthia's lye-raw hands were rubbed clean every few minutes, given that her many daily chores included preparing the family's meals, cleaning the family house, and washing the family's clothes.

Dorothea was not afraid of dirt. She was afraid of Cynthia, and what her presence might accomplish.

"I don't want the prince," she assured her stepsister in a rush. "I just want to attend the ball, like everyone else."

Stasia gave a dismissive wave of her hand. "Well, you can't go unless you manage to look as presentable as everyone else."

Dorothea slanted her sister a scorching glare.

"It's not going to happen," Stasia said defensively. "She doesn't *have* anything presentable to wear."

Dorothea gave a long-suffering sigh.

"But... if I did find a dress," Cynthia said hesitantly. "I could go to the ball then?"

Stasia glanced at Dorothea. "I don't mind if she comes along."

Dorothea shrugged. "Me neither. It's not as though she'll outshine us. But despite the Prince explicitly inviting all unmarried young women, Mother will never allow Cynthia to join us."

Stasia bit her lip. "I could say I need a maid to look after my hair."

"Your hair *does* require constant intervention," Dorothea agreed dryly. She turned to Cynthia. "We'll tell Mother we need you in order to look our best. You may accompany us for an hour or two, but you must return home by midnight. No matter what Stasia and I say, Mother will expect a fresh hot bath waiting for the three of us when we return home. And a full breakfast on the table first thing in the morning, ball or no ball. Midnight, and not a moment later."

Cynthia nodded eagerly. "Midnight. Thank you."

Stasia sent her a look of warning. "If you fail to do even one of your chores to Mother's satisfaction, she won't allow you to leave the house for frivolous activities again."

Cynthia swallowed hard. "Understood."

They reached the door just in time to hear Lady Tremaine shriek, "My kippers are cold! Where *is* that lazy wench?"

Shite.

Cynthia rushed into the house to prepare her stepmother a fresh meal. Between now and tonight's ball, she had to perform each task impeccably, lest Stasia's begrudging permission be snatched away before Cynthia could attend tonight's ball.

She cooked and cleaned with more vigor than ever before, but there wasn't a spare second to even think about where to find a gown for another hour, until Lady Tremaine and her daughters left for their customary early-afternoon promenade in Hyde Park.

Home alone at last, Cynthia finished her final chore and rushed upstairs to her relocated room in the attic to search for something to wear. The ladies were right. Cynthia's clothes were fit for nothing but rags. She didn't need any of the carefully folded items inside her broken wardrobe. She needed a miracle.

A rustle of feathers sounded in the small open window. Cynthia gave a wan smile to the pair of magpies she'd named Jack and Gus. Cynthia wasn't sure who had befriended whom first, but she was deeply grateful for their company. Oftentimes, the only nice thing she heard all day was the sound of their happy chatter.

She crossed to the window. "You didn't happen to bring me a ball gown to wear, did you?"

They dropped their offerings in her palm: a sparkling pearl button, a shimmering satin ribbon, a shiny new penny, a beautiful red leaf.

"Thank you," Cynthia said as she always did, and added the new treasures to the growing trove heaped inside a dilapidated old bucket.

Jack and Gus twittered and preened in pleasure.

Cynthia slumped to the scuffed wooden floor and rested the back of her head against the windowsill. From this angle, the attic looked even smaller than usual. Most of it was piled to the rafters with old household detritus. The battered wardrobe next to the lumpy mattress. A cracked clock, a broken table, a hatbox that looked as though it had been run over by a herd of bulls.

The remains of a life Cynthia and her beloved parents had once had. If her mother were still here, she would help Cynthia find a way to the ball.

Wait a moment.

Hatbox.

She scrambled over to it on her hands and knees and pried open the lid. The paper inside the box fell apart in her hands. The hat it was meant to protect was crushed and soiled beyond repair.

But where there was a hat... might there not also be other attire?

With frantic energy, she set about moving each old item from one side of the attic to another, searching for something, anything, that could aid her cause.

And then she found it: a scarred valise that used to belong to her mother.

Hands trembling, Cynthia brushed the cobwebs aside and eased the creaking hinges open. It was part of her mother's wedding trousseau! Fragile linens and embroidered handkerchiefs and... a plain white gown thirty years out of style, and slightly yellowed with age.

Cynthia clutched it to her chest and danced about the attic in gleeful circles. The gown was old and desperately in need of a good cleaning, but it was free of holes and patches.

How long would the rest of her family be gone? An hour? Two? They would wish to prepare for the ball, as well. Cynthia raced down the stairs to wash her new gown, then hung it outside in the sun to dry. With the July heat and constant breeze, it wouldn't take long.

But it wasn't quick enough. Her stepmother and stepsisters arrived home just as Cynthia was taking the dress down from the line.

"What do you think you're doing with that?" Lady Tremaine demanded in alarm.

"It's my gown for the ball," Cynthia explained. "Stasia said—"

"*Stasia*," Dorothea spat, casting a nervous look over her shoulder. "Mother told us that kindness is always a bad idea."

"She won't catch anyone's eye in that thing," Stasia said. "Except as an object of pity, perhaps. That dress looks older than we are."

"There's no holes or patches," Cynthia said quickly, hugging her mother's gown to her bosom. "That was the agreement. I could fix it up a bit more, if one of you were to loan me—"

"I need my hair washed," Dorothea announced. "And dried and set into ringlets."

"All three of us ought to be washed before the ball," Lady Tremaine added.

Stasia flashed Cynthia a look of apology. "I really was counting on you running to the cobbler to reheel my dancing slippers before it's time to leave."

Cynthia's heart sank. There would be no time to work on her own appearance. The best she could hope for was to wear the gown as-is and dash a brush through her hair.

"Of course," she said with resignation. "I'll do all those things straight away. Let me take this dress up to my room, and I'll be right back down."

"Leave it there for good," Lady Tremaine snapped. "It belongs in an attic."

"Just like you do," Dorothea informed Cynthia, earning a smirk of appreciation from her mother. "You smell as musty as that old dress."

Cynthia had bathed herself and cleaned the dress less than hour prior, so she knew this comment was meant to wound rather than be truthful. But her heart had long since grown calloused to scathing remarks such as these. Her step-family's biting tongues did not matter to her in the least.

The only opinion that mattered was that of Princess Ammalia.

And the only way to look her best for the princess was to complete her new spate of tasks as briskly as possible.

She dashed up the shallow steps and skidded into the attic so quickly, the side of her foot brushed the old bucket and sent the gifts from the magpies skittering across the wooden floor.

"Blast!" She cursed her clumsiness and poor timing. "It will take ages to—"

The entire floor glittered as though strewn with diamonds. Cynthia was fairly certain that none of Gus and Jack's baubles were more valuable than bits of glass, but some of the items certainly *appeared* to be real silk ribbons and pearl buttons.

If she adorned her mother's gown with trimmings such as these...

"Jack! Gus!" She set the gown atop her pallet and scooped up a pearl and a length of pink ribbon. "Can you bring me more treasures like these?"

The magpies chirped as if they understood the mission and its urgency, and soared off from the windowsill in tandem.

Spirits buoyant, Cynthia hurried through the washing of hair, the serving of afternoon tea, and the five additional tasks her stepmother and stepsisters dreamt up before she could finally break away to take a moment for herself.

"Dawdle at your own risk," Stasia warned her under her breath. "The ball begins promptly at nine, which means less than three hours until we join the queue!"

"We leave with or without you," Dorothea called out as Cynthia barreled up the stairs on exhausted feet.

"Hopefully without," Lady Tremaine added fretfully. "I know she's your lady's maid, but how fashionable will you two look if you're seen towing a bedraggled scullion about like a pet?"

Cynthia ignored them all as she hurried back to the attic.

There, atop the smooth folds of her mother's ivory gown, rose a mountain of colorful ribbons and sparkling baubles.

"Jack and Gus, you clever scamps!" she breathed in wonder, dropping to her knees to sift through the trove of pretty ornaments.

In no time, she had her sewing kit in hand, and briskly trimmed the sleeves and hem and bodice with bright pink ribbons, giving the ivory gown a gorgeous splash of color. She dotted the bodice with pearl buttons and added a faux diamond to the clip in her hair.

When she made her way down the stairs, her stepmother and stepsisters weren't merely horrified at the sight of her.

They were furious.

Lady Tremaine pointed a knobby finger at Cynthia's bodice. "So *that's* where the ribbon of my riding bonnet went!"

"My missing pearl buttons," Stasia gasped. "*You* have them."

"Is that..." Dorothea dropped the black cat from her arms. "Is that the diamond from my lost earring?"

Oh, no. Oh, oh, oh *no*.

"You thief!" Lady Tremaine slapped Cynthia's cheek. "Did you think we wouldn't notice?"

"*Rowr*," added Morningstar, racing up Cynthia's legs, claws out, scratching her skin and shredding her mother's gown. Her stepsisters joined in the fray.

"I... I didn't..." she managed, but it was too late.

The dress was ruined. It didn't matter whose fault it was. There was no time to make a new one.

Cynthia wouldn't be going anywhere.

Chapter Four

Ammalia's heart beat faster as the royal carriage drew up the cobblestone street. The parade had long since ended, though hours remained before the ball. All of the prior onlookers had returned to their homes to prepare. There were only a few souls in sight to give her curious glances. A street sweeper, a stray dog, a hunched woman carrying a basket of apples.

As usual, without Zurri by her side, Ammalia was of no interest. The woman with the apples didn't spare her a second glance. Even the puppy had better sticks to chase. And the street sweeper simply sighed, as he waited for one of the eight white stallions to deposit a royal mess to be cleaned up.

She lowered herself from the carriage and accepted a pretty box from Fabrizio, one of the footmen.

"Stay here," she told him. "I won't be long."

Fabrizio glanced askance at the humble houses before her. "And if you do not return swiftly?"

"Then you wait here until I appear," she said firmly. "I trust you brought a book?"

He grinned and held up the volume Ammalia had loaned him. "I'm on chapter seven."

"Good man." She smiled back, then turned toward the row of residences, in the hope that her hunch was right, and the woman she had seen lived nearby.

She was in luck—at the second door, the butler recognized Ammalia's description as that of one of the neighbors, a sweet girl who lived three doors down with her family, the Tremaines. Ammalia's spirits rose, and she hurried down the street to the indicated home.

The residence was old, but sturdily built. Three stories of pretty brick. It was nothing like the Parmenzan castle back home, but then, how many English houses were? The important thing was not the exterior. If Ammalia's luck held, the pretty maiden she hoped to find was somewhere inside.

Box tucked under her arm, she marched to the front door and prepared to knock.

Doing so was unnecessary. The front door was already ajar, and swung all the way open at the first brush of Ammalia's knuckles.

Inside was a scene of utter chaos.

A pair of magpies flew about the parlor in wide, swooping circles, as though caught in a tempest. A black cat with a loud hiss and sharp claws tore over the furniture to give chase, leaping and swiping at the air and skidding on the hardwood floor, only to sprint and leap after the birds all over again.

In the center of the room stood the young woman who had caught Ammalia's eye earlier, looking even more memorable now than she had before. Two well-dressed young ladies about Ammalia's age tugged at the mystery woman's ivory gown, which hung from her slender frame in tatters. The—sisters?—crowed with delight as they yanked pearls and bits of ribbon from what might once have been a pretty dress. An older lady in an extravagant ball gown reared back her hand as though set to strike Ammalia's angel's face... which already bore a red mark.

They all froze at the sight of her.

Her mystery woman gasped and dipped into an immediate curtsey, the torn strips of her skirts flying. "Princess!"

Ammalia inclined her head, then glared at the other three. "And you are?"

"This is my house and these are my daughters," babbled the older woman. "Well, not that one. That's just Cynthia. But these two jewels are my darlings Dorothea and Stasia. And I am Lady Tremaine."

"Welcome to our home," chorused Stasia and Dorothea, curtseying in unison.

Ammalia stared back at them impassively.

"Cynthia, go and get cleaned up and fetch some tea for the princess," Dorothea hissed under her breath. "Where are your manners?"

"Where are the manners, indeed," Ammalia said dryly.

Cynthia looked stricken and her eyes took on a suspicious shine.

"Not you, dear heart," Ammalia assured her. "You are the only one who did not appear to be perpetrating violence on other people when I arrived."

"It wasn't violence," Stasia blurted. "Not exactly. That is, Mother *might* have slapped her, but that was only because—"

"Now, now," interrupted Lady Tremaine. "Let's not bore the princess by airing our dirty linen, shall we? Cynthia, you heard Dorothea, did you not? The tea shan't fetch itself."

"She stays," said Ammalia.

Lady Tremaine and her two daughters froze.

"Then... how will we have tea?" asked Stasia hesitantly.

For God's sake.

"Cynthia, do you work for these ladies?" Ammalia asked.

"I..." Cynthia bit her lip and glanced at the others out of the corner of her eye, as if torn between loyalty and honesty. "I don't get paid, no. I live here because this is my home."

"*My* home," Lady Tremaine corrected her. "Settled on me when I married your father."

"May he rest in peace," Cynthia murmured, her eyes lowering in pain.

"I see." Ammalia sent Lady Tremaine her iciest glare.

"I'm afraid I do not see," said Dorothea. "With all due respect, princess, why are you here? Has your brother come, too?"

"He had better things to do, I'm afraid." Probably a nap. Or a glass of *vin santo* and a rubber of whist. "His royal highness sent me in his stead."

Or would have, if he'd thought of it. This visit was Ammalia's idea. She was the one who could not stay away from her mystery woman. Not if there was the slightest chance—

"Prince Azzurro sent you to do what?" Lady Tremaine asked, bewildered.

"My brother wishes to ensure that this family will be attending tonight's royal ball. As you may know, our father is increasing ties with England, which will soon include a royal wedding to unite our two countries. That is why tonight's ball is open to all unmarried women. The king believes my brother deserves no less than the prettiest English rose in all the kingdom."

Stasia and Dorothea exchanged delighted glances, rolling back their shoulders and puffing out their chests in preening self-satisfaction.

"I told you he was looking at us," said Stasia.

"At *me*," Dorothea said smugly.

"Of course we'll be there," Lady Tremaine assured Ammalia. "Not Cynthia; she's needed here. Someone has to do the chores. But my daughters and I would not dream of missing an opportunity to—"

"The entire family is to be present." Ammalia enunciated each syllable, ensuring her accent did not hinder their comprehension. "Which appears to include Cynthia."

Who, Ammalia realized, had clearly been in the midst of a lively struggle to attend the ball, only to meet with familial resistance. For the fight to have progressed to a level that left Cynthia's gown in tatters only underscored just how badly Cynthia had hoped to dance with—and perhaps enamor—the prince.

Ammalia tried not to be disappointed. She should not have expected otherwise. Young ladies in both countries would tear each other apart to be the one to wed Zurri. Ammalia had just hoped Cynthia might be different. That she might see beyond the prince's façade to the sister that stood in his shadows.

"Well... I mean, yes, technically, Cynthia is a part of this household," Lady Tremaine conceded, "but she's wearing the finest gown she owns, and as you can see, it's barely fit to sweep the cinders from the fireplace, much less rub shoulders with royalty."

Cynthia pressed her rosy lips together, as if forcing a retort back down her throat.

Perhaps something like: *This gown was perfectly serviceable until you three ripped it apart with your bare hands.* Or perhaps: *If the family coffers have money enough for your modiste, surely you could have spared a coin or two for me.* Or even: *I could open your wardrobes right now and find two dozen acceptable gowns you could have loaned me.*

None of it mattered. Even if Cynthia was destined to wed Zurri, Ammalia didn't want her to have to endure disrespect from to the Tremaine women ever again.

"As it happens," she said coldly, "his royal highness, in all his wisdom, has already provided the solution."

All four women stared at her.

"S-solution?" stammered Lady Tremaine.

Ammalia held up the be-ribboned box she'd been carrying. "My brother sent this gown, in case one of the young ladies needed it. It sounds to me as though that lady in need is Cynthia."

Stasia gasped in horror. "The prince... But *I* want..."

Dorothea whirled around. "Mama, you *cannot* allow that scullion to outshine us!"

Ammalia stepped forward and handed Cynthia the decorated box.

The tips of their fingers touched, sending a jolt of electricity crackling along Ammalia's skin.

She swallowed hard, to hide how badly the brief touch had affected her. "Good luck with my brother tonight. Mayhap your maid can help you don the gown."

Cynthia lifted her long eyelashes, her voice shy and her expression wistful. "I *am* a maid. I no longer have one."

"In that case..." Ammalia straightened her shoulders as an undeniable burst of wickedness rushed through her. "Do allow me the honor."

Chapter Five

Did the princess just say... *she* would be Cynthia's handmaiden?

The stunned expressions on her goggling stepsisters' faces mirrored Cynthia's own dazed reaction. Once she picked her jaw up off the floor, all she could do was stutter, "I... You needn't..."

"I'll tell you what we need," said Princess Ammalia, turning toward Lady Tremaine as if it had been Cynthia's stepmother who had offered to play lady's maid. "A hot bath, posthaste. Instruct one of your footmen to take it to Cynthia's dressing chamber at once."

"Er..." said Stasia.

"We haven't—" began Dorothea.

"Of course, your highness," Lady Tremaine interrupted, all scraping curtsies and saccharine smiles. "The girls will see to it personally. Won't you, girls?"

Stasia and Dorothea stared at her in horror, though neither breathed a word of protest. Both were more terrified of their mother than of making a poor impression on visiting royalty. They would not refuse any request.

"Go and ready Cynthia's bath," Lady Tremaine commanded her frozen daughters. "*Now.*"

Stasia and Dorothea scurried off, too rattled even to remember to dart accusing looks over their shoulders at Cynthia as they hurried toward the kitchens.

Cynthia wondered if they knew how to boil water.

Lady Tremaine gestured toward Dorothea's bedchamber. "Show the princess to your rooms, dear."

"But that's not my room." Anger flashed through Cynthia's veins. "You gave my room to your daughter and sent me upstairs to live in the attic."

Lady Tremaine looked as though she could happily throttle her, but settled instead on visibly grinding her teeth behind a tight smile.

"To the attic, then," Princess Ammalia said briskly. "I'm certain there will be no trouble carrying the hot bath upstairs."

No one had ever brought Cynthia a hot *anything* up to the attic. If she wanted a bath or even a cup of tea, she boiled the water herself down in the kitchen. The cramped wooden tub in the pantry was where she'd had the most stolen moments to relax.

"Of course, your highness," Lady Tremaine said, curtseying low, her tone fawning. "My girls will be right up."

Princess Ammalia inclined her head as though all of this was as it should be. Without further comment or attention to Lady Tremaine, the princess turned to Cynthia with her eyebrows raised. "Now then. Why don't you lead the way?"

"Of... course," Cynthia stammered, as used to leading the way to her attic bedchamber as her stepsisters were used to manual labor. Which was to say: not at all. In the years since she'd been installed there, the only living souls to visit her were her magpies, Jack and Gus.

Even Morningstar the devil-cat didn't bother climbing multiple flights of stairs to torment Cynthia by scratching at her door and her shins. It was just as easy to wait to attack until she was making her careful way down the steps with a heavy basket or precarious tray in her hands.

She hated that the princess was seeing her this way, bedraggled and browbeaten. But Cynthia could not help but want to please her, and Princess Ammalia's low rich voice with its Italian accent was too delicious to deny.

Cynthia hurried up the stairs at her usual *must-accomplish-every-thing* brisk pace before realizing the princess was likely unused to racing up and down flights of stairs. Most likely, Cynthia had left the poor woman in the dust back on the first step.

But when she paused, Princess Ammalia was right behind her. Due to the difference in their heights, and because Cynthia had not given warning that she was about to turn around, her bodice swung directly into the princess's path.

The princess had no time to slow her forward momentum before her startled face smushed directly into Cynthia's bosom.

"Oh," Cynthia gasped, her face flaming with heat. "I'm so sorry. I..."

She jerked backwards, rescuing the princess from suffocating in Cynthia's cleavage, then spun around and dashed up the final steps as though her slippers were on fire.

When she reached the top of the stairs, she flung open the door to her bedchamber and launched herself a safe distance inside.

Probably it was a safe distance. Maybe. She wasn't quite sure what she was running from—the princess, or her own reaction to having her so close.

If it was the latter, things were not about to get easier.

The princess glanced around the dim attic, taking it all in. The ceiling was low, but the wide chamber covered the full length of the house. Almost every inch was full of decades-old trunks and boxes and furniture, save for the small area Cynthia had claimed for herself, with just enough room for the broken wardrobe where she kept her few items of clothing, the straw pallet upon which she slept, and the heap of strings and sparkly bits the birds had brought her.

"Er," Cynthia said, then decided to forge ahead without further mention of accidentally force-feeding her bosom to the princess. "I'd offer you a seat, but as you can see, I've no chairs. The wooden crates are sturdy, if you'd like me to dust one off for you."

"You used to have a proper bedroom?" the princess asked.

Cynthia nodded. "It's Dorothea's now."

"This three-story house only contains three usable bedchambers?"

"No, there are others. But they're reserved for guests."

"Guests," the princess repeated. "Not to be used by the one person who grew up in this house, prior to the others' arrival."

"I get by, by trying very hard not to think about that," Cynthia said softly. "And by pretending I don't care how I'm treated."

"You should never have to pretend not to care," the princess replied. "*I* care how you are treated."

And now Cynthia would have to pretend that her insides weren't turned upside-down because of *that*. Her heart fluttered.

Before she could return the conversation to safer topics, such as which of the warped crates would be most suitable to dust off for a princess, a ruckus sounded at the foot of the stairs. Cynthia rushed to the open doorway to see what had caused the commotion.

Chapter Six

T here on the landing below were Dorothea and Stasia, red-faced and sweating, as they tried semi-successfully to lug Lady Tremaine's fancy bathtub up the stairs, rather than the shallow wooden tub left in the scullery for Cynthia. Their mother hovered right behind, candle in hand..

Cynthia hurried toward the stairs to help them, but Princess Ammalia caught her elbow before Cynthia could take more than a single step.

"They made it this far," the princess said quietly. "Allow them to complete their task—and allow yourself to enjoy it."

Cynthia *might* have enjoyed seeing her stepmother and stepsisters pitch in for once, if it signified anything other than what was about to come next. A tub meant a bath, and a bath meant disrobing—in front of Princess Ammalia, who had already experienced an unexpectedly close encounter with Cynthia's bosom.

The thought of being fully naked in front of the princess was almost too much to bear. And, if Cynthia was being honest, the effort was wholly unnecessary. She had bathed earlier, and was already perfectly clean.

She could not quite bring herself to voice this tidbit of information, however. Cynthia *liked* baths. And the sight of Princess

Ammalia taking charge and ordering the others about was simply too delicious to pass up.

In relatively short order, the pallet and a few crates were moved, and room made for the pretty tub. Dorothea and Lady Tremaine hurried out of the attic and back down the stairs to help Stasia bring up the first buckets of hot water.

"This would go faster if I helped," Cynthia said to Princess Ammalia. "At this rate, we'll be late for the ball."

The princess cocked an eyebrow. "Does anyone help *you* bring the water up the stairs when it is time for their baths?"

Cynthia shook her head.

"Then let them appreciate your efforts." Princess Ammalia leaned her shoulders against the wall next to the open window as though they had all the time in the world.

"And if we're late to arrive?" Cynthia ventured.

"Are you in a hurry to see my brother?"

"No," Cynthia admitted. "What I really... Who..." She cleared her throat. "I mostly wanted to see *you*."

"And here we are, in arm's reach of each other." Satisfaction flitted at the corner of the princess's lips. "Two wishes granted."

Cynthia frowned. Although it was undeniably true, she hadn't *said* she wanted to be in arm's reach of the princess. Was the princess simply assuming closer proximity was Cynthia's second wish? Or was Ammalia saying she, too, had been looking forward to a second meeting?

"Water," gasped a voice from the doorway.

Cynthia hurried aside as Lady Tremaine and her daughters staggered into the attic with the first round of brimming buckets. They dumped the steaming water into the tub, filling it halfway, then slumped back down the stairs for more.

"They're not used to physical labor," Cynthia explained. "Their muscles will be sore tomorrow."

"Good," said the princess. "Mayhap tomorrow they will appreciate you even more."

The truth was, Cynthia didn't want to think about tomorrow.

Today was the magical day. Tomorrow things would be back to normal. Worse than normal. If Cynthia had to guess, *appreciative* was not the word anyone would use to describe her step-family on the morrow when there was no princess in the room to command acts of kindness.

"I presume you have footmen at home who deal with such tasks?"

The princess snorted. "We have footmen everywhere. I could have snapped my fingers outside this window and summoned a full retinue of royal footmen to bring up enough water to form a waist-high thermal spring right here in your attic."

"Bathing in a natural thermal spring must be magical," Cynthia said wistfully.

"Have you never visited one?"

Cynthia shook her head. "The most popular thermal waters in England are in Bath, one hundred and twenty miles away. I'm afraid I've not had much opportunity to venture so far from home."

"Italy has many such thermal waters. Not just in Parmenza, where I am from. Hot, luxurious waters are found naturally around the base of several of our volcanoes. I think you would like them."

"I know I would," Cynthia said with feeling. "I've dreamt of traveling widely. But I'll likely never leave here."

"Won't you?" The princess's expression was unreadable. "I wonder."

Heavy steps sounded on the stairs, followed by loud panting and muffled swearing, then the appearance of Lady Tremaine and her daughters hauling the final buckets of steaming water.

Flushed and sweating, they dumped the water into the oversized tub, then turned to Princess Ammalia rather than to Cynthia. "Anything else, your highness?"

"That will be all for now." The princess's expression was now aloof and imperious. "I will summon you if I have need of your aid."

Stasia and Dorothea exchanged pained glances, but scurried down from the attic before Princess Ammalia could change her mind. As much as they despised being treated like servants, the abrupt dismissal was a relief too precious to ignore. They exited in such a hurry, a candle was left behind.

After depositing soap and a towel next to the tub, Lady Tremaine gave a final curtsey before closing the door and hurrying after her daughters.

"Now then," said the princess. "Where were we?"

Cynthia swung her alarmed gaze toward the clean, hot bath with a mixture of excitement and trepidation. She'd never undressed in front of a stranger before, much less a woman who set her pulse racing. Now that the time to disrobe had come, the moment seemed sharper and more real than anything she had ever experienced before. She did not want to disappoint the princess.

"I hope *you* know what we're doing," Princess Ammalia said in a conspiratorial whisper. "I've never remained on the outside of a bath I summoned before."

Cynthia laughed, and the moment was suddenly bearable. Whatever happened, the princess wouldn't judge her. She was in fact just as lost in this new landscape as Cynthia was. They were both on the same side.

"Fear not," Cynthia assured her. "All of my gowns are designed to be donned and doffed without aid of a lady's maid."

"That might have been a gown once," said the princess with a dubious expression, "but the material is now hanging from you in strips and tatters. I fear it is fit for the fireplace or the rag bin."

Cynthia nodded tightly. Her mother's gown... but she would not think about how Morningstar's claws and her stepsisters' hands had rent the once-fine fabric into fraying shreds. Over the past five years, there'd been a surplus of heartbreaking moments in which Cynthia had weathered some form of torture or another.

This moment was about Princess Ammalia. Cynthia was determined to make it a memory to cherish.

She stripped the ruined garments from her body with as much dignity as she could manage, then quickly stepped into the hot water before her nakedness could overwhelm her.

Only once she was immersed in the water up to her knees and

shoulders did she realize she had neglected to retrieve the scented soap from its position nestled atop the folded towel.

"Er..." She cleared her throat. "Would you be so kind as to hand me the soap?"

Rather than drop the soap into Cynthia's outstretched palm as expected, Ammalia paused, then dropped to her knees and began to suds Cynthia's curved back. Soon the bubbles rose to her shoulders.

The sensation was incredible. A mix of the relaxation that came from long-tight muscles being massaged into putty, and the sense of connection that came from another human being taking the time to care for her, with her full attention and gentle sweetness.

"Is this... all right?" asked the princess.

"I could marry you," Cynthia said on a sigh.

The princess stopped sudsing.

"Figuratively," Cynthia blurted out. "Metaphorically. All I meant was... Yes, it's all right."

"All you meant," the princess murmured. "Of course."

The sudsing of Cynthia's back resumed, this time in silence.

The resulting bathing experience was both more than she ever dreamt and yet not quite everything she wanted. Princess Ammalia was touching her, but not in the way Cynthia most desired—and only one of them was naked. There was a moment when Cynthia almost thought... but no. The princess was simply being extraordinarily, improbably *kind*.

When every inch of her back had been massaged into languid bliss, Cynthia forced herself to take the soap from the princess.

"I'll continue from here. You can... look about the attic, if you like."

The princess relinquished the soap, then rose from her knees. She dried her hands before turning her back discreetly and feigning great interest in the piles of rotted crates and the dismal view outside the window at the brick wall opposite.

Cynthia washed the rest of her body in haste.

She didn't bother with her hair because there wasn't enough time for it to dry. And by now, the water had begun to turn tepid.

Cynthia gripped the sides of the tub and pushed to her feet. At the sound of the sluicing water, Princess Ammalia spun around. Cynthia's face went bright red.

Unperturbed, Princess Ammalia wrapped Cynthia in the towel, and allowed her to pat herself dry whilst the princess opened the box she'd brought into the house.

Cynthia gasped to see a folded gown of rich blue satins and silks take up most of the interior, topped by a matching blue diamond tiara and a pair of dazzling slippers that glittered brightly, even in the fading sunlight. She used her stepsisters' forgotten candle to light the wall sconce in order to see the items more clearly.

"Are those slippers covered with bits of decorative glass?" she asked in wonder.

"Thousands of gemstones," the princess replied, as if such an extravagance was perfectly normal for a shoe that would be half-hidden beneath one's skirts and dashed against hard terrain all night.

"I couldn't possibly," Cynthia stammered. "Each of those gems must have cost... If I lose even one of them..."

"No one will know but you," the princess answered. "If even you can tell the difference. These shoes are yours now. You needn't return them. They're yours to do with as you please."

"Until midnight," Cynthia murmured. She had to be home by then, or she'd never get her chores completed on time—and she couldn't risk infuriating her stepmother and stepsisters any worse. They were already fuming. Once they caught sight of Cynthia in this gown and with these slippers...

"May I help you with the dress?" Princess Ammalia asked. "I fear it is indeed the sort that requires the assistance of a lady's maid."

"Please, that would be lovely." After sliding on her shift, Cynthia held perfectly still as the princess laced the cords along Cynthia's spine.

She'd expected the dress to be too big or too small, too long or too short, but it fit her as though it had been custom-tailored to Cynthia's exact measurements.

An appreciative smile flitted at Princess Ammalia's lips. "You look breathtaking. Even more beautiful than you did before. The blues bring out the bright cerulean of your eyes, and the cut of this gown..."

"It is a truly astonishing fit," Cynthia admitted in awe. "Your brother picked this out after a single glance at my stepsisters?"

"*I* directed the creation of this gown," Princess Ammalia corrected her softly. "After gazing at *you*."

Cynthia's throat went dry. Her heart beat faster—then sank. Those ambiguous moments, during the bath...

Had she wasted a golden opportunity she would never have again?

Chapter Seven

All Princess Ammalia wished to do was ogle Cynthia. Well, ogle her, hold her, kiss her, touch her, have her. Ogle with sensual flourishes.

Cynthia had piled her long blond hair high on her head with nary an escaping ringlet. Her bosom was plumped to perfection inside a low bodice of shimmering ocean blue, matching the underskirt below. The puffed sleeves of robin's-egg-blue complemented the sweeping, overskirt of flowing pale blue gauze. The lines accentuated Cynthia's lush hips and narrow waist and long legs, right down to the tips of the sparkling crystal slippers poking out beneath the floor-length hem.

Essentially, Ammalia wanted to engage in activities that would ruin their coiffures and wrinkle both their gowns beyond repair, so that the only solution would be to stay here in this room with Cynthia and not exit each other's arms for any reason until the morning light.

Unfortunately, the second Cynthia opened the attic door, her step-siblings pounced. From that moment on, they conspired to keep Ammalia separated from Cynthia by inserting themselves between the two.

They peppered Ammalia with an unceasing and utterly

exhausting barrage of inane questions, every one of which was about Ammalia's brother Zurri.

"Has he got a castle of his own?"

"How tall is he?"

"What's his favorite color? Is it blue?"

"Is he considering staying in England to live?"

"Does he prefer women who purse their lips like *this* or like *this*?"

"How many balls does he throw a week?"

"Must I learn Italian if I marry him?"

"Do Italians drink tea?"

"How many servants would I have if I were Queen?"

"Is the prince a good dancer?"

"Does he like pudding?"

It was enough to make Ammalia wish to scream.

The ball would begin at any moment, and she was supposed to be arranging her brother's dances with the prettiest of all the young ladies present.

Cynthia did not take part in the questioning. She simply gazed at Ammalia from the corner of her eye or from beneath her long lashes, and then blushed becomingly every time Ammalia caught her at it.

That was enough to make Ammalia wish to throw Cynthia over her shoulder and charge out of the house to the carriage, knocking over the mother and the two sisters like so many bowling pins.

"Come," Ammalia commanded, interrupting the endless litany of questions. "We can continue this conversation—" Such as it was. "— in the carriage."

"In the *royal* carriage?" squealed Stasia. "We can ride with you?"

"If we all fit," Ammalia said quellingly. "You may have to sit on each other's laps."

"I'll sit on the driver's lap if I must," Stasia said gamely, linking her arm with her sister. "Don't dawdle so, Dorothea."

Dorothea sent a triumphant glance over her sister's shoulder toward their mother. "See? I told you Stasia wasn't queen material. A queen would *never* sit on her driver's lap. I would never behave so indecorously. The prince should marry *me*."

"As long as he marries one of you." Lady Tremaine shooed them both ahead with her gloved hand. "Go on, we haven't got all night for him to fall in love with you."

As long as he didn't marry Cynthia...

Once Ammalia had entered the carriage, Lady Tremaine should have been next—there was an order of precedence to such things, in Italy as well as in England—but Ammalia pretended no awareness of such a custom, in order to ensure Cynthia sat by her side.

After all, once the uncommon beauty arrived at the ball... Ammalia should be lucky to steal a sideways glance, much less a spare moment of Cynthia's time.

"Doesn't your sister look marvelous?" Ammalia asked the other two, who had conspicuously refrained from commenting upon Cynthia's stunning transformation.

"Step-sister," said Stasia.

"I'm still prettier," said Dorothea, then cast a nervous glance at Lady Tremaine. "Aren't I, Mother?"

"Even a toad is prettier than a scullion," Lady Tremaine assured her daughter, without so much as a glance in Cynthia's direction.

Porca miseria, Ammalia could not allow Cynthia to return to a life of thankless servitude with these people. But while Ammalia might be princess to a population of half a million Parmenzans back home, she did not have the authority to govern Cynthia's choices or command a better home life for her here.

At least she'd given her the shoes. With luck, tonight's momentary escape would be enough for Cynthia to take stock of her unhappy surroundings and sell as many of the gemstones as it took to finance her much-deserved independence.

"Wait a minute." Dorothea spun to face Ammalia. "The Prince intends to dance with all three of us, not just the scullion, right?"

Ammalia smiled tightly. Her brother had indicated no such intention, because he hadn't even known of their existence. But as far as Ammalia was concerned, he owed her that much, in exchange for suffering through their company without breaking down in tears or shaking some sense into them. After all, Ammalia was supposed to be in the ballroom at this moment, lining up the prettiest young ladies for Zurri to dance with.

"Yes, of course," she promised an elated Stasia and Dorothea. "He is absolutely agog with anticipation to dance with each of you. In fact, he has specifically requested to dance with both of you the minute we arrive."

Stasia and Dorothea clapped their hands with glee, then began to tussle amongst themselves over which sister ought to have the first dance.

Ammalia didn't much care which one went first. The distraction at least gave her two full sets before Zurri set eyes on Cynthia...

And decided that the woman Ammalia wanted was the one he would take as his bride.

Chapter Eight

From the moment the princess's royal carriage pulled up before the open door to the grand ball, Cynthia was unbearably overwhelmed.

The assembly rooms were the largest in London, and filled with so many people already that she could not fathom fitting a single additional soul inside, much less all five of the women scrambling out of the carriage.

That was, Dorothea and Stasia were scrambling. Princess Ammalia did not scramble. She floated to the ground regally, as if thousands of exquisitely dressed lords and ladies in a single room was just another Tuesday back home in Parmenza.

Cynthia, on the other hand, had never been anywhere so fine, or around so many people this rarefied. Everything was so much *more* than she had expected. The colors were brighter. The lights, dazzling. *How* many chandeliers were overhead? And with hundreds of lit candles burning on each one?

All the doors and windows were wide open, allowing in the frigid British night breeze, which was immediately vanquished by the crush of so many warm bodies swarming like bees in a hive. Despite the lower temperatures out-of-doors, the ballroom was suffocatingly warm.

Even the smells were overwhelming. Acrid smoke from pungent cigars being smoked by well-dressed gentlemen standing just outside the open doors and windows permeated the breeze. Cynthia couldn't even make out the scent of the hectare of thick trees and fresh flowers in the gardens surrounding the assembly rooms because of the competing odors of thousands of different soaps and perfumes and pomades and eaux de toilette.

And the sounds—good God, the sounds! Thousands of voices talking over each other was more than a dull roar, and the thunder of so many feet pounding the wooden parquet in rhythmic patterns hammered its way into Cynthia's skull.

Yet the orchestra managed to be louder than all of it. The violins' soaring melodies and the cellos' complementary low tones vibrated the walls and the floor and the panes of glass and Cynthia's very bones.

It was, in short, magnificent. Despite her dizziness at the sensory assault, Cynthia was determined to commit all of it to memory. She had never seen such a spectacle, and could not imagine herself taking part in a circus like this ever again.

"Ah, there's my brother now," said the princess.

Stasia and Dorothea clutched each other and bounced up and down. "Where? Where?"

"Do you see the three empty chairs near the dance floor?" The princess gestured. "I'm to send his dance partners there. You two, take your mother and arrange yourselves conspicuously. I shall send my brother over straight away."

Stasia was the only one of the trio to hesitate. "What about Cynthia?"

"Yes," Cynthia said, hurt. "There's no chair for me? Should I assume there's no dance for me, either?"

Princess Ammalia's lips tightened. "Of course you shall have your dance. I cannot matchmake my brother to the most beautiful woman in England if you do not number amongst his partners. If you prefer being first to being third—"

"Third is fine," Cynthia said quickly. "I just thought—"

"I've not forgotten you. I thought we might play companion to each other whilst your sisters have their dances."

"Yes, Cynthia," said Dorothea, her voice cajoling. "Do let your beloved stepsisters have our chance with the prince before you flutter your lashes and try to ensnare him."

"If he falls for you, I won't stand in your way," Cynthia murmured.

"Thank you," Stasia said fervently. "Wish me luck."

"Wish *me* luck," Dorothea objected. "I'm older, which means—"

"Make haste," Ammalia interrupted. "The minuet is ending, and there is a waltz to come."

"A waltz!" Stasia looped her arm through her sister's and the two ladies barreled through the crowd, elbowing higher ranking lords and ladies out of her path like a pair of bulls charging through a field of flowers.

Lady Tremaine hurried in their wake without sparing a single glance for Cynthia.

Not that Cynthia minded. Her eyes were only for Princess Ammalia. And her hands and her mouth and her bosom and everything else. Cynthia would joyfully provide anything the princess asked of her—if only the princess should ask.

After exchanging a few words with a footman, Princess Ammalia took Cynthia's hand and expertly threaded her through the crowd to the rear of the ballroom, as far from the voluminous orchestra and turbulent dance floor as it was possible to get whilst still remaining in the same large chamber.

"Is this where you saw your brother?" she asked, as soon as conversation was possible.

"I never saw my brother," said the princess without remorse. "I wanted to be rid of your family."

Cynthia's cheeks flushed with embarrassment and pleasure. Her stepmother and stepsisters could be mortifying, and it was a dream come true to have a few more moments alone—well, semi-alone; as alone as two people could be in a crowded ballroom—with Princess Ammalia. And yet...

"They'll be crushed if they do not get their dances with the prince," she told the princess.

"They'll get their dances," Princess Ammalia replied. "Did you not wonder why there were still three empty chairs in a chamber filled with this many people? Those seats were reserved for marriageable young beauties."

Cynthia tried not to be hurt. "I am to stay in the back of the ballroom because I do not qualify?"

"You're the prettiest of them all, no matter where you're standing. Are you angry that I did not lead you directly to the first chair in line? We can go there now, and—"

"No," Cynthia said quickly. "I would much rather be here, with you."

I would much rather be anywhere *you happened to be.*

Princess Ammalia smiled as if Cynthia had voiced this last secret aloud, and with enough volume to be heard over violins and stomping feet and the noise of all the other voices.

That the princess should have a mystical gift to see into the depths of Cynthia's soul would not surprise her at all. Cynthia still couldn't quite fathom that the princess had picked her out of the parade crowd to begin with, much less any of the bewildering events that had followed.

"It's the Prince!" blurted an excited feminine voice. A clump of young ladies were walking past Cynthia and Ammalia's chairs. "He's selected his first dance partner of the night. Who is that? Have you ever seen her before?"

Cynthia lifted her eyes and straightened her spine, but there was no hope of seeing the dance floor from this angle.

"One of your sisters," Princess Ammalia murmured. "Their seats made them next in line."

Vicarious excitement filled Cynthia on her stepsisters' behalf. "Which one did he choose?"

"I don't know." The princess started to shrug, then gave Cynthia a piercing look. "Would you like to go and see?"

"No," Cynthia said softly. Her hand was still in Princess

Ammalia's. Between the crush of people and the volume of their skirts, no one could see their entwined fingers. The hidden touch was a secret in plain sight. "I'm happy here with you."

Princess Ammalia's gaze warmed. "As am I."

She motioned to a footman, who arranged for a pair of armchairs to appear.

Cynthia was impressed. "Do you do this sort of thing often?"

"Suffer through ballroom after tiresome ballroom stuffed with starry-eyed women fawning over my brother in hopes of becoming his bride? *Far* more often than I'd like. No one is happier than I am that he shall finally make his selection and we can have done with this infernal wife market."

But the princess did not look entirely happy.

"No," Cynthia said. "I meant pluck a scullion out of obscurity and bring her with you to one of those tiresome balls?"

"Ah." Princess Ammalia's cheeks turned pink. "No, this is the first time."

Cynthia was inordinately pleased by this answer as well as the princess's charming embarrassment. It felt nice to be seen, to be thought of as special. She certainly thought the same about Princess Ammalia.

"Do you wish you were fawned over in the same way?"

"*Col cavolo*, I would throw myself into the boiling lava of Mount Etna before I'd want to wade through a sea of salivating gentlemen intent on bedding me."

That was how Cynthia felt as well... but that was because she didn't wish to marry a man. She hadn't mentioned pursuing gentlemen suitors at all.

Did the fact that men were Princess Ammalia's first thought mean that she did not view Cynthia in that way after all? After all this, were she and the princess only meant to be... friends?

Silly scullion, she scolded herself. *Not even friends. At midnight, you must return to your world, and the princess shall return to hers.*

The thought squeezed Cynthia's lungs. She wanted to pull the princess out of her chair and run away with her then and there.

But even that was a hollow dream. Run away where? The princess was royally bound to her own homeland—or to the prince she inevitably married. They could no more run off into the sunset together than they could fly to the moon.

"Do you ever dance at these things?" she forced herself to ask.

"When I must," the princess replied. "If you can keep a secret, I'd rather be in the orchestra than on the dance floor."

"You play an instrument?" Cynthia asked in surprise.

"Several," the princess admitted. "Most string instruments. My favorite is the violoncello."

"I love string instruments," Cynthia exclaimed with delight. "I used to play the violin, back when I still had tutors. I miss it."

"If I had known, I would have brought you one in the box with your gown."

"I already cannot repay you. And yet, if I could ask for anything, it would be to hear *you* play."

"Sadly, all of my instruments are at home in our castle. Dare I suppose the promise of a private performance is bait enough to lure you there?" The princess wiggled her brows comically.

Cynthia laughed. "If I had the means to travel, your music room is the first place I'd visit. And since I do not have the means... Pray, pay no attention if one of your valises weighs ten stone more than expected. I'm certain it's definitely not a fugitive scullion, stowing away in a princess's traveling trunks."

"And if it is, I won't tell a soul," the princess promised. She rubbed the soft pad of her thumb against the back of Cynthia's hand, and sighed ruefully. "*Madonna mia.* My brother is absolutely going to adore you."

At this pronouncement, Cynthia's stomach twisted into knots. "W-what?"

Princess Ammalia dropped Cynthia's hand and rubbed her own temples instead. "You and Zurri have little in common, but he'd be a fool to choose anyone else. And Parmenza could use a kindhearted queen on our court. Father will definitely approve."

Cynthia's spirits sank. The princess was sweet and thoughtful and generous. Both women shared unexpected things in common, from standing in their siblings' shadow to an affinity for making music. They'd be a perfect match...

If Princess Ammalia weren't determined to match-make Cynthia to the princess's brother.

Chapter Nine

Ammalia hated the thought of her brother inevitably choosing Cynthia as his bride. Yet she could not block his path. Not because he was her brother, and the heir and future king. But because all the unmarried English women in this ballroom had come to the gala specifically in the hopes of being chosen as Zurri's future wife.

Whether her brother himself was the attraction, or the allure of becoming royalty, if it was what Cynthia wanted, Ammalia would not stand in her way.

Of course, she also had no wish to stand in the shadows of the happy couple, watching their connubial bliss unfold to the delight of the entire kingdom. Cynthia's dream of traveling widely was a good one. If the woman Ammalia desired married Zurri, Ammalia would take the first boat out of Parmenza and never return.

The music shifted. The previous set had completed. Whichever sister Zurri had chosen to dance with was now being returned to her mother, and the second sister led to the dance floor in her stead.

Which meant Ammalia had twenty minutes left to enjoy Cynthia's company before Zurri came to collect her. Thirty, if Ammalia was lucky.

After that... Once all of the other gentlemen present caught sight of the gorgeous woman in Zurri's arms, Cynthia's round derrière would not find itself relaxing in a chair the entire rest of the night. There would be no more time for Ammalia at all.

"You look fierce," said Cynthia. "Is something the matter?"

Not yet. Soon enough.

Ammalia schooled her features into a smile. "Wool-gathering, I'm afraid."

"What were you thinking about?"

"When you said you'd love to travel. So would I."

Cynthia looked surprised. "I assumed you *were* well-traveled."

"The more one travels, the more one realizes that there are more places to visit than even possible to experience in a single lifetime. I have traveled, but I will never have traveled *enough*. It is an infinite adventure."

"I love that," said Cynthia. "How I would adore to embark on an infinite adventure. And you're right. I don't think a day would ever come when I'd had 'enough' and never wished to have another new experience again."

"Perhaps you might begin with Parmenza," said Ammalia.

"I would adore *that*," Cynthia replied in Italian.

Pleasantly surprised at the smooth pronunciation, Ammalia responded in kind. "You speak Italian?"

"I told you I had tutors once."

"*Italian* tutors?"

"Italian, Greek, Latin... I'm fairly certain my father wanted a boy, but when he had me instead, he saw no reason to curb my education."

"But that's splendid! Speaking—or at least muddling through— the local language makes travel all the more enjoyable."

"Then should we switch back to English?"

"Beh. Deuced few of your countrymen speak Italian as well as you. If we continue like this, our secrets cannot be understood by uneducated passers-by attempting to eavesdrop."

Cynthia's expression was droll. "Are we going to share many secrets?"

"We can if you'd like. What's your worst memory?"

"The deaths of my parents," Cynthia replied without hesitation. "Yours?"

"Any occasion with Zurri in it. Which are, ironically, also some of my favorite memories." Ammalia wrinkled her nose. "Having a brother is complicated."

"As is having step-sisters." Cynthia made a face.

Ammalia laughed. "It's a good thing we're not in competition for the most complicated family ties. It's difficult to say which of us would win."

"Perhaps it would be a draw." Cynthia tilted her head. "Then again, you've had to live with your brother your entire life, whilst I've only had step-sisters for five years."

"Eh, I was only in the company of your step-family for five minutes, and I'm already tired of them." Ammalia made a faux shudder. "You might win the obnoxious sibling competition uncontested."

"I'd rather win... A night with you at the opera."

Ammalia grinned. She loved how easy it was to talk with Cynthia. They could both just be themselves. "Do you like the opera?"

"I don't know. I've never been. But my old voice instructor used to be a famous soprano, and she would sing all her favorite parts for me. That's the main reason I learnt Italian to begin with. I wanted to understand the words I was trying to sing."

Ammalia leaned forward with interest. "Do you sing?"

"I *try* to sing," Cynthia repeated with a self-deprecating smile. "You'll notice *I* am not a famous soprano."

"Forgive me if I doubt your family would let you join the opera even if you had the best lungs in all of Europe."

"If I had a talent like that, I wouldn't wait for permission," Cynthia said. "I'd run away and never look back."

"Would you?" Ammalia said in surprise. The sentiment was too close to what she had just been thinking herself. "I suppose joining the opera is better than joining the circus."

"I wouldn't assume the opera isn't a circus of its own," Cynthia said with a smile. "But I wouldn't mind either one. Both get paid to travel."

"A fair point. What other tutors did you have?"

"Dance, watercolor, embroidery."

"Embroidery! There are specific tutors who specialize in that?"

"Do you not know how?"

"Good God, no. It's too close to manual labor. My father would expire on the spot before he'd allow me to pick up a sewing needle."

"Then he'd be pleased to know I've spent the past five years not embroidering a single thing." Cynthia's eyes twinkled mischievously.

Ammalia narrowed her own. "I suspect you're leaving something out."

"Only that it's possible to wear out a sewing needle," Cynthia confirmed with a laugh. "For half a decade, I've sewn more buttons and let out more hems than you can likely imagine. I could take apart this dress and put it back together before the end of the ball."

"Don't you dare," said Ammalia. "Also, it sounds to me as though you *do* have a talent. Several of them, in fact."

"I suppose I could apprentice to a seamstress," Cynthia agreed. "But I've not been offered any paying positions for multilingual violinists."

"That is because the world is not a fair place," Ammalia agreed. "If I were queen, the first thing I would do is enact a law requiring every kingdom to employ a well-hemmed violinist conversant in English, Greek, Italian, and Latin. I'd make it the best paid of every possible royal post."

"Let me know when you're queen. I'll apply that same day."

"I'll never be queen," Ammalia said with a sigh. "The real reason Father wants Zurri to pick a bride is because he can't wait for grandsons."

"Create your own kingdom," Cynthia suggested. "I'd move there."

"Without knowing where it is?"

"*You'd* be there."

"Perhaps I'd be the only constituent. The Kingdom of Ammalia, population one."

"Population two," Cynthia corrected her. "The queen and her multilingual violinist, with her sewing-calloused hands and questionable singing voice."

"No more sewing," said Ammalia. "It's outlawed in my kingdom."

"Will we wear rags?"

"Why wear anything? Parmenza is very warm. And when it is not, the problem is easily solved by a dip in a thermal spring. You haven't known true ecstasy until you've relaxed in hot water on a gloriously drizzly day."

"I didn't know drizzle could *be* glorious," Cynthia admitted.

"Maybe it's the nakedness, and not the drizzle." Ammalia stroked her chin as though deep in thought. "We will have to research this carefully."

"I cannot wait," Cynthia said with feeling. "Can't we start now?"

"How I wish we could! But I fear we've missed the opportunity to run away."

"Have we? I'm not too busy."

"You will be in just a moment," Ammalia said grimly. The music had shifted yet again, and a familiar royal form was striding in their direction, a pair of footmen parting the crowd ahead of Zurri as he took each purposeful step.

"What is it?" Cynthia whispered. "You look as though you've seen a Kraken."

"Worse." Ammalia groaned. "A future king."

Before she could say more, Zurri was right there in front of them, visibly gobsmacked at the resplendent sight of Cynthia dressed in the gown Ammalia had designed for her.

Porco cane, Ammalia should have clothed Cynthia in burlap and shaggy fur—anything to hide her beauty from Zurri.

But it was too late for such stratagems. Zurri was clearly smitten. All thanks to Ammalia. And he hadn't even *talked* with Cynthia yet.

Once he did so, the game would be over. Cynthia was sweet and resourceful and clever. Any man—or woman—would want her by their side. And Zurri was no fool.

Watching her brother make Cynthia his wife would break Ammalia's heart. No... That wasn't quite true. Who Zurri did or did not fall in love with was beside the point. What was destined to rend her in two was watching Cynthia fall for Zurri.

Like every other woman before her.

Chapter Ten

Cynthia glared at the man before her in vexation.

This must be the prince. She vaguely recognized him as person in the carriage next to Princess Ammalia during the parade, but she hadn't paid much attention to him then and wished she needn't pay any attention to him now.

Oh, he was perfectly attractive and all that. Tall, black-haired, well-built—the masculine version of Ammalia.

Cynthia preferred the female version.

"You look ravishing," said the prince, lifting her fingers to his lips as he sketched a sweeping bow. "My sister has chosen well."

"Perhaps she wasn't choosing for *you*," Cynthia muttered.

"Of course she brought you for me." He looked bewildered. "Everything in this assembly room is for me."

Cynthia bit back a snort of derision. Was the dripping candle wax for him? The stray spiderwebs? But she was being petty and unreasonable. This ball *was* in his name. Most females present *had* donned their very best out of an explicit desire to catch Prince Azzurro's eye.

She was the odd one who didn't fit the mold. Bitterly resentful that attracting the prince's attention meant losing Ammalia's.

Cynthia said quickly, "You needn't dance with me if you don't wish to."

Ammalia's eyebrows shot up.

"Of course I do," Prince Azzurro assured her. "Tonight and every night, for the rest of our lives."

For the rest of their... *Oh no.* He was speaking as though they were already betrothed!

"I really think—" she began.

He pulled her up and out of her comfortable armchair before she could complete her thought.

Cynthia stumbled. Prince Azzurro caught her. And swirled her into his waiting embrace in a move so smooth and graceful, Cynthia would swear he'd spent a lifetime practicing it.

The onlookers closest to them *oohed*.

Most of the crowd, minus four notable exceptions. Princess Ammalia, who was inspecting her fingernails as though the state of her cuticles was far more interesting than anything or anyone in this ballroom.

And Cynthia's step-family, who had elbowed their way forward. All three of them were staring daggers at her, despite Stasia and Dorothea having just had their turn with the prince scant minutes earlier. Their jealous suffering was tangible.

A novel turn of events that was gratifying enough to spur Cynthia into smiling at the prince and responding, "In that case, I accept this dance with pleasure."

"I never doubted," said the prince, and led her onto the smooth parquet.

Cynthia regretted her compliance at once. Not because the prince was a poor dancer. He was uncommonly graceful, and could have doubled as a dance-master himself. Perhaps he hadn't even practiced the sweep-her-into-his-arms maneuver from earlier. He might just be naturally talented at such nonsense.

The real reason Cynthia didn't want to dance with the prince was not because of the proximity or the movements, but because of the *prince*. His single, unforgivable, insurmountable fault was that he was not and would never be Princess Ammalia.

That, and he made Cynthia's skin crawl.

"Once we're married," he said as they danced, "I shall throw balls like this every night. I will install you in a golden throne atop a dais so that everyone can gaze upon your beauty, but allow none of the spectators close enough to touch. Only I shall dance with my future queen."

Wonderful. When he looked at her, he saw a possession that he could not wait to put on a shelf and trot out for special occasions. He didn't want a wife. He wanted a new acquisition to show off.

Marrying the prince would be a disaster. Being close enough to see her true desire whilst Ammalia remained forever untouchable would be nothing short of torture.

That was it. There was no possibility she could go through with a courtship. Cynthia didn't want the prince or any man. She wanted Princess Ammalia, who was the only royal Cynthia cared to spend time with.

Which left Cynthia no other recourse but to make the worst possible impression on the prince. By the time this dance was through, he'd prefer to marry a candlestick rather than Cynthia.

"What's a throne?" she asked.

He blinked. "A large chair. The sort royals sit in."

"Why is it gold?"

"Because gold is expensive. That's how people know it's a royal throne and not for them."

"What if a non-royal asks me if they can sit in it? Can I let them?"

He looked horrified. "A non-royal would never ask you if they could sit in it."

"My step-sisters will definitely ask," she said with confidence. "Unless they *don't* ask, and just go and sit in it. In which case, I suppose I can sit in your chair until they're done with mine."

"You can't sit in *my* throne. The king's throne is for the king, and the queen's throne is for the—never mind. We can go over the finer points later. I'll employ a royal tutor to instruct you in any customs you may be unfamiliar with."

"And a mathematics tutor?"

"Mathematics is not a feminine pursuit, *tesoro*. You'll be queen because of your looks, not because I need you to do any thinking."

"I like mathematics. I'll probably do some while I'm sitting on my golden chair. I could use the Pythagorean theorem to determine the angle between our chairs."

"There's no angle. Our chairs will be side-by-side and perfectly parallel."

"I could utilize cubic equations to determine the volume of space beneath my chair."

"Why would you need to?" he asked in confusion. "Why would anyone need to?"

"To ensure my pet fits."

He looked less than thrilled. "Is it a furry pet? Have you a kitten? Or a puppy?"

"A long-eared bat. He likes to hang upside-down. Are there good footholds beneath my chair?"

"For a *bat*?"

"Technically, I have five bats."

"Five bats!"

"One for each of the chairs."

"There are only four thrones!"

"Then two will have to go under mine. Do you see now why cubic equations and golden footholds are of utmost importance?"

"My parents would never allow rodents like bats inside the castle, much less..." He took a deep breath. "We'll discuss it later. This is not the time or place."

"Of course not," Cynthia agreed. "Bats aren't rodents. I will need some time to put together a proper natural philosophy presentation to explain the difference to your family. Perhaps we can invite renowned experts to give instructional speeches on the subject throughout the kingdom."

The prince stared at her. "Perhaps we can skip the speeches. Everyone's speeches. Including yours."

Cynthia widened her eyes. "Do you dislike conversation?"

"I adore conversation. I am not certain that's what we're in the midst of. I find myself more confused with every word you say."

"Oh, dear," said Cynthia. "I can start at the beginning. Pay attention. Natural philosophy began in ancient Greece, although it wasn't until Aristotle posited the categorization of objects based on shared traits rather than—"

"Might we just... Can we simply dance? In silence?" the prince begged. "Perhaps we can play a game, wherein every time we're together, we see how long we can maintain the silence between us."

"I don't like games," said Cynthia. "And it's much easier to perform mathematical equations aloud."

He grimaced. "You shall certainly be a... unique... princess."

"I don't like royalty, either," Cynthia said cheerfully. "Or primogeniture."

To her surprise, the prince looked wistful rather than appalled at this.

"It's probably heresy to admit that I feel the same," he said with a crooked smile. "When the Cispadane Republic unveiled its tricolor flag symbolizing the unification of Italy, I was elated. Some other prince would be tapped to lead, and I could become a regular mortal."

"Really?" Cynthia was intrigued despite herself. "A royal prince felt that way?"

"Viscerally." His expression turned grim. "Imagine my reaction when Napoleon fell, and the Congress of Vienna restored the prior system of independent governments. Instead of one hegemony to rule them all, we were back to Habsburgs and separatists, each with their own set of thrones and heirs."

"Run away," she suggested. "Don't take a bride at all."

"I have responsibilities," he said simply. "And I would never disappoint my father. He's the one who announced the ridiculous contest for me to acquire the continent's prettiest bride. I shall win it, because that is what sons and princes do. It's what my people want."

"Why not find a bride that *you* want?"

He tilted his head and regarded her with intensity. "To my surprise, I think I might have done just that."

Oh, shite. Cynthia should have kept to bats and algebra.

Prince Azzurro wasn't as bad as she'd first thought. Perhaps there was nothing bad about him at all. But she still did not want him.

"I like you more than anticipated, too," she admitted. "Which is why I'm about to tell you the truth: I don't want to marry you. I shall *not* marry you."

"I'll change your mind," he promised. "I'll install footholds for your bats if I must. At least they're not furry."

"I also have magpies," she muttered. "Very feathery. Every sparkling gem in the castle will disappear by morning."

The orchestra finished the set. Prince Azzurro tucked Cynthia's hand around his elbow. "Come. I'll return you to Lady Tremaine, so that she can hear the good news from me, first. I'm determined to make you my bride. I've arranged fireworks for midnight. Join me on the parquet, and we'll do the official announcement then, arm-in-arm."

No. None of that.

"I told you," she said. "I won't be your wife."

"And I told you—"

She wrenched free from his grasp and launched herself into the crowd, losing a shoe in the process. He tried to chase her, but without his footmen, the unwed debutantes converged, allowing Cynthia safe passage whilst they swarmed around the handsome prince.

There, in the back of the ballroom, was the open garden door leading far away from royal matrimony and certain despair.

All Cynthia could think about was escape...

And Ammalia.

Chapter Eleven

A mmalia hid deep within the garden, her back against the rough bark of a wide tree. She'd slipped away the moment her brother took Cynthia's hand. No—that wasn't quite true. She'd sat there, in deepening horror, until Cynthia smiled her dawning-sunlight smile at Zurri and fluttered her eyelashes the way all women inevitably did when in the presence of Ammalia's irresistibly charming brother.

Sadness had filled her, a deep hollow ache, kneading her insides until she could barely breathe. She needed more than fresh air. She needed to see anything at all—or nothing at all—so long as whatever was before her eyes, was anything but Cynthia smiling happily at Zurri.

With everyone's attention on the radiant couple, it had been simple to slip out through the rear door undetected. Ammalia had dropped heavily and unceremoniously onto a fallen log amongst the flowers, and then when that still seemed too close, she'd stood and moved deeper among the trees and the bushes, until she could no longer see the light spilling from the open ballroom door.

The moon was her only companion, a skinny sliver curving high overhead, adding a faint sparkle to the leaves as the moonlight trickled through the trees to the empty garden below. It was peaceful, out here all alone.

Too peaceful. Without the distraction of thousands of merry-makers and the noise of the orchestra, Ammalia was alone with her own thoughts, which had turned decidedly maudlin.

She might have evaded any additional glimpse of Cynthia in Zurri's arms tonight, but what about tomorrow and every day after that? Unless she planned to run away—impractical, if tempting—she would likely have to travel back to Parmenza in the same carriage, on the same ship, dining in the same room across from the newly betrothed pair.

It could not be borne. And yet, what choice did she have? If wishes were raindrops, Cynthia would fall right into Ammalia's eager embrace. But the chances of that happening were—

Footsteps. Panting. A sound somewhere between a sigh of relief and a sob.

Ammalia peeled her spine from the tree and peeked around the trunk.

Cynthia. Wearing just one shoe.

Their eyes met at the same moment. Cynthia sprinted forward at a crooked run, launching herself into Ammalia's arms for a heartfelt hug. Ammalia fell to the grass, bringing Cynthia with her. Ammalia wasted no time turning them both around so that Ammalia was atop Cynthia, who stared up at her with wide, startled eyes.

Impulsively, Ammalia kissed her.

To her shock, rather than push Ammalia off, Cynthia grabbed on tight and kissed her back, as if she had been waiting her entire life for this precise opportunity.

She smelled like the soap from her earlier bath. A visual that had not strayed far from Ammalia's memory ever since she'd had the good fortune to glimpse Cynthia nude. And touch her bare skin. And massage her muscles. How Ammalia had longed to climb into the tub with her! Or take Cynthia to private thermal waters, where they could bathe naked beneath stars like these.

For now, she would settle for a kiss as sweet as *panettone*. In response, Cynthia sank her fingers into Ammalia's hair and held on tight.

This kiss made every lonely moment that Ammalia had ever suffered worth it. Cynthia's lips against hers was a lifetime of happiness, all in one kiss. It was a connection that grew deeper, stronger, with each brush of their lips and taste of their tongues, twining them together from the depths of their hearts.

Cynthia's embrace was like exploring new worlds and coming home all at once. Excitement and adventure and comfort and rightness. It was as if Ammalia's arms had waited for this very moment with this very person. Now that they were finally together, Ammalia never wished to part. She wanted more. Wanted everything. Cynthia's body, Cynthia's heart... now and forever.

As their kisses grew ever more passionate, Ammalia gave in to temptation and allowed her eager hands full rein to explore every one of Cynthia's warm, soft curves.

Fully clothed was not the same as nude, but Ammalia would take Cynthia any way she could have her. In or out of a gown, in or out of the water, as long as she remained in Ammalia's arms and out of Zurri's reach.

At the thought, Ammalia's kisses became imbued with urgency and desperation.

Cynthia responded in kind, utterly destroying what was left of Ammalia's chignon and the pouf of her sleeves. They rolled around the grass, wrinkling—and likely ripping—every inch of fabric as their fingers sought each other's most sensitive areas beneath the inconvenient layers of their pesky skirts.

Ammalia allowed her legs to part and gently did the same to Cynthia, devouring her with kisses as their fingers explored and teased and dipped.

Her heart pounded as the pressure built within her, rising all the way up to the sliver of moon and threatening to explode around them in a spray of shooting stars.

Ammalia could scarcely breathe between kisses, so invested was she in bringing Cynthia the same pleasure that she was stoking in

Ammalia. The more she tried not to climax, in order to extend the moment, the more impossible restraint became. She tumbled over the edge, gasping into Cynthia's mouth as the rhythmic spasms overtook her.

But they weren't finished yet. Now that the heavens had heard Ammalia's prayers and delivered Cynthia into her arms, Ammalia had no intention of letting her go without first giving her a memory to last a lifetime.

Chapter Twelve

ynthia's pulse raced and her blood sang. She'd fled to the garden, desperate to free herself from the prince's clutches, and found joy in the arms of Princess Ammalia instead.

She hadn't been running away after all. She'd been running *to*. Ammalia was everything Cynthia wanted. She could barely think. Her mind was too full of exhilaration, and her body too close to release.

As if sensing this, Ammalia pushed Cynthia's skirts up to her hips and lowered her face between Cynthia's thighs. An incoherent gurgle of pleasure escaped Cynthia's lips.

Good God, she could not possibly marry a prince. Cynthia didn't want him. She wanted *this*. And she could not bear to spend the rest of her life one throne away from the princess yet unable to touch her.

But by not marrying the prince, the future was just as bleak. Refusing his suit meant no betrothal, and no betrothal meant staying home for the rest of her days. Lady Tremaine would never again allow Cynthia to attend a "frivolous" activity like a ball. With no glowing employment references, she would remain a scullion in her own home until she was too old and bent and brittle to scrub a floor or lift a bucket.

Princess Ammalia wouldn't be seated beside her, but rather thousands of miles away, in a far-off country. Out of sight and out of reach forevermore.

But Cynthia could not dwell on this. Refused to allow the bleak truth to ruin this beautiful moment.

With every breath, she concentrated on inhaling every detail about Princess Ammalia, to carry her essence inside her always. The scent of Ammalia's hair, as sweet and floral as the flowers in the garden surrounding them. The taste of Ammalia's kisses, still hot and sweet on Cynthia's tongue. The feel of her warm soft body. How it had felt pressed against her, beneath her, above her. Its position now, between Cynthia's legs, with Ammalia's firm fingers gripping Cynthia's hips, holding her in place. As if there was anywhere else Cynthia would rather be.

She couldn't even keep cataloguing the moment. The pleasure was too acute, and release too imminent. She was no longer lying in the grass but floating with the stars above.

As the climax overtook her, the night sky filled with fireworks. Reds, greens, blues, orange. As if each of the delicious contractions were echoed in brilliant color overhead.

Fireworks.

Midnight.

As the booming explosions ceased, she heard the last of a distant clock tower ring the final bell of midnight. The night was over. Hadn't the Prince wanted to make his betrothal announcement at midnight? And Cynthia was supposed to already be back home at her post. There was no time to waste. If her vindictive stepmother arrived first and discovered the house and its comforts were not waiting for them as promised... There was no telling what retribution would await.

Cynthia scrambled to her feet, her limbs still trembling and weak. Princess Ammalia did the same. Cynthia gathered her into her arms for the briefest, tightest of embraces. She pressed a heartbroken kiss to the princess's temple, then let her go.

"Forgive me," she whispered into Ammalia's hair, then turned and ran as swiftly as she could with one shoe on and one shoe lost, stumbling and scrambling her way back home.

The night—and the princess—had been perfect.

Surviving on the sweetness of the memory would have to be enough.

Chapter Thirteen

T he next morning, Cynthia swept ashes into a dustpan before the fireplace. Her stepsisters gasped in unison when Stasia shook out the morning newspaper.

Cynthia turned in time to see them both abandon their hot breakfasts in order to peer in shock and dismay at whatever was written on the front page.

"What has happened?" she asked nervously.

Her stepsisters were too distracted by the upsetting news to remember to shoo Cynthia back to the cinders.

Stasia gaped at her like an awestruck fish. "It says... It says..."

Dorothea snatched the paper out of her sister's limp hand and shook the headlines at Cynthia. "It says the prince fell in love last night, and will be announcing his future bride today."

"Maybe it's one of you," Cynthia said hopefully. Perhaps she could travel to Italy as Stasia or Dorothea's handmaiden, and steal snatches of time alone with Princess Ammalia.

"It is not me." Dorothea stabbed her finger at an illustration sketched further down the page.

Cynthia crept closer to look.

The caricature was recognizably a portrait of the handsome prince... holding a sparkling glass slipper in his large palm.

563

Cynthia's missing slipper.

"It cannot be," she said in horror, clutching the wooden handle of her broom like a defensive weapon as she reflexively backed away from the sketch in the paper. She'd *told* him she wouldn't marry him.

Princes apparently did not understand or accept the word no.

Dorothea and Stasia were just as appalled—and they blamed Cynthia.

"We have both *our* shoes," said Dorothea. "It's all your fault."

"It's my fault you have your shoes?"

"It's your fault you left one of yours behind, to stand out from all the other young ladies dropping handkerchiefs in Prince Azzurro's path."

"That's not what I was trying to do," Cynthia protested. "I wasn't trying to tempt him or be mysterious. I was trying to disappear."

"Well, you did so in the most slovenly way possible," said Lady Tremaine, entering the dining room in time to glimpse the infernal illustration on the front page of the morning newspaper. "I would have locked you in that attic if I'd known you had no intention of fighting fair. To think, you weaseled your way into his sights by behaving like a slattern—"

"Lock her in the attic now, Mama," suggested Dorothea. "Keep her in there whenever she's not cleaning or cooking."

"Excellent idea, daughter." Lady Tremaine glared at Cynthia. "Make haste with the sweeping and the dishes, then hie upstairs without delay. From this day forth, I've no wish to see your face unless I've specifically—"

A knock sounded at the front door.

All four women froze in place.

"Well?" snapped Lady Tremaine, waving her fingers at Cynthia. "You're the servant. Answer it."

Cynthia leaned the broom against the mantel and hurried to the door.

The prince stood on the other side.

She choked on her breath and scurried backwards, nearly tripping over the broom in the process.

He stepped into the house as if invited to do so, followed by his father the king, then half a dozen royal footmen... and Princess Ammalia.

Before Cynthia's startled gaze could meet Ammalia's, Lady Tremaine jerked her out of the way, pushing her back toward the unlit fireplace so that her daughters could step forward, blocking Cynthia from view.

The king raised his brows at Prince Azzurro, then spoke in Italian. "You're certain about this, son?"

The prince shrugged and glanced at his sister, who sent him a furious look. Prince Azzurro blew her a kiss, then turned back to the king. "I'm certain, Father."

The king held up Cynthia's lost shoe and muttered in English, "This item belongs to the most beautiful woman in England? Beh. All of them look the same to me."

Cynthia melted backwards as Stasia and Dorothea arranged themselves in their most alluring poses, eyelashes fluttering and lips plump and pouting.

"Which of you left this slipper behind at last night's ball?" demanded the king.

Cynthia shook her head frantically. She would *not* marry Prince Azzurro.

"*Me*," Stasia and Dorothea replied in tandem.

"Sketch this moment," the king ordered a portrait artist, who began drawing as quickly as he could. "I wish it to appear in tomorrow's newspaper. The rest of you—as you were instructed."

Three royal footmen rushed forward. Two knelt on the freshly swept stone floor to provide their broad shoulders for each of the sisters to grab for balance, whilst the third attempted to fit the slipper to their feet.

Neither could make the shoe fit.

"It belongs to Cynthia," Princess Ammalia said softly.

Cynthia's jaw dropped at the unexpected betrayal. She sent the princess a hurt look and took another protective step backwards.

The king pointed at the crystal slipper.

"Put it on," he commanded imperiously.

Before Cynthia could do so, Lady Tremaine clapped her hands and hissed, "Morningstar! *Now!*"

With a *rawr*, the devil-cat sprang out from the shadows, arcing upwards to land paws-first on either side of the poor footman's cravat.

The slipper tumbled from the footman's flailing hands. Crystals scattered on the hard stone floor. Morningstar scooped up the ruined slipper in his jaws and leapt out through the closest window, leaving nothing but glittering debris behind.

Stasia and Dorothea exchanged smug expressions of satisfaction. For once in her life, Cynthia was in full agreement. Their petty vindictiveness had saved her from a fate worse than death.

The king turned to Princess Ammalia. "You're certain you wished to bring home the girl who belonged to that shoe?"

Lady Tremaine and her daughters blinked in confusion.

Oh no. Oh, no, no, *no!*

Cynthia stared at the littered shards in horror. It wasn't the prince who had come to make his match, but the princess arriving to claim hers? And Morningstar had ruined Cynthia's chance!

"It *is* me," she blurted out. "It was my shoe. It fits me perfectly."

"So you claim, scullion." Lady Tremaine's expression was triumphant. "I guess we'll never know. And what did I just tell you?" She shooed Cynthia toward the stairs. "Off to the attic with you whilst my daughters and I discuss what is to be done about the royal wedding."

Cynthia trudged up the steps, then broke into a run, taking them two at a time in eagerness. Up on the top floor, on the bottom shelf of her broken wardrobe, was the matching slipper.

She scooped it up, heart pounding. She cradled the crystal slipper carefully to her chest as though it were as fragile as eggshells and hurried down the stairs as fast as she dared, in the hopes that the princess and her retinue would still be there.

Lady Tremaine was extolling her daughters' many dubious virtues to the prince. He and his father hung on rapt to every word, exchanging the occasional approving glance.

When Cynthia arrived in their midst, all eyes swung to her—and the glass slipper in her hand.

"It's the mate," exclaimed the king.

"*My* mate," murmured Princess Ammalia.

Before Cynthia could set the shoe on the stone floor, the princess hurried forward, elbowing the footmen out of the way in order to be the one to kneel at Cynthia's feet with the glass slipper resting in her palms.

Cynthia eased her foot inside the slipper.

It was a perfect fit.

Grinning, Cynthia reached her hands down to Ammalia's and pulled the princess to her feet.

Lady Tremaine blanched and turned back to the prince. "But... But you said you didn't come for *her*."

"That is true." The prince flashed Ammalia a crooked smile. "I don't want anything my sister wants."

The princess blew him a kiss.

"No need to inconvenience Ammalia," the king agreed. "My son will take the other two."

"*What?*" blurted Stasia and Dorothea.

"Both, Father?" said the prince with obvious interest. "Is that not too indulgent?"

"You only get one wife," the king replied repressively. "The other will have to be your mistress."

"B-but," stammered Dorothea, "which of us is which?"

The king looked bored. "*I* don't care. Sort it out between the two of you."

The prince gazed at both young women like a glutton at a feast.

"*Now*," Princess Ammalia whispered to Cynthia in Italian. "Hurry."

They slipped from the house hand-in-hand, leaving the sounds of sisterly squabbling behind them.

Princess Ammalia pulled Cynthia up and into the empty carriage, then took the reins in her hands. "Where to, my love?"

Cynthia kissed her. "Is Italy nice this time of year?"

Ammalia grinned. "Why don't we go and find out?"

"When will you be expected to retake your throne in Parmenza?"

"Never, if I don't wish to. Our future is up to us. My only task was to see Zurri betrothed. Now that he's settled, you and I can travel the world to our hearts' content."

"You *are* my heart," Cynthia said with a smile.

Ammalia kissed the tip of her nose. "And you are mine, *tesoro*."

With the magpies chirping behind them, the two women drove off without a backwards glance, exchanging smiles and kisses with every turn of the wheels.

And they lived happily ever after.

About the Author

Erica Ridley is a *New York Times* and *USA Today* best-selling author of witty, feel-good historical romance novels, including the critically-acclaimed sapphic romcom THE PERKS OF LOVING A WALL-FLOWER, featuring the caper-committing Wild Wynchesters, as well as the heartwarming m/m romcom UNDRESSING THE DUKE.

Other popular series, such as the *Dukes of War, Rogues to Riches* and the *12 Dukes of Christmas*, feature roguish peers and dashing war heroes who find love amongst the splendor and madness of Regency England.

When not reading or writing romances, Erica can be found eating couscous in Morocco, zip-lining through rainforests in Central America, or getting hopelessly lost in the middle of Budapest. For more information, visit https://www.EricaRidley.com

CPSIA information can be obtained
at www.ICGtesting.com
Printed in the USA
LVHW010751150723
752573LV00031B/428